# CORRIDOR OF DARKNESS

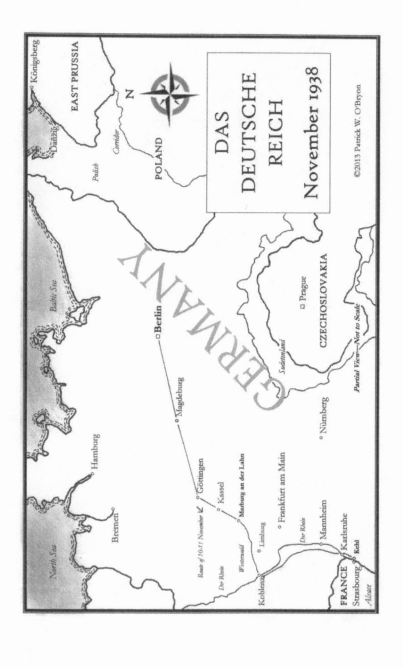

DAS DEUTSCHE REICH November 1938

©2013 Patrick W. O'Bryon

Königsberg

EAST PRUSSIA

Danzig

Corridor

Polish

POLAND

N

Baltic Sea

GERMANY

□ Berlin

Magdeburg

CZECHOSLOVAKIA

□ Prague

Sudetenland

Partial View—Not to Scale

Hamburg

° Göttingen

° Nürnberg

Bremen°

Route of 10-11 November

Kassel

Marburg an der Lahn

Westerwald

Limburg

° Frankfurt am Main

Der Rhein

North Sea

Der Rhein

Mannheim

Koblenz°

Karlsruhe

FRANCE

Kehl

Strasbourg

Alsace

# CORRIDOR OF DARKNESS

## A NOVEL OF NAZI GERMANY

## Patrick W. O'Bryon

Brantôme Press
NAPA, CALIFORNIA

Cover Design by G. S. Prendergast
Book Layout ©2013 BookDesignTemplates.com
Author Photo by Ashley Urke Photography

Corridor of Darkness/Patrick W. O'Bryon. -- 1st ed.
ISBN 978-0-9910782-0-2

*To my wife Dani, and in memory of my father*

# CONTENTS

Do not close your eyes to the fact that we are entering a corridor of deepening and darkening danger.

—Winston Churchill, May 1935

# PROLOGUE

## Marburg on the Lahn, Germany
### 29 October 1934

In the narrow passage between the inn and the brothel three men in dark clothing huddled in the shadows. The mouth of the alley opened to the upper market place, now mostly deserted. A young couple crossed the square, closely entwined, heading back to a warm apartment. A man with hat brim pulled low looked furtively right and left before entering the whorehouse.

"There goes one lucky son-of-a-bitch," said Stefan Brenner. "Wouldn't mind getting laid myself right now."

"Just concentrate on what's coming to that bastard Frenchman; that'll get you hard enough." Horst von Kredow glanced up to the second-story window of the inn where their target was celebrating the new semester with a few of his closest fraternity brothers. "I want that asshole ground to pulp."

"More meat for your sausage grinder, Horst?" Darkness hid the grin on the narrow face of Klaus Pabst. "Don't worry, once we finish with him tonight he won't lift a saber again."

Horst unconsciously placed a fingertip to the bandage on his cheek.

Wisps of fog drifted up from the streets below, diffusing the yellow cast of the street lamps. The clock face on the city hall was now barely visible, and across the square Saint George bled an ever-dying dragon into the gurgling fountain. The worn cobbles reeked of urine, stale beer, and dog shit smeared by passers-by in the course of the day just ending.

Their target had entered the inn almost two hours before, and the raucous gathering of comrades continued undiminished. One window high above the alley stood ajar, releasing tobacco smoke, celebratory toasts, and drinking songs to the cool night air.

The three waiting men had foresworn both distinctive fraternity colors and brown-shirted SA uniforms. Heavy wool overcoats warded off the chill, and wide-brimmed hats shielded their eyes and identities. The long wait itself was of little concern. They thrived on punishing those who lacked proper respect for their new Germany. The men now smoked in silence, the glowing tips of their cigarettes flitting about in the blackness of the alley. Horst drew cautiously on the harsh-smelling Roth-Händle, wary of overtaxing his damaged facial muscles with such a simple act.

From time to time other sounds reached them, male and female voices, barely perceptible beyond the closed windows of the bordello to their back. The night air shifted cautiously in the autumn chill, and acrid coal and wood smoke invaded the alleyway, hinting at the winter to come. At last they heard boots pounding down the wooden stairs, and the celebrants emerged from the inn to head home to bed.

Now only a scatter of friendly banter disturbed the quiet of the square. Taking leave of his last companion, their prey ambled down past city hall toward the old university building. An occasional misstep, ever so slight, betrayed the quantity of beer consumed that evening. His stalkers moved onto the main square and followed from thirty meters back. At one point their quarry, quietly humming a drinking song, braced one arm against a building and released a vaporous stream onto the paving stones. Then, with an audible sigh of relief, he descended the cobbled street toward the river bridge.

They knew where he would be most vulnerable. The gothic windows of the university church glimmered softly above the small square where grain once traded. At its end an arched passage pierced an ancient wall, beyond which a stone staircase dropped to street level. The corridor glowed dully under the iron lamps affixed to either side of the wall.

Their attack was swift. A crude hempen bag dropped roughly over the victim's head, and one assailant twisted it tightly around the drunken man's neck while the others restrained him. Strong arms whipped him around toward Horst, who slammed his fists relentlessly into the victim's abdomen and face. The well-aimed blows met no real resistance, for the student, his senses dulled by alcohol, quickly gave up his fight. Now on the pavement, he endured brutal kicks from all sides. His arms shielded his hooded head, leaving the attackers to concentrate on his unprotected back. There was little sound, just the repeated thud of heavy boots meeting flesh and the self-satisfied grunts of the attackers.

Once the man no longer moved, a dark mass on the stones beneath the arch, the attackers dragged him across the landing. They scanned the street below for late wanderers or a police patrol before launching him down the steps, and the body slid to rest, belly down, arms splayed to the side, blood darkening the coarse hood.

The men laughed as they stepped around him, descending the stairway. "Well, *Jungs*, a beer to celebrate?" Horst asked.

Once at street level they turned toward the Zentral-Hotel some blocks away, where a reserved table in the tavern awaited their arrival. A small flag displayed the colors of their *Corps*, alerting those not belonging to Horst's immediate inner circle to keep their distance. The low-hanging ceiling and dark wooden beams were pimpled with amber tar, witness to years of heavy-smoking patrons. Behind the bar the proprietor rinsed glasses to strains of martial music, his radio barely noticed over the students' singing and laughter.

Horst pounded his beer mug on the table to get the room's attention, then raised his voice to override the clamor. He took care not to strain his healing face. "To hell with all foreigners and stinking Jews!" He raised his stein, *"Prost!"*

Klaus and Stefan joined in, and the toast echoed at nearby tables. *"Prost!"*

A Nazi anthem announced on the radio led the bartender to turn up the volume. Chairs and benches scraped on wooden planks as the drinkers rose with right arms raised to bellow the lyrics:

*The flag held high, the ranks firmly closed, Storm Troops march forth with calmly assured step...*

Before the drinkers regained their seats, Horst von Kredow proposed a new salute, recently introduced at the Party Congress in Nuremberg:

*Ein Volk, ein Reich, ein Führer!*

The tavern resounded with the full-throated response: *Ein Deutschland!*

# DEUTSCHLAND ERWACHE!
## Germany, Awaken!

### 1929 - 1934

# CHAPTER ONE

R yan Leonard Lemmon smiled as he left the opulent lobby of the Woolworth Building to enter the bustling foot traffic on Broadway. The year was 1929, New York City was riding an irrepressible stock market with powerful men of finance at the reins, and the young Midwesterner was well on his way to becoming a citizen of this great metropolis. He already visualized a future office high atop one of Manhattan's imposing new skyscrapers, but in the coming year he would study finance in Berlin, for Irving Trust Company had encouraged him to accept the prestigious fellowship he had won. His departmental director predicted that the experience would make Ryan a greater asset to the International Division, and the bank had provided a Berlitz course in Business German to make the most of his opportunity.

Now Ryan headed to the noisy, uptown 42 Club on West 49th to join his brother Edward and Harvard School of Business friend Gene Lawton. He spotted them at a corner table and negotiated a path past other drinkers. There was no sign of Prohibition in the crowded speakeasy where the three gathered to celebrate Ryan's imminent departure for Europe.

Ed was the first to raise his glass. "To great times in Germany, my brother!"

"And I'll toast both my globetrotting friend and our beautiful Germany!" added Gene.

The glasses drained, Ed reached across the table for the bottle. "Not bad hooch. Is it really Jameson's?"

"As close as we'll find this side of the pond," Gene said, admiring an artfully-forged label. "You boys sure picked a top-notch joint. I'll bet this is where the Revenue boys unwind after busting up our fair city's bootleggers."

"Speaking of Feds, here's to your new position at German and Austrian Affairs, Ed." The State Department had recently recruited his older brother, and Ryan was sincerely proud. "With your talents and your new father-in-law's clout, you'll knock 'em dead in Washington."

"Well dammit, baby brother, I'm still jealous as hell. Shouldn't I be the first to live abroad?"

"Don't worry, Ed. You're destined for some lofty Foreign Service post while I'm still plodding along down in the trenches."

The Lemmon brothers were accustomed to both competition and success. A spirited icon of eastern Kansas society, their mother had demanded of them proficiency in scholastics, athletics and the arts, and their father, a respected dental surgeon, taught them to win respect with erudition and relaxed charm. Both brothers put their training to good use. Now in his early twenties and at the top of his game, Ryan stood ready to fulfill his overseas dream.

The previous summer he and Gene Lawton had escorted a group of Wellesley co-eds on a grand tour of Europe. It was Gene's second summer as a travel guide, while novice Ryan took responsibility for transportation, baggage, and seeing the girls gathered each morning for the next leg of the journey.

The experience had been an eye-opener for the Kansas native: horseback rides in Ireland, Alpine bicycle tours, mountaintop skiing at Chamonix, champagne-laced Parisian revues, and dancing into the morning hours in Roman clubs. For dashing Ryan, the tour had also provided a wealth of romantic opportunities. The three-month whirl from country to country, capital to capital, from museum to cathedral to art gallery, all had left him determined to make Europe his own.

"What a great time to live in Germany—the dollar's strong, the mark weak—and best of all, Berlin is wide-open," Gene said. "And knowing your success with the fairer sex, I look forward to hearing all about your new conquests over there." He paused to down another shot. "In intimate detail, of course."

"Gentlemen, I'll share my four-step secret for success with women." Ryan counted off on his fingers. "First, show genuine *affection.* Then, make a pleasurable *inspection.* And—very important—come up with a worthy *erection.*"

Edward grinned. "I believe you said *four* steps?"

Ryan lifted a fourth finger. "*Circumspection,* my friends, always *circumspection*...so don't expect any 'kiss and tell' from me."

"Well, in that case..." Edward held his glass high, "here's to great *untold* adventures!" Ryan responded with his broadest smile and signaled for a second bottle, the first still half full.

The next morning the three friends gathered in Ryan's narrow stateroom aboard the Redstar Line's SS Pennland, outbound for Antwerp. When the signal came to go ashore, Ed and Gene emptied a final glass of champagne, wished the traveler *bon voyage,* and descended the gangway to join all the other well-wishers on the Manhattan pier. Ryan waved good-bye through a cascade of colorful streamers before joining many other passengers at the starboard railing for the best view of the Statue of Liberty as the Pennland headed seaward. Under farewell blasts from the ship's whistles, the mooring lines dropped and tugboats maneuvered the massive liner out into the Hudson.

All three men cringed at the ear-numbing sound. All three were seriously hung over.

# CHAPTER TWO

The short train ride from Antwerp to Amsterdam proved uneventful, but Ryan's first experience with air travel—a rollercoaster hop to Berlin aboard a silver Lufthansa Junkers—left him queasy. Yet the excitement of both air flight and returning to Germany prevailed, and he arrived in high spirits, anxious to explore the German metropolis. For the first few months he would room with the von Haldheim family in a suburban villa, a door opened by his Harvard mentor, Dr. Otto Biermann, a native Prussian. The professor's letter of introduction promised entrée to Berlin's highest aristocratic circles, and Ryan would study finance at the famed Friedrich Wilhelm University.

Not expected by his host family until the following morning, Ryan hailed a cab at Tempelhof Airfield to bring him to the Hotel Metropol off Potsdamer Platz. Unlike Manhattan's rampant verticality, Berlin expanded in broad horizontal planes. The boulevards reached out from the grand plazas like spokes on massive urban wheels. The drizzle of a damp September afternoon softened the buildings and neon signage, and the glistening pavement reflected a constant ebb and flow of traffic.

After changing from traveling clothes, Ryan left the hotel in search of coffee. Berlin was vibrant, an urban world in constant motion. The flower stalls glowed in muted color beneath green and gray canopies, and newsboys shouted headlines amidst the passing parade of umbrellas. Ryan stopped in front of a tea room on a main boulevard, attracted by well-dressed patrons basking in the glow of soft lighting and pale yellow table linens. The *Konditorei* was brimming with suited business men, elegantly-dressed women, and starchy governesses with dutiful children, all indulging in rich desserts. From his table near the front display he watched the steady stream of passers-by until his coffee arrived, accompanied by a jelly-filled pastry which the waiter called *ein Berliner*. For Ryan it was a satisfying first taste of his new life in the German capital.

Beyond his plate glass window men in fedoras plowed briskly through the crowd with briefcases under one arm. Two stylish women stepped from a dress shop and spread their umbrellas, their latest fashions mirroring the chic mannequins behind them. Poised matrons with small dogs on leash sailed along the crowded sidewalks. Everywhere shops enticed consumers with handsome merchandise and special sale prices, a lively world of business opportunity. *Sarotti, Tietz, Grünfeld*—a heady new vocabulary of brand names and shopping destinations.

He had scarcely covered a city block before a smoke-filled tobacconist's shop lured him in with its cabinetry of deep-toned wood and a wealth of pipes, cigarette holders and cigar cases beneath the glass counter. Jars of exotic tobacco blends rose to the ceiling on polished shelves. Ryan used his basic German to purchase a briar pipe with gently-curved black stem. The tobacconist also recommended a special *Latakia* blend from Syria, and Ryan chose an airtight leather pouch to protect its freshness. He tamped the pipe loosely and lit up, then raised his umbrella and rejoined the crowd on the street.

On the broad Potsdamer Platz a flood of Mercedes, Horchs, Opels and Fords fought for right-of-way, ignoring both the policeman's whistle and the raised white glove giving pedestrians the go-ahead. Strident horns and bell-ringing bicycles encouraged Ryan to step aside, brightly-bannered trams rumbled past, and double-decker buses edged forward in fits and starts, fighting a strong tide. Once back on the sidewalk he lost himself in the roiling sea of humanity, mimicking the purposeful stride of the German citizen.

On side streets he found nightclubs already welcoming patrons in the early afternoon hours, their canopied entrances advertising exotic revues with leggy dancers. Touts forced flyers into his hand, flimsy sheets showing women in various states of undress. No German skills were needed to understand all that was on offer. And everywhere he looked, people consumed alcohol, openly and in great abundance. How parochial America seemed with its speakeasies and posted look-outs, its puritan attitude toward sex.

The less-trafficked back streets offered far more modest wares than those of the grand boulevards. *Hans Papier's Tauben-Handlung,* cages stacked five high before the entry, displayed live pigeons for consumption, breeding or racing. *Heinemann's Obsthandlung* overran the sidewalk with crates of oranges, red apples, and green bananas. The sausage-plump proprietor, red cap pulled low at his brow, gave a friendly greeting, so Ryan tipped his hat politely and bought an apple, slipping it into his topcoat pocket.

Reaching the Spree River, he watched tugboats finesse heavily-laden barges upstream. Above him on an iron bridge a train shrieked and rumbled past, bringing life and livelihood into the heart of the bustling metropolis. Ryan ate his apple, gave the core to a worn dray horse, then headed back to his hotel, at home in Europe at last.

The following morning the von Haldheims welcomed him into their home as a long-lost son. His fine room overlooked the garden, he could take meals with the family as often as he wished, and he received a standing invitation to take Saturday-afternoon tea with the remnants of the Hohenzollern aristocracy. With the former Kaiser exiled to Holland, the family patriarch assumed responsibility for keeping alive the monarchist tradition in Berlin, and regular attendees included others whose influence dated back a thousand years or more.

Surrounded by an imposing wall and approached through columned iron gates, the turn-of-the-century stone villa in Grunewald expressed the wealth and nobility of the clan. A circular drive brought limousines to the entry portico, where guests ascended broad steps to the foyer. A massive double staircase rose to the upper landing, the high-ceilinged rooms were framed by moldings and friezes, and Persian carpets covered rich stone and parquet flooring. It was truly as grand a home as Ryan had ever seen.

Manners were refined, but the tone surprisingly down-to-earth. Manfred von Haldheim, known to all as "The Old Major," regaled the group with indecorous stories of his misadventures, first in the Franco-Prussian War and more recently in the trenches of the Great War. He occasionally wore his Iron Cross and other medals acquired as an officer in both the Brown and the Black Hussars. A handsome man of seventy-one, von Haldheim was delighted with the young American whose polished manners and easy smile pleased his guests.

Ryan brought a sense of humor as well as an occasional soft-shoe routine to break the monotony of political discussion and ribald stories at the weekly teas. Conversation flowed in German, French, and English, with the occasional quip in Italian or Spanish, and Ryan demonstrated a natural aptitude for languages. With the start of his university studies and further Berlitz work he was soon at ease in rudimentary German, and learning French.

The von Haldheim formal dinners were as impressive as their mansion. Dress was evening wear or military uniform for the men, gowns of damask or silk brocade for the women. The butler Erich greeted the guests with aperitifs or cocktails, and wit, flirtation and *double entendre* set the tone for the evening's gathering. After drinks, the party moved into a dining room sparkling with silver, crystal and candlelight. Staff in white-on-black presented tureens of beef bouillon or rich fish soup, followed by oysters, mussels and eel, fresh from Berlin's Koln fish market. Next came pork and veal, sausage and venison, platters mounded high with roast potatoes and Brussels sprouts, thick gravies and, finally, ornate desserts. Both sparkling and still wines flowed freely, and the meal ended with coffee or tea. At long last the men retired to the smoking salon for digestive bitters or brandy, taken with cigars from the Old Major's humidor, or cigarettes drawn from a silver case monogrammed with the family crest. Ryan preferred his new pipe and *Kantorowicz Curaçao*, a pale triple sec.

Later, up in his room, his stomach aching from overindulgence, he folded himself over the back of an armchair to put pressure on his abdomen and ease his suffering, and vowed that, next time, he would show more self-control. The cure worked, the oath failed.

"Care to be my guest tonight for some of our city's notorious night-life?" Rolf von Haldheim, scion of the family and as yet unmarried, was Ryan's senior by a good ten years. Tall and fashionably clad, he radiated the confidence of one born to wealth and accustomed to getting his way through charm and savoir-faire. He cultivated a thin mustache and a slightly world-weary air. "And while we're at it, shall we use given names?"

"I'd be delighted, and first names do make sense for fellow night-clubbers."

"Excellent! So, state your preference, Ryan? Dance, music, stage entertainment?"

"You're the guide, Rolf, so surprise me."

He did.

Club Orion was an intimate cabaret near Potsdamer Platz. Dom Pérignon waited at their reserved table, and the younger von Haldheim was obviously a well-known patron. Rolf toasted Ryan's introduction to Berlin nightlife, a fast-paced duet sung by the tuxe-do-clad emcee and a dazzling blonde. A quarter hour later Rolf excused himself to see a friend and went backstage with the solicitous head waiter.

Ryan took in a musical revue enlivened by bare-breasted dancers before the emcee leapt to the stage again, his rapid-fire Berlin patter outpacing Ryan's German skills. Judging by the crowd's reaction to the antics and pantomime, the presentation was salacious and riotously funny. When the five-man house band took a break, an American jazz trio from Harlem came onstage to entertain the enthusiastic crowd.

Young hostesses worked the room in high heels and very little else. A petite redhead caught his eye, her lipstick matching the bobbed hair. Some invisible textile bound her scanty costume of sequins and feathers, its secret mystifying Ryan in the dim light of the club. She slid in beside him on the curved banquette and he signaled the waiter for another flute. Pleased with the first sip of the champagne, she snuggled close and draped one leg over Ryan's.

"What's your name?" he asked, his voice competing with the raucous music, and she leaned in closer still. The perfume was inexpensive, but enticing all the same. "Your name," he shouted, "what is your name?"

"Call me Lexi," she said, crimson lips pressed to his ear. He caught a trace of Eastern Europe, Roumanian perhaps. She took another sip of bubbly, her leg still straddling his as it marked time to the music, and he hardened in response.

An abrupt ring from the tabletop phone interrupted those thoughts, and Lexi beat him to the receiver with a *"Ja, sofort."* She set it back in the cradle. "I go now," she pointed to the stage, "but stay and we see more of each other later, okay?" No sooner was her glass drained than she was gone, only to appear moments later onstage, freed of the scanty costume and luminous in a backlit vignette. He found her "more" most pleasing.

Ryan knew the table phones were not just to summon show girls for a performance. A patron could contact any guest in the club, for small cards displayed the room's layout and the assigned number for each table. Many of the women patrons were young and attractive, some expensively dressed in furs, jewels and long gloves, and alcohol flowed freely during the spectacle. Some had male companions, others huddled and laughed with girlfriends, a few sat alone. Ryan considered trying his luck with an unattended blonde, but Lexi's invitation remained fresh in his mind.

He had drained two more flutes before Rolf returned to the table and suggested leaving for another club. "It grows boring here, my American friend. Perhaps we should try something a bit more daring?"

"That's hard to imagine, Rolf, but this evening's in your hands, as agreed, so lead on!"

Wind and pelting rain buffeted the taxi as it pulled onto a narrow side street close to Alexanderplatz. Club Adam greeted guests with a large neon apple in red and green, and beneath a flapping sidewalk canopy a studded double door was manned by two imposing doormen. Attired in little more than leather Speedos and bandoliers, they appeared immune to the frigid night air.

Rolf and Ryan carved a path through the din of loud music and the haze of smoke to a table on the far side of the raised dance floor.

All about them, drunken groupings indulged in sexual play, a motley mix of same- and opposite-sex partners. Both patron and entertainer alike did give new dimension to the concept of "daring." Rolf laughed at Ryan's obvious bemusement but said nothing, waiting for his new friend to come to terms with Club Adam's idiosyncrasies. Nothing the American had witnessed in New York burlesque houses came close, and the refined allure of the Folies Bergère in Paris seemed very distant.

A performer in stiletto heels moved about rhythmically under the spotlight, her partner an impressive rubber dildo, and to either side athletic males danced accompaniment with leather-sheathed penises bobbing merrily to the beat of the music. The woman was striking, an Amazon clad only in luminous gilt from head to toe and bearing no trace of hair. Pendant earrings matched a delicate chain hanging off her hips, its baubles swinging from side to side as she moved.

The dancer squatted low, facing the rowdy guests closest to the stage, and gradually took possession of the dildo to the delight of her immediate audience. With hands-free abandon she manipulated its rise and fall in time with the music, and those closest to the stage found her performance uproariously funny. As the band reached its crescendo, she drew forth the plaything with one great flourish, swung it in a wide arc, and swatted the nearest guest across his po-maded scalp. His colleagues drew back in drunken delight as the stricken man ran a hand over his hair, then regarded first his damp-ened palm, next the laughing dancer, and finally his ruined beer.

"Well, Ryan, what do you think? Is our Berlin to your liking?" Rolf reached over and squeezed Ryan's thigh, leaving his hand in place.

"Honestly, Rolf, my tastes run more toward that little Lexi at Club Orion." Ryan gently placed Rolf's hand back on the table. "No offence, but to each his own, right?"

"Nothing ventured, nothing gained, my friend." Rolf's English was flawless. "You'll soon learn many of us here are very set in our ways, and new ideas can frighten us. But God knows, our old way of doing things has certainly gone to hell." He patted Ryan's shoulder reassuringly. "Quite a few of us however are more open to life in all its diversity, so we do seek fresh inspiration for our tired German souls."

"Well, Rolf, perhaps a return to Club Orion? It may be old hat to you, but I'd like to seek some fresh inspiration with a certain red-headed hostess."

October 1929 arrived on a changing wind, and European papers reported with ill-disguised glee the financial ruin that had befallen "rich Americans." Wall Street had panicked at the collapse of the stock market, America's financial world was in free fall, and relatives in America would no longer lord it over their poor German relations. The arrogant "Kings of Finance" were finally getting their come-uppance.

Few anticipated the catastrophic consequences already spreading worldwide, but Ryan's background in economics and finance made him cautious. His stipend seemed secure, but he began to count his marks daily, recording expenditures to the *Pfennig* in his diary and holding to a tight budget. Rampant inflation became his constant concern, and the prospect of a long-term career anywhere near shell-shocked Wall Street faded quickly. After much deliberation, Ryan decided to make Europe his home for the foreseeable future.

Academia and its guaranteed, albeit modest income now held more promise than did banking in a world of economic turmoil. It was a difficult decision, but one with which he finally came to terms. He applied for a fellowship at the venerable university town of Marburg on the Lahn, and in the following spring semester he would pursue a doctorate in European history. His fixed stipend would be renewable annually for the duration of his studies.

In a matter of months *Schadenfreude* over America's economic woes had rapidly turned to dismay across Germany. Unemployment lines were growing longer, factories were laying off workers, and many doors were shutting altogether as markets for German exports dried up. The country already had huge numbers of impoverished citizens in the aftermath of a disastrous war, and the rural country-side was especially hard hit. Now the Weimar Republic suffered from high interest rates, inflation, heavy debts and foreign competition.

Panhandlers and matchbox vendors appeared on street corners, soup lines queued before National Socialist storefronts, and the rambling shacks of the unemployed sprang up in parks and unused urban lots. Gangs of violent youths made Ryan's customary evening strolls treacherous even along the main boulevards, and he took to daytime explorations of the city. The financial challenges were not lost on the well-to-do aristocrats at the von Haldheim teas.

"Germany will never last, you know," noted Helmut Graf von Landau-Bresewitz, one of the bluebloods tracing family name and seat back to the twelfth century. "Mark my words," said the count, "we'll never overcome these debts, and the Versailles powers have drained all our resources and stolen our most productive land. Next they'll absorb us piecemeal, region by region, then take us for what little we're still worth."

"A bit melodramatic, don't you think, Helmut?" The Old Major offered a wry smile. Their families had been linked by wealth, marriage and mutual benefit for generations.

"To the victors go the spoils," von Landau-Bresewitz responded in perfect English. "I'd do the same thing in their place. Face facts, my dear friends, the opportunity for a strong, unified Deutschland is past." He acknowledged nods of concurrence from several attendees and took a sip of his brandy. "It's agreed then, our dear country is well beyond saving, *nicht wahr?*"

The Old Major offered his own solution: "Personally, I say we make Germany an American protectorate; think Canada's relationship to Great Britain. The Americans will invest here again once they're back on their feet, our debts will be covered by their enlightened self-interest, and—if a few of them are as pleasant as our young Herr Lemmon here—we could do a lot worse." He smiled at Ryan.

"You know, I've spent some time already in the poorer districts of the city," Ryan said, addressing the increasingly-inebriated von Landau-Bresewitz. "This National Socialist movement is taking on quite a life of its own. Don't the Nazis favor the same strong leadership you want for Germany?"

Ryan was no stranger to the brown-shirted Storm Troopers, often youths with no job prospects, thrilled by the freedom to bully and harass in the name of "awakening" Germany. Brief attempts to outlaw the Brownshirt uniform were openly challenged in the city, and random violence and street demonstrations had become everyday events. Committed Nazis told him that only a racially pure Fatherland and a strong, fearless leader could resurrect the glory that had once been Germany's.

"Demagogues, that's what those blasted Nazis are, damned demagogues, with no respect for our institutions." Now the count was riled. "This Hitler is a ruffian of the basest order, not fit to polish our boots, much less lead us back to a united Germany." His words elicited hearty harrumphs of agreement. "But I will grant that upstart one thing: he knows how to rouse the rabble. Mighty fine theater, if you ask me, and an Austrian private, no less. God help us, he's actually gaining seats in the Reichstag." The count released a cloud of cigar smoke. "We might as well go on bended knee to the Americans and beg for protection."

"If Germany would just give the Weimar Republic a bit more time to prove itself, perhaps the American government might welcome that idea," Ryan said. "One democracy does favor another."

"That ship has sailed, young man. You Americans have it easy with only two real political parties to contend with. We've dozens, and more cropping up every day. How the hell can we get a consensus? The Nazis and I do agree on one thing: Germany's weakness lies in weak leaders, and these infernal foreigners, these Jews, Reds, Socialists, they're wiping out a millennium of German culture and civilization." He turned to the attentive butler. "Pour me another."

The Old Major spoke up: "Germany needs to honor its long tradition of authoritarian leadership, but we need a true Kaiser, a man of genuine rank and culture, not some Austrian who lathers up like a whipped horse and has the personality of a store clerk. And it's the responsibility of all of us here in this salon to find that great man."

And with that, the women rejoined the men and they all prepared to call it a night.

Two weeks later, Rolf von Haldheim arrived late to the weekly tea. He wore an open collar with yellow ascot, and something new gleamed on the lapel of his hound's-tooth jacket. The finely-worked, enameled pin bore a gold-rimmed black swastika, standing proud against brilliant white, the party name circling on a crimson field. It took mere seconds for the Old Major to spot the reviled symbol.

"Get rid of that monstrosity immediately, Rolf. Your joke's in extremely poor taste."

"I'm sorry, Father, but this is no joke. I've joined the National Socialists."

"The hell you have! No son of mine conspires with that band of thugs!" His voice dropped to a growl. "Where's your respect for centuries of noble leadership?"

"Father, face it, times have changed. Your beloved Kaiser isn't coming back, but our German people are," Rolf reached out to his father's arm, "if we give them their chance." The Old Major jerked back, and all in attendance focused on this jagged tear in the fabric of teatime propriety. "Please, Father, just take a look around. How many here are still young enough—ambitious enough—to make this country strong again? How many here have new ideas worthy of pulling Germany out of this sewer they've put us in?

"How dare you insult our friends and guests? Apologize and leave immediately! We'll speak later when you've come to your senses."

"I will apologize, but only for this disruption, Father," he turned to Frau von Haldheim, "and to you, too, Mother, for the breach of decorum." Rolf remained steady and controlled. "But I certainly will not apologize for speaking up for our nation and our *Volk*. Your old ways have failed miserably. Had you taken stronger steps to oust the Communists, the Socialists and Jews, we would be the victors now, rather than wallowing in pitiful weakness and disgrace." He turned to von Landau-Bresewitz. "My dear Count, you speak incessantly of the irretrievable loss of Germany as a nation, and my father constantly calls for our becoming America's vassal. Why? Simply because Wall Street holds our purse strings." He nodded toward Ryan, their resident symbol of American finance, and his voice became firmer still. "Surrender is unacceptable for any true German, and you have all lost the will to fight."

The elder von Haldheim's cheeks reddened, his voice was low and menacing. "*Raus, verdammt nochmal!*" *Get out, dammit!* He held his shaking fists to his chest as if, unrestrained, they would lash out at his son.

"Yes, Father, that makes good sense—" Rolf tapped his heels together and acknowledged the shocked by-standers with a slight bow, "and again my regrets for the disruption of your esteemed tradition. But I will never apologize for Germany. Accept it yet or not, Adolph Hitler knows what's best for us. Here you bemoan the loss of a failed Kaiser, when you should be welcoming our destined Führer."

The Old Major pointed to the door. "Go now or be thrown out! You are no longer welcome here till you come to your senses!"

Frau von Haldheim grasped her husband's arm, and he shook her hand away. "Manfred, let it be, don't say something you'll later regret."

"I'll say what I damned well please, and that is—" he pivoted back to Rolf, "get the hell out!"

Rolf nodded curtly and left. The Old Major stormed from the salon, his wife close on his heels. Her voice quavered as she dared reproach him, "But Manfred, he's your only son and—"

"We've lost our son, Klara. No follower of that man, that Austrian, is worthy of this family name."

Ryan stared after the departing hosts. The tranquil tradition of the von Haldheim teatime had changed irrevocably. It seemed that Rolf had finally found that fresh inspiration for his German soul.

# CHAPTER THREE

Ryan returned by train from Marburg to pursue his doctoral research at the Berlin university library and catch up on the tumultuous scene as the Weimar Republic faced the 1931 general elections. Political discord rode rampant. The aging Hindenburg stood for reelection as president backed by the centrist Social Democrats. Other, smaller parties that favored the Republic fought to block the rise of Hitler, who was gaining strong support from both middle and rural classes. The Communist party fielded its own candidate, while the Nationalists' aspirant demanded restoration of the monarchy. Many agreed on a general direction for Germany, but few concurred on specifics.

The university reception for a visiting American linguistics professor left Ryan bored stiff with incessant political discussion and dull academic small talk. He stood off to the side of the hall, trying to appear involved but smiling vacantly. He thought of returning to Grunewald, where the von Haldheims had made his old room available once again. But the evening was young, and escape to a cabaret or cinema had become his number one priority.

"You need the mustache." The husky female voice approached from his left. "Were it up to me, I'd give you a nice slender one, pencil thin."

"Pardon?" Ryan turned to meet the smile of a striking young woman, her forefinger pressed against her lower lip as she studied his face with mock seriousness. The bright eyes reminded him of a dancer from the Folies Bergère whose letters had pursued him since the two first met in 1928. "Well, hello there," he said, breaking into a broad grin of his own.

"I've had my eye on you from across the room," she said at last. "The smile and rakish look are about right, but a thin mustache would definitely complete the image of the archetypal hero." She laughed. "I'm sure you read Jung." She looked into his half-empty champagne glass. "Buy a girl a drink?"

"With pleasure, but shouldn't we introduce ourselves?"

"I'd prefer getting to know you first; a name limits the archetype, you know. But, fine, if you insist...Isabel Starr, reporter extraordinaire for the Chicago Times."

"Ryan Lemmon, former impoverished banker, now student of history, and doing my own bit of journalism on the side." He raised his glass to toast her acquaintance. "Plus, thank God, receiving a study stipend to make ends meet!"

"Well then, we can forget about *your* buying *me* a drink." She surrendered their glasses to a passing tray and reached for two fresh flutes. "Allow me to treat you to further refreshment." She moved closer to Ryan, pressing one breast firmly against his forearm, and Ryan suffered a momentary lapse in concentration. "Now then, Herr Lemmon, tell me all about your adventures in our bold city on the Spree. *Sprechen Sie Deutsch?*" Her German held no trace of an American accent.

He switched languages: "I do rather well with it, with only a year or two of practice." The university reception had taken an interesting turn. "Actually, I really enjoy it, a bold language for a country that admires strength."

"Well, let's see what you've learned. Give me your best German 'r.'"

Ryan growled the consonant.

"No, not that lazy, guttural 'r.' I want the actor's 'r.' Go on now, vibrate your tongue."

He trilled his best tip-of-the-tongue stage version.

"Not bad for an American, but I could definitely teach you a thing or two." She pressed closer still, daring him to pull back.

"Well, I'd be delighted to study under you," Ryan said.

"Tell you what. If I'm to give you lessons, let's start with something that—when done correctly—will eliminate those linguistic inhibitions." Isabel set their champagne glasses aside and took his arm, guiding him across the hall toward the cloakroom. She gave a quick glance up the hall as she shut the door and turned the lock. With her hands to his chest she backed him up against a rack of coats, one exploring hand sliding down past his belt as the other encircled his neck. Her lips forcefully found his.

Ryan broke the embrace to mumble, "What about the hat check girl? She could be here any moment."

"Let her find her own guy," Isabel said, squeezing and caressing. "Or maybe if she's bored she should join us?" Ryan looked at Isabel quizzically, not convinced of the joke, and she laughed. "Don't worry, my handsome archetype, I bribed her to take a smoke break in the powder room." Ryan drew a quick breath as she dropped to her knees before him. "Watch and learn, Herr Lemmon, watch and learn." He liked the huskiness of her voice. "Next it'll be my turn, and I'm expecting you to have mastered that tip-of-the-tongue 'r.'"

There was always something new to be learned from an attractive woman, Ryan conceded to himself, even if he didn't plan to grow that mustache.

Later in the evening they sat over a nightcap in a smoky bar near the university. Isabel confessed her distaste for the roles traditionally assigned to men and women. She found them nonsensical and anachronistic in the twentieth century. Ryan acknowledged she had proven her point quite ingeniously in the cloakroom. She also spoke of her preference for European men, but admitted that Ryan had appealed to her at first glance.

"So how did you know right off I wasn't German?"

"Simple enough—" Isabel said, "no European stands around smiling without a reason. Unless, of course, he's newly released from the local asylum. You're not, are you?"

"Not what?"

"Just out of the asylum?"

"Not recently."

She reached over and ran a finger across his lower lip. "Good, because I must say, you do have a damned fine smile."

The daughter of a Chicago newspaper editor, Isabel was determined to make a career in foreign correspondence without her father's financial support. Two years Ryan's senior, she had studied Journalism and German at the University of Chicago and was now three years in Berlin.

They agreed to speak nothing but German in each other's company. Isabel proposed trying to pass for *Berliner* in all public situations, the first to be unmasked paying for the other's dinner. Initially Ryan found his carefully-watched budget heavily strained. Isabel mercilessly corrected any error in his word choice, grammar or social custom, and cast a critical eye on his American wardrobe, obliging him to shop for new clothes, another budgetary burden. She suggested he switch to cigarettes, teaching him the German man's habit of constantly rolling the butt between thumb and first two fingers, but he remained true to his briar. He learned to count his thumb when signaling for steins of beer across a crowded pub so as not to order an extra mug. And in a café he requested *Präservative* for his breakfast roll, only to have his new friend laugh herself hoarse as the waitress looked on in consternation. Once she had caught her breath, Isabel finally clarified: he had asked for condoms, not fruit preserves.

Unlike Ryan, whose occasional reports to the Kansas City Times earned him a few dollars, Isabel relied on her journalism for a living. Together they sought out interesting stories with appeal for the American reader. At torch-lit rallies the Nazi leaders worked adoring crowds to a fevered pitch, and Isabel and Ryan reported home on Hitler's oratory genius, its manipulative power touching both peasant and professor alike. The couple walked alongside Communist street protests marked by clenched fists and red banners in the poorest sections of Berlin. And when the conservative *Stahl-helmer* gathered for a parade, the two young journalists worked the crowd and took notes. Political fervor often turned to violence, and they witnessed several dangerous clashes, exciting moments of living history.

They also spent some evenings at *La Taverne*, an Italian restaurant run by a German and his Belgian wife, where correspondents from major overseas agencies gathered to share stories and rumors and drink until the early morning hours. Ryan felt a bit unworthy, representing a small paper rather than the big guns like United Press and International News Service. He and Isabel eavesdropped, gleaning insights into current events in the Reich. Ryan had never felt so alive and involved.

One morning in February Isabel invited him on a promising nocturnal adventure. She revealed no details, but told him to dress down and expect a good story out of it. "Think of it as a costume party," she said, "think laborer or dock worker."

From his first days in Berlin Ryan was determined to explore every aspect of German life. Immersed almost nightly in the city's high society, Ryan had chosen to experience by day the underbelly of Berlin. He rode the elevated *S-Bahn* past Alexanderplatz to lose himself in the labyrinthine streets and dives along Mulackstrasse, a district notorious for crime and political unrest. And he had found in Isabel the perfect partner who knew no fear when it came to exploring this underworld.

So Ryan had no difficulties dressing down for Isabel's latest outing. He borrowed well-worn trousers, a pullover, and a formless jacket from the von Haldheim chauffeur Ulrich, and changed in the driver's apartment above the carriage house. A threadbare overcoat and woolen cap with narrow brim completed the costume. Ulrich commended his proletarian look and required no explanation for the masquerade, telling Ryan he knew a woman was involved.

To avoid inquiries from his host family—the "Old Major" could never fathom Ryan's interest in Berlin's low-life—he snuck through the back garden under cover of darkness. A cottage well to the rear of the estate was home to the butler Erich and his wife, and a small gate just beyond gave access to a service alley. Ryan walked the few blocks to the nearest *S-Bahn* station. He passed Café Braunitsch, where he was already well-known as a guest of the von Haldheim family, and his customary waiter eyed him with suspicion. The disguise was clearly effective.

The rendezvous was set for a workers' dive in Wedding, a rough urban neighborhood known as a hotbed of Communist activity. He and Isabel had ventured into this borough only once before, posing as radical students and playing the role of an amorous drunken couple when their cover appeared blown. The *S-Bahn* had spirited them back across the river in the early evening hours, while rundown shops were still open and the main streets teemed with down-and-out crowds rather than hoodlums and thugs.

On this evening he exited the station at Müllerstrasse. The ravages of the depression had badly scarred the neighborhood. He ran a gantlet of prostitutes vying for his attention, offering discounts from the typical ten marks to a low of four marks seventy-five. One streetwalker cursed him brazenly when he ignored all invitations. A crippled curbside vendor hawked a booklet for twenty pennies on "The Passions of Berlin," and Ryan received with his purchase specific directions to a narrow side street off Ackerstrasse where a flickering neon sign marked his destination.

Behind the bar stood a burly man of indeterminate age, his heavily-greased hair dyed an unnatural black. A cigarette with a mind of its own dangled from the man's lip as he picked absentmindedly at a scab on his cheek. Ryan scanned the dive for Isabel, but was not overly surprised at her absence, for she was often late. Placing a few coins on the counter, he ordered a beer. He winced at first taste and the second proved equally disappointing, so he requested a *Bötzow-Privat*, his regular choice at Café Braunitsch. The bartender rolled his eyes, mumbled something incoherent, and continued to rinse a glass, no cleaner for the effort.

Ryan turned his back to the counter. Grime-dulled lamps struggled with the thick haze of smoke. Three groups of heavyset men, crumpled fedoras and caps low over their brows, hunched over half-empty glasses. They concentrated on loud games of *Skat*, slamming down the cards and occasionally muttering to each other in the Berlin dialect he had yet to master. The place reeked of stale beer, fried onions, and unwashed bodies.

At a back table a hooker smoked a cigarillo and casually observed the card players. Once she knew she had Ryan's eye she leaned forward to straighten the seams of her white stockings, revealing both shapely legs and the swelling mounds of her breasts, so he carried his beer to her table. She glanced up as if surprised by his presence and smiled sweetly, raising one eyebrow. *"Kommst Du mit?"* she asked, the customary hooker's invitation with flirtatious inflection and often a wink.

"Gladly," he said. He leaned down, lifted the half-veil of her hat, and brushed his lips lightly across her cheek. The Chanel belied the brassy costume, but fought a losing battle against the stench of bar and cigarillo. "Another beer first?"

"No time for that, *Liebchen,"* Isabel mimicked the dialect effortlessly. "I am, after all, a working girl, and on duty. Besides, the beer here is worse than disgusting."

She snuffed out the slender cigar and headed toward the door, swinging both handbag and hips in exaggerated fashion. The *Skat* players finally looked up from their cards. She nodded toward the barkeep, also suddenly attentive, and directed: "Give him a mark, it's his cut." Ryan reluctantly pulled the coin from his trousers and placed it on the counter. The bartender acknowledged the tip with a desultory nod before returning to the scab on his cheek.

"You owe me big time," Ryan said, taking her long coat with worn fur collar from the rack and holding it open for her. They stepped out into the chill evening air. "Did you catch that? Big time."

Isabel only laughed. On the sidewalk she belted closed her coat. The temperature was dropping quickly. She steered him to the right down the dimly-lit street. "Not exactly my favorite neighborhood for an evening stroll," Ryan said.

"Then you should get out more often." she suggested.

Street lamps guided them past interconnected five-story tenements. Signs faded from years of neglect marked the shuttered storefronts, and a cobbled pavement strewn with trash and broken glass slowed their progress. Wind-gusted newsprint gathered at the stoops, and weather-shredded posters advertised years of political turmoil, with hastily-wrought swastikas competing with hammer-and-sickle graffiti and the slogans of belligerent political movements. *Down with Police Terror! Now Berlin stays Red!* The gutter reeked of urine, and a deflated child's ball sat incongruously in the middle of the street, reminding him that children, whole families, lived out their lives in this miserable neighborhood. They passed portals opening to inner courtyards. The stench of privies and spoiled garbage was all-pervasive, and from time to time Isabel held her handkerchief to her nose but made no comment on their surroundings. Somewhere above their heads a woman traded obscenities with a man, perhaps a husband, a lover, a pimp. Beneath a streetlamp a cloud of vapor rose from a viscous, purplish puddle, and the ragged trail of heel marks pulled the eye into a nearby courtyard.

Ryan drew the obvious conclusion.

Isabel shrugged. "Welcome to the real Berlin."

Ryan was less sanguine. "You could at least tell me where we're headed, just in case I ever have to explain what brought us to this god-forsaken place."

Isabel chuckled and described the evening's agenda: Leftists were gathering for a march of solidarity in the fight against the reactionary right. Violent clashes between brown-shirted Storm Troopers, Communists and sympathizing Socialist *Reichsbanner* were becoming more common, and bashed heads and knife injuries were not unusual. Some fatalities had been reported. The invitation had come from two of her "Red" acquaintances, and they encouraged her to bring Ryan as long as they both dressed to fit in. "What a fascinating moment in history," she said. "And we're right in the middle of it! How lucky is that?"

"Sure, lucky...if we live long enough."

"Don't worry; you look suitably proletarian to witness a class struggle." She reached up and stroked his chin. "Although a bit of stubble might have helped. Must you always look so clean-cut?" Ryan was surprised by his own wariness. "Leave it to my friends to look after us," said Isabel. "There's no real risk, I'm sure."

At the approach to the next tenement Ryan suddenly grabbed her elbow. A solitary figure in wide-brimmed fedora had stepped from a passageway and halted mid-street. Cupping his match to shield it from the wind, he lit a cigarette. In the flare Ryan saw the battered mug of a boxer. The man stared directly at the couple, slowly released a cloud of smoke through his nostrils, and acknowledged their presence with a nod. He then turned abruptly and strode off, only to disappear into another passage a block farther up. As they passed that spot no lights shone in the windows above.

They pushed onward until a narrow side street finally matched the route she had memorized. A broken gas lamp high on a wall and the shards of its shattered globe underfoot marked their turn. Ahead lay a stretch of brick buildings, and some hundred meters beyond loomed a large industrial structure. A vehicle hugged the wall on either side of the narrow street. Silhouetted figures gathered before an open doorway pouring light onto the cul-de-sac, and two guards flanked the entry.

"This must be the place," Isabel said, "and it looks like we've got a welcoming party."

"You're pulling my leg, right?" Ryan marveled at her composure.

A rope stretching across the street from bumper to bumper linked two brewery trucks with canvas panels. Suspended from the cord was a barely legible, hand-lettered sign warning police to keep their distance. They stepped over the barrier.

A voice called out to Isabel, and a petite woman broke free from the group to greet them warmly, her Communist friend, Doro. "I've been watching for you. We're about to start inside."

Despite the cloche hat obscuring much of her face, Ryan could see a narrow nose, pointed chin, and warm smile. She took Ryan's other arm and escorted them past the two guards wielding wooden bats. Doro's friend Jürgen waited inside at the door. He was heavy-set with watery eyes, either from the chill outside or from the pall of smoke in the warehouse hall they now entered. They appeared to be the last to arrive. Jürgen solemnly shook their hands and directed them to standing room at the back of the crowded hall.

"Love your outfit," Doro flashed Isabel a grin, "somehow it suits you."

"Enough solidarity with the working class?" Isabel asked, assuming a provocative pose. "I'm trying to win advocates to your cause."

Ryan and Isabel leaned against a wall plastered with safety placards and union notices, and she hung her veiled hat on a nail. Her two friends stood nearby, Jürgen with his arm around Doro's waist as she leaned in close to him. He whispered something and she smiled. A man noisily shut the entrance doors and secured the latch, the guards remaining outside before the entry.

The meeting hall was a sorting room for crates of industrial goods, but the containers appeared abandoned, and attendees were using them now for temporary seating. A man rose and approached the make-shift podium, a patch of dust obvious on the seat of his topcoat. The packed hall quieted as he stepped up on the platform to address the crowd, a lanky, bearded Abraham Lincoln in worker's garb and a crumpled hat. The speaker welcomed all the "worker soldiers," then urged the crowd to take up torches and placards to confront the enemy. He challenged the assemblage to fight the repressive tactics of the police and the growing anti-labor sentiment of the National Socialists. His fervor weakened as he droned on, a stark contrast to the Nazi rallies where Hitler worked a fevered crowd. The speaker tediously detailed repressive new government regulations, and then told the crowd to make its march loud and unforgettable, to turn on every light in the district as they passed through. There was a resounding shout of support and a salute of raised fists.

As the speech neared its conclusion Ryan sensed a muffled thump, its volume increasing steadily like some huge industrial machine gearing up. Those nearest the rear of the hall turned their heads and exchanged whispered comments. The heavy tramping began to override the speaker's voice, until all attention focused on the disturbance, and Ryan finally recognized the synchronized pounding of boots on cobbles.

A crash of smashed wood and shattered glass shook the rear of the assembly. Loud shouts and angry voices rose outside, joining the cries of warning within the hall. The meeting collapsed in pandemonium at the breach of the entry, and Brownshirts and long-coated men flooded into the hall. Many carried wooden clubs, iron crowbars, or flaming torches, and they plowed into the crowd, swinging brutally in all directions. A free-for-all erupted. Communists without pocketed weapons tore boards from the packing crates, beating back the attackers with matching ferocity. Clubs battered flesh and bone; fists, blackjacks, and boots hit home. The attackers trampled the fallen and brutally kicked or struck. A pistol shot rang out, followed by another from the opposite end of the hall. Ryan saw a Storm Trooper swing a *Stahlrute*, the narrow, spring-loaded pipe releasing a spray of steel bearings into the crowd. A man fell, his palms covering his bloodied eyes.

*My God*, thought Ryan, *we're going to die here!*

In the midst of the brawl he stumbled toward Isabel and grabbed her hand. They fought their way toward a side door, searching for a way out. Jürgen dropped with a bloody gash to his throat. Ryan reached out to drag him along, but the surging crowd pushed from every direction, and they were quickly separated from the downed man. Doro was nowhere to be seen.

Someone now ignited the stack of torches set aside for the march, and the hall filled rapidly with acrid smoke and soot. Violent coughing overtook those aggressively fighting as well as others merely trying to find shelter from the violence.

Ryan reached for a broken beer bottle at his feet just as a fist flew past his head. He came out of his crouch seething and swung the jagged weapon in an arc. The attacker dodged, blocked his arm and came up with a powerful upper cut to Ryan's belly, leaving him gasping for air. The thug, a broken-toothed grin visible beneath the brim of his hat, came in for another blow when he was felled by someone wielding a makeshift wooden club, and the attacker fell unconscious at Ryan's feet. Ryan, doubled over and fighting for breath, spotted the brass knuckles. *No wonder it hurts like hell.* Then he recognized the well-worn boxer's beak, the same tough they had seen lighting up on the street less than an hour before.

He rose to catch sight of Isabel planting a fierce kick to the groin of a fallen Brownshirt. Ryan felt his own pain pale in comparison to that of the Nazi, but felt no pity. Two men were forcing open a side door nearby, so he reached again for Isabel's hand. Still intent on her prey, she turned on Ryan in fury, ready to take him on, as well. "Come on," he shouted, "Let's get the hell out of here, now!" Her eyes cleared and she followed his lead.

A small group forced its way through the door into a hallway, the corridor dimly lit by fixtures high in the exposed metal rafters. At the end they reached a courtyard congested with industrial parts and huge shipping crates. Shouts arose from the passage behind them, and Ryan spotted brown-shirted pursuers entering the opposite end of the passageway. He helped two other men move a heavy length of conveyor track to barricade the exit.

A tall gate stood at the rear of the yard, its doors linked by an oversized chain with rusting padlock. The group shoved a massive empty crate alongside the gate, and a smaller container extended the height of the platform. Once up on the make-shift tower, Ryan and Isabel wrapped their topcoats around the barbed wire. Ryan sensed the ragged points pierce the material as he eased himself over and dropped. Isabel followed, her landing cushioned by his arms.

One by one their group clambered over the heavy coats, only to hang briefly before dropping to the pavement below. The last man held his hands tightly clenched to his chest. The coats had finally shredded on the jagged wire, and beneath the dim street lamp Isabel opened the man's fists to examine the bloody flesh. Ryan offered his handkerchief, ripping it in two, and Isabel placed a wadded section in each palm and closed the man's hands tightly over the material. He thanked her before running up the side street.

Their breath formed quick puffs in the chilly air. Flames from the burning factory reflected in the dirty windows of the warehouse across the alleyway, as acrid smoke and a snow of falling ash blanketed the area.

"You've real nursing talents," Ryan said as he took her arm.

"And you sure know how to land on your feet."

"Track and field in college. Next time, we try pole vaulting."

"Well, I'm up for the footrace part now," she clapped her hands to his cheeks and kissed him. "Your sports events are ruining my white stockings." Isabel laughed, exhilarated by the danger, then grabbed his hand and pulled him down the street.

They ran down blind alleys and back up narrow passageways between brick warehouses, all the while seeking an exit from the labyrinth. Muffled shouts and clamor from an ongoing battle echoed from afar, and police and fire sirens wailed in the distance. Their companions left them along the way, choosing alternate routes to skirt the turmoil, until Isabel and Ryan found themselves alone.

A half-hour of relentless back-tracking finally led them to a taxi stand before a dimly-lit bar. A black Opel sat at the curb beneath a streetlamp, its driver slumped behind the wheel, his head resting against the window. Ryan rapped lightly on the glass. The drowsy cabbie looked skeptically at their filthy attire and left his window up. Warehouse worker and whore, no overcoats, faces smudged with dirt and soot. Ryan pulled out a banknote and held it to the glass, an advance look at the fare, and thus reassured, the driver unlocked the rear door. Relieved to be sitting at last, Ryan gave Isabel's address. The driver clicked on the cabin light and consulted a well-worn city plan before starting the meter, and Ryan glimpsed a small Nazi flag affixed to the dashboard. *No wonder he's cautious about fares around here.*

Isabel's bathroom was common to all five tenants on the second floor of the *Pension*. Thankfully, the room was unoccupied at that late hour, and Ryan heated the boiler with coal from Isabel's private reserve. The landlady only fired the heater for Saturday baths—first come, first served—so Isabel squirreled away lignite bricks filched from the weekends-only coal scuttle. They took their time, slowly washing smoke and grime from each other's hair and body.

Back in her room they made love, Isabel on top and taking the lead. The faint neon glow illuminated the bare walls of the room and rendered the marks on his belly a purplish blue. She gently traced the pattern left by the brass knuckles.

Later they lay side-by-side, her head resting in the crook of his arm, exhilarated and exhausted by the long evening. "I do thrive on danger," she said. She teasingly bit his nipple, then kissed the bruised muscles and moved down. "Could it be an aphrodisiac?" she whispered.

They tested that theory again, very slowly, very carefully.

# CHAPTER FOUR

Isabel had disappeared. Ryan phoned the day after their close call in Wedding and set a rendezvous for the following weekend. But during the week she called to say a great new "adventure" was on for that very evening, a gathering of the same Nazi unit responsible for the mayhem at the warehouse.

"You have to come," she said. "It'll be a real kick!"

"You're out of your mind, Isabel. Those thugs won't care much for surprise guests, and I sure didn't see any women in their gang."

"Just one more good reason we have to go, Ryan. They need a woman's calming influence to keep them sane."

"Calming? You didn't exactly pull your punches the other night. I suspect at least one Brownshirt still can't pull on his trousers, thanks to you. Face it, Isabel—they'll spot you for sure."

"Nonsense, all they saw was a 'working girl.' Even you won't recognize me tonight; I'll go drab with no oomph. And you could easily pass for one of those better-groomed Nazi-types. I might even scare up a Storm Trooper uniform for you."

"You've got more balls than I do, Izz."

"Come on, Ryan, don't go spineless on me. It'll be perfect. First we reported the Marxist viewpoint, now we give our readers the Nazi perspective. My editor will simply die when he hears what I've done."

"Sorry, but I'm obviously more thinker than fighter." He ran his hand over the still-tender muscles of his belly. "One close call a month is enough for me. Please reconsider."

"Okay, if that's the way you want it," she said, "I'll go it alone."

"But wait, Isabel—" The line was dead. She was pissed.

The following Saturday she failed to show for their scheduled date, and phone messages left at her rooming house went unanswered. Sunday afternoon came with no word, so he dropped by her rooming house. The landlady, a starchy widow whose husband had fallen in the trenches, responded with cold reserve to each of Ryan's questions. She said Isabel had not been home for days.

"Have you tried her room?" He offered a smile he didn't feel.

"I'm well aware *you* have," she said, "on several occasions." His smile hadn't worked its magic.

"Does she normally go away without informing you?"

"That's certainly none of my business," the tone indicating everything was her business. "As long as I see monthly rent, the room's hers to use as she pleases."

"But perhaps—" Ryan continued undeterred.

"Fräulein Starr will be back soon, I'm sure." The door closed in his face.

Ryan stopped by the Chicago Daily News office at the Kranzlerecke. *No idea, but do let us know when you hear from her; her father's concerned.* He visited their usual haunts. Bartenders, artist friends, waiters in restaurants, the corner newsstand vendor, and no one knew her whereabouts. Even a cautious daylight excursion into Wedding to seek out the Communist storefront in Joachimstrasse proved fruitless.

No one recalled her, nor pretty Doro, nor teary-eyed Jürgen. Isabel had simply failed to return. The police were of no help, but he left his address should something come up, and for weeks he watched the papers—a woman's body found in a squatters' tenement, a wife strangled by her unemployed husband in a drunken rage, the occasional unidentified victim of a robbery or rape, a streetwalker's body found in an alley. Isabel rarely left his mind.

Over a month passed before the butler told Ryan, just back from the city, that a police inspector was waiting in the von Haldheim salon. The man sat drumming his fingers on one thigh, an empty tea cup perched on the other. He looked around somewhat uncomfortably, trying to decide where best to place the empty cup and saucer as he arose from his chair. For want of a better choice, the detective used a folded newspaper as a coaster and set the cup on a side table. He fished a slim leather case from his coat pocket and flashed his police identity card. Ryan glimpsed the man's name, a photo, an official seal stamped across one corner: Police Inspector Brandt.

"I'm here in the matter of Fräulein Isabel Starr." Polite, not overly cordial. "A friend, I believe?"

"Yes, a close friend—you've found her? What have you learned?"

"Nothing, I'm afraid. Shall we sit?" He motioned Ryan to the opposite armchair. "You've been looking for her, as have we. Perhaps you can help with details of your last time together?" His eyes held Ryan's.

"We were at a political gathering in Wedding, about six weeks ago now. There was a fight, a fire, but she was fine when I left her rooming house later. She had plans the following Wednesday to sneak into a Nazi meeting, across the Spree again. She asked me to go. I said no." The investigator nodded but said nothing, so Ryan continued: "I've heard nothing from her since."

Brandt put on glasses and withdrew a notepad from his jacket pocket. Ryan caught a glimpse of a tight, cramped script. "We're familiar with the Wedding incident. A number of casualties, and one fatality, as well. Not to mention the loss of a warehouse or two. It seems a dangerous business, this foreign correspondent work, don't you think?"

"It can be," said Ryan.

"To the best of your knowledge, is the Jewess involved in anything other than newspaper work?"

"Jewess?"

"Starr, Stern. They often change their names as they move about."

"What's that to do with her disappearance?" Ryan was surprised by the reference.

"One never knows these days, right?" The inspector glanced again at his notes. "As for you, your registration with the city indicates university enrollment and a Marburg student's residency. I see no mention of a journalist's permit."

"I freelance for the Kansas City Times, an American newspaper."

"Sorry, never heard of it. However I am very familiar with the Chicago Daily News, the reason for my visit. Our young Fräulein Starr works for the News, and her father's demanding an investigation. He's well-connected with my chief, so there you have it." He removed the reading glasses. "She was alone when you last saw her, when you left her apartment house?"

"Yes, it was late, she was alone."

"Perhaps she entertained another guest? After you left?"

"No." Ryan felt hollow. "Not possible."

"You have other names, friends, acquaintances to direct us to, people outside her newspaper sphere?"

"No, no specifics. I'm sorry."

"Then that's all there is to it, is it not?" The inspector rose from his chair.

"What can I do to help, anything at all?"

Brandt shook his head once again. "We get cases like this all the time. Your friend obviously has no problem getting about on her own." Ryan registered the implicit *perhaps she doesn't wish to be found.* The detective used a thumbnail to smooth down an imperfection on the leather cover of his notebook. "My guess? She's off on a story." He returned the notebook to his pocket. "So many causes these days, don't you agree?" He handed Lemmon his card. "When you hear from her, let us know immediately and we'll put her father's mind to rest."

Ryan followed the detective out into the foyer where Erich waited. "Do stay in touch," he said. The butler helped him into his overcoat and he was out the door.

Ryan could sense Brandt had done his duty by rote, expecting no insights, anxious to be on his way. He could still hear the undertone. *Sometimes such disappearances are better left unexplored.*

Weeks passed without further word. He attended a few university seminars, wrote an occasional letter home. He had no desire to return to Marburg. Mostly he visited familiar streets and haunts, remembering her insight and wit, her laughter, her passion. He missed her.

Then one morning a single letter sat on the credenza in the foyer. He rarely received anything other than air mail flimsies from America and the occasional note from his dancer in Paris. The envelope was postmarked Berlin, with no return address. He slit open the cheap cover with his penknife. It held no note, only a carefully-clipped rectangle of newsprint, the previous day's date jotted in a tight, cramped script in the upper corner, a bureaucratic hand at work.

The decapitated body of an unclothed woman approximately 30 years of age was found overnight in the Spree. Further investigation is pending, awaiting clues to the identity of the deceased. Anyone with information is asked to contact the Berlin Police Department.

In the silence of the foyer, lost in anger and self-blame, Ryan slumped against the wall.

He stopped checking the papers. He preferred uncertainty.

# CHAPTER FIVE

René Gesslinger's mother Jeanne, born in Alsace but thoroughly French, lost her heart to a German, the strapping, entrepreneurial boatman Heinrich Gesslinger from across the Rhine in Kehl. The pair met at a wine fair in Strasbourg, where each year her parents marketed the wares of their small winery south of Colmar. Jeanne was seventeen, young, pretty, a country girl to whom Strasbourg was a metropolis and the center of the universe.

At first sight she knew he was the one for her, and her parents encouraged her choice. The young couple danced that first evening in the fall air, and she charmed him with her wit and shy smile, intense blue eyes, and dark tresses tied up with a yellow ribbon. He wanted to give her hair its freedom and see the black curls drop to the pale skin of her neck.

Jeanne saw in Heinrich a serious, intelligent young man with the goal of owning a fleet of ships before he was thirty. He already captained a small riverboat and a crew of two, traversing the river from dock to dock with local cargo. The vessel was a meager inheritance from the uncle who raised him after his parents died from tuberculosis in his youth.

Heinrich and Jeanne married the following spring. Within a year, a difficult birth produced a hefty son, two weeks overdue and christened Reinhardt. Jeanne soon called the baby René, and the nickname stuck. The Great War came and Heinrich was called to the trenches. In his absence Jeanne looked after the business and raised their son, and she herself nearly fell to the Spanish Flu of 1918. Miraculously, her husband came home to her with limbs intact, but errant shrapnel from a British shell meant no future offspring for the couple. With the end of the war, Heinrich and Jeanne built a profitable shipping business, their small fleet of transports and barges plying the waters of the Rhine under the orange-black-white house banner of Gesslinger Shipping.

The boy spent many hours on the decks and docks with his father, gaining a deep respect for the river and the men who worked it. His parents were generous with employees and town folk alike, and René took their compassion to heart. The Gesslingers were Social Democrats and the first of the local shipping families to encourage unionization of their workers, much to the disgust of the other affluent shipping families. René divided his growing years between the river, his schooling, and exploring the dense woods and fertile fields behind his home. He fished and hunted, and spent long evenings under the stars, dreaming of traveling the world.

Geography became his favorite subject. His parents hoped he would assume the family business, but René fantasized of destinations far beyond Rotterdam, of taking his own sea-going ships to tie up at New York wharves or drop anchor off Rio de Janeiro and Hong Kong. He read constantly, spending his evenings in the family's small library devouring tales of international travel.

This longing was a gift from his father. Heinrich thought his son ready at age fifteen to appreciate the reach of the family enterprise, to experience his first taste of the great world beyond the Upper Rhine. As the early-morning mist rose from the river, they brought their bags on board, and the low-slung, broad-beamed vessel turned its prow northward, roiling in the first surge of spring melt out of the high Alps. They headed down-Rhine toward the great harbor at Rotterdam. René was thrilled by the nautical demands of the beautiful but treacherous Middle Rhine. Later he saw the great industrial cities of the Ruhr, where billowing clouds of soot and smoke smeared across the urban landscape, stinging his eyes and searing his lungs. Finally the Lower Rhine merged with the Meuse, and at the mouth of the great river they encountered vessels of every shape and size: barges and river boats, ocean-going trawlers, small skiffs and lighters, and massive ore-carriers. Heinrich was pleased to witness René's enthusiasm.

As evening settled over the vast harbor, huge vessels riding at anchor loomed overhead, the Gesslinger boat a child's toy alongside the ocean-going freighters. Tall cranes, channel markers, and wharves sent light dancing across the water, and unfamiliar music drifted from open portholes. Seagulls rose and fell on the oil-slicked waves, or huddled on buoys bobbing in the wake of the passing vessel. Their transport moored across from the main terminals, and René observed the warm reception his father received from the foreman, and the polite respect from the stevedores.

While their cargo was off-loaded, the youth tagged behind his father and the foreman as they crossed the tracks to a seaman's dive. In the smoke-laden bar he had his first sip of gin, taken from a greasy shot glass. His inexperienced palate, accustomed to smooth family wines, recoiled at the harsh taste, much to his father's amusement. Raucous laughter from all sides made it difficult to follow the adult conversation, so he turned his attention to denizens of the bar, an intriguing mix of unfamiliar races, languages and gestures, weathered tattoos, and many a missing digit or limb.

After a greasy meal of pork sausage, cabbage and fried potatoes accompanied by several beers, Heinrich and son left the crowded bar. They passed chandler's shops, still seedier dives, and deserted shipping offices, until Heinrich found a certain narrow alleyway sharp with the odor of saltwater and urine. A well-weathered sign distinguished this passage from the others, its image of a man paddling a red canoe directing knowledgeable visitors up the alley. They entered the courtyard of *De rode Kano,* a surprisingly well-kept three-story tenement.

Beneath the rosy glow of lanterns a dozen or so women waited, some leaning with a foot propped against the wall, others smoking or chatting softly in small groups. René gaped at long legs in mesh stockings, ample exposed flesh, heavy rouge and lipstick and dark mascara. Heinrich put his arm around René's shoulders, gave him a solid hug, and said, "Son, this evening you've finally experienced a bit of the wider world, and now it's time to learn what it is to be a man."

The father singled out a pretty girl, perhaps eighteen, slender in the hips, small in the bust. Dutch with Dutch East Indian, he surmised. She offered a grin of complicity when he gestured to the young René, and her dark eyes flashed in the soft light. Her skin was smooth and dusky. Heinrich negotiated quietly while René tried not to stare. Anxious, he worried how he would conduct himself once alone with the girl. Terms were settled and a few small bills changed hands. Then Heinrich handed his son a tiny package. "Don't worry; she knows how to use it. Just relax and have fun."

The girl, so exotic to a youth whose only prior experience of non-Europeans had come from books and magazines, led him up the stairs. His eyes followed the sway of her hips as she ascended the stairway a step or two ahead of him. They entered a tidy but cramped room, one of several lining the dimly lit hall. It held only a neatly-made cot, a scarf-draped lamp on a side table, and a simple wooden cross hanging above the bed. A narrow window with open lace curtains stared out to the dark night beyond. Her smile was reassuring.

For twenty minutes his father kept silent watch in the courtyard, smoking his pipe, politely declining invitations to go upstairs, remembering his own first time with a woman.

By 1934 René's chest was broad and his arms powerful. His unconscious attempt to hide his height gave the illusion of clumsiness, but few at the university knew he had perfected his balance on the rolling decks of river craft and was quick and agile despite a somewhat lumbering gait. And those who underestimated him in the past had quickly learned to respect the power of his frame and the speed of his responses. In Kehl more than one bully had been sent home bruised, wishing never to have provoked the shipper's son.

René had chosen the Philipps University at Marburg for its admired school of economics and business. He might have preferred a nautical trade school, but accepted the obligation to carry on the family concern. His parents encouraged him to pursue scholastic studies in the hope that he would build Gesslinger Shipping into something even greater. Almost immediately he was drawn to the camaraderie of student life, alternating lectures and seminars with frequent social gatherings to belt out drinking songs and down huge mugs of beer.

German fraternities, arising out of the independence movement of the early nineteenth century, consisted of *Corps* and *Burschenschaften*, some committed to German idealism, others to political activism, anti-elitism and abolishment of the aristocracy. After his first year of study, René had applied to one of the fraternities still dedicated to traditional academic fencing, a rigid form of stationary dueling in the name of honor and courage, and he was welcomed into the fellowship. As most such fraternities became fervently National Socialist, he found a few brothers in his own *Corps* who shared his social consciousness in the face of growing fascist sentiment.

He practiced extensively in the cellar of the fraternity house, mastering technique and delivering impressive strikes to the head of a mannequin. In his first match facing an actual opponent he acquitted himself well and in subsequent contests he became ever more skilled. A respectable mesh of scars on cheek and forehead soon won the admiration of his brothers-in-arms.

René's fascination with international travel drew him to the foreign students at the Dr. Karl Duisberg House. He joined a weekly session to hear stories of their distant homelands over beer or schnapps. His new friends included an American Jew from New York with German roots and plans to establish an international business in his ancestral homeland. The resident Parisian seemed intent on polishing the provincial edge from René's Alsatian French. Besides several other Germans in the group, there was a Spaniard, an Italian, two Brits, and a charismatic American whose language skills were all but perfect, Ryan Lemmon. In this international group—much to the dismay of the Parisian, who found it laughable— René became known as *der Franzose*, the Frenchman, due to his Alsatian roots.

Of all the participants in their "Little League of Nations," René was most intrigued by the dashing American. A few years his senior, Ryan had a worldly air and switched without hesitation from fluent German and French to passable Italian and Spanish. The American had already traveled extensively and done graduate studies in economics, although he now pursued a doctorate in history. Here was someone whose cosmopolitan ways René could emulate. They became solid friends, walking the woodland paths surrounding Marburg, smoking pipes filled with Ryan's favored mix while discussing international issues, economics, European history, religious themes, anything and everything. René listened and learned, all the while copying the unaffected mannerisms of the American. He even modeled his gait after his friend's confident walk. Ryan became the brother and mentor he had sometimes wished for in his childhood.

Unlike his new friend, René was self-conscious with women. The local Kehl girls had actively encouraged his attentions, perhaps because of his looks, perhaps because of his prospects as the son of the area's richest shipper. But in the university setting he felt self-conscious, the female students a bit too self-assured for him to trust his instincts and make a romantic move. He knew he was not unattractive physically, with intense blue eyes set well back under a bushy brow over a strong jaw line. And social gatherings were fine, where women welcomed him without hesitation as a member of the group. But once alone with an attractive girl, he usually fell silent, listening intently but adding little to the conversation, and the relationship went nowhere. His new friend Ryan was only too happy to share his knowledge of women, and set him up with several attractive prospects, and René gradually discovered his own worldly confidence.

As ever more brown-shirted uniforms replaced the traditional fraternity garb, the Nazi students began to mock René's claim to German blood. His hometown of Kehl had often been under French control, although following the war it had reverted to German territory. Official Nazi doctrine maintained that all of Alsace and Lorraine—as well as Flemish lands and the Netherlands—were historically Germanic, so the insult rang hollow.

Whether the ridicule stemmed from self-indulgent xenophobia or simple disrespect for a competitive member of a rival dueling fraternity, René didn't care. He cherished his mother's heritage as deeply as his father's. He viewed himself as an amalgam of both nations, stronger for the diversity of bloodlines and worthy of both.

But he worried that someday he would have to stand up to the arrogance and intolerance polluting Germany, and he vowed to be prepared.

# CHAPTER SIX

The summer of 1934 was a muggy slog through overcast days with little rain and the rare scorch of the sun to break the monotony. The drought was oppressive, leaving the Lahn River at its lowest level in decades, and the woodland paths through the beech forests prematurely carpeted with leaves. Heat and humidity had tempers flaring. City dwellers slept at open windows, sharing every intimate sound and argument with irritable neighbors. Shopkeepers propped their doors open, waiting in vain for a hint of a breeze, and butchers and cheese mongers spent long months at the mercy of flies and spoiled goods.

The public pools had been packed daily. But now the enervating heat had lifted, the crowds thinned, and Erika Breitling found room to swim laps again. Mid-afternoon sun finally pierced the cloud cover, and the stranger behind the sunglasses watched her every move, making no effort to disguise his interest. She glanced his way as she took a break, chest deep in the water, her back to the concrete coping. He reclined on a lawn chair several meters distant, his body bronzed, dark hair combed straight back from a high forehead, a pipe in his hand and a book open on his lap. The sunglasses were a rarity in Marburg, usually seen only on dashing Hollywood or UFA types on the town's movie screens.

Erika emerged from the pool slowly, pulling the swim cap free of her blond hair. She knew the swimsuit showed off her long legs and the contours of her breasts. She bent for her towel on the grass, then tugged down the back of her suit as she rose. He broke into a broad grin and she returned the smile.

"I couldn't help noticing your`tan," she called out. "Rather self-ish to use more than your share of sun, considering most of us spent a miserable summer here in Marburg."

"Had I known we were to meet, I'd have brought back a little extra." He removed the glasses and rose from the chaise.

"Italian Riviera or Côte d'Azur? Certainly nowhere north of the Alps."

"Nice guess! Villefranche, near Nice, two weeks with friends."

"Well, next time consider the less fortunate before hogging all that tan for yourself."

Erika casually dried off, one foot resting on the end of his lawn chair. She smiled into his blue eyes, prolonging her introduction.

She offered her hand. "Erika Breitling."

"Ryan Lemmon. A great pleasure." He held it a fraction longer than necessary.

"Your German is excellent," she said. "Without the interesting name I would have placed you for a Berliner. Are you English?"

"American."

"And a student?"

"History under Professor Engels. The dissertation's printed and orals only a few weeks off. And you?" He flashed that warm smile. "What—besides swimming laps to brighten my afternoon—brings you here to Marburg?"

"This semester will be my third year in medicine; gynecology."

"I'm surprised we've never met."

"Most days I'm stuck in the *Frauenklinik*. Unlikely I'd see you there." She wrapped the towel around her hips. "In fact, I've met very few Americans. Is it true what they say: you're more relaxed than German men, not quite as rigid?"

"Have a beer with me and be your own judge of that." He reached for his book and pipe, not waiting for her response.

Minutes later they met outside the changing rooms. Erika liked his casual look in a loose pullover with jacket and tweed cap set at a jaunty angle. She assumed that Speedo and book remained in a rent-ed locker in the bath house. She wore her pale-green summer dress, the hemline short enough to reveal her legs as she moved. She had brightened her cheeks with rouge and added some lipstick.

The couple crossed the river and climbed the stone stairway past the old Dominican cloister, now serving as the heart of the university. Marburg ascended steeply from the Lahn River valley, its narrow streets, stone stairways and half-timbered structures staggering up to the stately castle at the crest. The steeples of medieval churches and facades of Renaissance buildings punctuated the picturesque Old Town. On the main market square the city hall clock struck four, startling the pigeons.

They seemed at ease with each other almost immediately. Ryan shared his expectations from a planned teaching career in America, where a Midwestern university had just offered him a position. He spoke of his early travel misadventures, leading a group of co-eds on their first European Grand Tour, of Harvard Business School and a brief stint as a banker on Wall Street before making Europe his home.

"I've only traveled as far as Frankfurt with some friends, and once by train from East Prussia with my parents, but I was quite young then. Pretty pitiful in comparison with all your adventures, isn't it?"

"You come from East Prussia? What does your father do?"

"Professor of Internal Medicine. My mother also practiced briefly, but now she volunteers in the clinic."

"Did they meet at the university?"

"An unusual story, actually. They grew up in the same household as siblings. You see, my father's adopted. He studied at Königsberg, and then my mother came there to study, as well, and they spent time together as adults and it just happened. So in the end, I guess medicine brought them together."

"I hear that all students will soon have to take at least one semester in East Prussia." *Ostpreussen* had been landlocked from the heart of Germany by the Polish Corridor since the end of the war, and Hitler wanted to draw attention to its isolation. "Why'd your family leave?"

"My parents weren't fond of our friends to the east."

Ryan knew the danger. The Soviets had no hesitation about forcefully absorbing their neighbors.

"Well, I'm glad your parents made the move here. Otherwise I'd never have had this afternoon with you."

Erika was used to being noticed for her looks. A casual walk through town often drew the attention of men, and not infrequently the disapproving glare of matrons. More than once her mother had warned her of the malicious gossip of neighbors. But surprising to her was Ryan's obvious interest in what she had to say, something she rarely experienced, so she found herself speaking openly about her life and her dreams.

They sat away from other guests on the open terrace of Büchings-Garten, a popular restaurant on the castle ramparts where the panoramic view was the prime attraction. Below them rose the off-kilter spire of the Lutheran church. Student legend had it that a virgin graduating from the university would automatically right the ancient tower to perpendicular. Far off to the left, the gothic spires of the Elisabethkirche shone in the late afternoon light. The view extended to forested hills across the valley and neatly-groomed fields in the distance, and the main rail line beyond the river resembled a toy train set.

Between them on the table sat two glasses of *Philippus-Bräu*, barely touched. A middle-aged waitress stood near the terrace entrance, absent-mindedly smoothing her apron as she awaited the next order. Dappled sunlight danced on the white tablecloth, and an occasional leaf skittered across the graveled terrace in the light breeze. Erika sat back and crossed her legs, revealing a bit more thigh. Occasionally she reached over to touch his arm while making a point.

"Want a sample of the fun we med students deal with?" Her smile suggested a secret confidence. "Just imagine, some of our peasant women still stitch themselves into their undergarments the moment the weather turns cold. In the winter they come to the clinic and we must cut everything away for the doctor's examination. The stench can be just dreadful. In some ways, Germany still lives in the Middle Ages."

"And this draws you to medicine?"

Erika laughed. "I suppose it's in my blood. It's hard to put into words. Both my parents love it so, and the work in the women's clinic *is* fulfilling."

"But?"

"But I'd really rather travel, see more of the world, experience society, the big cities." She was silent for a moment. "That does sound quite shallow of me, doesn't it? But I do feel limited here, where everyone knows your every move. It's certainly not the exciting world you describe with all your international adventures."

"If it isn't what you truly want, look at alternatives. After all, I've already left finance for academia."

"That's not the German way, you know. More German rigidity, I suppose. Once we choose a career, it stays chosen." She hesitated. "And when I do finally marry, I'll devote myself to my husband and children, of course."

Ryan heard the echo of the National Socialist propaganda on the role of women. "So that's what you really want?"

"I do love children. And my parents are proof that family—after the State, of course—takes priority. They gave up everything— friends, family, university positions—all to get away from the Bolsheviks, all for my sake."

"Well, the German Reds certainly aren't much of a threat anymore." Hitler had eliminated open political opposition after only a year in charge, and his purge of the SA a month before had put full control firmly in Nazi hands.

She regarded him intently. *Do we really have to talk politics?* Living with the propaganda on a daily basis was bad enough. One had to be wary, even with friends and family. Denunciations were commonplace, usually anonymous, and people had been hauled away for being too open with their views. She knew what needed to be said.

"The Führer's already done so much to improve things, don't you think? Unemployment's down, people are no longer starving, everyone's more confident, even optimistic. We're finally sharing a sense of unity, of self-worth."

Ryan lowered his voice and scanned the other guests on the terrace, aware of his sensitive ground. "Don't the newest laws concern you, the severe restrictions on the Jews, the nighttime arrests?"

*Could this American with his perfect German be something more than chance-met?*

"Listen, Ryan, hard times demand strong measures." Erika put confidence in her voice. "All the bickering among the parties and politicians had to stop. And now they've finally gotten rid of those SA bullies who were such leeches. The Führer's a good man with a good heart; he's just had some bad people advising him. I'm sure it'll get easier for everyone from now on."

Ryan thought of girls who professed loving Hitler more than their own fathers, of the uniformed seven-year-olds on parade, marching and saluting with military precision. He let the subject drop.

From the castle they wandered down through the narrow streets and entered the Elisabethkirche, taking time to admire the worn tombstone figures of medieval knights and ladies before finally agreeing that dinner was in order. Ryan suggested a family-run restaurant in the nearby Rittergasse where they could avoid sharing a table with strangers. Instead they shared sauerbraten and fried potatoes. The wine was ordinary, but neither seemed to mind.

On the walk back up toward the market square Erika remarked on the chill, a first sign of fall finally on its way. He wrapped his jacket around her shoulders, leaving his arm in place. Plans were made for the following day, an afternoon walk in the woods once she was free of clinic duties. He would bring a light picnic and a better wine. At the door to her parents' apartment he drew her close.

He took his time walking back across the valley to his room, intrigued by her charm and laughter, disturbed by her unflinching acceptance of the new Germany.

# CHAPTER SEVEN

The Duisberg House at the foot of the castle ramparts had long been the most desirable housing available to foreign students. For three years it had been Ryan's delight to climb up from the Old Town toward the fine old building, the canopy of ancient trees gradually opening to reveal this stately structure, his Marburg home.

His favorite pastime was to grab a book and walk up from the house through the arched gate to the outer yard of the castle, climb over the battlement, then settle on the slope of a buttress. There he would tamp tobacco into his pipe, sit on his folded jacket, and lean back against the stone wall warmed by the sun. With his home, the city and the valley spread out below him in grand panorama, he would immerse himself in his history studies.

Strength of character and academic excellence were the historical guidelines in determining who won a coveted room in the Duisberg House. Now "racial purity" was taking precedence. Jewish students were being evicted from all university-sponsored housing, and the Nuremberg Laws instituted during the summer by the National Socialist government meant that soon no Jew would study in the Reich.

Tensions had mounted as the majority of the university's students joined the wave of enthusiasm for the Nazi regime, and whole fraternities voted to join the SA as a group. Many of Ryan's friends and acquaintances swore allegiance to the new regime out of concern they would otherwise lose the right to continue their studies. In that year the drab brown-shirted uniforms had become commonplace, where earlier the flashy colored sashes of the fraternities had fought for attention.

The furtive knock on Ryan's door one evening startled him from his reading, and he opened the door cautiously. "It's Franz, Franz Meyer," the voice barely a whisper. His friend from their "Little League of Nations" appeared distraught. "Got a moment? It's important."

Franz was in his final year of law study. The slight-of-build German was distinguished by an unruly mop of auburn hair which hung off his forehead in unconscious mockery of the Führer. The wire-framed eyeglasses with round lenses gave him a studious air. Ryan enjoyed his company and dry sense of humor, which always enlivened the gatherings of their international group.

Tonight, however, an obviously distraught Franz slipped into Ryan's room and closed the door with utmost care, as if normal shutting might draw attention from the entire house. No one had yet retired for the night, so strains of radio music and subdued conversation still pervaded the floor. Somewhere below a student fretted with a violin. Franz stepped to the open window and shuttered it before turning to his baffled friend.

"Ryan, I'm in trouble and need to talk." Ryan read the stress on his friend's face. "You're American, so you're my only choice in this."

"Take it easy, Franz. Have a brandy and tell me what's going on."

"No, nothing for me, thanks, I can't afford to relax, this is too important. No one here knows yet, but my mother is..." He glanced again at the closed window, as if expecting it to burst open to expose his secret to the world. "My mother's Jewish." Franz slumped to the sofa, unburdened at last. "There you have it. I'm Jewish." He stared at the polished tips of his boots.

Ryan was instantly on alert. Now he cast his eyes quickly to both door and window, for there was much spying within the house and several of his friends had been denounced for purported lack of "political dependability."

"Who else knows?"

"That's just it—by tomorrow, everyone will. There's a student in my civil law seminar I've had words with, Kurt Schlosser. I bested him in a debate and he couldn't stomach the loss. As luck would have it, he spent the weekend in the Ruhr visiting some girl. My father has a good-sized foundry and we're well known thereabouts, and somehow he found out about my mother. Who knows who'll squeal these days, right? In any case, word's out."

"Have they been harassed?"

"They've pretty much left them alone despite the racial laws, because the foundry's vital to rearmament. They put a Nazi at my father's side to learn the business, but so far my family's still in charge. But now my folks know it's a short fuse, and this afternoon that bastard Schlosser stopped me after seminar and broadcast publicly that I'll be kicked out of the university. My God, Ryan, I only have one semester left before my state exams! Once the university finds out I'm Jewish, it's all over." He shook his head. "Three years' study into the toilet." His eyes remained glued to the toes of his boots. "Dammit, I'll probably end up shining shoes."

Ryan actually knew little about the Jews. He remembered helping black-ball the Buick dealer's son who wanted to join his Kansas University fraternity, but certainly not out of prejudice or hatred. The student simply wouldn't have fit in. After all, he wasn't one of them—not Presbyterian, Episcopalian, not even Methodist. The Jewish boy would not have felt at home, and Ryan had given his action no further thought. Until this evening.

The anti-Semitic tirades of the National Socialists had become so omnipresent lately that he paid them little heed. After all, the Jews lived primarily in a world apart, much like the Negroes in Kansas. The Catholic seamstress who darned his socks was convinced of Hitler's greatness, that Nazi venom against her own faith would have no lasting effect, but she warned him only to visit his Jewish cobbler's shop by night should he continue to frequent a non-Aryan business. And then, in a small village east of Marburg, he had heard an old peasant woman rant as she swept out the rustic church with a twig broom. She condemned the Jews for her poverty, periodically punctuating her argument with a swig of schnapps from a flask hidden in her heavy skirt. He asked about Jews she personally knew. "You don't have to know vermin to despise them," she spat out, "they should all be dead." This intensity of hatred revealed a prejudice more virulent and deeply-rooted than he had imagined. And now he was witnessing first-hand its effect on someone he knew and liked.

"I'm sorry for my ignorance, Franz, but won't this anti-Semitic thing fade away once they consolidate control? It has to be just a matter of time before taking back pre-war German territories takes priority."

"Come on, Ryan, you're the history student, anti-Semitism is never out of fashion. First off, we're the Christ-killers. We supposedly crucified your messiah just because he called official dogma into doubt. One can't allow the questioning of authority to lead to torture and murder, right?"

The allusion to the Gestapo hung in the air. Ryan poured himself a brandy and handed one to his friend. "Have a small one, as long as you're here." Franz tossed back the amber liquid with a nod of thanks.

"Then we Jews brought the plague to Europe, of course, because only God's Chosen People could be responsible for such divine wrath, right? And, unlike the Christians, we weren't forbidden to lend money at interest, so some of us did get very rich subsidizing their noble lifestyle, their wars and crusades. Then these same noblemen killed us off to confiscate our fortunes." Franz held up the glass for a refill. "And now, depending on the day of the week, we're either the most rapacious capitalists manipulating the world's wealth at Germany's expense, the most virulent communists robbing every German of the fruits of his honest labor, or both in one, no matter how self-contradictory that may appear."

A sudden thump in the hallway. They stared and waited. Nothing. Ryan approached cautiously, put an ear to the door before opening a fraction, checked out the corridor. Relieved, he slid the bolt home. He found some patriotic music on the radio and turned up the volume.

"My favorite of them all, Ryan? We Jews are determined to pollute the Germanic bloodline. Yes, it's true! We'll either poison the purity of the Aryan race by marrying their good women, or, failing that, rape their daughters and wives at the drop of a hat." Franz's arm shot up in mock salute. "Lock up your women, *Kameraden!*"

His eyes returned to the toes of his boots. "You know, my American friend, we're really just *Menschen*, some stinking rich, many more miserably poor. Good, honest ones who'll give you the coat off their backs, and cunning ones who'll stab you in the back. But when anyone needs a convenient scapegoat, we take the historical prize." Franz sat back on the couch, grabbed a cushion and gave it a powerful punch.

"So what will you do?"

"It's not just me, Ryan. There are more of us here than you would ever guess."

Franz revealed that several of Ryan's other friends were hiding their Jewish heritage, and all were terrified. Ryan had felt their fear but not known their special cause, because everyone he knew was frightened: afraid to speak on the phone, to write letters, to whisper a comment on a street corner. Windows were kept shut when students gathered in a room so that nothing was overheard. Foreign radio broadcasts were avoided for fear of denunciation and arrest. A friend had asked Ryan to notify his family in case he suddenly disappeared. The local minister was removed from his church in the night and presumed to be in a concentration camp, where "enemies of the state," political opponents and those unwilling to work were incarcerated for the good of the Reich.

"I can't see how I can help, Franz, as much as I might wish to."

"But you can, Ryan, take me with you back to America," he pleaded. "Come on, I'll be your janitor, I'll run your lift, haul your garbage, do anything you ask. Just get me out."

The plaintive note left Ryan searching for a suitable response, and he found none.

For days afterward he agonized over his standing in the doctoral rolls were he to side with the Duisberg evictees. A personal choice became clear to him. He certainly wasn't bold enough to speak out publicly against the injustice, but would silently protest by relinquishing his own beloved room, the castle above, the city below. It was a gesture of support for his friends, hollow perhaps, but with far-reaching consequences. With little time remaining before his passage home, he was able to rent a basement room across the Lahn beneath the hillside home of the local chief of police, and he began to pack up his belongings.

He and his evicted friends were assembling possessions outside the Duisberg House when five uniformed men strutted up the road, seemingly headed toward the café terrace of Büchings-Garten at the foot of the castle. The Brownshirt attire foretold possible trouble for the evictees, and the Nazis immediately circled Ryan's group, mocking and taunting. Then one of the gang stepped forward to knock over a stack of suitcases and boxed books. When the owner tried to protest, he too was shoved onto the tumbled pile in the street.

The obvious Nazi leader was cut in classic Teutonic mold, with a strong chin, narrow face and piercing blue eyes. He immediately singled out Ryan when the American offered a hand to the bullied student. "Perhaps we should have torched more than just their books," he said, gesturing to the fallen student trying to rise to his feet. Works by "degenerate" authors black-balled by the government had been burned in Nazi bonfires across the country in the spring of the previous year. The state-sponsored pyres had been made even more incendiary with vicious beatings inspired by the Propaganda Ministry.

"If you spent more time reading books than burning them, perhaps you'd learn to temper your ignorance," Ryan spat out, wishing immediately he'd held his tongue.

At that moment an old Ford rattled up the hill, its raucous horn and backfire announcing the arrival of transport for the evicted residents. Several young men sprang from the automobile and joined the increasingly angry evictees in facing down their uniformed tormentors. Now outnumbered, the troublemakers heckled the new arrivals with a few final insults, then turned toward the beer garden, laughing as they went.

At the top of the rise their leader turned and shouted down to Ryan: "This isn't over yet, Yid-lover."

Pointedly ignoring the challenge, Ryan removed his pipe from his jacket pocket, tamped the bowl, and struck a match. Releasing smoke into the air above his head, he turned and smiled up the hill.

The announcement of the visitor to his fraternity house came as a surprise to René. He had been trudging through Richard Dana's *Two Years before the Mast* when Ryan showed up. He hurriedly set the memoir aside, admitting at last that he should have chosen the German translation. They hadn't planned to meet until the following day. René had just returned to town, and Ryan, preparing for the oral defense of his dissertation, had been less available for walks. Seeing his friend in the foyer, René knew at first glance something was amiss.

"Catch you at a bad time?" Ryan's habitual smile was missing.

"It's quite urgent,"

"Come in, we can talk in the library."

René led the way into the room, its walls heavy with sabers, shields and etchings of fencing matches from earlier eras. On either side of a stone fireplace, iron-tipped poles bore the fraternity colors. Above the mantel an oil painting depicted a medieval battle, knights on horseback flailing with swords and foot soldiers wielding long lances. The opposite wall was dedicated to leather-bound books. A solitary skull, its original owner and reason for residing there long forgotten, sat forlornly as a dusty bookend, a lone candle affixed to its brow. The odor of stale tobacco was all-pervasive.

"Out with it, what's put you in such a sour mood?"

"It looks like I've offended one of your fraternities, and now I'm to fight a duel," Ryan said. "Care to give me some lessons with the saber?"

"Better yet, give me details. First off, you aren't allowed to fight a duel; you're not German. Dueling with a foreigner is off-bounds. Even we *Corps* brothers have to be careful since academic fencing is now officially forbidden. If a foreigner were hurt, they'd clamp down hard and the sport would really be over for everyone." He took a seat. "Secondly, do you even know which end of the saber to hold?" He grinned. "Now tell me what happened?"

Ryan paced before the musty couch as he told his story. His mind overburdened with cramming for the exams, he had taken his usual morning break and headed up toward his old haunts at the castle. Unexpectedly, two Corps brothers had stopped him in his tracks and upbraided him for passing the Sachsen-Wachonia fraternity house and failing to lift his hat to their blue, red and gold flag. Ryan had tried diplomacy and an apology: he had not known a salute was expected. The explanation fell on deaf ears. A third student then strode out and faced him down. Ryan immediately recognized the obnoxious Brownshirt leader from the Duisberg House incident.

"Obviously you have no concept of honor." The man was in his face. "Perhaps you need a lesson in manners."

Ryan took a reflexive step backwards. "My lessons are academic, and no business of yours. I'll tip my hat now and be on my way."

"Far too little, far too late." The Nazi pulled an embossed calling card from his jacket, tore it halfway through, and handed it to Ryan. "Shall we say tomorrow afternoon, four o'clock, Marbach? I assume you can find your way?"

The three had turned abruptly on their heels and entered the fraternity house, leaving Ryan staring in disbelief.

"And that was that." Ryan handed the calling card to René with a quizzical look. "You know him?"

René nodded. He rose and shut the door to the library, then took a chair facing his friend. "Quite a piece of work, this von Kredow. Arrogant bastard, but a damned strong fighter, well respected in a *Mensur*, likes to pose as the old-school aristocrat. He heads Wachonia this semester, as well as the Nazi student group, and has quite a following."

"So I've managed to piss off a good one."

"Sounds like a set-up to me."

"Probably so," Ryan acknowledged. "He sure had a problem with me the other day, and their house is on my customary walking route. I've never been asked to doff my hat before."

"What could you expect? Wachonia has gone full-bore Nazi, out to cleanse the country of anyone not "pure" German. And it gets worse: this von Kredow heads the AWK, as well."

The euphemistically-titled Academic Research Employment Office, *das Akademische Wissenschaftliche Arbeitsamt*, organized Reichwide military training under the guise of character-building "defensive weapons practice." Its regional offices bore the acronym AWK. All the fraternities had now joined the movement, along with many of the student organizations, until every non-affiliated student felt pressured to participate. It was as much as mandatory for anyone not a foreigner.

"Speaking of such nonsense, how was your AWK 'vacation,' anyway?" He lit his pipe and handed René the tobacco pouch, relieved to have a friend in a dueling fraternity to advise him.

"I'd hoped for the nautical training, of course. But signing up and getting in aren't the same, especially when things are run by our archrival, your friends at Wachonia. They shunted me off for three weeks in the countryside." He tamped his pipe.

"Not your typical camping getaway, I suppose."

René's voice dropped to a whisper, "A shitload of Nazi crap about the 'Jewish threat' and 'holy duty to the Fatherland.' My favorite: 'strengthening the defensive will of German youth.'"

"Boot camp, then."

"No, merely 'defensive training,' remember?" Both chuckled at the absurdity. The country was re-arming at a feverish pitch, right under the nose of the nations that had signed the despised Treaty of Versailles.

Ryan returned to his personal dilemma. He knew he did not have to *Heil Hitler* at every hello and good-bye, but most foreign students toed the line and used the salutation, and he had quickly adjusted, finding it easier throughout the day. It was very uncomfortable—and in some situations dangerous—to be viewed as lacking respect for the new Germany. Not a few had been soundly thrashed for failing to salute a passing SA parade, even though as foreigners they weren't obliged. And now Ryan had shown some unintentional disrespect to a local Nazi powerhouse.

"So what is von Kredow's angle, anyway? He must know I'm American and can't duel."

"Public humiliation. If you don't show for the *Mensur*, he spreads the word you haven't the guts. If you do show up, he makes you a laughingstock in front of his cronies. Either way, he validates his power. Remember, you're dealing with bullies. They dishonor the very concept of honor daily, and get away with it."

"All right, let's say I just ignore all this?"

René considered carefully. "Face facts, my friend; you'll be crossing the Atlantic soon, so maybe you can pretend this never happened." René struck a match. "But we both know the Nazis now own the student council...and the faculty." He exhaled a plume of smoke. "And there's your big risk: once a *Corps* brother, always a *Corps* brother. Your exam committee will be stacked with Wachonians—they're the oldest and strongest of the corporations—so your degree's at risk if you piss off the wrong people. Willing to chance failing your orals?"

Ryan shook his head in disbelief. "So what's my answer?" The inadvertent slight of a colored piece of cloth, and his doctoral work imperiled.

René abruptly stood and assumed the dueler's start position. "I am." He creased the air with the imagined saber in rapid flicks of the wrist. "Frankly, I'm fed up with these assholes, and wouldn't mind putting that one in his place, so I'll take the challenge on your behalf. You can second me, there's no rule against that."

"You know I'm grateful for the offer, René, but you just said he's a strong dueler, and you tell me repeatedly you're still learning the ropes? I couldn't ask that of you."

"No one's asking, my friend, I'm volunteering. I'll land this *Scheisskerl* on his pompous ass. As your champion, I'll show up for the challenge and we'll shake up his plan."

# CHAPTER EIGHT

Horst's summer had been a great success. He had organized and spearheaded the AWK training in the Hessian countryside, and then marched and celebrated with his comrades at an impressive National Socialist Party Congress in Nuremberg. But upon his return to Marburg for the fall semester he learned that much had happened in his absence. His reputation stood at risk, and now he had set the wheels of retribution in motion.

Horst had anticipated an enthusiastic reception from Erika Breitling after the lengthy separation. The girl's lithe body and desirable looks suited his own physical attributes, in bed she yielded to his demands without question, just as a woman should, and in public she earned him the envy of every man in the crowd. In short, she was worthy of him, and the right wife was integral to his master plan. The Party demanded an obedient wife to bear perfect German children for the Reich, and Erika's considerable charms were to play a fundamental role in promoting his career.

Reichsminister Göring himself had congratulated Horst on his taste in women, giving a conspiratorial nod toward Erika in appreciation, man-to-man. That brilliant evening back in February had been a triumph. Göring had paid an official visit to Marburg, and Horst represented the student association at the reception for the Reich's most powerful police official. Göring had recently separated the political and intelligence units of the Prussian police and formed the *Geheime Staatspolizei*, the secret state police known as the Gestapo. Erika stood at Horst's side, and his handsome fraternity uniform had mirrored the striking outfit of the man who now commanded the nation's largest law enforcement group.

The celebration of their powerful guest was a memorable affair held at the castle, and the weather cooperated with a winter sky sparkling with stars. Göring emerged from the Grosser Mercedes resplendent in his white uniform, the *Pour le Mérite* cross at his throat and a dagger at his side. Horst and Erika were introduced in the reception line, and Göring, after an appreciative nod to Erika's beauty, mentioned his familiarity with Horst's local efforts to further the Party cause. Toward the end of the evening an aide drew Horst aside, inviting him to meet with the state police leader in a private room off the main hall.

"You come well recommended," Göring said, signaling a steward to offer Horst a glass of champagne.

"I'm honored to serve in any way I can, Herr Reichsminister." Horst took the glass.

"We'll need more men of your strength and dedication in the months and years ahead. The local chief of police is a friend of ours, and he says you've helped him identify local troublemakers standing in the way of our progress."

"I do my best, sir."

"And I'm also told that you assist him—unofficially, of course— by setting straight such enemies of the state?"

"An honor and an obligation, sir."

"I've recently made some changes in the structure of our state police force, and I shall be requiring young men of proven skills to undertake difficult tasks. We are destined to win back our rightful place in Europe, but it will take work." He sipped his champagne. "I believe you have these merits. Interested?"

"Nothing would please me more, sir."

"I'm told you study law."

"I'll have my degree by the end of the year, sir."

"Then we'll be in contact once you finish your studies. It's important to have well-educated men of caliber on our force, don't you think?" He grinned. "And it certainly favors your cause having that attractive blonde on your arm. Makes things more pleasurable for everyone, don't you think?"

With those words a door had opened to Horst's future. Police work on behalf of the State. Secret police work, where he might write his own rules, all in the name of state security. Here was a goal to strive for, and he would need the wife, the family. He would need Erika.

Months of silence followed. A representative of the Academic Research Employment Office arrived from Berlin to review Horst's university-wide promotion of the defensive military training. He was commended for bringing the student government into the fold and regimenting the training camps. The functionary noted in passing that an agent from Gestapo headquarters had recently inquired about Horst's work with the local AWK branch, so he knew he was not forgotten.

But April came and Horst read with dismay in the *Völkischer Beobachter* that Göring had transferred leadership of the secret police. The duties of running a consolidated police organization nationwide had now passed to Heinrich Himmler. Horst heard his door of opportunity slam shut.

Then in mid-summer Klaus Pabst, his right-hand man, climbed the stairs to Horst's private room to announce an unexpected caller. The gentleman waiting for him below in the foyer of the Wachonia house wasted no time with formalities. "Join me for a little ride," he said. Horst got a quick glance at the identification card, *Kriminaloberassistent. Geheime Staatspolizei.* Gestapo. Recalling his conversation months prior with Göring, Horst felt his hopes begin to recover, and he followed the man without hesitation.

When they reached the street he slid into the back of a spotless black Mercedes driven by a uniformed policeman. The agent sat beside him but turned a deaf ear to his questions, so Horst kept his peace and waited to learn their destination. They drove south toward Giessen, stopping after half an hour at a roadside inn where a solitary, similar Mercedes stood on the gravel lot, its engine idling. The driver, a sullen-looking Storm Trooper, propped a Nazi newspaper before him on the steering wheel and barely gave a glance as the new arrivals entered the *Gasthaus*.

The apron-clad innkeeper's eyes never left the sole patron, a well-dressed man about thirty years of age in an expensive suit who sat at the table farthest from the entry. The agent pointed Horst in that direction but withdrew before introductions. The slender stranger rose to greet the younger man, and Horst noted an equine face, cool blue eyes, a strong nose and jawline.

"Heydrich," the man said in a surprising tenor. He extended his hand but gave no rank or title, no document of identification.

"*Heil Hitler!* Horst von Kredow, at your service, sir." Horst saluted and offered his own hand, regretting the sweat on his palm.

"Herr von Kredow, you come well recommended, so let's get straight to the point. If you're still interested in law enforcement—I have it on good authority you are—we've need of your services, and soon."

"How can I help?"

"Please take a seat."

Horst complied, and waved away the innkeeper who approached the table to take his order.

"As you're undoubtedly aware, our movement still has enemies at every level of society." Heydrich took a sip of tea.

Horst nodded.

"Even in the local and regional governments we still have those who would oppose our greater plan for the Reich. It's the desire at the highest level that we set up strategic offices for our police force to draw these people out, to expose their crimes against the Reich. And we'll need diligence from the *Volk* as well to help uncover sedition. From what we understand, you and your comrades have already done an excellent job within the student population and the local AWK. From now on, we'll offer you training in tools and techniques that will make your job—and ours—easier for all concerned." He clarified with a grin: "Easier for all but our enemies, of course."

"Of course, sir." Horst showed his appreciation of the jest with a smile.

For the next hour he sat in rapt attention as the man laid out his future. He was to develop his investigative skills with professional instruction, continue disciplining those who failed to fall into line, and follow Party orders, no matter where they might lead. He assured his host in return that his devotion to the Party and the Führer knew no bounds, that he had already taken this assignment to heart. It was to be a glorious future.

Only upon returning from the Nuremberg Party Congress did he learn that Erika had been seeing an American doctoral candidate in his absence. Klaus Pabst reported the embarrassing discovery, and Horst could barely control his rage. It wasn't that Erika had made him any promises, and he certainly continued to bed any attractive girl he chose. In fact, he had undoubtedly fathered a brat or two in Nuremberg. But this development was a blow to his pride and social stature, and an unacceptable threat to his career plans.

He had called on Erika midday at the women's clinic. "Erika, my beauty, still remember me?" He knew he looked handsome and fit in his SA uniform.

"Horst, you're early, you're back! When did you arrive?" She rose clumsily from behind the desk.

"Not glad to see me?" He feigned concern.

"Of course I am, but you weren't due for another week," she said, coming around to embrace him.

"Well, here I am now, and I'd hoped for a warmer reception."

She kissed him. "Warm enough for you?"

"That's more like it. I couldn't stay away from you any longer. After all, a couple of months apart can be dangerous to a relationship, right?" Her cheeks flushed, yet she said nothing. "But certainly not to a friendship as close as ours, of course. Did you find ways to keep yourself occupied? You weren't bored, I hope."

"It's been pure havoc here at the clinic, so many away on vacation, you know. Not a moment's rest, but I never stopped thinking of you...of us, that's for sure. Was field training good, and Nuremberg?"

"We grow stronger by the day, Erika, soon nothing will hold us back. So yes, very fulfilling. Sorry you couldn't find time to relax while I was away, but I'm going to make that up to you, I promise. Dinner at eight tonight?"

"I'm so sorry, Horst, nothing would please me more, but I'm handling two shifts today, so I'm already exhausted and wouldn't be any fun anyway. Another time?"

"Count on it, my beauty. I'm sure you'll find time for me...and soon."

# CHAPTER NINE

René tested the balance of the heavy saber. The steel basket of the fist guard hovered just above his scarred brow, the blade angling past his shoulder toward the worn oak flooring. The padding at neck and shoulders felt restrictive, and the leather arm guard added to the heft of the blade.

"Crouch low and stay to my left, and for God's sake, keep your head down." He turned to reassure his American friend. "The mask and shielding will protect you."

"What about my saber?" Ryan appeared pale, his winning smile noticeably missing. "It does feel a bit foolish, my just holding this thing." He cautiously swung the blade from side to side.

"Fine, think of it as a stage prop." He limbered up his wrist. "As my second, there's little else for you to do. Von Kredow's man will use his blade to block the duel when the umpire cries 'halt,' so just crouch low and stay out of range of our sabers, and please don't cut yourself in the meantime." He gave Ryan a smile. "Or anyone else."

Late afternoon sun raked the crowded guild hall, the rays diffused by dust and haze. Smoke rose to dissipate in the mote-filled light. Silhouetted against the bank of paned windows, fraternity brothers from the two opposing camps gathered in separate groups, sharing jokes and cigarettes. Colored sashes and small-billed caps revealed their *Corps* affiliation.

"And how long will it last?"

"Can't say. Could be fifty rounds, could be over in one."

A commotion at the entry drew Ryan's attention. Flanked by admirers, Horst von Kredow entered the hall. Placing bets on the university's most accomplished academic fencer had put many a *Reichsmark* in his comrades' pockets, so he had many fans. The tall Nazi projected self-confidence as he shook hands with the well-wishers. Ryan turned back to René. "So...you fight until first blood?"

"First to flinch, first to weaken, rarely first blood. The medical students call the match if it goes too far, but stamina usually wins out. Earning these handsome scars..." René traced a finger across the marks on his forehead, "can be exhausting."

The warm autumn day was giving way to evening, and a heavily-laden farm wagon rumbled past on the roadway, briefly casting a shadow across the tall windows. Local farmers busy with harvest took little notice of the students gathered within the hall. Though the contests were now officially outlawed by the National Socialist government, the local authorities turned a blind eye as long as the dueling fraternities remained discreet, and this tiny village of Marbach just outside Marburg had become their favored site.

"He certainly seems to be enjoying himself," Ryan focused once again on René's opponent.

"This von Kredow does thrive on adulation...that, and any opportunity to humiliate someone he considers inferior." René grinned at his friend and tapped the toe of his blade against the floor. "Which pretty much includes anyone other than von Kredow himself? But perhaps the stamina of a Rhine boatman will surprise him."

A sudden murmur moved through the crowd. "Ah, here's our umpire now, so let the fun begin." René nodded toward a slender student with a pencil-thin mustache working his way between the two waiting factions. The man carried a wooden chair in one hand and small writing block in the other. The crowd settled down. "He'll note the rounds, hits and penalties on that pad," René explained.

Perspiration beaded on René's forehead as heat built up beneath the body armor. A fraternity brother seated the leather-rimmed goggles which left René's forehead and cheeks exposed. Round iron meshwork protected each eye, a metal guard the nose. Once again René flexed his arm. "It's all in the wrist action, the parrying of the other blade. Watch for the blood, you'll never see the actual strike."

The combatants assumed positions less than a stride apart, sabers in hand. Horst gestured to René's damp brow and said with a sneer, "Is our big Frenchman here nervous facing a true German?" Before René could answer, Horst cast a contemptuous glance at Ryan and added, "What a pity your Jew-lover here isn't man enough to fight his own battles." Ryan remained silent but wished he knew how to use the saber in his hand.

"You know the American's untrained, von Kredow," René said. "So even were foreigners permitted to fight, it would be a rather pitiful victory for you, don't you think? Now, shall the two of us settle this perceived 'insult' to your house colors?"

Horst grinned but said nothing further as he loosened up his saber arm. His second adjusted the goggle strap across the combatant's ears. The umpire stepped onto the chair to announce the rules of combat and number of blows allowed in each round: six. The fighters' seconds now donned full-face masks of metal mesh, held their sabers off to the side and crouched low to the left of each combatant.

The umpire's call of *"Silentium!"* stilled the observers.

*"Mensur!"* Distance was established, the fighters' free arms held to their backs.

*"Hoch bitte!"* Sabers rose.

*"Fertig!"* All set, a second's pause, then *"Los!"*

As if self-willed, each blade broke loose, whipping toward the head of the opponent to meet with force. Sunlight flashed off the finely-honed edges. The blows repeated in blinding succession, each strike coming with the pivot of a wrist, saber clashing against saber, the metallic impact ringing across the hushed room.

With the sixth strike and the umpire's call, Horst's second sprang from his crouch, using his blade to halt the competing sabers. The crowd exhaled as one, the duelers caught their breath and took a moment to resume positions. The umpire made a note on his pad. No blood drawn.

"Up, please! Ready! Go!"

The sabers renewed their spirited dance. Nine more rounds came and passed without a meaningful hit. A pause was called to give the combatants a brief rest, both now drenched in sweat and beginning to show the strain of extended combat.

The change came abruptly. In the tenth round René's weapon deflected his opponent's blade and continued its unerring path. Crimson gushed from the severed tip of Horst's ear, and in that same instant the edge bit cleanly into bone, cutting a deep furrow through the flesh of cheek, grazing teeth and gums. Horst barely flinched, and both sabers finished the round before the extent of injury was known.

Two medical students leapt forward to halt the blood coursing down Horst's face, but the damage was too severe for novice medical skills. Unable to stanch the bleeding, the medics compressed his wounds and two fraternity brothers carried the stricken fighter out to a waiting car. The excitement over, the students moved toward the exit, some in jubilant mood, others cursing their lost bets.

"Well done, René!" Ryan set aside his untested mask and saber and a fellow student untied the American's protective vest. "I believe you made your point." He chuckled at his own joke.

"Our Nazi friend will think of me every time he sees his reflection, but don't expect any sign of respect from that one." René wiped clean his bloodied blade and handed it to the American. "Here, keep a souvenir of your first—and hopefully last—*Mensur*. Now, how about some beer to celebrate? I have a murderous thirst!"

The boisterous remaining students crossed the darkening street to the *Gasthaus zur Post*. At their approach, the inn's proprietor rose slowly from a bench behind the bar, having taken a moment to massage the dull ache in his knee, reminder of youthful enthusiasm for battle in the Kaiser's army. A well-smoked Meerschaum drooped beneath a graying brush mustache. Tonight he hoped for an unusually large crowd. These honor challenges were rare these days, and foretold a steady flow of beer and schnapps and a full till when the last drunken student headed home.

The innkeeper stood the celebrants a round for their success. Later his young niece placed fresh mugs of beer before the students and took to the lap of the victorious "Frenchman," rewarding him for a duel well fought with an enthusiastic kiss and a glimpse of her full breasts. René nestled his face in her cleavage to the applause of his comrades, then raised his stein to toast her personal contribution to their celebration.

Back at the university clinic, Horst awaited relief as the morphine entered his vein and the physician prepared to suture. His damaged face shuddered in agonizing spasms, and blood gathered relentlessly in his throat. The razor edge of the blade had severed the fifth facial nerve, the trigeminal. Horst had yet to learn the magnitude of his wound, but rage at his own failure burned in him, and an ominous plan for vengeance began to take form.

Humiliation and public ridicule of the American had seemed a punishment worthy of the insult to Horst's supremacy, and he had been certain of satisfaction. But somehow the duel had gone awry, and he had allowed himself to be bested by a racial inferior. Horst knew he controlled his own destiny, yet he had permitted others to intervene, and now his face bore a lifetime reminder never again to relax his guard.

For Horst, retribution was now very personal. He had lain in bed for three long weeks after the duel, waiting for the crust on his inflamed cheek to turn to scar, his newest badge of honor. The severe damage to his facial nerve would warrant a lifetime of caution, where searing pain could be triggered by the gentlest touch. He was learning to get by with ever smaller doses of morphine, but the agony could surface at any time with burning intensity, announced only by a tentative prickling near the wound, and—truth be told—he did enjoy the drug, even without immediate need for it.

During his recuperation, first in the clinic and later in his room, the wounds slowly knitting, he welcomed Erika's daily visits to encourage his recovery. But all the while he silently plotted his path of revenge. The meddling Alsatian who foiled Horst's plan for the duel and tarnished his reputation in the process was to be put in his deserved place. And then Horst would crush the American. This time for good. He would take personal pleasure in that final fatal blow.

René Gesslinger felt as if he had fallen beneath a streetcar. Weeks after his return to Kehl he regained full consciousness, but he still had no memory of the attack. By now he had been told many times of the vicious beating that had left him near death, and just as he knew that no streetcars plied the *Altstadt* of Marburg, he was equally sure Horst von Kredow had crippled him.

He lay propped against pillows in his room overlooking the Rhine, the drapes open to welcome a sunlit fall morning. Traces of morning frost sparkled from the few remaining leaves of the plane tree beyond his window. At his bedside gathered unread newspapers and books, gifts of well-meaning family and friends. His pipe and tobacco were close at hand, but smoking now nauseated him.

Again and again he demanded to know what happened, but the reawakened memory was ephemeral, momentarily clear, then slipping into a confusing mist of recollections. Repeatedly they told him of the policeman who found him bleeding and unconscious below the university church. He had lain unconscious in the hospital for days before finally coming home, and there were serious doubts regarding a recovery. The frustration in the family's responses finally silenced him.

The family doctor suggested René would need many months to regain both health and mobility. At first he could barely move, his right side numb, his right hand failing to respond to his commands. Now he could walk short distances around the house with a cane, but his right leg lagged behind, and he did not tackle the staircase. He wondered if he would ever lose the limp, and regretted the loss of his recently-mastered "American" gait. His chest ached with the gnawing pain of broken ribs trying to knit, so getting up from bed proceeded with agonizing slowness. But each day brought progress, and the earlier vertigo had given way to an old man's unsteadiness.

His mind was inexplicably altered. He waited for the accustomed precision, the ready access to words and concepts he could share with others. His sense of self also seemed off-kilter. Others recognized him as the same person, but he knew he had changed, and deep anger had replaced the measured self-restraint which had been his guide before the assault. But for now, still hampered mentally as well as physically, René knew things would never be quite the same. The more he regained his powers of analysis, the more he reached several convictions.

He knew he would never write Ph.D. after his name. The studies in economics were not a great loss to him. He doubted his professors would ever condone his liberal ideas in light of contemporary Nazi economic theory, and he rebelled at the *Gleichschaltung* within the Reich, as public thought and spirit were "coordinated" with the Nazi creed. He rebelled at surrendering creative thought to blind acceptance and rabid enthusiasm. One saw it in a suspicious glance, a hesitation to speak openly, a near autonomic concession to the propaganda, and everywhere the unquestioning submission to the will of the state.

Gone, too, was the prospect of forging his way through international waters at the helm of a great ocean-going vessel. Instead, he would now apply his talents, such as they might be when he recovered, to the family business of river transport.

And finally, with a conviction as clear as the sky on that crisp fall day, he knew that he had lost the physical strength to avenge von Kredow's insult, and would never again fight a duel of honor. He could however use his family's money and influence to counter the escalating brutality preached by Horst's brethren-in-arms. René's hatred of bullies had survived intact, and he would find a way to take personal revenge on this whole class of cowards, but on his own terms. He would draw together a trusted band of workers and comrades, Rhine men who valued independence, rebelled at central authority, and scorned bureaucratic niceties. Together they would fight a good fight.

One long day of recovery rolled into the next, mirroring the unending stream of river traffic below his window. From time to time he would spot the orange and black banner of Gesslinger Shipping, transporting fine Alsatian wines from the slopes of the Vosges to Rotterdam, returning with cargoes destined for the ports of the Upper Rhine. With every passing day he grew stronger and more determined to put Nazi "coordination" to the test.

In the genteel atmosphere of one of Marburg's most pleasant cafés, the three Nazi comrades planned their next attack. "Our brave cops have finally called off the extra night patrols." Klaus Pabst grinned at the memory of their assault in the Old Town a few weeks before. "I guess it's safe for us to go out after dark once again."

Horst responded with only the hint of a smile. Anything more expressive might trigger that ugly spasmodic tic, even under the comforting effects of the morphine. But too much of the drug dulled his mind, so he was learning to avoid laughter as well as overt anger. From the enclosed terrace of Kaffee Vetter a panoramic view of the river valley spread out below them. The cake sat untouched on his plate, but he did take a small sip of coffee. He now avoided eating in public, for careless chewing could easily bring the agonizing pain to his healing face.

His eyes scanned the clientele and staff for a female worthy of his time. The young waitress was obviously interested, a robust girl in a less than appealing white uniform, small black apron cinched at the waist. *Too easy, no challenge there.* The two fashionably-dressed women, interrupting shopping to enjoy some Vetter specialties, stole occasional glances in his direction. Horst was well aware of his classic Aryan looks and self-assured air. His face would be an even greater asset once the scar was no longer inflamed. Today however he found no worthy feminine challenge and returned attention to his comrades and the task at hand.

"Tonight we finish off the Jew-lover," Horst said. "I'd prefer grabbing him at his room over by Spiegelslust—we could handle it quietly in the woods—but unfortunately he's now lodging beneath the police chief's house. Too close for comfort, despite my understanding with the old man."

"Finish off?" Klaus raised an eyebrow.

"This one goes down for good."

Klaus Pabst's eyes were lifeless, his face and head remarkably slender. The receding hair was slickly pomaded and combed straight back. As Horst's first lieutenant, Klaus evoked fear, but never respect or admiration. Horst relied on his "dagger" to solve those problems where he himself preferred to keep some distance.

His second lieutenant, Stefan Brenner, was a different story. Stefan lived to fight, a solid man and valuable addition to the team. His was a martial family for generations back. But now Stefan's father relived the terrors of trench warfare in drunken stupors and horrifying nightmares, and Stefan despised the old man's weakness. Stefan's mother, three years gone and only a memory, had died of spousal abuse and a broken heart for all she had lost in her husband. Stefan's own beatings at the drunken hands of his father had only made him stronger, and he never let Horst down.

"So what's your deal with the chief of police?" Stefan asked, sitting as always with his back ramrod straight.

"He's giving us full encouragement—off the record, certainly—to help clean up the streets," Horst said. "As long as we don't draw public attention to ourselves, there'll be no official interference. So we'll handle the American here in town, and this time the body disappears."

"How do we pull that off?" Getting rid of a corpse in a town the size of Marburg was problematic for Klaus.

"The *Abdeckerei*." Horst gestured toward the heavily-forested hills of the Lahnberge on the far side of the valley. "I already have a key to the gate, and there's an incinerator at our disposal. Our American should fit right in with the ashes of diseased animals and road kill."

He reached to still the incessant itch beneath the facial bandage, withdrawing his hand quickly as he remembered the agonizing pain that would cause.

# CHAPTER TEN

The river Lahn lay shrouded in dense fog, its luminous tendrils winding up through the town's narrow streets toward the castle. A crescent moon hung close to the horizon. Across the valley two figures stood on the open platform of the Kaiser Wilhelm Tower as Marburg slowly disappeared into the mist.

Ryan wrapped Erika in the folds of his topcoat, her back pressed against him. Warmed by her closeness, his thoughts drifted to the more intimate pleasures soon to come in the comfort of his featherbed. He slipped his hand beneath the cashmere and smooth silk, feeling her nipple rise against his fingers. She moved more purposefully against him.

Her gaze lay on the distant town. "It's really quite beautiful, don't you think?"

"They both are," Ryan teased, moving his hand to caress her other breast and pulling her closer still. They spoke softly, wary of disturbing the fragile stillness. "But it's also getting late. Your parents expect me to play the perfect gentleman and have you home by midnight, and I'll have to beat the one o'clock curfew or the SA patrols will pick me up." He nuzzled her neck.

She turned and brought her lips to his, a lingering kiss.

"I wish we could stay longer," his lie without conviction, "but I can imagine a far warmer place I'd rather be right now."

She laughed and broke free, grabbing his hand to pull him toward the staircase. "Then let's go find that place for you."

Ryan switched on his flashlight. The dark stone stairwell was treacherous enough in daylight, impossible in the enveloping blackness. He held a protective arm around her as they descended the curving staircase to the grassy yard. Only a small lawn area and a fence of rough-hewn rails separated them from the valley below. To their right loomed the old inn, its terrace now desolate and uninviting. Just weeks before this beer garden had been alive with families taking in the last sunny days of the year. Small children had played tag beneath the massive beeches, as waiters scurried in and out of the *Gasthaus* with mugs of beer and heavily-laden plates. Now a damp shroud lay over the inn, its terrace abandoned, the chairs removed, the tables left to face the winter months untended.

Leaves crunched underfoot. As their eyes adjusted to the feeble moonlight Ryan switched off the flashlight. The couple moved quietly arm-in-arm along the broad woodland path that he now knew well, having walked it almost daily since taking his new room on this side of the valley. His European years coming to an end, he had chosen a last nighttime walk with Erika to mark this turning point in his life. He pulled her closer. The groomed trail circled round to parallel the valley below, and the woods opened up from time to time to reveal the distant, veiled town. Here the fog drifted in spectral wisps through the barren trees.

For all Ryan's cosmopolitan charm, Erika had known very quickly that this romance could not last. He was the shining movie star of films, all dark hair and flashing teeth, golden tan and witty banter. But her "American boy" would not be the type to settle down anytime soon, and she knew it. At first she imagined their falling in love and being whisked away to tall skyscrapers and a vibrant, open society. Although she wasn't sure Kansas fit that bill, she was certainly done with living in her parents' Marburg home, and she longed for social interaction and challenges beyond the dull university gatherings and the tedium of the clinic. She imagined lavish parties with exciting new friends, urban adventures in metropolitan centers like Berlin or New York where her future could be far more enriching and far less predictable.

Horst was the far better gamble. She had first seen him the year before, striding boldly into the main market place where table upon table had been set out to celebrate a festival day. He wore his fraternity regalia as if born to it, ancient nobility reflected in his carriage and demeanor. He reminded her of the old carved images of knights, as handsome as Ryan perhaps, but taller. Here was refinement with strength, the all-conquering Germanic hero.

Over their first beer together he told her he would be a leader in the new Germany, and she believed him, for he had already presided over his fraternity for one semester, and had a powerful position in student affairs. He had an unsettling drive and dark mystery, but she found his aggressive self-confidence irresistible, his public manners impeccable.

She had surrendered willingly to his advances. He was not her first—she had learned from a few fumbling encounters with a school boy and later a medical student or two—but Erika was ready for a serious relationship, a prospect. As the propaganda made abundantly clear, she should marry and bear solid, obedient German children. Horst treated her more roughly in bed than she had expected, but his fire was contagious. He awakened a surprising response in her, and left her drained.

Her parents were wary of Horst on first meeting, and encouraged her to keep her options open. *We know this type, he can be trouble.* Erika demanded details, but her mother's face darkened and she returned to her book. Yet Erika enjoyed the excitement, and she saw great possibilities in Horst's connections and drive. She knew he was destined for greatness. She saw herself on his arm, her couture expensive to complement his dashing uniform, dazzling their admirers over cocktails in Berlin or Leipzig.

He was ardent in his support of the new government and institutions, and tutored her constantly in the values of National Socialism. He recommended *Mein Kampf* and Rosenberg's *Myth of the 20th Century.* She begged off—*too much going on in the clinic*—but he kept pressing, and she finally thumbed her way through a few chapters of the volumes he brought her. *So much propaganda,* but she kept any doubts to herself.

Horst had taken her to a memorable civic reception to welcome Göring. With Hitler's ascent to Chancellor, Göring had become Interior Minister of Prussia, and the great flying ace cut a fine if somewhat portly figure in the enthusiastic crowd. The street leading up to the castle was lined with uniformed Storm Troopers holding aloft flaming torches. Banners were draped from lampposts and buildings, and huge flags decorated the archway leading to the *Schloss*. In the castle courtyard an orchestra played rousing anthems as the arriving guests saluted all around.

The grand hall, once host to Luther and Zwingli, was festooned in red and black bunting, and each table flew a tiny swastika flag. Here a smaller band played Party favorites and dance tunes, and a banquet table displayed a whole roast pig as centerpiece, its crackled skin curling back to reveal the juicy flesh beneath. Uniformed servers cut thick slices for the guests, rich gravy flowed from silver boats, graceful swan-shaped pastry shells held mayonnaise and other condiments, and heavy chargers offered a feast of delicacies.

Horst, as leader of the National Socialist German Student *Bund* at the university, shared the honor of welcoming the prestigious guest. The slit in Erika's crimson gown revealed just enough leg to draw admiring glances from the handsome men in attendance. She had fashioned it herself, and that flirtatious attention confirmed that she was a fitting social companion for Horst. "Such a stunning couple" was a constant refrain. Göring himself had complimented her beauty with a knowing wink. Toward the end of the evening the guest of honor left the hall with his entourage, and shortly thereafter Horst disappeared for half an hour, only to join her afterwards filled with unbridled enthusiasm.

"Well? Come on, tell me, out with it," she demanded, not used to seeing him so obviously upbeat.

"My time is finally coming, and soon. Watch for even greater things from me, just wait and see." It felt good to exit on his arm under a canopy of fascist salutes.

She knew he was hers if she wished. Back in his room there had been no foreplay, her new dress never again fit for wear. She was shaken by his forcefulness, but excited all the same. That night he had seemed so powerful, but somehow distant, perhaps deep in thoughts of his own future.

And now, in the darkness of the woods with Ryan, she drew herself closer and forced all else from her mind, focusing instead on the few remaining hours before she would send her American home. They followed the fog-laced path in silence.

Ryan wondered if he would ever see Erika again after this last evening together. They had so much in common—a love of nature, of children, of wry humor and uninhibited sex. Studying had been so demanding that he had relished the rare moments when they could be together, but it disturbed him to hear her voice more and more the platitudes of intolerance and obedience.

This adopted homeland had once won him over with the richness of its culture, the celebration of life found in every village festival and city beer hall. Now, as the German people embraced the Nazi dogma and moved forward in goosestep, he was leaving disillusioned. Neatly-painted signs at the entry to villages proudly proclaimed *Jew-free Town* or *Jews Unwelcome*, places which hadn't seen an actual Jew in centuries. Hitler Youth marched through the streets of Marburg, singing of Jewish blood spraying from their knives, and by-standers raised arms to salute both crimson flag and bloody sentiment. Friends were evicted from the university for nothing more than their heritage. *What became of the high ideals of great German thinkers, where was the tolerance?*

He had been so naive. Where once he might have encouraged an animated discussion, he now held his tongue, and he was equally disillusioned with himself for not speaking up. He knew full well that any critique of the government—even with exams successfully passed and his doctorate earned—could still cost him the diploma, which needed official issuance by the university to follow him home by mail.

But what he wished to pursue on this last night together was neither politics nor social change. He would soon take Erika to bed and feel her warmth, and he pushed aside other concerns in anticipation. Now in the blackness of the forest, with only a glimmer of starlight directly overhead, they stopped and he pulled her close. His top coat once again engulfed her.

Without warning, havoc surrounded them. Suddenly alerted to human presence on the path, a herd of deer pummeled the couple as it thundered past in panicked flight. Just as quickly, it was gone, leaving the couple breathless in the re-found stillness. Ryan and Erika held each other tightly before separating in the laughter of relief.

"Were those red deer?" He peered into the dark woods. "They were amazing!"

"Come on, quit wasting time, get me to bed and I'll show you my amazing animal side." She pulled him off the path and toward the valley below.

Erika reached for matches next to the ashtray and lit a small candle. "Much nicer, don't you think?" Ryan switched off the floor lamp. He had left the coal banked in the heater, and the room was warm. The space, devoid of clutter and character, suggested hotel lodgings rather than a student's chamber. Gone were his books, the writing implements and pipe rack. No scatter of magazines and newspapers at the foot of the easy chair. His unframed etchings and other souvenirs of five years abroad lay in the steamer trunk already waiting dockside at Bremerhaven. A brown leather valise stood near the door, open for final packing in the morning.

"You really are leaving," she said.

He tossed his hat on the desk and removed overcoat and jacket. "*D-Zug* for Bremen at 7:35."

Erika dialed past radio static and strident voices to find soft music. She draped her coat and scarf over the chair and slowly rolled down her silk stockings. Ryan imprinted every gesture, every moment in his memory. She moved to the window overlooking the valley and he came to massage her neck and shoulders.

"Your place seems so different, so lonely, as if you've already left."

"I'm still here with you now." He caressed her neck with his lips before drawing the sweater over her head. She turned to face him, opening his shirt to run her hands down his chest. He revealed her pale breasts to the flickering candlelight.

"You will miss me," she whispered. "And I you, my American boy."

What little clothing remained gathered quickly on the floor. She led him by the hand to the bed. Urgency now, kisses of longing and growing heat and a deep embrace as her legs encircled his hips and drew him in, and they moved feverishly as one until all became still. Then she lay for long minutes in the crook of his arm while he traced the gentle curve of her breast and the rise of her nipple. Her hips rose to meet his searching fingers and a low moan escaped her lips. She reached for him, and this time they moved slowly, drawing out these last shared moments together until neither could wait longer. With the release, the reality of parting flooded back.

Ryan drifted toward sleep in her embrace, but Erika bit him lightly on the neck, then kissed him deeply and rolled aside. She took her time gathering fallen clothing, providing him one last, lingering appreciation in the flickering candlelight.

"My father knows where you live, you know," she teased, and began at last to dress. "And now you must get me home before he comes looking for me."

Hands arched behind his head, he leaned back in the pillows and watched her re-apply her makeup at the mirror over the wash basin. The candle was extinguished, the floor lamp burning once again. "You predicted I'll miss you." His eyes followed the lipstick as it traced its path. "I do already." She glanced his way, and he saw sadness in her eyes.

The narrow lane at the upper reach of Spiegelslustweg inclined steeply to the valley floor. Once across the railroad line they ascended toward the heart of the old town. Haloed streetlamps guided their way in the dense fog. The *Altstadt* had tucked itself in, leaving the narrow streets hauntingly still except for an occasional drunken shout from a student heading home. Ryan and Erika stood together on her parents' landing as he sought the words for that final goodbye.

"I'll write from Kansas," he said, only half believing. Such a promise came easily, but life and new romances always seemed to interfere with its fulfillment. A clean break might be preferable to any hollow expectation of a future relationship. Both their lives and their countries were on such diverging paths.

"And I'll share all the exciting news from Marburg." Tears brimmed as she spoke. "And might you come back soon?" She slipped the key into the lock.

"Who knows? Perhaps next summer, maybe between semesters." He drew her back into his arms and held her close, breathing her scent, denying the coming separation.

"You *will* see me again."

And she broke away and was gone, the latch falling into place. Ryan waited several moments on the street below, looking up at the apartment. Light still framed the windows, so she had not left the living room, but no drapes parted to reveal a wave of the hand, a final smile. He turned back into the fog, a lump in his throat. Ryan knew this was not love, but he genuinely liked this girl. And he was taken by the sensual freedom she embodied, so at ease with herself, so different from most he had known. In fact, until then Isabel had been the one great exception. In some ways Erika reminded him of Isabel, and he knew he would miss her, too.

Perhaps he would find a way to make her final prediction come true.

# CHAPTER ELEVEN

The clock on the main square tolled midnight, and the narrow streets remained densely shrouded. Only a tomcat on nocturnal rounds disturbed the silence of the Old Town. The upper stories of the half-timbered buildings disappeared into the thick fog, and every surface glistened in the muted glow of the streetlamps. Ryan crossed the medieval Haymarket and descended Butcher's Lane toward the towering gothic university building.

Despite the wool coat a chill ran through him and his senses heightened. The hair at the nape of his neck stood on end. There was nothing he could clearly put his finger on, no obvious sight or sound to disturb the quiet envelope of fog. He glanced back to see the cat disappear between buildings, tracking a rodent or a female in heat. A second look revealed nothing, but he knew that in those labyrinthine streets something lurked unseen.

The attack on René weighed heavily on his mind. Ryan had accepted the official explanation—a random act of thuggery, his friend's inebriation and lack of discretion making him a victim. There had been no witnesses, and such violence was rare in a university town like Marburg. His visits to René's hospital bed had left him shaken. His previously vibrant young friend lay half-comatose, unable to speak, his prospects shattered.

A dull thump caught Ryan's attention, and his pace quickened. The prickling sensation intensified. *Damn cat.* The explanation fell short. Projecting his homeward path, Ryan sorted out the possible twists and turns ahead, exploring options. He approached the small square where René had been attacked.

Ryan felt himself the prey and did not like it. He was a competitor, an achiever, an athlete used to the win. He quickened his pace and sensed immediately that his pursuer had moved off to the right, perhaps looking for advantage in the shadows of a side alley. Now a jarring thump on his left, metallic and discordant in the still of the night. A garbage pail knocked over by a quickly-passing hunter, intent on his quarry? *Two hunters?*

Once the decision was made, reflexes took over. He veered abruptly to the left, turning down the cross street and lengthening his stride to a run. A sharp cry of alarm, its origin distorted by the dampening fog, erased any lingering hope of an overwrought imagination. Heavy, pounding steps descended from above and behind. He knew what he would find on his right, a precipitous passage of narrow steps dropping to the lower town, easily overlooked by nonlocals. He had climbed its worn path numerous times, knew the uneven stone risers and treads, the twists in its narrow course, but now he would negotiate the stairway in the dark of the night.

He took the abrupt turn on the run and leapt down two and three steps in a bound, grabbing at iron railings and the slick stone walls, hoping to retard his speed and prevent a disastrous slip and fall. He heard excited voices behind him, but knew better than to take his eyes from the treads below. He put himself in the race, his focus solely on the finish line he had set in his mind. But only with a good head start would he make it. His lungs began to rebel and his heart to pound and he regretted the long woolen overcoat. At the landing he veered right into the empty street without a backward glance wasted on his pursuers.

The Lahn Bridge was now in sight. Through the enveloping fog the lampposts glowed dimly, the guardian lions barely visible atop their columns at the head of the crossing. The bridge was bounded by stone parapets and iron railings which disappeared into the mist. Ryan had gained distance on the pursuers, but could hear their dampened footfalls behind him. The fog on the river was his shield. Taking the sharp turn onto the bridge at full speed, he immediately vaulted left, bracing on the iron rail and swinging himself over toward the darkness below. He slid down on the iron palings and prepared himself. *It's never the fall that kills, it's the landing.*

He released his grip and dropped, sensing the ground rise up to meet him, and tucked his shoulder and rolled onto the sloped bank fronting the river. His hat flew off into darkness. He checked for injuries, but the thick coat—cursed moments before—had blunted his impact as he rolled riverward over sharp-edged field stones. He found his footing and loped several yards northward along the river bed, feeling for solid footholds on the slanting rocks and grass. From above on the bridge he heard cries of anger from his frustrated pursuers. Now he moved stealthily, hugging the rock wall for stability in the deep fog.

A short distance ahead lay his hope for escape. Centuries-old tunnels reached up into the bowels of the mountain, long-abandoned passageways for goods from riverside to market square and castle. Recessed indentations in the old stone walls hid heavy doors barring access. His doctoral advisor had told of exploring the sealed passageways in student days, and since his safety now depended on it, Ryan only hoped that nothing had changed in the intervening years.

Abruptly, he felt the wall veer inward. Stumbling over the uneven ground, Ryan ignored the first tunnel mouth and moved on to enter the hollow of the second entrance. He was thankful for the flashlight he had brought to guide them up the Kaiser Wilhelm Tower. Now his cupped hand shielded the beam of the Ever-Ready as he surveyed the heavy door before him. Bolt heads secured solid metal braces binding the thick planks. The age-encrusted iron lockset was wider than his hand. The ends of the planks had rotted from exposure and occasional high water, creating narrow openings for rodents and small birds to pass. Barely his height, the door appeared solid and secure. A thick metal stanchion ran from the rock threshold up through the lockset to seat in a cavity in the upper stone facing.

Ryan returned the light to his pocket. He set his shoulder to the door and pushed upward, straining at the task. According to the professor, the years had not been kind to this particular door. The rot had weakened its alignment, and the rusting of the hardware had loosened the stanchion. A hefty lift upward should shift the lower pin from its mooring and allow the door to swing inward. It did not.

Ryan's mind raced. If the professor had readily managed this door over forty years before, it should be even weaker now. He slammed a fist-sized stone against the thick iron hinge pins, then against the lockset itself. The thumping was muffled by the damp air, but he still heard a clamor of voices in response coming from south along the riverbank. *Three of them now, moving closer.*

"Here, he's here!" A gruff voice from near the first tunnel entrance.

"No! The next one!" A whoop of pleasure at fixing upon their prey.

Ryan pounded again and again to jar the metal loose, then dropped the stone and heaved upward with all his might. The door edged partially open on the rusty hinges. Once through the tight opening, he shouldered the door back into place. There was a reassuring click as the stanchion rod found its way home.

A sweep of the flashlight and a quick survey of his surroundings. The landing was littered with fallen stone, collapsed barrels, iron rings, wooden and metal staves. Wrought-iron torch holders had decayed to skeletal remains. Stalactites of moss and cobwebs reached for his head, and a sharp metallic odor lay heavy in the air. Stone steps rising into darkness were hewn directly into bedrock below a low-arched ceiling. He breathed a sigh of relief.

The door rocked as his pursuers tried to bully the barrier into submission. Their voices were audible, their words garbled. Ryan grabbed an iron bar and wedged it against the door and set out up the stairway. Orienting himself to the river, he knew he was climbing toward the market square. The treads were steep and slick, treacherous where the stone walls had surrendered in falls of rubble. Exhaustion was taking its toll, his breath coming in gasps. The air was close and dank, laden with mold and decay.

A loud crash reached him in the darkness as the door below was forced open, and enthusiastic shouts echoed up the passage. Ryan now bounded up two steps at a time, the beam of his flashlight playing against the uneven stone and fooling his eye with shifting shadows. Off to his left a blind alcove suggested a former refuge for those descending empty-handed to give passage to workers hauling up heavy loads.

He discovered a wooden pallet at the rear of the recess, an upright grid of decaying planks cobbled together with iron strips. Setting down the light, he put his shoulder to the barrier, and it moved a fraction. He tugged until it gave way with a moan, revealing a low door barely waist-high. He tested the iron handle and the hinges shrieked in protest as the door opened. Grabbing his light, he crawled through the opening and pushed the door shut behind him.

The stone floor was littered with rock debris, and even on his knees he barely cleared the damp ceiling. He lodged several larger stones against the door to slow his pursuers. Now began a tedious crawl along the narrow shaft, as broken stone forced a snail's pace. This cramped tunnel was clearly designed only for escape. His faltering flashlight picked out observant red eyes along the tunnel above. Faint chirping cries echoed down to him as the rats scurried into the darkness. At the end of the passage Ryan reached another small door. The rodents had disappeared. He hesitated a moment, holding his breath and listening intently. The dank air was suffocating, the silence a relief. No sounds came from below.

The handle would not budge. Ryan pushed with all his remaining strength. *No give.* He sat back, braced his arms on the uneven stones, and using both feet, kicked with all his might. The door surrendered with a moan, and he dragged himself into a narrow storeroom. His flashlight braced on a derelict cabinet, he used crates to build a makeshift barrier as thick and high as the low ceiling and cramped space would permit.

Satisfied at last, he collapsed against the wall, drenched in sweat, flashlight back in hand, his trousers filthy and torn. He slid off the switch to preserve the dying batteries and relaxed, letting his eyes adjust to the total darkness which enveloped him.

A rat approached, its whiskers quivering, and paused to sniff his fingers, but Ryan didn't notice. He slept.

# ERNTEZEIT
### Harvest Time

1938

# CHAPTER ONE

Horst crept into consciousness with eyes tightly shut. He steeled himself for the physical trial ahead. By dawn the morphine had usually released its pain-dulling hold and his neck ached in penance for a night on his back. He fought the urge to rub his face, to force aside the drowsiness. Any pressure on the scarred cheek could trigger a convulsive spasm of pain lasting excruciating minutes. And always he suffered the throbbing headache, payback for the drug and alcohol of the previous evening.

This daily trial had initially been an agonizing insult to a man for whom self-control was everything. As the wound had knitted, the sensitivity worsened. Now, four years later, he accepted it as a rite of inner strength. He consciously willed himself forward. Once the pain was in his control no challenge of the coming day would be too great, for he was once again his own master. He would not touch the drug again until evening.

He cleared the fogged mirror with a hand towel, and then drew the straight razor skillfully and methodically across his face in even, measured strokes. A safety razor had proved less precise at shielding the scar tissue from any inadvertent touch. Horst always saved the area near the scar for last. That stubble was spare but required careful attention. The process was measured in long minutes as he avoided any facial movement, an artist applying careful final strokes to his living canvas.

Horst admired his reflection, the epitome of racial purity, the Germanic ideal. The bold mark of honor and the shortened left ear were enhancements, and faded scars from earlier duels paled beside these bold statements of courage. Whether standing naked before the mirror, later in his daily civilian attire, or in black SS uniform at Party functions, his bearing was always self-assured, for Horst von Kredow dominated his world. Once free of the residual morphine, his mental and emotional states were equally well-honed. Co-workers and subordinates wondered at his unfailing composure.

No one suspected that Horst had mastered an inner discipline even more demanding than that suggested by his aloof persona, for any strong emotion could also play havoc with his appearance. A mere frown might trigger a searing jolt of pain. A full smile could turn one side of his face clown-like in contrast to the other, the classic guises of comedy and tragedy in grotesque juxtaposition. Horst's placid demeanor was a defensive shield for his one area of weakness, and he would tolerate no curiosity or pity. And it was this handsome mask, never betraying emotion, which unnerved subordinates and terrified detainees.

In the early days he had vowed to destroy both the man whose saber transformed his life and the American who dared vie for Erika's affections. Vengeance had seemed the ultimate response, and he had set in motion plans to fulfill that commitment. Yet as time passed he also found redeeming value in his own suffering, for it taught him unyielding strength in the face of adversity, and it goaded him into avoiding any show of weakness. Now, to be worthy of his interest, an opponent had to show strength equal to his own, and if his challenger did not have that same steel, he deserved no consideration, an unworthy animal.

Even in his childhood, pain had been his close companion. Raised without siblings, his father fallen in the Great War and his mother a devotee of self-reliance, he often spent hours alone in the woods and fields. He was adept with hunting knife and rifle, weapons inherited from the father he had hardly known. He took down game or the occasional dog or cat, hoping to injure rather than kill so that he could observe the slow deaths. Control and domination always at his fingertips, he inflicted agony with impunity. His excitement grew in the animal's slow struggle, and he regretted the moment when it surrendered to his manipulations and died.

In his youth a peasant girl had caught his eye. She lived outside Gerbach near his family's estate, and he observed her from a distance for days. He guessed her to be about fifteen. When he found the moment right, the anticipation no longer bearable, he surprised her as she gathered windfall beneath an ancient apple tree, its heavily-laden branches supported by crude wooden posts. She bent to her task as he approached, her spread apron rapidly filling with fruit. A toddler sat on a rumpled blanket in the shade, a brother entrusted to her care while the parents tended the fields. She was pretty, her innocence appealing, yet what attracted him most was her vulnerability.

He teased her relentlessly until fear rose in her eyes, then threw her to the ground, one hand held roughly over her mouth, the other forced between her legs. He took her violently, drawing out his moment of absolute power, finding his pleasure less in the act than in the pain and terror he caused. He left her there on the trampled grass, skirt high at her waist, the apples once again scattered beneath the tree. She sobbed softly as the untended child wailed the cry of an injured animal.

Later that day the girl's father made his way up to the family villa and requested an audience with Horst's mother. He was a bent man, prematurely aged by a hard life in difficult times. A worn felt hat turned in his nervous hands as he entered the library, and his words came haltingly, the fury difficult to express in terms suitable for addressing his landlord. He related his daughter's shame.

"How dare you suggest my Horst would do such a thing?"

"My daughter doesn't tell lies, *gnädige Frau*. We all know your son."

"He has no need to resort to such nonsense. I can think of several local girls of superior station and breeding who would be delighted should he wish to indulge his natural urges. Might your daughter just be looking for a little extra spending money?"

"In God's name no, *gnädige Frau*, all we seek is justice. My wife and daughter are devastated, and no girl is safe if such an act goes unpunished."

"I'm truly sorry for your girl's troubles, though she may well have brought them on herself. However, should you feel obliged to press this matter with the constabulary, consider carefully the long-standing working relationship between our families. I would hate to have you compromise the situation to your detriment."

"My daughter has been shamed, and your son is responsible for this vile business. What would you expect of me?"

"Here, take this," she handed him a few banknotes from the desk drawer, "and see that she gets medical attention, should any actually be required. Or, for that matter, use it to supplement your harvest income. It's all the same to me. But no further nonsense regarding my son or the repercussions will be unpleasant for all. And no one wants your girl's shame bandied about the countryside. Understood?"

Horst had eavesdropped from behind the library door. He moved to the window to watch the defeated man leave the grounds. As the farmer descended the drive he appeared even more stooped than before.

His mother summoned him to the spacious salon lined with polished oaken shelves and leather-bound volumes of classical works. Here he received his lessons in the arts and sciences as well as in demeanor suitable to his station. He anticipated her anger, some strict punishment, but her rebuke struck him as tacit approval.

"I understand that young men have needs, but you must always be discreet. Find your pleasures in town, not on our lands."

He nodded understanding but kept his silence.

"Always remember, *noblesse oblige*. Your station in life demands certain obligations to these people under our care. And you *will* respect the memory of your father."

He carried away two valuable lessons: first, honor your own needs, but always with discretion. And second, stay close to the powerful, for they protect you until you have no further need of their power.

Now himself a man of influence, Horst found it fitting that infliction of pain found such a satisfying role in his professional life, even though he took care to hide from his colleagues the personal gratification it brought him. And he did indeed enjoy the support of a very powerful mentor, Reinhard Heydrich.

On this morning he took pleasure in his mastery of the razor, and imagined creative uses for the blade in the basement cells of *Prinz-Albrecht-Strasse 8*, Gestapo headquarters, Berlin.

# CHAPTER TWO

"*Fahrkarten, bitte. Fahrkarten.*" A drowsy Ryan came instantly alert as the railroad official asked for his ticket. The train official held military posture, his jacket keeping an expansive paunch in check. The odor of mothballs now pervaded the compartment, but the conductor wore the aged blue uniform with obvious pride. A brush mustache sprouted below his broad nose, wire-framed eyeglasses resting near its bulbous tip.

"*Schönen guten Morgen,*" The trainman's greeting acknowledged both Ryan and the elderly woman seated across from him.

Ryan drew his ticket from his vest pocket, and the conductor took the narrow card in hand, tilted his head back and squinted through the glasses, then punched and returned it with a quick nod of satisfaction. He turned to the neatly-dressed woman seated at the window, her ticket out of her handbag, ready for its authorized blessing. He was gone as quickly as he had arrived, the door shutting with authority and once again dampening the steady rumble from the passageway. His fellow traveler returned to her needlepoint.

Before long the cadence of the wheels, the metallic rub of the carriage bumpers, and the occasional far-off screech of the locomotive joined forces to lull Ryan back into memories, recalling his final train ride out of Marburg four long years earlier.

He had awakened that morning in the pre-dawn hours, slumped against the wall of a dank storage room deep below the university church. His shirt was still clammy from the exertions of his frantic escape, his trousers torn at the knees, his coat filthy from the scramble along the river bank and up the tunnels. He shivered with cold and ached from hours on the hard stone surface, and he was hungry. His pursuers had somehow lost his trail. Ryan reviewed the chase but could make little sense of it all. Yet there in the darkness, surrounded by musty crates and abandoned furniture, he knew that the attack had not been random. They had been too determined, the pursuit too calculated. It was no coincidence that René had suffered a brutal assault under similar circumstances, and the only suspects were von Kredow and his Wachonian comrades. The commonality was the duel. *So much for honor.*

He had used the dimming beam of his flashlight to find a narrow stairwell leading up into the church apse. At that hour no one stirred, and the massive front doors remained locked. He circled around the center rank of pews seeking access to the university building next door. The towering gothic windows glowed faintly with the first light of dawn. The latch at the side exit was unsecured, and Ryan entered a long hallway. A door opened somewhere distant, then a light flared, but his passageway remained in shadow. He hid in a deep alcove alongside a cabinet, listening as footsteps on the stone floor grew closer. He was not prepared for a new chase. The night guard ambled past, humming to himself and leaving a trail of pipe smoke in his wake.

Ryan waited for him to disappear at the far end of the corridor before moving cautiously toward the front of the building. The door to the street was unlocked. He spotted no one on the square and slipped out onto the street. Nearby a bakery readied wares for the morning deliveries and early clientele. Ryan's stomach rumbled, but he chose to ignore the enticing aroma, traversing instead the damp square and moving down the stairway, past the site of his drop from the bridge just a few hours before, and swiftly crossing the river through the fog. He did not stop to look for his hat.

Back at his room Ryan changed clothes, brushed the caked mud from his coat, and hastily threw the rest of his belongings into the valise. He left a scribbled note of thanks to the police chief and his wife along with the room key, happy his account had been settled and personal farewells exchanged the morning before. The landlord's tabby, patiently waiting on the stoop, received a last scratch between the ears. Ryan scoped out the lane for any unusual activity before closing the door on his Marburg years.

Holding to the far side of the valley he strode northward until he could cross the tracks to the station, where he scanned the scattered crowd and found the waiting room free of fraternity men. Two policemen at the newsstand exchanged gossip with the vendor, a janitor mopped the floor. Satisfied at last that all was clear, Ryan grabbed a roll and coffee in the station canteen. While waiting for his train, he bought a postcard and a stamp at the newsstand, and jotted down a quick good-bye.

> *Thank you for the wonderful times we shared.*
> *Affectionately,*
> *Your "American boy" Ryan.*

He paid for a second-class ticket and stepped out onto the covered platform. His express north was due to arrive at 7:35, depart at 7:40. There was no delay.

By afternoon he had passed through Bremen, and the Norddeutsche Lloyd steamship *Europa* was moored dockside in Bremerhaven, ready to carry him home.

# CHAPTER THREE

Klaus Pabst was pleased with his long day's work. It had been well worth rising early and enduring the hours of travel from Berlin, crossing the Polish Corridor in a train sealed to prevent boarding or detraining on Polish soil. He had enlisted Dieter Sprenger, a Gestapo associate from the Königsberg office, to drive him out to the country village of Praddau. Sprenger had done the local research and legwork that made this final step so simple and satisfying.

The parish church was easy to find, as was the aging pastor who greeted them in his office. The frail man sat uneasily behind a cluttered desk, his pale skin almost translucent and stretched tightly across sharp cheekbones. Blue veins and age spots stained arthritic hands. His eyes however were soft and fluid. Despite the civilian dress the old man knew immediately that his visitors were on official business, policeman, undoubtedly Gestapo. The look and demeanor was easily recognized and feared. He rose from his chair with difficulty.

"How may I be of service, gentlemen?"

Pabst drew a warrant badge from his vest pocket. The oval metal disc bore embossed lettering—*GEHEIME STAATSPOLIZEI* — and a four-digit identification number stamped below. The mere sight of the badge intimidated most citizens into immediate cooperation with its bearer. It had that desired effect here.

"Yes, of course, officers, what may I do for you?" the pastor said. One gnarled hand held fast to the other, both trembling in a dance of nerves. The pastor found his chair and waited expectantly.

"You have a quiet little parish here, well out of the mainstream of church politics, we presume?"

The minister hesitated, knowing that every spoken word had consequences. The last few years had been especially trying for the Protestant church as well as the Catholics. Untold hundreds of his fellow pastors had been arrested for refusing to adopt the precepts of "Positive Christianity," the Party creed shifting focus from belief in Christ as Son of God to faith in National Socialism as the one true expression of God's will. "You must already know that the other diocesan pastors and I have sworn our personal oath of obedience and allegiance to the Führer." He willed his unsteady hands still.

"Indeed you have, and I'm confident your parishioners are pleased that you now direct your prayers to the Reich and its Führer. So much more sensible than revering an insignificant Jewish carpenter, don't you agree?" Pabst gave the old man a smug look, challenging him to respond.

The pastor stared at the officers. "Is my loyalty in question?"

"We're here on a different matter, a question of certain birth logs. The local civil records aren't all that helpful. In fact, they raise more questions than they answer. Perhaps you can help us fill in some blanks using your family records here in the parish office?" Pabst and Sprenger took seats before the pastor's desk without being invited.

"Yes, forgive me, please be seated. And of course, I'm happy to help in any way I can." The minister appeared anything but happy. "Which family is of interest?"

Klaus smiled at his colleague before responding to the cleric. "Why yours, of course. As I just said, it's *your* family that interests us."

The pastor's translucent skin appeared to grow paler still, had such a thing been possible.

# CHAPTER FOUR

The locomotive rolled at high speed, a trail of gray smoke whipping behind. From time to time excess steam vented from the boiler in white bursts, and the shrill whistle alerted the countryside to the priority of the express over less important rail traffic. Fallow fields and farmsteads gradually gave way to tiny plots of garden land with summer cottages, where city dwellers raised crops and bonded with nature. Steel girders flicked past, the bridge trembling beneath the speeding train, while heavily-laden barges on the waterways below moved at a far slower pace toward the city's markets.

Ryan barely noticed the landscape passing before his eyes. He felt a pervasive lethargy as his thoughts drifted back to Kansas, recalling the events which had led to his imminent arrival in Berlin.

Starting his new duties at Baker in the spring of 1935, Ryan had quickly fallen into the routine of academic life. His classes had been well-attended, the students interested in the volatile state of European politics and the first-hand experiences of the young German professor. Their curiosity appealed to him, a sharp contrast with the unquestioning single-mindedness of fellow students in his own final years in Marburg. Standing before the blackboard with chalk in hand, Ryan took satisfaction in sharing what he had learned in the streets and lecture halls of Germany.

He had rented a one-bedroom bungalow not far from campus. Arising daily at six, Ryan rolled his newly-acquired Indian Sport Scout out of the garage in back. Storing his briefcase in one saddlebag and suit coat in the other, he donned a fleece-lined leather jacket and took to the country roads. He would stop at a café in some small town near Baldwin City for fried eggs over-easy, bacon and hash browns, toast and coffee, then head back to campus to trade leather for wool and prepare for his classes. It was a satisfactory—though boring—routine.

The letter in his mailbox in the Admin Building had come as a surprise. In clear, feminine script covering three thin sheets of air-mail paper, Erika wrote of her short courtship and recent marriage to Horst von Kredow. She expressed deep affection for Ryan, her desire for change and challenge evoked by Ryan's international adventures, and her recognition that she and Ryan were of different worlds and could never be together. He stared at the pages in his hand.

> *Horst offers a real future in the new Germany, for he is strong and well-connected, and I see in this marriage an opportunity to move beyond the narrow confines of Marburg.*

She hoped Ryan would wish her well. He noted the postmark and return address: Berlin. *With love, Erika.* He read through the pages again, this time more slowly.

Several weeks passed before he felt he could reply. His one-page letter acknowledged her motivation, recalled the wonderful times they had shared in the previous autumn, and sent best wishes for a happy life in her new home and marriage. *With lasting affection, Ryan*

He had taken the motorcycle out that endless evening on unmarked country roads, carving a path of light through the spring night, deep in thought on the unpredictable nature of life, and of relationships.

# CHAPTER FIVE

Pedestrians quickened their pace as they passed Gestapo head-quarters in Königsberg, the capital of East Prussia. Muffled cries or an occasional scream rising from the shielded basement windows resonated in the mind of any hapless passer-by. Mothers with small children in tow crossed the street a block before reaching the former hotel. Why bother with implausible explanations for frightened little ones?

Klaus Pabst found the basement interrogation facilities to his liking. A common aisle gave access to a row of narrow cells, re-vamped storage closets once used for supplies. Small shuttered open-ings in the compartment doors allowed a visual check on occupants, but each of the six cubicles, when unoccupied, held nothing but a distasteful bucket pushed into one corner. Small grills in the back walls allowed eavesdropping on detainee conversations. A metal basket over the ceiling light prevented unauthorized access to the glaring bulb, or to the electrical wires. Little was left to chance. Vents drew oppressive heat into the cells in summer, and when win-ter arrived the brutal Baltic winds turned the basement rooms into cold storage lockers.

Across the corridor stood two interrogation rooms and a soli-tary toilet facility, exclusively for staff use. The situation of the rooms forced cell occupants to hear the sounds, if not the specifics, of interrogations in progress. Painted a clinical white with pale green doors, the rooms had sparse furnishings. Two metal chairs faced either side of a small table. Above one chair hung a shaded lamp, and at its feet iron shackles were attached to the floor. In the center of each room sat a tall bench fitted with leg and arm restraints. Another metal table displayed implements of interrogation in neat order: an automobile battery with cables, an electric drill, a soldering iron, and a selection of hand tools, both sharp-edged and blunt. Cudgels and whips with metal-tipped leather cords hung on a wall rack. To the side of the table sat a mop bucket.

A white hospital cabinet occupied one corner, vials and hypodermic needles clearly visible through the glass door. In the opposite corner stood a wash basin with towel rack and small metal wall mirror. Near the ceiling a thick iron rod traversed the room, fitted with a pulley system of ropes, shackles and wires, and a meat hook. The concrete floor, painted gray, sloped slightly toward a center drain. Additional heat when required came from a coal stove, also useful for bringing iron implements to a steady glow.

Unlike his friend and mentor Horst, who was ever ingenious in developing interrogation techniques but always stoic in their use, Klaus took obvious pleasure in their application, even when little of immediate value was learned. As Himmler himself had said, everyone has something to hide. *Even should you interrogate the wrong suspect for a particular crime, be confident you have gained information in the process which will lead to an enemy of the Fatherland.*

But this time, Klaus already had what he wanted.

Strapped naked across the bench, the pastor made a sorry spectacle. His once colorless back and buttocks were flayed raw from the metal whip, his flesh torn in ragged strips. The early cries of pain and denial were now barely audible moans. Sprays of fresh blood streaked table and floor, and urine and excrement ran down his legs.

His prayers had gone unanswered, for the torment had not stopped; in fact, the pleas had been mocked by his interrogators. It was only a matter of time before he confessed all he knew. Perhaps he already had. Judging by the shallow breathing, Klaus doubted the fragile old man could take much more, so he suggested a brief break in the proceedings. Klaus already knew enough for his purposes, even if the pastor gave up the ghost before they were finished.

"Best light a match to clear the air," he suggested to Dieter Sprenger as he left the room, the interrogation record in hand. "The stench in here is barbaric."

# CHAPTER SIX

Utility poles ticked past in rapid succession, and suburban rail stations recalled once-familiar names for the outlying towns. A uniformed stationmaster on each passing platform waved his flag to clear the passing express. Commuters in shades of gray and brown lined the tracks, shielded from the cold by heavy coats and scarves. Viewed from Ryan's compartment it was a surging sea of hats and umbrellas. Raindrops tracked across the carriage window in horizontal rivulets. He watched the droplets race along, choosing from moment to moment seemingly-random course corrections which would ultimately determine their destination. *How often one misses a destiny-changing choice.*

A few months earlier the clamor of the phone had startled him awake, and a pile of student papers flew from his lap as he stumbled toward the phone in the hall. A late call meant illness, accident, a death in the family.

"Ryan, did I wake you?" Edward sounded calm enough.

"Of course you woke me. What's wrong? Are you and Grace okay?" Ryan hadn't heard from his brother in months.

"All's good at this end, but something came up at work you need to know about."

"Listen, Ed, always happy to hear your voice, but have you checked your watch?" He checked his. "It's past midnight, my time. What on earth keeps you up so late in Virginia?" Ryan thought of his comfortable bed waiting in the next room.

"Plenty of excitement coming over the wires tonight. The Czechs ordered partial mobilization over this Sudeten thing."

"And this couldn't wait till the morning papers, Ed?"

"Interesting as it is, I've got something even better for you personally, and it couldn't wait. How'd you like to fly to Europe this summer at government expense?

"You're kidding, right?"

"Nope, giving it to you straight, brother."

The prospect of travel shoved all thought of sleep aside. Ryan's annual salary from Baker barely carried him through the academic year, and summers he was on his own. A birthday gift each June from his parents helped out financially, but after nine years of depression the economy was only marginally improved, and international travel was expensive, especially by Clipper.

"You did say 'fly,' right?"

"Plus an assignment right up your alley."

"So whom do I have to kill? Come on, spill it!"

A throaty chuckle. "No one, and nothing we can discuss over the phone. You'll still need to sell yourself in person, but it's for real, and urgent. Can you be here before the weekend?"

He looked again at his watch. "My God, Ed, I've a class to teach in a just few hours, too late to cancel that one. But I can clear my schedule for the rest of today through the weekend. Listen, I'll aim for tonight's overnight from Chicago, that'll put me in D.C. by Friday noon at the latest. You'd better be serious about this, because if not, you're the one I'm gunning for."

"Dead serious." Again the deep chuckle. "The job should be yours for the asking; just come impress my guys in Washington tomorrow. And give a call with your arrival time, so I can have a car waiting. Union Station, main concourse, front entrance. I'll keep an eye out for that smile of yours, baby brother."

Ryan had only revisited the Continent once since his return home to Kansas. A shared third-class berth to Bordeaux, a couple of weeks in Nice—sunbathing and swimming in the azure waters and practicing French while avoiding his bedbug-infested room—then two weeks in his beloved Burgundy village near Dijon before crossing the Rhine to see René.

His old friend had recovered remarkably, although some motor skills still gave him difficulty. The family shipping business was doing adequately well, but René freely expressed to Ryan his rage over the changes in Germany.

The final few days with the von Haldheim family in Berlin were saddened by the Old Major's pessimism. *These bastards have us coming and going, and we don't dare say a word to anyone anymore.* Some of their closest friends had fled the country, or simply disappeared overnight. The weekly teas no longer took place.

Back in Kansas, Ryan had sought satisfaction in his daily teaching and back road excursions on the Indian, but he found himself living in the vivid memories of his European life. The routine of daily preparation and endless classroom hours had dampened his initial enthusiasm for teaching. The concerns of colleagues seemed so trivial: inter-departmental bickering, meetings over minor issues with never a resolution, complaints about students and administration. And his brief romances had been equally shallow and unfulfilling. He had missed the liberated women of Berlin and Marburg.

The night of his brother's surprise call, Ryan slept in fits and starts, parsing Edward's words for hidden clues, and by morning he headed straight for campus on foot, carrying a small valise along with his briefcase. He muddled through the morning class, a review of verb tenses he could teach by rote, and then posted a cancellation of his Friday classes on the office door and classroom bulletin board. The departmental secretary was asked to explain his absence to the dean: a family emergency.

By one that afternoon he sat on the train for Chicago. As he smoked his beloved Berlin briar and watched the fields of Illinois race by, he tapped fingers nervously at his knee. He'd be in Washington by morning to learn more.

# CHAPTER SEVEN

Horst cautiously blotted his face and combed back his pomaded hair, slicking down the closely-cropped sides. The dark-gray suit hung on the rack, carefully brushed for lint and dandruff. He straightened his tie before the metal-framed mirror on the dressing room wall and was pleased as always by his appearance. He knew the car would be waiting in twenty minutes. His valet and driver Schimmelbach suited him: taciturn, attentive, and obedient. Oskar was both a solid SS man and a reliable chauffeur.

In the dining room the maid had set out fresh bread rolls, jam and cheeses, and a porcelain pot of coffee. He split a poppy seed roll with his knife and smeared it with butter and elderberry preserves. Taking a cautious bite, he chewed slowly. The coffee, served on his demand more warm than hot, energized him, and the caffeine helped relieve the headache.

He hoped to delegate any regular office duties this morning in order to complete a final point-by-point review of the protocol. The master plan was due in two days for presentation to Heydrich, who now headed the Gestapo as well as the SS counter-espionage service, the *Sicherheitsdienst* or SD, and stood second only to Himmler himself.

For four years now Heydrich had held Horst under his wing as one of his protégés. He brought him to Berlin and encouraged Horst's special passion for dealing with Jews and foreigners who undermined the Reich. Horst felt it was his breeding and education that established a kinship with Heydrich and set him apart from so many of his fellow secret police officers. It was a good match, and they made an intimidating pair. As tall as Horst, Heydrich had close-ly-spaced, pale-blue eyes and blond hair. His education was as pol-ished as his manners. Only that inordinately high-pitched voice and almost feminine hips were discordant in an otherwise harmonious picture of the Germanic masculine ideal.

Heydrich had masterminded the wide-spread network of plain-clothes agents and administrative personnel that made the Gestapo so powerful. Most important to the success of the organization was a vast web of informants and spies, everyday citizens who made the system efficient by keeping eyes open and ears alert. Every citizen had the duty to report any suspicious thought or activity, and an anonymous phone call would bring the now notorious nighttime knock at the door.

In the last two years their work had become even easier. The recent Gestapo Law removed secret police actions from all judicial oversight, and the Führer himself had declared that any means, whether supported by existing law or not, were legal, as long as they served his will. That *carte blanche* opened every door.

Barely four weeks had passed since Heydrich had summoned Horst into his office for a special conference. Heinrich Müller, chief of Gestapo operations, sat to the right of Heydrich's desk, a cup of coffee in hand. Müller extended his arm in casual salute, but failed to rise. Heydrich stood behind a mahogany desk framed by brilliant flags and motioned Horst to the unoccupied leather chair. Horst declined coffee with a shake of the head, and the SS orderly with-drew from the room without being asked.

"How is your lovely wife?" Horst recognized the look in Hey-drich's eyes whenever he spoke of Erika or flirted with her at social gatherings. Rumor had it his mentor was a less than attentive hus-band.

"Thank you, very well indeed." Something important was clearly on hand, the small talk a formality. "I trust you and yours are doing well?"

Heydrich accepted the inquiry with a gracious nod. He took his seat behind the desk, its broad polished surface bearing two phones, an inkwell surmounted by a bronze eagle clutching a swastika, and a silver charger laden with refreshments. No files or portfolios. He directed Horst's attention to the platter of small cream cakes, which he politely declined. Müller helped himself to a cake.

"Tell me, my dear Horst," Heydrich said, "what do you make of the disposition of the Jewish problem to date?" He gave an encouraging smile. "Please speak freely, and keep in mind we share a common goal."

"Well, on one hand I'm confident the Reich has made a tidy sum with the Aryanization of Jewish businesses and the confiscation of their wealth. And our national efforts aim to encourage emigration, especially to Palestine. But there seems to be no coherent plan, and at this rate we won't eradicate the vermin for years."

"So what would you suggest?"

"Let's face it, we've little consensus on the ultimate goal. The Führer made clear over a decade ago that eliminating this menace was a high priority. It's obvious we need to free up our own youth to protect the Reich, and that means using fit young Jews to work in industries and farms. But as for the rest—the old, the feeble, the worthless—we say we encourage emigration, but then make the process so burdensome and expensive relatively few actually leave."

"There are others at the top who feel we should milk them before we set them out," Heydrich said. "The Reich needs money. Our friend Eichmann is having great success in Vienna and the Ostmark moving things along. Perhaps we should implement his operation throughout the Altreich?"

"I'm not convinced they'll go willingly. We've taken away civil service jobs, business opportunities, and access to commerce, educational and cultural opportunities—all very effective at impoverishing them, and they certainly know they aren't wanted. Yet many just hunker down and refuse to take the hint."

Heydrich nodded but remained silent as he refilled his cup. Horst looked over at the bull-necked Müller, who took another bite of his cake but added nothing to the discussion.

"If I may, gentlemen," Horst said, "we're promoting their exodus—pardon the poor pun—and thousands leave weekly. But our inconsistency in both treatment and goals means a troublesome slog before we're rid of this scum."

Heydrich's response was measured: "The German People know the time will come to solve the Jewish problem once and for all. We now have the broad support of our people, they're fed up, and their brutal response now occurs spontaneously." He set down his cup. "But I agree, Horst, piecemeal action will never be sufficient, and we must keep the bigger picture in mind. The Reich isn't stagnant, it must grow, and that means many more of these people coming under our control."

His gaze was intense. "Just take a look at our Austrian brothers, finally back within the Reich, and all the Jews they must deal with. The labor and detention camps alone won't suffice, and inaction gets us nowhere. Uncoordinated action, whether instigated by us directly or arising out of the people's fury, only delays the inevitable."

Horst nodded in agreement. Müller appeared bored, obviously already briefed on the agenda.

"There are and will be simply too many of them for us to handle without a clear blueprint, and the risk they pose can no longer be stomached. Exclusion from German society and expulsion from the Reich are only the first steps. There can ultimately be only one solution, and now, at last, it's time we plan for it."

He took a cigarette from a polished case, and a silver plume of smoke rose toward the ceiling. "Horst, you're to be our point man on this. I want a proposal for the Reichsführer-SS and ultimately for the Führer himself, a comprehensive, far-sighted protocol with practical methods to solve this burden as we assume our destined boundaries."

Horst was thrilled. "I was hoping we'd move in that direction, and am pleased to play my part." *An assignment made in heaven: work and pleasure combined.*

"Don't be hemmed in by the misguided scruples of foreigners and bleeding hearts. Those fools have no understanding of what we're dealing with here. Carry it as far as you wish, knowing that all of Europe will eventually be ours. Our requirement for vital space can't be denied, so put your creativity to work, clear?"

"Perfectly clear, and the opportunity is a great honor. I assume we focus first on our neighbors to the east?"

"Poland, Lithuania, and beyond, they'll be the worst infested, but again, don't limit yourself. When our political and military moment is ripe, we'll need a well-designed protocol to apply wherever and whenever we wish."

"I'll need to delegate some of my current projects, and make use of additional staff."

"But of course, and I suggest you coordinate with Eichmann, as necessary. I know you find him tedious, but he's our point man for SD research on the Jewish problem. In fact, he's just returned from Vienna, and he spent time last year in Palestine. He's a reliable source of information you may find useful." Heydrich rose. "So, there's your task."

Horst despised the dark little Eichmann, and suspected the un-educated, uncouth boor might himself have Jewish blood. He would avoid working with him. "How soon would you like to see it?"

"Shall we say a month, at least for the preliminary protocol?" Heydrich glanced at Müller, who nodded in concurrence before reaching for a second cake.

"I've personally enjoyed your creative procedures for the inter-rogation cells, von Kredow," Müller finally spoke, all the while wiping his lips with a napkin. "This should be right up your alley."

Horst allowed himself a hint of a smile in acknowledgement. Rising from the leather chair, he saluted sharply with outstretched arm, first Heydrich, then Müller, and took his leave. His excitement was as great as the evening he had first met Göring.

Now the month had passed and all the basics of the protocol were in place. The weeks of diligent planning and writing had flown by, with lesser assignments passed along to Klaus to oversee. Horst was confident of praise from his superiors, and his goal was personal oversight in the application of his suggestions. He stood at the desk of his study and briefly scanned the draft proposal in its black leather folder before slipping it into his briefcase and carefully latching the flap. As he passed the wall mirror, he assured himself that every hair was in place, and ran an index finger with extreme care along his scar. Just as a reminder.

Horst assumed his wife was still in her room. He seldom gave her much thought. She was still useful to him socially, her physical attributes a feather in his cap and her social graces a plus, but his sexual interest in her had faded. Early in the marriage her distaste for his domination had made taking her even more pleasurable, but with the birth of the boy he had lost interest. Compliant, willing women were everywhere, no matter what his demands. And his "dagger" Klaus stood ready to clean up any mess should an assignation prove more violent than usual.

Oskar waited patiently under the *porte cochère,* the engine of the sedan idling smoothly. He held the rear door for Horst, and then fed gas to the powerful Daimler engine as they left the gates. Horst removed the protocol from his briefcase. Morning traffic was spotty as they left Zehlendorf and headed east on Berliner Strasse. Despite the light rain, the black Mercedes carved a clear path through morning traffic toward Prinz-Albrecht-Strasse.

# CHAPTER EIGHT

The piercing steam whistle announced the imminent arrival at Potsdamer Station. Ryan stood to observe the rail yard activity and lowered his rain-swept window, but shut it again quickly as a departing locomotive, passing near enough for him to feel the draft, filled the compartment with coal smoke. His elderly traveling companion, small bag already on her lap, sniffed at the impropriety and held a handkerchief to her nose. As he singled out familiar Berlin landmarks from the elevated tracks, he thought of the trip to Washington, D.C. just four months earlier.

He had found the men's lounge of the Baltimore & Ohio *Capitol Limited* crowded at six in the morning. Standing before a bank of stainless steel sinks, their suspenders dangling at the waist, his fellow travelers sought to synchronize their razors with the rocking of the speeding train. Outside, the wig-way signals gave urgent warnings as the train shot by grade crossings, and less distinguished trains sat on sidings out of deference to the *Capitol Limited*.

Ryan waited his turn in one of the leather lounge chairs and read of Britain and France's rejection of the latest demands for concessions to Czechoslovakia's Germanic minority. Hitler was calling for self-determination of these Sudeten Germans. *The good Führer will get what he wants, just as he did in Austria.* The article ran to an inside page, but offered little else new.

Ryan had hesitated paying the extra fare for a deluxe "name" train, but the afternoon departure from Chicago with its early arrival in Washington was too good to pass up, so he swallowed the surcharge and had a decent night's rest in a Pullman sleeping car. Now freshly washed and shaved, he breakfasted on fine china in the dining car, the table decked in crisp linen. He sighted forward along the streamliner watching the two spotless diesel locomotives in royal blue-and-silver livery snake the train through the Appalachians. At the Martinsburg stop Ryan quickly used a pay phone in the station. The long-distance operator put his call through in moments and he reached his brother at home in Virginia with the anticipated arrival time. The train was on schedule.

Ed had been easy to spot across the crowded concourse. An inch shorter than Ryan and three years his senior, his brother was more slender in the face, but his smile was also his calling card. Edward wore an expensive checked suit and a trilby hat with deeply-creased crown. Ed had married a New England socialite of wealth and breeding just before his brother's move to Germany, and Ryan had been best man. He liked his sister-in-law, but found her too affected for his taste, preferring a woman who knew how to relax. The couple owned an expensive brick townhouse in Falls Church, across the river from the capital and Edward's State Department workplace.

Ed welcomed Ryan with a huge grin and bear hug before grabbing his brother's bag. He led them from the concourse toward a green Dodge parked in a no-parking zone. Ryan was impressed with finding a driver at the wheel and official government plates on the sedan.

"Okay, enough mystery, what the hell's going on? Getting here cost me an arm and a leg, and—unlike certain people I know— I've yet to marry rich." Ryan remembered his manners. "But before that, how's Grace doing? No little niece or nephew on the way for me to spoil?"

"Give it time, brother, give it time. Grace is doing swell, and looks forward to seeing you tonight for dinner, but more about that later." Ed signaled the driver to move out. "But first off, you should know things at State have been crazy lately. Secretary Hull feels we're doing too little to counter the dictatorships in Germany and Japan, and he's pressing for serious rearmament, but many of our countrymen and congressmen want us to stay out of both Europe and Asia."

"From what I've seen in Germany and France, that won't be possible. Just imagine Europe under Hitler. And the Brits and French continue to bluster and vacillate."

"That's where you come in. My boss Richard Kohl is Deputy Assistant Secretary on the German desk, a demanding guy to work for—never lets up, never satisfied—but I think you're going to like what he has to say." Edward tore the cellophane from a pack of Lucky Strikes and reached out the pack. Ryan shook his head, opting instead for his pipe. "Kohl's not convinced Hitler's ambitions reach as far as we might think, but he's willing to listen. And he's looking for people like you. Interested?"

"Certainly. At least in hearing what he has to say."

Edward had always tried to direct his younger brother's life to the smallest detail, perhaps as all first-borns do. But having now already experienced far more than his older sibling stuck in a Washington office, Ryan was not about to seize the bait at first glance. Listen, learn, weigh the consequences, then make the decision. Or so he told himself.

The State Department Building was a stone colossus, multi-storied towers and massive wings occupying five acres of lawns and terraces. The car dropped them at the South Wing. Spiral staircases of granite lined with bronze balustrades and mahogany rails rose from the lobby to wide corridors covered in black slate and white marble checkerboard. German and Austrian Affairs occupied one section on the third floor, and the front office bustled with clerks processing files. A receptionist ushered them into Kohl's personal office.

Richard Kohl was stout, in his early fifties with a ruddy complexion and thinning hair meticulously combed over. His manner was cordial and ingratiating. "Dr. Lemmon, a pleasure to meet you at last. And Edward, glad you managed to lure this famous brother of yours to Washington."

Kohl gestured toward the chairs in front of his desk. He spread the contents of a file out before him. Ryan recognized old newspaper reports from Europe carrying his byline, neatly mounted on thin cardstock, and spotted his name atop a government form with several pages of typed copy attached by a clip.

"We've taken a close look at your rather intriguing overseas career, thanks to Ed here," he nodded to Edward. "And I hear you're damned good in the classroom, as well. But more important, at least to me, you come highly recommended by some friends at Harvard Business. Always good to be well-connected. Right, Dr. Lemmon?"

"Thank you, sir, pleased to be invited here, and friends are indeed valuable. But tell me, I can't quite see what use Washington has for a small-town college professor."

"I trust Ed here managed not to reveal too much, so I'll start from scratch." A knock on the door brought a receptionist bearing coffee. "As you well know, Europe's a mess, Asia's equally unstable, and we Americans think we can stay uninvolved? Well, we didn't succeed the last time around and we'll soon be in shit up to our ears again. Now our immediate concerns here in this office are Nazi Germany and the expanding Reich, and you're already quite familiar with the situation over there."

"Yes, it's sad to see the changes, and even sadder for those living through it."

"All cards on the table, Dr. Lemmon, we think you can do us a great service by returning to Germany for a spell. Frankly, we need to get in touch with the grass roots. What you learn over there might help provide us with intelligence to defuse tensions a bit, or just change a few isolationist minds over here. Influential minds. And should we have to get involved—that's what Secretary Hull and President Roosevelt expect—you'll have made our job a helluva lot easier. Still interested?"

"Absolutely, sir, tell me more."

"Right now this country's woefully underequipped for an intelligence battle, much less another war. We need to know with what and whom we're dealing. As for our President, he plays his cards close to the vest, and prefers to hold several hands at once. So he's exploring a number of options for gathering clandestine information, and we're now one of them."

"Sounds intriguing."

"We need a few qualified chaps for an ongoing project. In a nutshell, a few of the President's friends—Harvard and Yale men, that sort of thing—anyway, these well-off buddies trot the globe, keep their eyes and ears open, and report back to him. But now we need to know what the less powerful and influential are up to." Kohl swept his hand over the news clippings. "You were in contact in Germany and France with many of the political movements, right?"

"Nearly all, I suppose: monarchists and nationalists, Nazis, Social Democrats, Communists, some of the fringe groups, too. But I'm told most opposition is now in the detention camps or in bed with the Nazis. Is anyone still fighting the tide?"

"That's your task to find out. We've a few connections within Hitler's government which could prove useful, but we suspect some opponents are still lying low and biding their time. We need to reach out to them, and know what they're capable of. But quietly, you understand."

"Of course."

"For now, we can offer you an assignment you might actually enjoy, and you'll fit in well with the existing talent within 'The Group,' as we call the project around here. Accept our offer, and you operate for us in the areas you know best, pretty much independently. I hear you easily pass for a German or a Frenchman?"

"I've done so before," Ryan said.

"Excellent. That's what our vetting people reported." He chuckled. "We had native speakers pay you a covert visit or two to confirm your abilities." Ryan recalled a couple of prospective students sitting in on classes who had seemed a bit out of place.

"You'll be a correspondent at large, doing stringer work as you've done before. With the necessary identity papers, of course. Feel free to file a few stories, to keep up the appearances, but your primary task will be identifying anti-Nazis still active behind the scenes, or willing to step up if and when the time comes."

Ryan took a few moments to consider. He sensed Edward's eyes on him. "I don't see any difficulties with that, I'm still in touch with a few of my old friends and acquaintances."

"We can offer them assurances of support—primarily financial at this point—but we'll intervene in other ways where we can. Committed contacts, that's what we really need, clandestine agents over there should Johnny march off to war again."

"Wouldn't trustworthy, German-born Americans handle this better?"

"We've a few in training, others already in place, but you yourself know what it's like. Having a family can be a detriment. Plenty of denunciations going on, and it's way too easy for the Gestapo to use parents or grandparents as collateral and turn our agents. We prefer Americans who can pass for European without the familial ties."

Kohl paused to light his pipe. "And you qualify."

The proposed undertaking was exciting, but he recognized the potential danger. He knew how the Nazis worked: Isabel's disappearance, René's near-fatal beating, and his own close-call in Marburg. But to return to Europe, to actually spy for his country, was more than intriguing compared to the humdrum life on campus. "Are we talking months, or longer? I've commitments at Baker."

"No worries there. You're almost free of this semester's classes, and we can make a leave of absence easy." He smiled and set down the pipe. "We're government, you know. A few weeks of training before we fly you over, and then you're basically on your own. An open-ended summer vacation, paid by Uncle Sam himself. Ed here tells me you're fond of airplanes?"

"I've flown a number of times within Europe, but never across the Atlantic. Plus a few glider lessons in Marburg. It's beautiful up there."

"Tried it once, came down sicker than a dog. But we need our people in place quickly, so you fly."

"No problem there."

"Once in Europe, we'll keep you on the ground—forgive the pun—indefinitely, mostly in the Reich, but France, as well. It's anybody's guess how long the French will hold out if Hitler turns west once he's finished with the east. Things are moving at a rapid pace, and if we wait too long, getting this type of information will become seriously problematic."

"At least a year abroad then. And the financial arrangements?"

"I'll let the accounting boys handle specifics. Suffice to say that travel and living expenses will be covered, including incidentals, here and abroad. And extra for inducements, you know, bar tab one day, grease a palm the next. Still a lot of guesswork on our part, we're just now getting a good handle on all this. But you'll be living much better than a college professor."

"And specific assignments?"

"Occasional requests from here, information from outside sources to verify, some special piece of intelligence needed, perhaps. But for the most part, just track down your own contacts and material. Ed here will be your control. Your shared family background should make things easier with codes, that sort of thing."

Ed finally spoke up: "We might use some of the Cherokee we picked up as kids when Mother took us out to the reservation for her charity work."

"By the way, Dr. Lemmon, you've done some acting at..." Kohl glanced again at the papers, "Kansas University?"

"A little."

"Good, because solid acting skills will help if you run into trouble, and we can't promise to be there to help." Kohl closed the file and leaned back in his chair. "So, are you in our little game?"

Edward watched his brother expectantly. Despite Ryan's determination to take his time, to instill a bit of doubt in Ed's conviction, his decision was already made. A broad grin spread across his face as he reached to shake Kohl's hand.

"I'm in," he said, and Edward smiled.

# CHAPTER NINE

The secluded farm lay in rich, rolling country outside Alexandria, Virginia. It consisted of a large white farmhouse, several former stables converted to relatively comfortable dorms, and a vast horse barn, now equipped for classroom training without an animal in sight.

Upon his arrival Ryan wore a distinctive ring he had purchased on the Ponte Vecchio in Florence. Now he had to surrender the gold band to the indoctrination officer, along with any other personal belongings. They disappeared into a sealed pouch for the duration of training. He was issued a simple uniform of khaki. The recruits were to know nothing of the fellow participants' former lives, and each trainee received a code name. Personal information in the wrong hands could put both agent and classmates at risk. His heavy gold ring bearing an onyx cameo of a gladiator did however inspire Ryan's code name, "Firenze." Ryan did not tell the officer about the ring's finely-crafted compartment, ostensibly a replica of a Roman original designed to carry poison. *Ideal for a spy*, he thought, and laughed at the absurdity.

He quickly mastered the tradecraft—shortwave radio communication and simple codes, couriers and drops, hand-to-hand fighting and small weapons use. He was familiar with shotguns from shooting skeet on a cousin's farm in Missouri, but the handling of pistols was new, and he practiced his aim—both short- and long-distance—on the firing range and in a section of the barn fitted out to resemble a German alley and hotel room. The more complex code work proved challenging, and he hoped never to rely on it.

Yet boredom occasionally set in when their instructors devoted long hours to aspects of German daily life already familiar to Ryan from his years in the Reich. He had to force himself to pay close attention. The instructors, just back from Germany, were fluent in the up-to-date vocabulary and behavior required in the police state, where any deviation from the norm was immediate cause for suspicion.

The trainees learned what to expect when showing identity papers to authorities, what publications were acceptable to read in public, and how to spot the secret police on sight. *When you believe yourself observed by a Gestapo agent, approach the observer directly and request directions; a guilty person always looks the other way or tries to evade detection.* Checking over one's shoulder, the so-called "German glance," was a dead give-away that could leave you dead.

Edward came out to the farm to meet him in private and work on personal communication codes. He, too, was required to don the khakis. Once close as youngsters, the brothers had spent little time together since Ryan's move to Europe. Now together again for days, the two reconnected. They reviewed a list of Ryan's European acquaintances, identifying those who might prove willing to help undermine the Nazi machine. With maps spread out on a drafting table, they agreed on potential contact points as Ryan followed a pre-planned itinerary across eastern France and into the Reich. Normal communications with Ed would be through contacts at American embassies or consulates, although cables or phones were always available in an emergency. Since lines were uniformly tapped, the code language would come in handy in such cases. His cover as a correspondent for the Washington Post provided a drop point at their offices in Paris and Berlin. Ryan memorized names and numbers which might prove useful, and he and Ed agreed on a few Cherokee words to express special needs or verbally alert the other to danger.

It felt good to exercise strenuously again. He hadn't noticed how years of sedentary teaching had robbed him of the stamina taken for granted when he had walked and bicycled throughout Europe and swum at every opportunity. He and the other recruits ran several miles a day and did demanding calisthenics, and he left the training camp in peak physical condition, feeling himself once again the college athlete.

At a final dinner with Edward and Grace, they announced that a niece or nephew would arrive in the coming year. Ryan found himself pleased, but also envious. Over his years at Baker his dating had been a constant search for the spirit and passion he had found in Isabel and Erika. As the day of his departure approached, the idea of settling down suddenly became appealing. He realized the dangers he would face made any promise of stability in an unstable world all the more tempting. But Europe was in his blood, and he knew it was time to revisit Germany, time to reconnect with his past.

# CHAPTER TEN

The North Atlantic, always challenging for ships due to its fierce seas, storms and icebergs, was now putting their large aircraft to the test. The Sikorsky Clipper III was the world's largest passenger plane and it bucked and shuddered in the face of severe and shifting winds. Pan American was running survey flights from Newfoundland to Ireland in anticipation of setting up a new passenger route, and a small group of unidentified guests was along for the bumpy ride.

Someone in The Group had pulled serious strings to get the five unrecorded passengers onboard, each of whom had anticipated taking the established southern route via Jamaica, the Azores and Lisbon. Ryan and his companions were experiencing what Pan Am hoped to offer wealthy paying passengers soon—shorter transatlantic flights at speeds far superior to the sluggish dirigibles. But instead of the luxurious trappings planned for commercial application, the passengers were roughing it without stewardesses or cocktails. They probably would not have kept the drinks down, anyway, as evidenced by the widespread use of airsickness bags. Ryan, however, reveled in the flight, and as the seaplane approached the British Isles the clouds below opened to welcome him back to Europe under bright rays of sun.

He caught an Imperial Airways flight from Foynes to London where he found a modest hotel near Victoria Station. July was ending, the weather hot and muggy. Escaping the confines of his room, took an evening stroll and noted anti-Semitic graffiti scrawled on walls and sidewalks, British Fascists and Nazi sympathizers making their opinions clear. The next morning, hungry and rested, he hurriedly downed eggs and sausage with Earl Grey at his hotel before boarding the first available train to Dover.

The Channel crossing was uneventful, and by late afternoon he was in Paris. The streets were somber. A palpable tension filled the air, as if all Parisians held a collective breath. Ryan missed the *joie de vivre* he remembered so well. Newsboys shouted reports of violent protests in the city, and of pro-Nazi demonstrations in Alsace and Lorraine.

He found a small table at a sidewalk café on Saint-Germain-des-Prés and read *Le Monde* over an espresso. He scanned a long article on recently passed anti-Semitic legislation in Germany. Jews could no longer work in the stock market, real estate, lending, and most commercial fields, and must declare their assets and sell their businesses. All Jews would now carry police-issued identification cards. A related news report followed up on the July 5th international conference convened by Roosevelt at Evian on Lake Geneva. Most of the participants, including the United States, indicated a desire to further restrict Jewish immigration. *Where will Jews forced out of the Reich go?* He set the paper aside.

His covert game was finally in play, and it was time to link up with old friends in Paris, Burgundy and Alsace. Ryan mentally reviewed the list of people he planned to contact in eastern France before crossing the Rhine. He already dreaded entering Germany, not from fear, but simply because he knew it would erode the last cherished memories of a country that had won his devotion nearly a decade earlier.

His first phone call was to a small night club in Montmartre, and he arranged to drop in that evening at eleven. Ryan had first seen Marita Lesney in 1929 when she brightened the stage at the Folies Bergère. He had waited outside the stage door for three nights in a row before she had consented to go out with him. Their affair was brief, but over the years she had written him regular updates on her life. His old Berlin address served as *poste restante*, and the Old Major had forwarded her letters and cards on to America, usually with a suggestive comment of his own. Ryan had only responded once or twice. But upon learning he would return to Europe in the summer, he had sent an air mail letter suggesting this rendezvous.

Two years before, Marita and her sister Marie, herself a former dancer, pooled their savings to open *La Chatte bottée* in a converted movie theater. The burly doorman with shaved head led Ryan across the lobby toward a narrow staircase. Beyond the red velvet curtain a musical revue was in progress as scantily-clad young women danced to the raucous accompaniment of a small band. Couples occupied tiny tables with room for little more than small shaded lamps, ashtrays, and beverages. The lively flurry of feathers and bare flesh turned Ryan's thoughts to happier days in Paris.

Her office—obviously the former projection room of the theater—overlooked the crowded club floor. Marita had barely aged in nearly ten years, though a hint of sadness in her eyes suggested significant changes in her life. She welcomed him in a lacy red dress and pearls, her dark hair pinned up off her shoulders. Her high heels were crimson.

He'd forgotten how petite she was; he remembered the perfume. She offered only her cheeks for a kiss, held him for several seconds, then stepped back to look him over. "You hardly answered my letters or postcards," she said. "What's a girl to do to get your attention, dance naked for you?" Her pout turned to a wry smile. "Oh yes, I've tried that already. It used to work." She turned to close both the door and the shutters at the projection window. The emcee's amplified patter dropped sufficiently in volume to allow conversation.

"I have but one excuse," Ryan said, his expression serious. "Your letters only made me miss you more, and I couldn't afford to spend all my time thinking of you." He broke into a grin. In truth, once he had left Paris years before and her letters became more serious, he realized how much emotion she had invested in their casual affair, and he had not felt it fair to prolong the correspondence.

"You're as handsome as ever, so I assume life treats you well?" Marita indented his chin with the tip of her finger, eliciting his full smile. "Ah, that's the Ryan Lemmon I remember, all flashing teeth and irresistible charm."

"My only complaint is my failing memory. I'd forgotten how damned beautiful you are." Ryan caressed her cheek.

"*Non, non, et non!* We won't start all that nonsense over again. I've finally gotten over you."

Ryan was relieved to recognize her former sense of humor. She offered him the small chair next to her writing desk, whose surface lay half hidden by neat stacks of invoices, a crystal ashtray, and a pack of Gitanes. "Champagne? We do offer some bubbly worth drinking, but only for favored guests."

"Let's drink to our reunion."

She opened the shutters and extended her head out the tiny window, her hips toward him and swaying to the rhythm of the band. She shouted down to the bartender below, "Laurent-Perrier, *s'il-vous-plaît!*" She caught him smiling appreciatively as she turned around. "You never lose the urge to dance," she said with a wink.

Within moments a waiter arrived with a tray and withdrew just as quickly. Ryan popped the cork, filled the flutes and toasted her. Marita laid a hand on his knee. "You said in your last letter—I'm having it framed since it's probably the last from you I'll ever see—that we've something important to discuss. Since I'm obviously not pregnant," she straightened her back and ran a hand over her flat belly, "and you're obviously not here to propose marriage, tell me what brings you back to me?"

Ryan had thought broaching the subject would be easier. Instead he was hesitant to abandon flirtation and move on to serious matters. "It has to do with my work."

"A professor of history now, I believe?"

"French and German, actually; my doctorate's in history. But I'm here to report on European politics and to do some research."

"And...?"

"And I need to know a little more about what you're up to before I dare ask for your help." His own nervousness surprised him. "I recall your mother's Jewish?"

Marita stiffened slightly, but didn't drop her smile. "Yes, you guard my great secret, and please don't tell me you've become one of those nauseating anti-Semites after spending all that time in Germany. I'm not sure I could deal with that."

"*Moi non plus*. But I do know France has its share of home-grown anti-Semites. Have you had troubles here? Have your parents?"

"Ah, my parents." A shadow passed over her face. "Well, I seldom see my mother; I guess she just doesn't approve of dance." Marita gave a sad half-grin. "But I've stayed in touch with my father, and his health could be better." The grin was gone.

"They're here in the city?"

"Le Marais, in the *quatrième*. Why?"

"I couldn't recall, that's all. Are you concerned about the plight of the German Jews?"

"Concerned? Yes, but what of it? Does anyone know exactly what will happen? There or here?"

She offered him a Gitane. He shook his head. She nervously tamped hers against the desktop, waiting for his match. The acrid smoke escaped her lips and curled to the ceiling.

"It's clear another war's coming, and you must hear what's going on in the Reich." Ryan bent forward. "The Nazis are looking east now, but who really thinks—given history—they won't turn west again when it suits them, despite all their protests of peaceful intentions?"

"*C'est juste*, of course, it's the talk of the town."

"I've only just arrived and hear nothing else. My God, your prime minister can now govern by decree in case of war. And from what I'm reading, the generals bluster as usual but don't prepare. They think the Maginot Line's the ultimate solution to everything." He laid his hand over hers to still the incessant tapping of her fingers. "You and your family need a plan."

She stubbed out the cigarette, still barely smoked, and raised her hands in resignation. "Marie and I plan to keep our little business going, and if the Germans make it here, we'll find a way to keep them entertained. *Mon Dieu*, I deal with them almost every night anyway. They can't keep their hands off our dancers." She mimicked an obnoxious drunk, squeezing her breasts as she rocked her head back and forth. "Oompah-pah, oompah-pah. But these *Boches* throw around the francs and drink our cheap booze, so they're welcome to come here to make fools of themselves."

"Listen, Marita. Fools are one thing, these Hitlerites another. One reason I'm here now is to find people America can trust should things go sideways." "Doesn't sound exactly like newspaper reporting to me." She smiled. "But America won't fight this time; it'll be up to just us Europeans. It's no secret how your countrymen feel about getting involved over here again."

"Many of us think it's unavoidable, and I'm one of them. And right now we're preparing for the worst, so we need people we can rely on for help. It seems you're in a unique situation to help me, if you're willing."

"What could I do here in our little cabaret?"

"Just keep eyes and ears open for reliable people for me to meet. Maybe your girls could pick up useful information—" he reached for his own chest and rocked back and forth, "from those 'oompah-pah *Boches'* you're talking about." Marita didn't respond, so he dropped his hands. "Nothing loosens tongues like that cheap champagne," he said.

She glanced away, took another cigarette from the pack, put it back.

"And meanwhile, I'm going to look for a way to help you and your family, if it comes to that. Even if you're not concerned, I'm worried for your sake. I know what's happening to Jews across the border." He squeezed her hand. "Does any of this make sense?"

She had watched him intently, the sadness in her eyes more evident than ever. Now tears surfaced. She drew a handkerchief from her purse and dabbed them away, and when she spoke he heard the fragility. "Our local Nazis attacked my father in the street, left him lying in the gutter, all because he loves a Jewish woman. *Mon Dieu,* she's his wife for over thirty years. Now he fears leaving the building, and Marie and I can do little for him. He just sits and stares out the window. So you see, I don't have to wait for the *Boches;* we already have our own fascists to do their filthy work for them."

The tears welled again, this time coursing down her cheeks. He knelt beside her chair and took her in his arms, and her head dropped to his shoulder. A few moments passed before she composed herself again, turning to the mirror above her desk and dabbing at her eyes.

"My mascara's a mess." She gave a feeble half-smile. "Now tell me how I can help."

# CHAPTER ELEVEN

"Ryan, how good it is to see you again!" René was burlier than ever and full of warmth. His powerful hug almost took Ryan's breath away. "I thought our paths had parted forever."

They descended the steps from the imposing Gesslinger home to an iron table and chairs set out on the flagstone terrace. A green bottle of pinot blanc and two glasses awaited them. The promenade above the river was bordered by balusters and urn-capped pedestals, an expansive setting overlooking broad lawns which descended gently to the bank of the Rhine. The gardens were park-like, the foliage just reaching fall color. Ryan noted that his friend favored his right leg. They sat and talked.

René's shipping concern still found business despite the challenges of both the unsettled economy and political reality. The Nazis had brought tremendous pressure on the dockworkers and boatmen, shutting down the unions and forcing out the few remaining former SPD members. They had arrested his father Heinrich briefly in 1935 for investigation of "seditious thought," the denunciation coming surely from an envious competitor. He was released again when his French shipping customers refused to deal with the Nazi "temporarily" placed in charge of the Gesslinger contracts and threatened to boycott the other shipping firms in the Kehl region. Heinrich had returned from two weeks' interrogation a weaker man, intimidated by the police power of the government and unwilling to continue his political struggle. Then in the previous winter he had returned exhausted and coughing from a trip downriver meant for his relaxation. The official cause of death was pneumonia.

"He just couldn't face living in our Third Reich," René said with a sigh. As for his mother Jeanne, her health was still good, but her bouts with depression disturbing. "Fear forms the backdrop to all we think and do. You never know who's listening, who's informing," René said. "Don't expect to hear anyone voice democratic sympathies now. No one even jokes about it."

"Even among friends?"

"We seldom get together anymore, no festivals or parties. Too dangerous, even a few inebriated words can land you in a concentration camp. The only social clubs are those approved by the state, and they're controlled by Party members. Our homes are searched and we're hauled off in 'protective custody' at no provocation whatsoever. And then our businesses end up in the hands of local Party group leaders. Some surprise, no? *Heil Hitler.*" The bitterness in his friend's voice was new.

As the steady river traffic passed below them they spoke at length of René's recovery, which appeared complete despite the dire warnings of the doctors. He mentioned occasional forgetfulness, but boasted he could still physically assist his stevedores and boatmen as well as before the assault. Ryan shared his own close call with von Kredow and the Wachonians, his narrow escape through the old tunnels of Marburg. And then Ryan told him that Erika Breitling had married the Nazi.

"What a loss." René shook his head in disgust. "A fine-looking girl, I thought the two of you made quite a pair, and she seemed a bit more clear-thinking than many, but weren't we all at one time?" René's right hand trembled as he lifted the wine glass, and he made light of it by switching to his left. "Good thing I don't lift sabers anymore."

"I'm afraid at day's end I got away much better than you, my friend, under the circumstances," Ryan said.

"You also weren't the one soused to the gills. I only wish I'd been at your side when they came after you," said René. "Together we would have given them something to think about, assuming those bastards knew how to think."

"Oh, they think all right, they just don't allow others to think differently." Ryan acknowledged a perverse admiration for the skill involved in the Nazi takeover. "After all, they engineered a brilliant legal coup through intimidation and manipulation, and the Republic didn't stand a chance."

René nodded. "They appealed to our basest fears of economic ruin, and played to our love of social gatherings, spectacle and music. A winning combination, I have to admit."

"Don't forget violence, the ultimate political tool."

"We thought our *Reichsbanner* would crush a military coup head-on, but there was never a *Putsch* to put down. Instead they picked us off one-by-one with political maneuverings, and by the time we realized it, they already controlled the government and the people." Rene's stared down at his clenched fists. "*Mein Gott,* what cowards we became."

"So, are all the fighters gone?"

"Not all. For most of us, apathy is all we have left. But luckily, there are still a few willing to even the score where we can."

"Are you closely monitored, I mean personally?"

"Oh, we have our block wardens, of course. Mine's a sniveling bureaucrat, an office Nazi appointed to his post, and as long as I make my regular financial contributions to the cause he marks me 'politically reliable' on his monthly report and moves along. But thank God he doesn't know what we're really up to."

"Up to?"

René winked and suggested a tour of his home. "Come along, my mother's so anxious to see you again."

Jeanne welcomed Ryan graciously in the salon, but with an air of distraction. *Still an eye-catching woman, so very French.* Her raven-black hair was now silver, her brow lined with ill-disguised worries. "Of course you'll stay and dine with us." She suggested an aperitif on the terrace before dinner and then excused herself to give direction to the cook.

René led Ryan into his study and pulled a book from the shelf. Ryan looked quizzically at the illustration on the dust jacket of a cowboy on horseback. "The Lone Ranger?"

"A gift from America, sent by a former dock supervisor. We couldn't keep him on, of course, a Jew. He's now in New York with his family." René pointed to the rider rearing up on his stallion. "That's me these days, do you know him?"

"I've heard a few radio episodes," Ryan said.

"Certainly no Siegfried when it comes to slaying dragons, but this cowboy avenger is a man after my own heart. Our dear Führer insists our children play 'Aryans and Jews' rather than 'Cowboys and Indians,' but I think we're living in the Wild West now with bad guys and robber barons fully in charge. So I've taken up the fight with some trusted companions who'll come to the rescue when needed."

Bottles of Cointreau and Courvoisier were waiting on the terrace table when they returned. They turned their chairs to face the Rhine. A parade of river boats and low-slung barges floated through the warm autumn afternoon. René related how he and a trusted circle of former *Reichsbanner* militia men and river workers had squirreled away weapons and gone underground. No gathering in public, only occasional exchanges of ideas and information in private homes and at the docks, and a communication network to call for aid when needed. They watched for loyal republicans who shared their hatred of the regime, and kept eyes and ears open for persecution of the weak and enemies of the state.

"Just take a look over there," he pointed to the far bank of the Rhine, his eyes squinting into the long rays of the afternoon sun. "France, of course, but for anyone who wants out of the Reich, practically an impossible goal. Can't swim it with your family, and river traffic is watched like a hawk."

"So how do you help?"

"They can't find us, so we find them. We have eyes on the border checkpoint. It's mostly Jews now who run into trouble, even though their departure is officially encouraged. Those few with sufficient valuables to grease a Nazi palm or two get across the rail bridge to Strasburg. The others are sent back packing, or picked up by the Gestapo and shipped off to the camps. It's heart-breaking."

René described whole Jewish families—grandparents, parents, little children—scattering across the train station in abject fear while hounded by Gestapo, with helpful citizens directing the police to the fugitives' hiding spots.

"So how do you intervene?"

"We slip them across by boat at night. Easier to mask what we're doing, of course. We may dent a few Nazi heads in the process, but who's counting?" René laughed. "We've learned quite a bit about head-denting from those bastards, and we confiscate a few good weapons in the process." He took a sip of the Cointreau.

"*Frei Heil*," toasted Ryan with his snifter. Hail freedom, the old *Reichsbanner* salute.

"*Frei Heil*, indeed," responded René. "There's one we don't dare use anymore."

Ryan knew he had struck gold. He explained his assignment in detail, and René was on board before Ryan could finish. "Tell us what to do, and we're there for you," he said. "I already have an escape network on both sides of the river." He gestured to the water traffic below. "Just watch for the orange and black of Gesslinger Shipping."

Ryan scanned the river and within moments spotted one of René's boats. "Those are Princeton colors, *mein Freund*—you must remember I'm a Harvard man."

"Please do overlook that. I assure you they're friendly colors, and it's a bit late to make a change." He refilled Ryan's glass.

"Always happy to fight under your colors." Ryan was thrilled to discover this network.

Before dinner they drove down to the Gesslinger docks. The facility was enclosed by high chain-link, an access road separating it from woodland beyond. A long loading platform paralleled the boat basin, which lay obliquely off the river. Several smaller buildings squatted dockside at even intervals, and four large warehouses bordered the landward side of the rail tracks servicing the docks. A barge was being loaded by a crane operator and a crew of stevedores bent to the task.

The friends climbed the external staircase to an office above the main warehouse. *Gesslinger Rhein-Fracht* stood proudly in orange and black high on the corrugated metal siding. René wanted Ryan to meet his closest associate and long-time chief of operations, Hugo Gerson. "You won't find a more loyal man than Hugo. He's my

Tonto. Should something happen to me, rely on him as my alter-ego."

"Are they on to you?" Ryan wouldn't risk making his friend's life any more dangerous than it already was. "Have you been threatened?"

"Threats only make me mad, so we don't wait for a second threat." He did not smile. "But we stay as covert as possible. A fact of life in the glorious Reich is that even our school kids denounce family and neighbors, so I only trust those I've known forever, who've proven I can trust them. That's Hugo, through and through."

They entered the office. Banks of tall windows overlooked operations up and down the docks. Gerson rose from behind a crowded partners' desk to shake Ryan's hand. A stout balding man, perhaps fifty years old, Hugo was still fit from years on the waterfront. His skin showed the aging that comes with a lifetime spent outdoors, and he squinted even in the subdued light of the office, as if constantly peering across reflective waters. The shy smile under a bristly mustache appealed to Ryan.

"I inherited Hugo from my father; best gift he ever gave me when it comes to business." René smiled appreciatively at Gerson, who seemed genuinely touched by the praise.

"Welcome to our humble office, Herr Lemmon. May I offer you a beer?" Gerson gestured to a white-enameled icebox in the corner.

"Thank you, but no. I believe we're expected for dinner soon, and we've already had a bit to drink. What a pleasure to meet you in person, after René has sung your praises so loudly."

"Ryan's one of us, Hugo," René said. "He's bringing in some outside help for our struggle, so be as open with him as we are with each other."

"Then welcome a second time, this time to our fight." Hugo's smile widened to a large grin. "As we say to reassure each other, we may never bring them down, but at least they'll feel our bite."

René and Ryan spent several weeks traversing the Upper Rhine countryside in an Opel sedan, stopping at farms, villages and small towns. Ryan was pleased to see his friend's slight limp didn't cause any serious problems getting around. René introduced him to members of his resistance group, and together they set up means of covert contact and a list of assignments for the men and women involved. Ryan memorized their code names and passwords, all inspired by the Wild West novel. René wanted to be certain that Ryan would have direct access to his "sidekicks" without him, should the need ever arise. The American sensed a deep-seated melancholy in his friend, a ragged fatalism in the face of overwhelming odds.

Everywhere stood hateful anti-Semitic signage, contrasting boldly with the colorful posters promoting Party rallies with marching bands, guest speakers, gymnastics, and food. The Hitler Youth and League of German Girls paraded through the narrow streets, flags flying to the accompaniment of singing, fife and drums. In every town blood-red swastika flags flew from public buildings, and many private residences also bore banners. Movies promoting the achievements of the Reich and Nazi values played in cinemas throughout the region.

A plain-clothes policeman stopped them as they entered a country inn near Rastatt for lunch and called for their papers. Ryan handed over his press identification along with his passport bearing a swastika-stamped entry visa. He explained that he was reporting for an American newspaper on the wonders of National Socialism. René offered his own identity card. The policeman grunted his satisfaction and returned the documents, and they all exchanged perfunctory Hitler salutes before the man stepped back outside.

"I think we need a glass of *Weissburgunder* after that," René said. They split a bottle on the terrace of the *Gasthaus*, folk tunes drifting down to them from an unseen flute-player in a farmhouse up the lane.

Ryan felt his first three months in Europe were proving a success, and he relayed back to Edward his sense of real progress. Much as he had wished to use the aid of Marita and her sister, so similar in looks and manner to be almost twins, he had opted to leave them out of the contact chain, and he told Ed to strike them from the report. Their family's distress was too immediate, the emotional weakness a potential liability. But they did provide him with links to the Parisian Jewish community and a coterie of French republicans, regulars at *La Chatte bottée*. His old friends in Burgundy had also gathered commitments from sympathetic anti-fascists fearful of German aggression. They remembered all too well the killing fields of the Great War, the miles of deadly trenches at their doorstep. And now he had enlisted a covert network of anti-Nazi patriots on German soil with the means and the know-how to intervene, albeit on a limited scale.

Finally, on a crisp early morning in the first week of November, René had driven him in his Opel to the train station in Kehl. "Just remember this, my dear friend, the Reich conceals very few whom you can truly trust. Assume the worst—it's truly all around you." He shook Ryan's hand, smothered him with a great bear hug, and watched his friend board the train.

René waved as the express pulled from the station, headed for Karlsruhe and on to Berlin. He was still standing there when Ryan lost sight of the platform.

He used several hours of the journey to organize his thoughts for a report back to State and The Group. In Berlin he would put it to code and deliver it to the U.S. consulate for the diplomatic pouch. The balance of the trip was filled with memories of that early, uncritical love he had found in this beautiful country and its people. Arriving once again in Berlin after an absence of years, planning to operate covertly in the heart of a police state, Ryan began to sense the challenges which awaited him in the very heart of the Reich.

The clatter from the wheels of the carriage grew louder as the express rattled over merging rail lines and the train slowed for the stop. Passengers rose from their seats, pulled luggage from overhead racks, noisily opened compartment doors and began to crowd the aisles. Mothers made young children presentable for family awaiting their arrival. Somewhere in his carriage an infant wailed, displeased at being awake and hungry.

Ryan remained seated as the train slipped under the canopy of Potsdamer Bahnhof. He was hesitant to leave his fond memories for the stark reality of Hitler's Berlin. Sad thoughts of Isabel flooded back, her vivaciousness, her disappearance. But his curiosity about changes in the capital was strong, and he looked forward to seeing the von Haldheim family once again.

The train came to a standstill to the hiss of brake lines. Passengers in the aisle lowered the windows to pass through suitcases to waiting hands on the platform. Ryan allowed the aisle to clear, then took his valise and stepped down onto the familiar concrete. He moved with stragglers alongside the locomotive, its running gear already being serviced by train personnel. Nazi flags hung from the smoke deflectors on the massive snout.

Two sullen men in fedoras and topcoats checked papers as the passengers filed past toward the concourse. They reviewed his American passport, made a note on a pad, and waved him on through. The acrid smell of coal smoke gave way to the aroma of grilled sausage coming from within the station. He was hungry. He would have lunch before making his first call.

# CHAPTER TWELVE

Erika sat in the quiet of her childhood room, absent-mindedly stroking Leo's fine, silky hair. The child lay asleep with his head in her lap. Still dressed in his traveling clothes, the boy was exhausted from the sudden late night train ride to see his grandparents in Marburg.

She thought of how it was, learning you have something incurable which will soon wrench you away from those you love, from those who love you. She had watched the process often enough in her student years at the *Frauenklinik*. She would summon the patient to the doctor's office where the open file lay before him. The sick woman, fearing the worst, sat nervously fidgeting with her handbag, the ring on her finger, a handkerchief. She would shake her head in disbelief before beginning to sob softly as the enormity of the news sank in. Erika would stand nearby to help her from the room, to answer questions about the course of treatment which always arose once the reality had settled in, all the while knowing that—in this case, as in so many—no cure was possible.

Erika's affliction also had no cure. She had married a committed National Socialist, a true believer and arch-achiever. Her marriage was a failure. Her powerful husband was a monster brimming with hate and brutality, a respected Nazi, a Gestapo big-wig. But ironically, she had achieved the social life and position she had sought. She was wealthy and lived in an envied mansion near the Wannsee. And she had a darling little boy who brought tears of joy to her eyes. And here, in the glorious Reich, married to the ultimate

Aryan success, Erika had just learned a truth which would destroy all she loved.

The social gathering of the previous evening had turned her world upside-down. All the Gestapo powerhouses had been present, even Reichsführer-SS Himmler himself. As with all Party functions, attendance was mandatory. The men were dashing in their black uniforms and polished boots, all gleaming insignias of rank and flashing smiles. The wives displayed their finest gowns and jewelry. Everyone traded witty small talk while sipping champagne and balancing plates of hors-d'oeuvres.

Horst looked splendid as usual, and was, as usual, surrounded by women basking in his masculine glow. She hadn't cared. Erika tried to stay as far away from him as socially acceptable. In private she also had kept her distance, especially now that she understood what for weeks had been the object of his dedication, knew its enormity and its horror. And the thought of living under the same roof with such a mind terrified her.

She rarely ever entered Horst's study. It had been a Sunday morning exactly one week before the event, and Leo had led her there. Horst was still in his bedroom, sleeping off the drug and inebriation, she assumed.

She had discovered her son playing hide-and-seek beneath the heavy desk at the window. The boy refused to abandon his hiding place, so she waited for him to change his mind, sitting in her husband's chair and absent-mindedly opening the leather portfolio embossed with eagle-and-swastika to peruse the meticulously-typed pages, now studded with Horst's hand-written revisions and corrections. She could not stop reading despite her revulsion. So clinical, so precise, so typical of Horst von Kredow.

There before her lay a monstrous plan to systematically kill the Jews of Europe in the wake of a path of conquest. *Einsatzgruppen* he called them, task forces designed for the mass slaughter of innocents. The protocol detailed the creation of paramilitary commandos, death squads comprised of SS and Gestapo. Their sole task was to follow advancing Waffen-SS troops, identify and round up Jews, Marxists, and other undesirables, and lead them to slaughter.

The captives would be shot in the head or machine-gunned en masse. Local fascists would be recruited to assist in the murders. He recommended executions take place at the site of pre-dug mass graves to expedite disposal of the bodies. Men, women, children; no exceptions unless of some value to the occupiers, such as an expendable supply of slave labor.

Erika sat back, shuddering at the heinousness buried in the cold, administrative language. Leo called up from beneath the desk, "Come find me, *Mutti!*"

"One moment, *Liebchen,*" her voice as lifeless as those slaughtered innocents she pictured in her mind.

She turned the following pages clumsily, her fingers as numbed as her mind by the cruelty and cold-bloodedness. A chill crept through her as she imagined the consequences for families sitting down to breakfast at that very moment with no idea of the coming horror. There were pages of numbers, charts. Projected Jewish populations to be "processed" based on SD research. Estimates of quantities of death squads required as the forces slashed their way across Eastern Europe. She found similar charts for France and Italy, as well.

There were proposals for other means of extermination, as well. Horst's suggestions were as varied as they were diabolical: mobile killing chambers on military trucks using exhaust fumes to suffocate those trapped inside, fatal injections disguised as inoculations, temporary—"perhaps permanent"—detention camps with dedicated extermination facilities. Recommendations for enlisting chemical works and pharmaceutical houses to see what products might already be available or convertible for such application.

He advised that certain of the younger, stronger detainees should be worked to death as slave laborers, or extorted to help seek out and bring in Jews in hiding, once the killing began. It was suggested that some Jews could be coerced into guiding their fellow captives to slaughter at the killing sites with the promise of extending their own lives.

"*Mutti,* you're supposed to find me!" Leo tugged at her skirt to get his mother's attention.

She reached down and drew the three-year-old into her arms as tears streamed down her cheeks, then ran from the room, clutching him to her as tightly as possible. The report lay open on the desk.

As the SS gathering had gained momentum, copious quantities of champagne flowed and the guests eased from one group to another, exchanging pleasantries and tired jokes. She was introduced to a tall, distinguished *Sicherheitsdienst* officer in his forties, hair graying at the temples, worn longer than the style chosen by most of the closely-shorn minions. His manner was aristocratic, his mood a bit somber for a get-together of this nature. He was presented as a newcomer to the SD team liaising with the Gestapo. Erika had been startled by the familiarity of his family name, and then made the connection.

"Von Haldheim?" she asked, suddenly alert. "A friend of mine in Marburg knew the von Haldheim family here in Berlin, an American, Ryan Lemmon. Do you remember him?"

"Yes, of course," Rolf von Haldheim smiled briefly in recognition. "He and I shared interesting times in the city's hottest night-spots some years ago. He lived for some months in our Grunewald home as a family guest." His eyes flashed in remembrance before a hint of unexpressed melancholy returned. "As a matter of fact, I just learned he returns to Berlin in a week or so."

Erika hesitated, overcome by an unexpected wave of emotion and melancholy for times past, opportunities now lost. *Ryan, in Berlin.* Before she could ask more they were joined by other celebrants. Von Haldheim gave her a short bow and warm smile, clicked his heels and took his leave, forgoing the customary *Heil Hitler.* Erika sensed that his discomfort in this crowded setting was as great as her own.

She glanced around for their host, ready to claim a headache and escape early. Instead she found the weasel-faced Klaus Pabst staring at her from across the crowded room. His cynical grin confirmed that he had caught her unwanted attention. He nodded slowly before moving in her direction. Since reading the protocol Erika had tried her best to isolate herself from Horst as she sought to process the damning information. Just knowing about it was tearing her apart, but she saw no way to intervene. She had withdrawn into a private shell, devoting her attention solely to Leo. But in public she went through the motions of a dutiful Gestapo wife. And now she had to face one of the most contemptible of her husband's cronies.

She tried to pick up on a conversation with others nearby to avoid speaking with Klaus, but to no avail. Even as a student she couldn't abide the boot-licking Wachonian, the one Horst called his "dagger." Klaus consistently made sexual overtures despite her protests that Horst would not appreciate such advances, but his lackey seemed unfazed by both rejection and implied threat.

In reality, she doubted her husband would give a damn were it not for the insult to his own reputation and "honor," and she knew that the sycophant was only interested in goading her. His devotion to Horst went far beyond admiration and respect; she viewed it as a form of worship. Klaus was his acolyte, a mindless devotee who found his purpose in the adulation of his Gestapo god. She sensed his jealousy of her relationship with Horst, but little did the weasel know he had nothing to envy.

That evening however something had changed. Klaus appeared overly confident, not his usual unctuous self. "My dear Frau von Kredow," he said, "A few moments of your time on this lovely occasion?"

Erika honestly couldn't recall the purpose of the event; there were so many and each as empty as the last. "But, Klaus, what could we possibly have to discuss?"

"A matter of some delicacy. Perhaps a word in private?" He nodded toward the adjoining salon, momentarily free of guests.

"You know that wouldn't be appropriate."

"Then I'll be discreet in this less-than-ideal setting." He bent closer to her ear and spoke just above a whisper. Erika strained to hear against the background of the loud party in progress. Someone nearby was trying to organize a group sing-along of Party favorites. "As you know, we spend a good deal of time investigating family histories. Simply to maintain the purity of the *Volk*, of course. Regrettably I've stumbled upon something quite unpleasant for you personally and for your loved ones, as well." His look of concern was transparently insincere. "But only should it get out, of course."

Erika—suddenly attentive despite her aversion for the speaker—suspected some devious trick. "And that information is?"

"Details here would be too distressing." He gestured to the crowd surrounding them. "If indeed you don't already know, I suggest you have a little talk with your parents. Delve into your family history a bit more closely." Klaus's smugness was repugnant. "For the moment I've been able to keep this under wraps, but I can't say how long I can hold off telling your dear husband." He squeezed her arm, didn't let go. "Once you understand the nature of your problem, perhaps we can work out a mutually-satisfactory accommodation?"

No words came to her, and she shook loose his hand. Klaus stepped back and grinned. He saluted sharply and turned on his heels.

Erika stared dumbly after him, trying to understand what had just happened. The implication, however, was clear. Some discovery had turned the sniveling Pabst into someone with whom she must reckon. *Would he dare try this if he couldn't back it up?* For the moment, Erika was truly perplexed.

The rest of the evening passed in a blur. The distraction of the warning never left her, even when she was drawn into inane conversation and forced to feign interest as she attempted to get away. Seated in the car with a drunker than usual Horst, she found further time to question and worry as they rode home in silence. Once the chauffeur dropped them at the front door she immediately ran upstairs to check on Leo, asleep in his bed. She knew that Oskar would help Horst find his own way.

She relieved Frieda Loos of her duties for the evening. Erika couldn't abide the governess. Horst had added her to the staff after Leo's birth, ostensibly to make Erika's life easier with the baby. Her work record gave her age as eighteen, a girl from the country serving her obligatory household year in domestic service. But Erika knew immediately this woman was in her twenties, and much more than just domestic help. And when the year was up, Frieda had remained a fixture in the household. Erika acknowledged Frieda's attractiveness to men in a buxom, peasant way, with full breasts, narrow waist and broad hips, and self-assured in her own sexuality. None of this bothered Erika, but Frieda was anywhere and everywhere in the house. Erika often came upon her in rooms where the nanny had no business. She was certain that the young woman was there to spy on her, and she felt robbed of any privacy, a prisoner in her own home. Horst insisted on complete control, and that included his marriage and household.

Erika also assumed that her husband demanded more personal services from the nanny, having heard Frieda leave his room at the oddest hours. But she neither expected nor desired fidelity from him. When drunk he boasted of sexual conquests in repulsive detail, and she was grateful not to share a bedroom as in the first months of their marriage. From time to time he still visited her at night and took pleasure in her degradation. Despite the pain she was thankful that his demands didn't risk another pregnancy. And now that she understood the depth of his depravity, his callous disregard for the lives of others, she was even more relieved that no additional child had been born into their household.

This night, as on most evenings, she knew he would call for her to give him his morphine injection. He was fully capable of doing it himself, but enjoyed the revulsion she couldn't hide when forced to serve him in this way. "Remember, my dear, you studied medicine," he would taunt, "so prove your worth around here."

How her marriage had changed over the years.

Once her "American boy" was gone from her life, she had felt an unexpected emptiness. Handsome, debonair Horst filled that loss with a promise of permanence and position. His imminent rise in the new Germany was a given, and he offered her a life she would never have found in Marburg. He changed in so many ways after the prolonged recovery from the deep cut to his face. She sat with him often during those weeks, despite finding pleasure elsewhere with Ryan.

Horst's dueling scar didn't bother her any more than his lesser ones, but he had lost both smile and laughter in his convalescence. Instead, he met the world with a self-assured stoicism which many found intimidating. This new demeanor did not distract from his fine Aryan features and icy blue eyes, and she knew women envied her because of him. If they only knew the price she paid for such this dashing husband.

Horst had proposed marriage just weeks after Ryan's return to America. Her acceptance would put a premature end to her studies, and they would move to Berlin, the new capital of Europe. He treated her more gently than before, introduced her to his powerful local allies in the Party, and she fell under the spell of his power. When she discovered her pregnancy, she readily agreed to share his life. Her parents seemed less than pleased with her choice, but gave their consent when faced with her expectant condition.

Her first experience with his *tic douloureux* left her stunned. He had inadvertently struck his cheek against the open door of a cabinet and dropped to his knees in agony. His head wrenched violently to the side in spasms, and tears streamed down his cheeks as he fought the urge to touch the afflicted area. The low howl from deep in his throat was agonizing to hear. The suffering lasted minutes, and there was nothing she could do for him. He shoved her away when she reached out to help. Afterwards he showed her the morphine and needles, and had her inject him.

The second surprise was also not long in coming. Following the wedding ceremony they left for a brief honeymoon in Bavaria. They were expected in Berlin within the week. Although they lodged in Garmisch-Partenkirchen, Horst spent most of each day away in Munich with Party associates. She spent hours alone on the hotel terrace admiring the Alpine views and reading.

Returning late on the final evening, Horst was drunk and his callousness inflamed, as always when he drank too much. He threw her on the bed, forcing himself into her as she buried her head and tears in the pillows. She was fearful for the child growing within her, and realized she had married a man she didn't know.

The pregnancy brought an end to his attentions, a relief. When the doctor and midwife arrived at the beautiful Berlin home near the Wannsee the night of Leo's birth, Horst was nowhere to be seen. He came home early the next morning, but waited a full day before coming to her room. Giving Erika barely a glance, he briefly examined the infant and declared his son a fine specimen. Obviously, other than as evidence of his adherence to the Nazi demand to create perfect Aryan offspring, children held little interest for him.

She understood nothing of his actual work in the secret police. Everyone knew and feared the Gestapo, but she had always assumed his contributions were necessary to protect the people and the Reich. And their life had certainly improved in the years since the Party had taken control under their Führer. Now, having read the protocol, she realized the enormity of the Gestapo's role. Shaken by that discovery, she felt a foreboding of what was to come. And it was coming to her personally. Her parents had tried to warn her away from the marriage. She should have listened.

She gave a gentle knock on Horst's bedroom door. Receiving no answer, she entered quietly and found him lying across the bed in an inebriated stupor. He was still in uniform but for the visor cap on the chair and tall boots at the foot of the bed. Oskar had done his best to make his master comfortable. She took the hypodermic kit from the dresser drawer and injected him with the morphine. Horst twitched slightly but didn't awaken.

It was nearing midnight when she had placed the call to her parents in Marburg. The operator made the connection quickly, and Erika heard in her mother's voice concern at the late hour of the call.

"Is everything all right with you? With Leo?"

Years before, on the eve of her marriage, Erika was invited to her parents' bedroom. Behind closed doors Minna had spoken quietly of the dangers inherent in the big city, made even more ominous by the political situation and Horst's work with the police. *Should you ever be in trouble and need my help—we mustn't trust the phones, you know—we need a special word.* A trigger word settled upon, a term of endearment used for a shrunken old woman, something Minna had always promised she would never allow herself to become. Now Erika trembled as she pulled that trigger:

"*Mütterchen*, are you and Father doing all right? I had a bad dream about you."

An anxious silence. "Your *Mütterchen* could be better. Can you get away to visit us?" Her mother's voice broke.

"Yes, Mother, but..."

"Then come, Erika, come home to us immediately."

"I'll be there by morning." Erika resigned herself to a few more hours' wait. She told Frieda to prepare the child for an emergency trip, phoned Oskar, and wrote a note for Horst: *Mother ill. Leaving for Marburg. Back in a few days.*

She quickly packed a small suitcase with Leo's and her own needs. Frieda offered to accompany them to look after the boy, but Erika declined, saying that her father would be there to help. The last thing she wanted right now was a spy in her family circle. She left the note on the foyer credenza.

Oskar was waiting with the car when they stepped out the front door. They drove quickly to Potsdamer Station, the nighttime street free of traffic. It was now well past the one a.m. curfew. The terminal was a mausoleum, her clacking heels echoing eerily in the near-empty hall as Leo shuffled along beside her. The chauffeur had stealthily followed them through the entry, and she spotted him, half-hidden by a column, as they crossed the concourse. Tickets acquired, mother and child boarded the next train to Marburg.

As Leo slept most of the long hours of the trip, Erika ran scenarios through her mind. Whatever Klaus knew, it had to be political, and very damning. Communists in the family? Someone who fought against the Nazi take-over? A family member with dangerous information about someone in power? An active seditionist?

It clearly had nothing to do with ancestry. After all, the pure bloodlines of her forebears were fully documented and certified for four generations back, as required by law for her father to keep his position at the university.

But she was wrong. Erika von Kredow, born Breitling, was a Jew.

# CHAPTER THIRTEEN

M inna's eyes shifted constantly from her husband to Erika sitting beside her on the sofa. Holding her daughter's hand, she tried to read the reaction to her husband's narrative. They had hoped never to share this burden, held secret for years, and now it had come home to haunt them and the small family they loved. In fact, it could destroy them.

Joachim hunched forward in his well-worn armchair. Stacks of patient files and medical texts lay forgotten to either side on the rug. His elbows rested on his knees, his hands hanging loosely between them, shoulders sagging under the burden of the story they had learned from the pastor, their father.

In 1881 Tsar Alexander II had been assassinated in Russia. The bomb thrown by a member of the radical People's Will movement shredded the Tsar's lower body. In the violent aftermath, reforms that might have led to a constitutional monarchy were shelved, and fear and repression took hold. His successor, Alexander III, cast blame for his father's death on the Jews, and Imperial Russia erupted in violent pogroms. Jewish men, women and children suffered assault, death, forced poverty and destruction of their homes and livelihood for three miserable years.

Amidst this pain and suffering, a young woman emigrated from the Imperial region of Lithuania. She had lost all her family to the violence. It was rumored in the terrified Lithuanian villages of the Pale of Settlement that Jews were well respected in Prussia and not persecuted, so she headed west.

Nadia Arens was sixteen years old. She was slender and fit, her hair golden blond. In a cloth bag slung over her shoulder she carried the few personal belongings rescued from the burned ruin of her family home. She lived on stolen fruit and vegetables and water from wells and creeks. From time to time strangers took pity on her as she moved from village to village, and she received something more nourishing to eat or drink. Nadia walked kilometer after kilometer, avoiding main roads and Tsarist patrols. She often slept away the daylight hours in barns or hayricks, then returned to her trek as the sun went down.

At the edge of the east Prussian village of Praddau she stumbled upon a parish church. She was hungry for the affection she had known in her family before the terror of the pogroms. She was starving for food. A young Lutheran minister, fresh from the seminary in Königsberg, found her unconscious on the steps of the church in the first winter days of 1884. Awakened to their Christian duty to care for the less fortunate, Pastor Johann Kessinger and his wife Lotte took in the young woman. Nadia spoke almost no German, but Yiddish carried her through, and they made her comfortable and fed her from the church pantry, until she regained her strength.

The Kessinger marriage was barren, so they had adopted an orphaned toddler from the village. His Christian name was Joachim, his surname Breitling. The small boy took an instant liking to the young Lithuanian woman with the gentle voice and tender touch, and the Kessingers decided that she should stay on as his nanny. She would earn her keep with child care and cleaning of the parish house and church.

For six years Nadia thrived in this loving household. She learned to speak and write fluent German. She shared meals with the pastor's family. She sometimes cried herself to sleep with the sorrow of her loss, but treasured the new family she had discovered in Prussia. In her first year she converted to the evangelical faith. Her former beauty blossomed once again. And in her sixth year in Praddau temptation overcame piety for Pastor Kessinger, and he came to her bed in the night.

The child of that union was an underweight baby girl. Nadia refused to divulge which of the village men was responsible, and no one stepped forward to claim the child as his own. She was baptized with the Old German name Minna. After much private counseling from the minister, Nadia agreed that the pastor and his wife would adopt the infant as their own. Johann Kessinger emphasized that the baby would thereby never face even the possibility of persecution for being half-Jewish. Nadia had seen the wisdom in the decision. The baby girl grew healthy, nourished at her birth mother's breast. She loved her nursemaid, and as a child never learned the truth. The clergyman entered Minna's name in the church registry as the daughter of Pastor Johann and Lotte Kessinger.

Barely a year after the birth, Nadia began to experience muscle weakness. She fell repeatedly and had difficulty coming down the stairs from her attic room in the parish house to look after the baby. She found swallowing increasingly difficult and lost weight she could not afford to lose from her slender frame. The doctor came and could give no explanation for the sudden decline in the young woman's health. Mucous filled her throat and lungs, and breathing became a painful trial. Nadia was buried at twenty-four after a month of suffering.

The boy Joachim grew into a tall, fine-looking young man with a sharp mind. He adored his younger "sister," and she him. At eighteen he moved to Königsberg, leaving behind his parents and ten-year-old Minna. Pastor Kessinger had only one close relative, his brother Albert. The brother had done well with his tannery and remained a bachelor. Albert offered to pay for Joachim's study of medicine at the university, and the young man declared his determination to find the cause of the illness which took the family nursemaid. His studies so impressed his professors that they invited him to lecture at the university and upon graduation join the faculty of internal medicine. He occasionally returned to Praddau to see his family, and watched Minna mature into a beautiful young woman.

In 1906 fever took the life of Frau Pastor Lotte Kessinger at only thirty-seven years of age.

When Uncle Albert also offered to pay for Minna's education, she gladly moved from the village to the big city. Sharing a love of medicine with her "brother" and thrown together in the rambling house of their uncle, it was only a matter of time before Joachim and Minna—siblings in name only—fell in love.

They went hand-in-hand to the pastor and declared their devotion to each other and desire to marry. The minister buried his head in his hands and prayed to God for forgiveness. He then said that, despite his misgivings, he would not stand in the way of their marriage, but suggested a city marriage to avoid any hint of impropriety in the gossip-ridden parish. Joachim and Minna thanked their father for his blessing, returned to Königsberg, and were married in a civil ceremony. Uncle Albert and a friend stood as witnesses, and the Prussian state blessed the union. In the first year of their marriage a baby girl was born. Johann came to Königsberg to christen his grandchild Erika.

The couple lived and researched and taught at the university, but then came the Great War. Joachim served as a field doctor at the western front, tending the wounded and witnessing the tragedy of mangled bodies and soldiers blinded by mustard-gas. The Treaty of Versailles created a Polish Corridor to the Baltic Sea separating East Prussia from the Weimar Republic, and the young parents found the growing threat of Bolshevism from the east too unsettling. Joachim applied for a faculty position in the Hessian university town of Marburg. He readily won acceptance based on recommendations from his peers in Königsberg and his impressive clinical work.

The years passed and Pastor Kessinger preached the Gospel, counseled his flock, and enjoyed the occasional letters and phone calls from his distant family. Travel between Prussia and its eastern arm was restricted to sealed trains across Polish territory and ship ferries along the Baltic coast, so family visits were difficult to arrange.

Then in 1935 the Nuremberg Laws "for the protection of German blood and German honor" changed everything. All who wished to acquire or maintain civil service or teaching positions in Germany were required to prove their pure Aryan heritage for at least four generations, untainted by Jewish blood. An *Ahnenpass*, a certified documentation of ancestry, would provide that proof. Anticipating no problems, Joachim sent a letter to his adoptive father requesting completion of the form, since the pastor was official keeper of the Praddau parish records.

The request stunned Johann Kessinger. There was no problem with Joachim's bloodline. His natural parents—the mother dying in giving him life, the father killed shortly thereafter in an agricultural accident—were of pure German blood, fourth-generation Praddauer stock. The church records confirmed this.

But the harsh new laws also made Gentile marriage to a Jew a crime, *Rassenverrat*, betrayal of race. Pastor Kessinger feared for the safety of his beloved children. He painstakingly altered the date of Minna's birth in his parish records, giving his daughter a pure Aryan heritage, as well. Then he went to the town hall to view the civil records. They showed that a Jewish woman, Nadia Arens, residing at his address in the same year, had borne a girl child of unknown paternity. There was nothing he could do to change that document. He could only hope no one would ever compare the entries. With trembling hand Pastor Kessinger signed the *Ahnenpass* and attested to the pure bloodline of Joachim Breitling and his family.

At seventy-five, exhausted from bearing his secret for almost fifty years, the minister then boarded a train and made the strenuous trip from Königsberg to Marburg to deliver the truth in person. Minna finally learned that her birth mother was the beloved nursemaid Nadia, and that Johann was her natural father. She also learned that her mother had been a Jew. With that revelation Minna became a first-degree half-breed by National Socialist standards, and her daughter Erika, "tainted" by birth as a second-degree *Mischling*, was now married to a fervent anti-Semitic Nazi and ambitious Gestapo officer. Fear for her family clenched Minna's gut, and she and Joachim had vowed to hold the secret forever.

Erika sat in the room of her Marburg childhood and took the devastating knowledge to heart. She had told her parents of the SS plan for conquest and extermination. Now she tried to reconstruct in her mind the complex structure of the 1935 racial laws, which had never before had serious meaning for her. One thing was certain: she, her mother and the peacefully-sleeping child whose head rested on her lap were officially tainted by the blood of an "inferior race." She thought marriage between a full-blooded German and a second-degree half-breed was officially allowed under the laws, with any offspring considered *deutschblütig*, but she had heard her husband's anti-Semitic rants, knew his venom. All laws be damned, Horst would still categorize her and Leo as sub-human, worthy only of death.

She had rarely seen Jews in Marburg. The tailor Edelstein, for one, a master of the needle and sewing machine who could make any piece of clothing fit, according to Minna. Erika recalled a gentle man with scraggly beard and bushy eyebrows. He always had a kind word and a piece of hard candy for the child when she and her mother visited his basement shop with items for mending or alteration. She also remembered seeing in the *Altstadt* a bearded man in black hat with twists of hair dangling at his ears. But in Berlin she had seen Jews on the streets, and asked herself why they didn't dress and act like real Germans.

All Erika really knew about Jews was learned from Nazi propaganda. The constant barrage over the past five years had instilled the message that Jews were responsible for the collapse of the German Empire and the loss of the Great War. They were Marxists and Capitalists all in one—a political conceit which Erika found difficult to grasp, even given her limited understanding of Karl Marx's tenets of class struggle. The Jews undermined all Christian and German tradition and virtue. German women and children were not safe in their company. Germans no longer shopped in their businesses; and the venal Jews were forbidden to buy in German shops. The Jews were being forced out of the Reich in any way possible for the good of the *Volk*. Yet this anti-Semitism had not resonated because she had nothing to which it truly related in her life. Until now.

*Rassenverrat, Rassenschande, Blutschande*—there were many terms in the Nazi lexicon for criminal defilement of blood and race, the betrayal of Aryan purity through sexual relations with a Jew. To her father Joachim, professor and physician, it was one more proof of the collapse of German idealism into the cesspool of racial and religious intolerance and cruelty.

Though her marriage was not technically forbidden, Horst would feel betrayed by this devastating blow to his "purity" and all legal technicalities would mean nothing. Should word of his "shame" reach the upper echelons of power, blackmail and coercion would follow, and his career—his very reason for being—would be over. And now here was Klaus Pabst, the sycophant who desired her and also despised her for standing between him and his idol Horst. Pabst had uncovered the secret and would use it.

Without a plan, they were already dead.

# HEIMKEHR
## Homecoming

November 1938

# CHAPTER ONE

R yan set his tray on one of the tall tables in the station canteen. Standard traveler's fare: grilled bratwurst, bread roll, potato salad, a small beer. Other patrons stood nearby with luggage at their feet as they grabbed a quick meal between trains. Most ate in silence. One thumbed through a magazine. Another stared vacantly toward the platforms, holding the crisp-skinned sausage in hand, stirring it in the mild mustard.

Ryan observed the man more closely. His skin was sallow, a thick stubble showed gray. The Iron Cross at his throat hung in stark contrast to a stained collar and frayed overcoat. The veteran ate slowly, his toothless mouth giving him difficulties. Bit by bit he slid the sausage into his mouth, gumming intensely at the fatty meat.

Just above the bridge of his nose sat a triangular depression at least a thumb's thickness in depth, each of the three indented sides perfectly symmetrical, as if an object had struck his forehead with great force. Perhaps he had been thrown into some unyielding, canted object. The skin of the indentation appeared remarkably smooth and unscarred. Ryan looked away. He thought of his own good fortune. With a last sip of the beer he decided to be on his way.

While still in Paris he had mailed Major von Haldheim, telling of his anticipated return to Berlin the first week of November. Two weeks later a letter arrived in general delivery at the rue du Louvre post office. The obvious enthusiasm of his friend was gratifying. The Old Major welcomed his "American son" back to Germany and invited him to call the moment he reached the city. His old room in the villa would be waiting, "just as in the good old days." Ryan looked forward to seeing his Berlin family once again, his mind filled with fond memories.

The public phone in front of the canteen offered nothing but a busy signal. He waited a few minutes before a newsstand, reading the headlines. All the German papers appeared written by the same hand. By the end of September war had seemed a certainty, and the foreign press drummed a steady warning as Hitler demanded Czechoslovakia's surrender of the Sudetenland with its three million ethnic Germans. Ryan had met pessimism everywhere he traveled, fear and gloom were palpable, and it was obvious the German people themselves had no enthusiasm for another armed conflict. No crowds came out to cheer the long troop convoys on their way south and east. Then England had appeased Hitler, and France had once again caved rather than live up to its treaty commitments, and the Sudetenland fell under German rule. Hitler had further expanded his Reich without unleashing a new European war. *The rest of poor Czechoslovakia doesn't have a prayer,* Ryan thought, *just wait.*

Once again the busy tone. He rang the operator to make a third attempt and learned someone was using the line, which came as a surprise. He remembered well Frau von Haldheim's constant admonition to the household that the telephone was for brief and important business only. Casual conversation belonged in the salon amongst friends, best enjoyed over coffee and cake.

Ryan gave the taxi driver the Grunewald address. The cabbie seemed pleased with the prospect of a drive into one of the city's wealthier suburbs and the attendant higher fare. On the way they exchanged small talk about the weather, and the driver chatted about his children. He pointed proudly to a small photo attached to his visor. Two young boys in Hitler Youth uniform stood to attention. He asked if Ryan had children of his own.

"No, not yet married. I'm American, a correspondent." Ryan noticed the arching eyebrows in the rearview mirror. "Tell me, have things settled down a bit here after the crisis in September? Are Berliners worried about war?"

The warmth had disappeared, replaced by unvarnished cynicism. "Life's good. We celebrate each of our Führer's bloodless victories, and Germany has no further territorial ambitions in Europe. What's not to enjoy?"

Political candor, even within the confines of a cab, obviously made the driver wary, and Ryan remembered René's warning. He let the matter drop.

The fall day was rich in color, a brilliant blue sky streaked by a few white clouds, the woodlands and gardens still in autumn gold. An occasional breeze scattered leaves across the manicured lawns. Within the walled estates teams of gardeners swept the errant foliage from the walkways as quickly as it fell. Ryan had run into austerity drives across the Reich, encouraging Germans to cut back for the benefit of the state. The rattling tin cans of the *Winterhilfe* summoned citizens to donate to the poor for the coming cold months. René had explained that overseas trade embargoes on German goods were affecting the massive military buildup of Göring's Four-Year-Plan. As a one-time student of economics, Ryan knew that without foreign currency the economy had to be on the ropes. Yet, here in this wealthy enclave, prosperity showed no signs of abating.

Not far from Brahmstrasse he had the driver wait outside a flower shop. Bent, arthritic Beckemann still remembered the young American from his occasional visits in the early thirties. After the exchange of pleasantries and a discussion of the shopkeeper's ailments in excessive detail, Ryan left with a bouquet of long-stemmed yellow roses, Frau von Haldheim's favorite.

The taxi entered an elegant row of villas and the von Haldheim home came into view. A stone wall topped with ornate wrought-iron separated the mansion from the street. From a distance he spotted a dark sedan parked at the gated entry. Black uniforms stood to either side of the gate with guns shouldered.

"Trouble." The driver slowed his vehicle to a crawl and pulled to the curb.

"Wait for me here," Ryan said. "I'll go check it out."

"Thanks, but I'd best be going." The driver's eyes never left the SS guards. "Those fellows are seldom in the friendliest of moods."

Ryan reached for his wallet. "Café Braunitsch, it's easy to find. On the left, two streets back. Keep the meter running and I'll make it worth your while." Ryan added a generous tip and stepped out.

"Good luck." The cabbie touched the brim of his cap. "You may need it." The taxi carved a wide turn and headed back.

Pedestrians in this neighborhood of grand mansions were rare: an occasional resident out for fresh air, a mother with baby carriage, a servant walking the dog or running an errand. Ryan intended to stroll past his old residence, but realized that a valise in one hand and roses in the other suggested something more than a casual walk. With some distance between villas he was bound to be noticed, and he didn't want the armed SS to suspect his interest in the von Haldheim home. *Always remain as inconspicuous as possible to the authorities,* his trainers had admonished. But Ryan saw no choice now but to find out what was going on with his Berlin family.

To the rear of the grounds sat the brick cottage of the butler Erich and his wife Luisa, head of the kitchen and housekeeping staff. A tall manicured hedge shielded the house from the villa gardens. Ryan recalled the service gate from the night he snuck out for his final adventure with Isabel. Approaching the corner of the grounds, he turned and headed up toward the alley which ran along the back perimeter. He stopped to stash both bag and flowers in the hedge paralleling the wall. A flock of starlings rose with a startled chorus of cries. *So much for keeping a low profile,* he thought.

Reaching the gate, Ryan peered cautiously beyond the iron bars and saw no guard at this approach to the mansion. He gave the button a single brief push and a muffled bell responded within the cottage only a few paces away. Movement at the window caught his eye, as Luisa drew back the edge of the curtain. He knew she had recognized him. The curtain fell back into place.

Erich emerged. Grabbing the handle of a garbage bin he dragged it slowly down the walk to the gate. Before Lemmon could greet him, the butler slowly shook his head twice, his eyes then cutting toward the main house in warning. Ryan stepped back into the shadow of the portal. The butler opened the locked gate and pulled the refuse container into the alleyway. He didn't acknowledge Ryan, but spoke in a whisper, as if muttering to himself. "Something terrible has happened." His throat caught. "You must leave, Herr Lemmon, now, for your sake as well as ours."

"What's going on? The von Haldheims—are they home?" He wouldn't leave without an explanation.

"We mustn't talk out here. Give me a moment to reassure Luisa." The old man made his way back to the cottage.

Ryan found the gate now unlatched and the house door also stood ajar. He let a minute pass before deciding enough was enough. Only the roofline of the main house extended above the dense foliage or the gardens, and no one appeared to be watching from that direction. Nothing moved amidst the cultivated plantings. Ryan approached the cottage, then hesitated a moment and listened. Only the splashing of the moss-covered fountain could be heard.

He let himself in with a gentle knock and surveyed the room at a glance. The house was impeccably clean despite porcelain figurines cluttering every free surface. Brightly-colored banners and embossed pewter plates celebrated tourist destinations from across Germany. Ryan couldn't recall that Erich and Luisa had ever traveled, had ever been anywhere but attentively at the beck and call of the von Haldheims. The walls displayed framed portraits of children and grandchildren, parents and grandparents. He had never seen any offspring. *Service staff truly does live in a world apart.* The cottage predated the villa by many decades. Rugs covered the rough-hewn plank flooring, notably worn by years of use. A pastoral North German landscape hung above the beamed mantelpiece. A burgundy velvet sofa faced the hearth and overstuffed armchairs flanked the window, lace doilies protecting wood and cloth. The all-pervasive smell of wood ash came from the fireplace, where untended embers still glowed. Erich and Luisa stood in the center of the room, his arm about her shoulder. She dabbed at her eyes.

"I apologize for the interruption, but what's going on here?"

"They took them this morning, Herr Lemmon." Erich pulled his wife closer and kissed her forehead. "They arrested them both, the Major and Frau von Haldheim." He lowered his arm and took Luisa's hands in his. The old man's jaw was trembling.

"Who took them?"

"One high-ranking SS officer, three troopers, two Gestapo. The rest of the staff was sent home or confined to their rooms. We're to stay here until summoned."

"What charges?"

"Sedition, fomenting rebellion against the Reich, at least that's what they said." Erich smiled thinly. "You know the Major; never one to keep his opinions to himself."

"Had he become more open about it?"

"Unfortunately, yes, with all the war talk in September. No one thought the French would turn their backs on Czechoslovakia, that England would go soft. Some of our generals were here at the villa, meeting in the salon. They were discreet, but I heard talk of overtures to the British, of taking back our government from the Nazis. The Old Major wouldn't leave it alone."

Luisa spoke up, her eyes brimming with tears: "But the *Gnädige Frau?* What's she ever done to deserve all this?" Erich tucked a loose strand of hair behind his wife's ear, but the question went unanswered.

"Any idea where they've gone?"

"They told us nothing, but with the Gestapo, we all know." His eyes did not leave his wife's. "Prinz Albrechtstrasse, and then Sachsenhausen." Luisa broke down in sobs and lowered herself to the couch. Erich pulled a handkerchief from his vest and dried his own eyes.

Ryan felt infuriated by his own impotence. "There must be something we can do. Perhaps they'll release them after questioning? The Old Major has powerful friends."

"The SS commander allowed them each one small bag." He cleared his throat and blew his nose. "It was a sham, they won't be back. I helped him gather a few things, but there was little time."

"What about Rolf, their son? He's been in the Party for years now, right? Can't he help?"

"Too late, I'm afraid. The young von Haldheim was here only a week before last. The first time in ages—you do know they were estranged for years over politics?" Ryan nodded. "He showed up with a car at the gate and demanded to speak to his father."

"Why'd he come back?"

"I wish I knew, but I withdrew, of course. They talked for some time privately in the library. He did caution his parents to be discreet; his final words at the door were 'be careful.' They were all in tears. Over the reconciliation, I suppose."

"And then?" Ryan noticed Luisa repeatedly glancing toward the door and window. He had no wish to endanger them further. He should hurry.

"The Major did tell me that his son was once again welcome in his home. Frau von Haldheim was visibly shaken and retired to her room for the day."

"And that's it?"

"No, Herr Rolf was back again yesterday, very distraught. This time they didn't call for Frau von Haldheim. Voices were raised; they argued. I know only that they embraced when he left. I'm now convinced he was warning them about all this." The older man gestured in the direction of the villa.

"Any ideas on how I might contact Rolf?"

"I'm sorry, no—there'd been no word from him for ages, and he didn't leave a card, at least with me." In afterthought, he turned toward the sofa. "The Herr Major did leave this for you." Erich removed an ivory-colored envelope from a photo album on the end table. "He had told me of your coming visit; he was so very excited to see you. Despite all that was happening this morning, he slipped this to me as he gathered his things and told me to get it to you if possible."

The butler handed the envelope to Ryan. Recognizing the distinctive pen of the Old Major, Ryan slid it into his jacket pocket unopened, more pressing matters at hand. The SS could call for the couple at any moment.

"And what's to become of the two of you?"

"Who knows, perhaps we're to be arrested, as well. Or they could keep us in service here. It seems there will soon be new residents in the manor. The officer in charge was quite taken by the formal salon. I overheard him say the Reichsminister will find all this even better than he'd hoped."

"The mansion?"

Erich joined his wife on the couch and laid his arm around her shoulders once again. "Were it my guess, this has nothing to do with sedition or criticizing the Reich, it's all about real estate. Some big-wig from Wilhelmstrasse wants the villa as his own."

Ryan shook their hands and wished them well. He knew nothing more to say or do, so he left in deep gloom, frustrated by his own helplessness. The gate clicked closed behind him, and he recovered his valise from the hedge down the alley. No birds rose this time in protest.

He returned briefly to the cottage gate to leave the yellow roses, perched between its bars.

# CHAPTER TWO

No taxi waited at the Café Braunitsch, which didn't surprise Ryan. Greeting the familiar waiter, still on the job after years since his last visit, he hung his overcoat on the rack at the door and found a table toward the rear of the elegant room. He needed a break to collect his thoughts.

The words of the butler ran through his mind again and again as he tried to formulate some plan to help his adopted German family. The arrests came from very high in the government. Nothing seemed doable; at least, nothing without risking his cover and compromising his assignment. An inquiry with the Gestapo would draw dangerous attention. Nazi officialdom, especially the police, would not take kindly to an investigation by a foreign reporter. He still had to register with the authorities and had no local press pass, and it would not do to be thrown out of the country on his first day in the city.

Ryan had counted on the aid of his monarchist family to reach sympathetic contacts in Berlin and beyond, hoping to find dissident groups similar to René's operation here in the heart of the Nazi capital. In Washington Ryan had been briefed on discontent with Hitler's leadership at the highest levels of the Wehrmacht, but there had been no guidance on whom he might contact. Without introductions, it would be difficult to tap into that resource and earn their trust. Now he needed a new plan.

The waiter set coffee before him in a white ceramic pot, a plate of small cookies to the side. Ryan reached into his jacket pocket for his pipe, which always relaxed him and helped organize his thoughts. His fingers brushed the envelope from the major, forgotten in his shock at learning of the arrest. He slit open the cover to reveal a short note from the major alongside a smaller, sealed envelope, addressed in care of von Haldheim at the Brahmstrasse address. No return name or address; Berlin postmark three days prior. He set the small envelope aside.

The major's loose note was written on linen stationery embossed with the family crest:

> *My dearest Ryan,*
>
> *I had hoped to deliver my welcome to you in person, but there is now   only one certainty in the Reich—we can predict nothing. How very much things have changed here since you were first our guest.*
>
> *If you are now reading these lines, know that I am reconciled with my fate, whatever it proves to be. So I write to wish you my best should we not meet again.*
>
> *The enclosed arrived for you two days ago. The hand is obviously feminine, so I pass it along gladly, trusting that it will lead to something warm, welcoming and pleasurable for you.*
>
> *As always,*
> *Your Old Major*

Ryan allowed the sadness to wash over him. He set down his unlit pipe and opened the smaller envelope. Erika's second letter in four years was as brief as it was enigmatic:

> *My dear Ryan,*
>
> *I hear you return once again to Berlin and send you my fondest greetings.*
>
> *How well I remember our last time together the eve of your departure from Marburg: the view of the city from high atop the tower, the cathedral bells marking the hour, even my very last words to you.*
>
> *With enduring affection,*
> *E.*

His mind raced. Somehow Erika knew he was back in Berlin, wanted to reestablish contact. But how to find her? He sought veiled meaning in her concise lines. Erika hadn't penned this note merely to reminisce, and he vividly recalled that final evening, so full of promise, their passion and parting, and finally the dangerous and frantic escape along the river and up the tunnels. He scanned the enigmatic lines word by word, setting that last Marburg evening in a Berlin context.

Gradually answers clicked into place: *The view of the city from high atop the tower.* Replace the Kaiser-Wilhelm-Tower in Marburg with the Kaiser-Wilhelm-Memorial Church in Berlin Charlottenburg, both memorials to the same Kaiser, and the massive bell tower would offer a fine view over the city.

*Cathedral bells marking the hour.* What time had they rung from the fog-bound valley that night four years past? He pictured Erika in his arms, enveloped in his top coat, and mentally backtracked from the final farewell at her family apartment, just before midnight. It had to have been about nine.

*My very last words to you.* They were as clear in his mind as the very night she uttered them before slipping into the apartment, her eyes filled with tears: "I will see you again."

But what day could she mean? When should they meet? *The eve of your departure.* He remembered leaving Marburg on a Wednesday for a Thursday morning embarkation in Bremerhaven.

"My God!" he muttered aloud, drawing back abruptly in the chair. "Today's Tuesday! She means tonight!" He glanced around quickly, surprised at the sound of his own voice. None of the other patrons had noticed his outburst. He checked the postmark again. She had sent this four days prior. She wants to meet tonight at the church!

Ryan tossed coins on the table, grabbed his bag and ran for the Grunewald S-Bahn station a few blocks distant. It was mid-afternoon. He could be in Berlin-Charlottenburg within the hour. Nothing would prevent his meeting her when the church bells struck nine.

# CHAPTER THREE

Charlottenburg lay at the city's heart, where money gathered to celebrate Berlin's commercial vitality. At the convergence of four heavily-trafficked boulevards vehicles of every description rumbled and rattled past around the clock. Trams with clanging bells swerved in and around Breitscheidplatz, and lanes of taxis, cars and double-decker buses merged only to separate once again. Crowds of pedestrians gathered to shop, dine out, and enjoy the latest releases at the *Gloria-Palast Cinema* and the *UFA-Palast am Zoo.*

In the center of the lively square and surrounded by the serpentine traffic, the massive Kaiser-Wilhelm Memorial Church could not be ignored. This Protestant cathedral dwarfed its neighboring neo-Romanesque buildings, all raised in celebration of the pre-war German empire. Its four secondary towers stood as faithful minions to the huge central spire. Large rose windows faced the main boulevards, and an entry portal with three impressive gables welcomed the devout as well as the tourist.

Ryan arrived at the Zoo rail station shortly after four and immediately headed to the church to check out the floor plan. He anticipated meeting her high in the central tower, but found that access to the viewing platform closed at seven each evening. He decided to return later to keep watch from the pews closest to the tower entry. For now, nothing could be done for the poor von Haldheims. Perhaps reuniting with his former lover would be a different story, an opportunity for action. He reminded himself of her long marriage to a dangerous man, but could not quiet his remembrances of her passion in bed.

An inquiry at a local bar found him a relatively affordable hotel on Marburgerstrasse a few blocks from the square. The street name seemed fitting for a reunion with his last university flame. He paid for a small attic room, the fifty-penny surcharge for heat seemingly money well spent.

The narrow bed was crammed beneath a steeply-sloped ceiling, a small window opened to the street, and a sink supplied running water. He tested the tap. *Reasonably warm.* The bath and toilet were down a flight of steps on the next floor. Ryan found the lodgings satisfactory at the price in this expensive district of the city. Now, without the anticipated accommodations at the von Haldheim home and no other personal connections in Berlin, Ryan had no idea how long he would remain. Everything depended on Erika.

The narrow street below his window was still congested with pedestrians and vendor carts. A horse-drawn delivery wagon clopped by, followed by an occasional slow-moving truck or automobile. He left the window open to air out the musty, overheated room, whose radiator handle revolved endlessly to no effect. The heating surcharge had been wasted; he had no choice in this space but to sweat. He washed his face and underarms, combed his hair, and changed to a clean shirt. He spread his shaving gear on the glass shelf above the washbasin, and his spare clothing went into the creaking wardrobe. A quick survey of the room, and he decided he was home for the foreseeable future.

Ryan felt the nervous energy of a first date, wondering what Erika would look like after four years and whether the old attraction would still be there despite her marriage. The hours crept by.

He left his room for a café on the Kurfürstendamm, where foot and vehicle traffic passed noisily by as he read a newspaper and drank a *Pilsner.* The Berlin press screamed lurid tales of anti-German atrocities in Czechoslovakia. He picked up an abandoned Times of London but found its take on the Prague crisis equally favorable to the Reich, if not as lurid. It seemed no one elsewhere in Europe really gave a damn about the inevitable assimilation of Czechoslovakia. His order of Königsberger meatballs, an old favorite, arrived with unwanted capers swimming in the thick gravy. A few bites of the onion-laden meal and he pushed the plate aside, signaled for a second beer, and smoked another pipe to calm his nerves.

At seven he settled the bill and stepped out into the colorful neon glow. At the main intersection of the boulevards he crossed heavy traffic under the direction of a policeman and entered the cathedral once again. Only a few visitors remained at this hour. The church was ornate for a Lutheran house of worship, and he made several rounds of the interior, regarding the stained glass windows backlit by the signage on the grand square outside. He scanned the large mosaic portraying Prussian history. Finally, having exhausted all possibilities for distraction, he took a seat two rows back from the tower access and waited. And waited.

He tweaked the front brim of his fedora. He ran a finger down the furrow in the crown and set the hat beside him on the bench. He wound his watch to assure it was functioning correctly. It was. From time to time the heavy front door opened and closed, and a new arrival's footsteps resounded in the vast space. Convinced of the clandestine nature of the rendezvous, he did not turn his head, despite the strong urge to see Erika arrive to meet him.

Someone took a seat directly behind him but said nothing, so he continued his impatient wait. Should he turn to look? He heard the whisper of a prayer book being drawn from the rack behind his pew. A few moments passed before the visitor rose abruptly and retreated toward the entry. When he could wait no longer, he turned his head and caught a glimpse of a slender woman in plaid overcoat and gray hat leaving the church. Seconds later, a tall man emerged from behind a column and followed her out. He checked his wrist. Eight thirty-eight. Ryan stood and turned, concerned that he had blown the assignation. Had he somehow missed her signal?

On the bench behind him rested an open hymnal, a visiting card inserted between its fanned pages. *Erika von Kredow.* He reversed the card. In the dim light of the cathedral her fine script was barely legible: *Tomorrow 10 a.m. Tiergarten at the canal lock, south end. Please take care! Being watched!* Ryan raised the ivory-colored card to his nose and sensed a lingering trace of perfume.

He glanced at the songbook in his hand. His eyes found the hymn she had marked: *Wenn wir in höchsten Nöten sein.* When we are in most dire need.

# CHAPTER FOUR

The Tiergarten, a vast parkland in the heart of Berlin normally alive with walkers and horseback riders, felt deserted on that frigid morning. Autumn gave way to winter before his eyes, the air cold and damp and leaden. The waters of the canal ran sluggish gray, the woodland foliage a blemish of bronze on a monochromatic landscape. He stood below an abutment at the lock bridge and watched her move along the canal path. He could not take his eyes from her, from the small boy holding her hand.

*Of course she would already have a child, perhaps children.* Until this moment she had been that sensuous young woman of his past. Now she was much more: a wife, a mother, and—apparently—a friend in serious trouble. As Erika and the child neared the bridge he searched in vain for any sign of the tall man from the previous evening.

Her face brightened when she caught sight of Ryan. Her cheeks rosy from the chill air, a cashmere scarf framing her face, she appeared as lovely as before, and Ryan felt the surge of old feelings. "Come, Leo, run with me," he heard her tell the little boy. The two moved hand-in-hand down the embankment, Erika keeping her steps short to match the child's. Her long coat parted to reveal those legs he remembered so well, and Ryan stepped up to greet her. She released the boy's hand and fell into his arms, where he held her tightly, emotions coursing through him.

"I've missed you," he said.

"You came for me—" amazement in her voice, "you got my message." Relief was there, but also something deeper, anxiety perhaps, her old self-assurance displaced by wariness. "Ryan, this is Leonhardt. He's three." The boy stood obediently to attention and made a little bow, then reached up for Ryan's outstretched palm. "Leo, here's my friend, Herr Doktor Lemmon."

Ryan shook the small hand and grinned broadly. "A pleasure to meet you, Leo."

The child smiled cautiously and nodded, but said nothing. She squatted down to put her arm around his narrow shoulders and squeezed him lovingly. "He's seldom shy with strangers." The boy received a radiant smile of reassurance from his mother that warmed Ryan, as well. He noted the child's deep blue eyes and slender frame. Tufts of blond hair showed beneath the woolen cap. The boy wore a plaid scarf and child's herringbone topcoat over short pants and calf-high stockings. The fine features of the face, perhaps, but no sign of the von Kredow arrogance.

"A beautiful boy, with his mother's looks."

"He sometimes shares her stubbornness, as well. But we must talk quickly, there's little time." Again he noted something, a caution deeper than mere anxiety; fear clouded her eyes. She took a small paper bag from her pocket and offered it to her son. "Here, Leo, go feed the ducks while I talk with my friend." She gestured toward the waterfowl huddled near the water, a mix of migrants resting on their way south and locals accustomed to braving the Berlin winter. Leo, who had eyed the flock from the moment of their arrival, thanked his mother enthusiastically and ran down to a welcoming cacophony of honking and quacking. "Not all at once," she called out to him with a mother's smile. The boy waved to acknowledge the rule.

She turned to Ryan and the smile faded as the words came spilling out. "Ryan, I'm in such terrible trouble, and I need your help. Hearing from Rolf von Haldheim that you were coming back to Berlin was a godsend. And that you actually understood my message, that you are here now, is such a relief." She dabbed her eyes with a handkerchief. "But now I must fear for you, as well."

He touched her cheek, familiar and yet distant. "Slow down, Erika, just tell me what's going on; we'll figure it out together." He led her to a nearby bench, brushing aside the damp leaves before they sat down.

The story came in rapid bursts: the loneliness and cruelty of her marriage, the threatening words of Klaus Pabst, and now the revelation of her bloodline. "You're sure of the Jewish blood?" He understood immediately the ramifications in the Third Reich.

"There's no denying it. My parents are terrified, and rightly so. Horst lives to destroy his 'enemies of the Reich.' I've been a good Nazi wife, accepted the abuse of the Jews. My God, Ryan, I've even played that board game with Leo, tossing the dice, moving the pieces around the board, collecting Jews to ship off to Palestine!" Her eyes sought out the boy surrounded by water fowl. "And now I am the target of my own prejudice." Leo waved, and she responded. "Ironic, isn't it?"

Ryan took her gloved hand in his and encouraged the rest of her story, all the while racing through the implications for them, for him. She revealed her suspicions about the governess, and how the driver spied on her every activity.

"Someone followed you out of the church last night. The chauffeur?"

"Oskar hardly lets me from his sight. My pretense to get out last night was a League of German Women meeting, and I made him stop at Breitscheidplatz. I had to know if you'd gotten my letter, understood it, if you'd be there..." Her voice trailed off and she squeezed his hand. "I was scared crazy you wouldn't be, and then there you were, and I was petrified you'd turn and speak to me. Thank God you didn't."

"In all honesty, I was afraid to turn around to see if it was you."

"This morning Oskar dropped us off at Tietz," she continued. "We switched elevator cars on the third floor, went back down to the second and took the stairs. Leo thought it a great adventure—he loves the department stores—and at the side entrance we caught a cab." Erika paused to catch a breath. "I think we lost Oskar at the first elevator, but he'll report it all to Horst. We'll have been gone for hours, but I had to see you, see if you can do anything to help us get away." She drew back Ryan's cuff to check his watch. "Horst will be fuming, and he's more dangerous than anyone imagines, so we have to hurry."

"We must get you and the boy out of here—out of Germany— as soon as possible." The danger was real, frightening.

"I've already made a plan for Leo and me, for my parents, too. I certainly can't leave them to face Horst. Word of this will destroy his career, and he won't allow it to get out. Under the laws we should still be safe, but the law means nothing to him, he's a monster; he'll kill us all, or have that foul Pabst do it." She checked on her son, her eyes brimming with tears. "He can, you know."

"I know his brutality. He went after me that last night we were together, he and his cronies. It was a close call. I'm sure I'd have suffered as René Gesslinger did, if not worse."

"Horst did that to René?" She hesitated a moment. "Of course he did, who else?"

"No one crosses Horst without payback."

"Did René recover? I know it was bad." She and Ryan had visited him briefly when René was in the clinic, still severely battered and unconscious.

"Far better than you'd expect. But time's short, so tell me your plan."

"I was set to move forward on my own, and then I heard you were back in the Reich, and I remembered how you stood up for Jewish friends in Marburg." A melancholic hint of the old Erika's grin came through. "I thought: now I'm a Jewish friend, too." She gestured to the little boy holding a cracker high above the birds' heads to make them work for the treat. "And he'll pay the price, too." The fear returned to her eyes. "I'll understand if there's nothing you can do."

"Don't worry, I'm here for you now, and we'll find a way out of this mess."

"There's more, Ryan, much more, it reaches far beyond my family." She shuddered and drew her coat more tightly around her. "Horst and his Gestapo plan something monstrous. You'll think me mad for even believing it all."

"You can't shock me when it comes to this bunch." He tried to keep his voice reassuring. "Tell me the rest?"

She stared down the slope to her little boy and the noisy flock. "They plan to conquer all of Europe, and methodically wipe out every Jew along the way." She dried her eyes with the handkerchief.

Ryan had been wrong; he was stunned. He had read *Der Stürmer* and *Der Angriff* from time to time, and had often heard Goebbels in person and on the radio. He knew the depraved anti-Semitism expressed in those Party rags, the unwavering vilification of the Jews. But to systematically kill them? This was new, horrifying in its ramifications.

"You're sure this isn't just Horst's braggadocio, some sick fantasy?"

"It's in writing, Ryan, and appalling, a plan to exterminate all of them..." now her eyes fixed on the boy below, "all of us. Special killing units to follow the SS troops. Believe me, Czechoslovakia's only the beginning, Poland and the Balkans are next. Our beloved Führer will have it all. My God, Ryan, we're talking children, families, human beings whose only fault is being Jewish!" Her face flushed with anger and sorrow, her eyes damp with tears, she could not go on.

He held her in his arms as she sobbed softly. Ryan kept an eye on the boy near the water's edge. The child sat on the sloping bank, surrounded by ducks, geese and two swans, talking to them and trying to pet their heads while avoiding their arching, demanding beaks. The crackers appeared gone.

Ryan sorted through their options, choosing and discarding ideas. If this outrageous plan for conquest and extermination were verifiable beyond a doubt, the proof could change the way many Americans thought about the Third Reich and European politics. Could change the minds of those who thought Hitler's anti-Semitism was a casual whim. Put the lie to his oft-stated desire for peace, for having no further territorial demands in Europe. If such a plan were known as a certainty, many from America's isolationist camp might change sides. Here was knowledge of incomparable value to the State Department and to President Roosevelt, but only if he could get irrefutable proof back to Washington. And that would put this woman and her child at even greater risk.

Once Erika had recovered sufficiently she sketched out her escape plan. *It could work,* Ryan thought. But it would have to happen quickly, and there could be no errors. Horst was indeed more dangerous than Ryan had suspected. And Ryan could see why she was increasingly nervous at being away so long.

Leo ran back up to his mother to get more crackers. Learning there were no more, he spread himself out between them on the bench, any shyness forgotten, and soon drifted off to sleep, his head cradled in his mother's lap, his legs crossing Ryan's. He noted flecks on the boy's coat and shoes from sitting in the grass with the waterfowl, removed his handkerchief and brushed the droppings away as best he could before discarding the soiled cloth beside the bench. Erika, distracted by her own thoughts, seemed not to notice.

He knew she was losing herself in the horror of Horst's plan as she stared down at the sluggishly flowing water. Ryan drew her attention back to the escape plan, reviewing it in detail and adding a few strategic changes. Then he made a proposal which might further endanger Erika, but could have momentous consequences if successful. Erika listened carefully and agreed it was worth any risk. They set a list of tasks and a timetable for the next twenty-four hours. Although it would further delay her return home, she reluctantly agreed to meet Ryan again at two that afternoon.

Bending over the dozing child she kissed Ryan gently on the lips. "Thank you, my American man."

The boy opened his eyes and smiled.

# CHAPTER FIVE

The afternoon proved hectic as Ryan tied up loose ends around the central city. He hoped Erika could keep her nerves under control, for so much depended on what she accomplished that evening at home. From a public booth she was to phone her parents to confirm in coded terms an arrival time in Marburg for the following day, but make no mention of his participation in the plan. *The less said on any phone, the better.*

Ryan's first consideration was how much to tell Edward of this ominous turn of events. His itinerary had been carefully planned so his brother knew at any given time where Ryan was and whom he intended to contact. His assignment obviously did not provide for the rescue of a former girlfriend, now married to the Gestapo. In France Ryan had received a coded letter from Ed acknowledging his brother's successes, and this afternoon Ryan planned to drop off at the consular office an encrypted update on the "Lone Ranger" network to accompany the next courier to Washington.

Ryan was very aware of the positive contribution his efforts were making toward Ed's promotion within German Affairs. Grace's father had worked his magic to bring his son-in-law into the Foreign Service under the aegis of The Group, and the senator was undoubtedly watching closely for Ed's quick advancement. Ed knew of the close call that final night in Marburg and shared Ryan's conviction that the pursuit was by the man Erika married. Now Ryan's helping that same woman and her son escape from this powerful Nazi could undermine an assignment whose success depended on the most clandestine of covers. Ryan's rocking that boat was not a risk Edward could condone.

His brother had always balked at Ryan's finessing of the rules. In their youth, conflicts often arose when Ryan had chosen a different path than that proposed by Edward. As adults, Ed still felt obliged to render sage advice. Ryan suspected his brother secretly envied his own ability to be spontaneous, certainly no trait for a future diplomat, where calm deliberation and plodding attention to protocol was the proven path to success.

Ryan decided to follow his gut. He would not mention the next day's undertaking until it was a *fait accompli*. He would remove Erika and the child from danger before returning to Berlin and his assignment. Once his friends were safe with Marita in Paris, and proof of Hitler's true criminal intent reached Washington, all the risks taken would prove a feather in Edward's cap and full justification for Ryan's bending of the rules. So he delivered the report into the hands of his contact at the consulate and sent a cryptic cable from the main post office telling his brother to await an important update within twenty-four hours. *May as well give him something to look forward to.*

Ryan visited two photo shops before finding what he needed at the Reuter Foto-Haus off the Linden. When he met them again in the back booth of a small café off the Ku-Damm he handed her a camera, a Minox sub-miniature as small as the palm of her hand. She was to photograph Horst's damning protocol. His Virginia trainer had demonstrated the use of this new device, "the perfect tool for espionage," he had called it. Now Ryan repeated the lesson with Erika, showing how the tiny camera opened telescopically to reveal lens and viewfinder, focused as closely as eight inches, and took fifty shots to a film cartridge. They discussed how best to light the subject and she practiced manipulating the controls before he loaded the miniscule cartridge. Ryan gave her an extra canister in case the document exceeded that length.

The French consulate had readily issued visas for her and the child's entry into France. The notation of her husband's SS rank and police position expedited the process, and she indicated a pleasure trip to visit friends in Paris. Erika had instructed her parents to take the hour-long trip to the French consulate in Frankfurt to get their visas. Ryan checked his own and found it recently expired, but decided to return alone later in the afternoon to renew it. They should not be seen together anywhere the Gestapo might later check and a clerk remember. They left the café and went their separate ways.

At the Dresdner Bank on the Ku-Damm Ryan withdrew funds sufficient to cover their expenses to the border, remembering Erika's assurance that she would bring marks from home, as well. German currency had little value outside the Reich and could not be exported, but extra money might come in handy should they run into unexpected difficulties en route. He was required to register his presence in the city as a reporter within twenty-four hours of arrival, and the Gestapo agents at the railway station had undoubtedly added his name to their list. But now knowing that his departure was a matter of hours rather than days or weeks, he decided to forgo that requirement and hope for the best.

Later in the afternoon Erika put Leo in the care of the governess. The boy was exhausted by the strenuous day's activities, but remained well-behaved, just quieter than usual. She knew Horst would learn soon enough that she had escaped Oskar's oversight, but she decided worry had no point. She knew her husband was preoccupied with finishing off his appalling report, so he might not even care. For a week he had spent every evening hour at his desk, poring over the black file, giving her the relief of not having to interact with him at all. She expected he would likewise disappear the moment he arrived home that night.

After an early dinner with Leo, she told Frieda to get the boy prepared for bed. While the nanny was occupied, Erika slipped into Horst's study. The Minox was in her pocket, but the report was nowhere to be found at his desk. She realized he must have it with him in his briefcase, so she would have to wait until his return from Prinz Albrechtstrasse.

To pass the time, she locked her bedroom door and began packing. Traveling without luggage might draw attention, since their visas indicated a vacation getaway, so they had agreed to carry one small case apiece, with hers to include the boy's clothing. Only necessities; she would shop when they arrived in Paris. She passed the study and headed for the boy's room. Leo was already fast asleep, and the nanny long gone to her upstairs quarters in the opposite wing. Erika gathered a few of his items before kissing the damp brow of her sleeping son. At the last moment she also grabbed Leo's favorite toy, a small *Steiff* bear, a gift from his grandparents on his first birthday. Back in her room she made a quick survey of the suitcase, found it adequately packed for immediate needs, and slid it under her bed.

Erika remained there until Horst arrived home. The gravel beneath the car's wheels warned of his approach, and she watched through the gap of the curtain as the sedan pulled under the covered portico. He stayed downstairs for what seemed an inordinate period of time, then finally climbed the staircase and entered his study. She expected him to deposit the briefcase there and return to work on the file once changed from his suit coat to the customary smoking jacket. A few moments later she heard him move down the hall to his own bedroom. The door closed quietly. Erika waited for what seemed forever, listening for him to re-emerge. Finally, hearing no sound on the landing, she stepped cautiously out into the hallway and moved along the corridor, noting a sliver of light beneath his door.

Horst grabbed her from behind and slammed her against the wall, the force knocking a painting to the carpet. He brutally wrenched her to him with an arm around the neck, then smothered her mouth with his other hand and dragged her into her bedroom and threw her on the bed. Erika tried to rise, to push him away, but he shoved her down again and straddled her. She could smell the alcohol. His face remained a stoic mask as she cried out and struggled to get away. He let her loose to slam a fist into her belly, and she curled up and fought for air, the pain shooting through her solar plexus. As she lay gasping, he rose and strode to the dresser and removed several silk stockings.

"What the hell are you doing?" The words came in short bursts from her bruised throat, her voice gravelly.

"Nothing you don't deserve, my beloved little whore." Only the hint of a smile creased his face.

"Get out of this room or I'll scream, dammit!" A meaningless threat; there was no one who would help her now. Horst straddled her again, pinning her arms to the side, and forced a stocking into her mouth, binding it in place with another tied around her head, and stuffed the others into his pocket.

"That should shut you up for a while." His voice was brittle. "Time to examine your transgressions, my dear wife. For now—I speak, you listen and learn." Terror gripped her. She could hardly move, the pain in her belly nauseating. "Don't worry; you'll have plenty to say later."

Horst picked her up, crushing her body against his to make struggle impossible, and carried her down the hall into his own bedroom. His bed was already stripped down to a tautly-stretched sheet. He threw her belly-down and tied her wrists and ankles to the bedposts. Her body shook, her mind raced. He had taken her forcefully in the past, but that had been the limit of his physical abuse. At those times he had seemed uninvolved, more insensitive observer, not active aggressor. But this assault was wantonly malicious. She was terrified by the pure cruelty, the cold hatred new and unexpected, the gag and restraints brutally tight.

Having seen the protocol, she knew he was capable of anything, held no compassion or empathy, lived disconnected from the feelings of others. She sought some means to coax him back to rational behavior, but, without speech, she was helpless. She could only focus with dread on what was to come next. Erika twisted her head to the side to keep him in sight, her eyes tearing with fear, anger and frustration. There was no controlling the trembling. Her hands grew numb from the constriction of the bonds, and her belly was on fire. An awakening cramp in her calves promised still greater agony. The gag made swallowing difficult, and saliva gathered in back of her throat, threatening to choke her.

Horst returned from his closet with a black and silver object, and she recognized his ceremonial SS dagger. He freed the knife from its scabbard and slowly and methodically slit her dress from neckline to hem, the finely-honed blade slicing easily through the material. He cut away slip and bra and garter belt and tossed them aside. Finally he notched the tip of the blade into her silk panties and split them from thigh to waist. With a deft hand he tore away the tattered remnants of cloth, leaving her fully exposed to his abuse.

He remained outwardly calm, unaffected by the torture of his wife.

# CHAPTER SIX

That Breitling bitch should have been his from the start. Klaus Pabst first saw her in the fall of 1933 as she left the women's clinic in Marburg, and he had trailed her home. Here was the girl he desired but never had: tall, attractive, vivacious. He approached her days later in the student dining hall to suggest a movie or a beer, and she turned him down politely—too busy with studies and duties at the *Frauenklinik*—but he saw in her eyes that same pity reserved for a street beggar or an unqualified job applicant. A few weeks later she was dating Horst.

He guessed his friend had watched his degradation at the *Mensa* and made his own move shortly thereafter. Naturally she would favor Horst—tall, debonair, superior in all ways, Horst who took all the honors and prizes. Klaus imagined Horst between those long, slender legs of hers, imagined stepping in to take Horst's place. But he never begrudged his mentor's conquests. Horst's success was always his success, and Klaus was, above all else, loyal.

Over the years he casually propositioned her in social settings, knowing well it would come to nothing, but finding pleasure in discomforting her. Although the SS prized honor, family-orientation, and fidelity in its leaders, Klaus knew that extra-marital affairs were commonplace among the officers and their wives. Sexual innuendo was a staple of social intercourse. He certainly would have liked bedding her, but he never would jeopardize his close friendship with Horst, even had she been interested. Her willingness alone would have given him the hook he needed to bring her down. And now that he knew she was racially impure, he was pleased to have never polluted himself by fucking her. At least that's what he told himself.

The failed attack on the American back in '34 had shown a surprising weakness in Horst. The three comrades lay in wait in the *Altstadt* ready to take down the bastard. Horst was seething, knowing his girl had just come from the American's bed. Once they realized he had leapt from the bridge, they lowered themselves from a retaining wall to reach the river bank below and followed the fugitive until they lost him in the tunnel. Unprepared to explore a dark passageway with nothing but lighter and matches to light the way, they gave up the chase.

Horst had lashed out at his cohorts, blaming them for the American's escape. Klaus expected Horst's outburst to open his facial wound, but instead a convulsive spasm twisted his head to the side. He slumped onto the damp bank with a terrible wailing, a keening cry from deep in his throat, and suffered through the painful attack. It was the first and last time Klaus had seen his friend and leader lose self-control. They had retreated to the Zentral-Hotel tavern and Horst drank himself into silence. A second attempt for the following evening was aborted with news the American had left Marburg, and then Horst impregnated the bitch and made her his wife.

For years now Klaus watched them together, knowing she was unworthy of his friend, hoping to find some way to discredit her, to prevent her from impeding Horst's rising star. And his own. A Gestapo truism stated that all men had something to hide, and he was determined to find the skeleton in the Erika Breitling von Kredow closet. He researched the family's heritage and its political leanings, and initially found nothing out of place. They were anti-Bolshevik, so much that they had left East Prussia to get to the heart of the Reich. He could find nothing useful in her parents' dossiers, except perhaps the curious fact that they had grown up in the same household, practically brother and sister. Was incest a possibility here? Stranger things had been found by diligent police work. Klaus ordered an examination of the grandparents' family records in East Prussia, which—intriguingly—were kept in the church archives recorded by her very own grandfather as parish minister. Klaus's intuitive sense tingled, and he ordered a trusted local agent to investigate the civil records, as well.

And there it was, his hook, his leverage to destroy her in Horst's eyes: Erika was a Jewess. A second-degree *Mischling,* to be precise. For Horst the distinction would be meaningless. The blood pollution was there despite two generations of baptism and conversion. She had—perhaps knowingly—snared a high-ranking SS officer now tasked with helping solve the Jewish Question, and he knew Horst would be appalled with his personal *Blutschande,* his sexual relations with a Jew. His mentor would have no choice but to eliminate all trace of her. That was Horst's way, and his "dagger" would see it happen at last.

It had been a full week since he had set things in motion at the SS gathering, and she had left immediately for Marburg to see her parents. By now she certainly knew what—for a few moments longer—only he knew. Klaus viewed this private knowledge as a beautifully-wrapped gift to himself, ready to open and savor at the right moment and in the right manner. He had hoped to hear her grovel upon her return to Berlin. Instead, only silence, which took guts. And he knew that in his world of constant surveillance, investigation and suspicion, someone else might step forward at any time to steal his thunder. But if he acted now, he alone could manipulate the destruction of the pompous Jew-bitch. Saving Horst from the public revelation and disgrace would be Klaus's greatest gift to his friend.

Sitting alone at his desk, Klaus placed the phone directly before him and planned how best to word his call. He saw no gain in waiting.

# CHAPTER SEVEN

Horst sat naked in the window nook of his bedroom, the leather portfolio open on the small table before him. Turning the pages, he considered a few final revisions. Such methodical editing was boring but necessary work. He considered using a stronger word, then let it be. He caught one misspelling. No longer was it a matter of content or sentence structure. To his aggravation, his fountain pen kept smearing. First thing in the morning he would have this final version retyped just before the presentation. *On the Resolution of the Jewish Problem in Occupied Lands of the Greater Reich* would have to be convincing, its recommendations flawless. Once accepted by Heydrich and passed along to Himmler, it would assure Horst's ultimate rise in the SS firmament. He might well be handed the primary role in implementing this mammoth undertaking.

He had been drinking, for this evening was to have been a celebration of sorts. The report was nearly ready to present to his superiors, and the timing was perfect. On the drive home the radio had broadcast Dr. Goebbels' latest raging harangue. Events in Paris had provided the emotional trigger so important to win hearts and minds, for a foolish Jew had assassinated a German diplomat. It was the great wake-up call to the German people. Suppression of the Jews in the Reich would no longer be a matter of a few laws. Hands-on action by the people would now to be the rule of the day.

He clumsily turned another page, focusing on the tables and graphs. The estimated numbers of Jews his *Einsatzgruppen* should handle on a daily basis was truly impressive. Many millions would have to be processed when the Waffen-SS and Wehrmacht rolled east. He promised remarkable results, especially if the SS followed these recommendations to the letter. Heydrich had stressed Himmler's insistence on the accuracy of all numbers and projections.

But the evening had taken an unexpected turn. Horst's excitement in the moment had wavered in the face of the newest revelations about his disloyal wife. Once again she had compromised his honor, and he was forced to take action. He took a long swallow of the Courvoisier, well beyond savoring the amber cognac, stubbed out his cigarette in the crystal ashtray, and glanced over at the bed.

Erika lay spread-eagle, face down, hands and feet bound to the bedposts—his favorite view of any woman, totally vulnerable and exposed to his predation. He would have preferred to hear her plea for his mercy, but she would not shut up when ordered, so the gag became necessary. *Wouldn't want to wake the household, would we?* She had lain that way now for over an hour, her ass streaked and welted from his belt. He had raped her as the capability struck him. Eventually she would reveal everything. *They always do.*

For over a week she had been up to something, avoiding him at every turn, unable to look him in the eye. She still had value to him as a social attribute to his professional career: Erika von Kredow, the officer's wife with the striking looks and witty personality. At the last SS gathering however he had watched her interact with the male guests. She appeared distracted, yet spent an inordinate amount of time with some officers, even briefly with Klaus Pabst. There was also a new SD officer present with whom she seemed unusually animated. This gave him pause.

Horst was surprised to learn the next morning that she had left with the boy, ostensibly to see her ill mother. Oskar had confirmed the trip to the station, and Klaus had set up a tail in Marburg. Klaus was invaluable to him. His "dagger" had discovered her disloyalty with that asshole American years before, and remained the model of loyalty and discretion in looking after his reputation and career. He wondered if Erika's sudden trip had been a ploy to meet with someone on the train.

Both the chauffeur and the child's governess had been directed to keep an eye on his wife at all times. Beyond the typical outings with the boy and shopping excursions, there had been little of interest until the previous evening. Oskar had reported Erika's visit to the National Socialist League of Women, a group he knew she avoided at all costs. And equally inexplicable was a stop at the Memorial Church on Breitscheidplatz—ostensibly for prayer—where no one had contacted her, *not even God?* He laughed at the absurdity, knowing his wife's opinion of religion. And why the Charlottenburg cathedral when others were so much closer, more accessible?

Then—thanks to Frieda Loos—he knew for certain his wife was making a fool of him. The child's nanny first reported Erika's reading of his private papers in the study, undoubtedly spying for one of his colleagues. Horst knew he inspired jealousy in many; brilliance always did. Then, that very morning, Erika had managed to lose Oskar's shadow for most of the day, the boy with her. Wife and son had returned home later by cab. With Frieda's encouragement the child revealed that his mother had met *"Mutti's* friend" in a park and the two had ‥hugged and kissed." *How long had she been fucking this bastard?* He would learn soon enough. Her lover was undoubtedly an SS colleague. Many would love to see him appear the cuckolded fool, so he had to act quickly and decisively. She would reveal the identity of her lover, and the man would disappear cleanly from her life. He would see to it personally.

Horst intended to go slowly, enjoy the process, even if it took all night. One thing for certain, he would do nothing obvious to mar her looks. She could still be a social asset when this was over, and she would never try anything so foolhardy again after what she would endure this night. He admitted his earlier leniency was partially responsible; he had left her on her own for far too long. She had become complacent in the marriage with little appreciation for all he had given her. Without him she would still be a Hessian *Hausfrau*—no luxury, no society, no public admiration. It was time she learned just how dangerous he was, and tonight's little lesson would be a good start. Horst tossed back the cognac and poured another double shot, the amber bottle now half-empty. He rose from the chair and approached the bed, steadying himself on the corner post.

"I'm being cruel, aren't I, darling?" he whispered in her ear, his voice as smooth as the cognac. "And most selfish." He took another swallow, enjoying the warmth of the alcohol. "Allow me to share a bit with you. Yes, let's sterilize your ass, my love. After all, it's seen so much activity lately."

He emptied the cognac over the raw welts. Erika's muscles clenched from the agonizing pain and she arched against the bonds, the ties tearing into her wrists and ankles, her cry stifled by the gag.

Horst held the ceremonial SS dagger a hair's breadth from her eye. His hand trembled. He ordered her to admire the weapon, pointing out the bluish sheen of the metal and sharp edge. She stared in terror. "There's an important lesson here for you, my dearest." He angled the ebony handle toward the lamp at the bedside, catching the light on the shining blade. "The words etched here read 'My Honor is Loyalty.' Do you even understand loyalty? Honor?" He rocked the blade back and forth, as if testing the balance of the weapon. "I would say no, you don't. And it was on this very day, November ninth just three years ago, that I received this beautiful weapon at my SS initiation. A fitting moment to put it to first use, wouldn't you say?"

She strained against the bonds.

"My dear Erika, you will always be my little treasure, and you do serve me well in public. Any man would be proud to have you." He lifted the hair from the side of her face with the sharp tip of the blade. "But obviously one too many has done just that, and sharing you with other men insults *my* honor." Horst spoke slowly to avoid slurring. He sat down heavily beside her and used the dagger to caress her shoulder, gently tracing down the length of her spine before slipping the blade slowly between her thighs. She shuddered.

The telephone startled them both. He stood, stumbled, then regained his balance by gripping the bedpost. He lifted the receiver. "Von Kredow here. What is it?"

The familiar voice of Klaus on the line: "Have you heard, Horst? Very big developments across the Reich this evening—Dr. Goebbels' work, we're told. Tomorrow should be very interesting."

"And for this you disturb me at this hour, and at home?" He glanced over at Erika, thinking of trying to take her again. He was probably too drunk to make it happen, but he felt the excitement growing.

"No, Horst, another matter, something you should know about as soon as possible." The usual deference seemed muted tonight, but perhaps it was just Horst's difficulty concentrating on the words. "This news affects you directly."

"Well, out with it, for God's sake. I don't have all night."

"It's better discussed in person, Horst. Your place within the hour?"

"As I said, I'm busy now, I can't be disturbed. I meet Heydrich at ten tomorrow. We'll discuss it right after. Now, *gute Nacht.*" He dropped the receiver in its cradle and stood still for a moment, swaying slightly. He felt ill, and realized he would have to be sharp for the morning.

Stretching across Erika, he severed her bonds on wrists and ankles with the blade and left the improvised gag in place. "Just know this—" he carefully enunciated each word as he rolled her to her back and dragged her toward him. Erika winced as her raw flesh smeared the rumpled sheet. He held the tip of the knife to her nipple. "Just know this," he repeated, "there are many ways I can make you less attractive to other men, ways which will never show in public. Clear?" She nodded. "And we'll be taking this up again later, after my personal investigation. Just be certain of one thing—I *will* find him." He shook his head to clear his vision, and felt a sharp stitch in his cheek. "Now clean yourself up. You're a mess."

He bent forward to slide the dagger beneath the stocking around her head and slit the silk. A small drop of blood rose on her cheek. Abruptly, he slumped across her. He was out cold.

# CHAPTER EIGHT

She held the syringe to the light, clearing the bubbles from the pale liquid. Her hands trembled. She could still sense the adrenaline, the terror, the pain. Her determination to give Horst a fatal overdose, decided in the throes of his assault, now gnawed at her conscience. She considered how much morphine would eliminate him from her life. She picked up the small vial, cradling it in her palm. She had often wondered at the transformative properties of this drug, for Horst's dependence had meant her independence for most of four years, had made her life with him so much easier to bear. Now she could remove him as a threat forever.

Erika rose carefully from the armchair and went to his side. He was spread across the bed, his crotch smeared with her blood, his flaccid penis exposed. He snored. She steadied her hand and slid the needle effortlessly into his arm. The hypodermic slowly surrendered the drug to his vein, and he barely stirred.

She released the pressure on the plunger and shook her head, disgusted with her own weakness in the face of such evil. She simply did not have what it took to kill him, no matter all he had done, all he had become, all he planned to do. She knew that killing him would not keep the Nazis from their plan, perhaps not even slow them down. Things had already progressed too far. Far better to let a powerful country like America intervene and prevent such barbarity. She withdrew the needle, half of its contents still unused. He had received twice the normal dosage. She could not kill him, but she also would not risk his awakening too early.

The future of her son and parents was now at stake. The revenge for her pain and humiliation might be sweet, but her husband would be missed in the morning, and any manhunt would be all the more rabid were he to turn up dead. She could not imagine the police accepting as coincidental his family's disappearance on the night of his "suicide." Horst had repeated often enough: *The Gestapo doesn't believe in coincidence.*

Carefully replacing both vial and syringe in the small case, she considered taking some of the painkiller into her own vein. She knew the damage from his brutality would test her resilience over the next twenty-four hours. She zippered shut the case, determined to remain sharp for whatever was still to come, but decided to take it with her. *Just in case.*

Only half an hour had passed since she had rolled him aside in both relief and disgust and dragged herself awkwardly from the bed. Back in her room she had cleansed her sensitive wounds and examined her tortured backside in the mirror. There was no way to bandage the welts, so she used a salve and cushioned her torn skin with extra underwear. The nick near her ear was barely noticeable. *A little face powder later to disguise it, should time allow.* Long sleeves and dark stockings should hide the marks left by the ties.

Before leaving her room Erika had placed a few pieces of the most valuable von Kredow jewelry in her handbag, and pulled the valise from under the bed. The throbbing welts and aching abdomen made everything an effort. She was hesitant to leave the unconscious Horst alone for long, knowing that Frieda might be on the prowl. Once back in his bedroom, she had forced a wad of tissue paper into the keyhole, and reinserted the key to turn the tumbler. No spy would watch her inject Horst and photograph the document, a beacon of evil in its lustrous black portfolio.

Once the drug kit was closed and the temptation to eliminate Horst suppressed, she reviewed the camera controls for focusing, shutter speed and aperture, then cleared the table, leaving only the lamp in place. She set the shade aside to give optimum light to the tiny

Minox. Page after page clicked off with solid precision, exactly forty-six sheets of sterile bureaucratese, promoting the murder of millions.

Erika steadied her shaking hands, her body wracked by pain, her mind overwrought by anxiety. For the first time since her student days in the *Frauenklinik,* she now knew she was doing something unselfishly, something solely to help others. She forced herself to relax. A discomforting glance at Horst found him still sprawled across the bed. He would be no further trouble tonight. The very sight caused hatred to well up again, but there were more important matters to attend to. She replaced the lampshade, organized the report in its folder, and left it on the seat of the chair where Horst had abandoned it. With the table and room returned to a semblance of normal, she switched off the light, closing the door to this horrifying segment of her life. She didn't look back. She intended never to set eyes on him again.

As she moved along the corridor toward Leo's room, two final matters came to mind. In Horst's study she opened a small wooden box on the desk, Horst's birthday gift from Heydrich the previous spring, its embossed-leather top bearing the eagle-and-swastika. She placed its contents in the pocket of her handbag. She then opened the right-hand drawer of his ornate desk and removed a ledger and a few letters. A false bottom hid thick stacks of banknotes bound with rubber bands. She helped herself to two bundles, all she could fit in her crowded bag. Again, *just in case.*

Ryan's call to René from a public phone at the S-Bahn station went unanswered. The operator reported the lines across the Reich especially busy that evening. He should wait for a call-back when the connection went through.

Ryan stood next to the booth and watched the passers-by enter the Zoo station. Working men and women hurried home after a long day in store or office, their collars up and scarves wrapped tightly to ward off the chill. Some carried mesh bags with foodstuffs intended for the evening meal. Many carried briefcases under the arm, or umbrellas, even though no rain was forecast despite the cooler weather. Helmeted policemen wandered through the crowd.

The occasional Brownshirts swaggered past in pairs, thumbs hooked in belts, rifles slung over shoulders.

A harried businessman in a long tweed overcoat, his cheeks flushed from the cold, approached Ryan's phone booth and hovered impatiently. Ryan apologized, explaining his wait for a connection on that line, and directed the man to the next booth a few steps away. The man mumbled a gruff response and moved away, but did not leave. *Obviously a lot on his mind.*

Ryan's phone rang. The operator confirmed his connection to the Kehl number.

"To what do I owe this pleasure?" René sounded relaxed. Ryan could picture a snifter of Cointreau in his friend's hand.

"It appears the Lone Ranger is needed sooner rather than later, my friend." Ryan kept his voice as low as possible, given the din at the station. He glanced casually to his left and right as he spoke, avoiding the furtive "German glance." Gestapo informants were common, especially in public gathering spots. "How's tomorrow looking? Have time to greet some old friends; perhaps arrange a river outing?"

"A bit chilly this time of year, but name your time and place."

"I'll know more by morning. Where's best to reach you, office or home?"

"At home, at least till noon, fewer distractions here. After that, use the other number." Ryan had memorized both.

"Travel safely," said René, "and stay in touch." They wished each other well and cut off the call.

Ryan turned back toward his hotel. The harried tweed overcoat now loitered a short distance down the grimy wall. He stared past Ryan toward the station entrance, as if waiting to meet someone. As the American headed toward him, the stranger quickly shifted his gaze toward the line of buses across the street. The man had not used a phone while Ryan was on the line with René. *Too early for paranoia?*

He stopped at a small restaurant off the Ku-Damm and ordered grilled sausage and pan-fried potatoes with a half-bottle of Franconian wine. During dinner he observed the street outside for any further sign of the tweed coat. No one caught his attention. Suitably fortified for a long night, Ryan returned to find the hotel elevator out-of-order, and climbed the five flights of stairs to his room. He set aside a few items he had purchased and made preparations for the morning, arranging his clothes in the brown-leather valise, checking for the third time to be sure his passport and visa were in his suit jacket. There was little to pack, just toiletries and a change of basics.

Minutes later he was done. He set the frail wooden chair under the ceiling lamp for better light and tried to read a newspaper he had lifted from the lobby on his way up. The words were clear enough, but the meanings escaped him. Tomorrow was too distracting—too many possible scenarios, too much that could go awry. As an actor in college he had never suffered from stage fright, but this role would put other's lives at risk, not to mention his own. His nerves were getting the better of him. Stretched out on the narrow bed in his underwear, the room still overheated and stuffy despite the open gable window, he found sleep elusive.

Dressed once again, Ryan went down to the corner bar to find a beer. An hour later on his way back up, he settled his bill with the night clerk. Around midnight he shaved before packing away all but his comb, hoping to speed his getaway in the morning. Sleep finally came fitfully, the plan surfacing again and again in his mind, turning and twisting, excitement and trepidation.

In the velvet darkness of Leo's room Erika shifted frequently in the overstuffed chair. She found no comfortable position. Her body ached, and the aspirin did little to alleviate her pain. Her nerves were as raw as her flesh, yet she still fought a mental numbness which threatened to engulf her and take away the will to act.

It was here in this armchair that she had nursed her baby and quietly promised him a future full of joy. She could hear the untroubled breathing of her son in the nearby bed. How lucky to still be so innocent, so free of worry, for just a few minutes longer. She wished his life could have turned out differently. Her Leo was such a sweet little boy, so attentive to her moods and anxious to please.

Horst had never shown much interest in the boy; she knew that the youngster felt no special affection for him. Not a surprise, given how distant and cold he was to all. She thought she saw a touch of fear in Leo, perhaps only a reflection of her own constant unease in Horst's presence.

Their life together had changed dramatically once they had moved to Berlin. She realized quickly that Horst had won her over with charm and social expertise solely to display an attractive wife to further his career ambitions. Once her pregnancy was known and they married, his attitude became neutral, then totally disinterested. He had other worlds to conquer. Now the relationship had devolved into hatred and abuse.

She and Leo would face a traumatic change in France. She knew a little French, perhaps enough to get by. Ryan had people who would help them find a new life in the French capital. He warned her things there could also be difficult for Jews, but not nearly as bad as under the Nazis. Yet Horst's proposal proved that Hitler intended to make all Europe part of his Third Reich. No place would be safe any longer. Perhaps Ryan could help them find a way to get to America, or even South America. She remembered that very few countries showed interest in finding Germany's Jews a home outside the Reich.

Money was not a problem, at least for a while. Her handbag hid valuable von Horst jewelry, wedding gifts from his mother shortly before she died. She had been a cold, distant woman, but generous with Erika at the end. Perhaps it was pity for her daughter-in-law that Erika had witnessed in the dying woman's eyes. After all, she must have known her own son for what he was. And the stack of bank notes from his desk reserve might ease the transition, as long as she was not arrested crossing the border with German currency, a violation severely punished. Ryan said *Reichsmark* held little value outside the Reich, but it was currency all the same. She chided herself for the foolishness of that thought. If detained at the border, she and Leo would never face charges. They would both die. Horst would see to that.

Perhaps the aspirin did indeed make the pain easier to bear; there was no way to know for certain. She had never been beaten with a belt before, never known the rawness from such a violent sexual assault. She knew some parents routinely strapped their children, and she was quietly thankful that hers had never resorted to physical violence. Perhaps she had been spared because she was an obedient child, unlike many of her friends who rebelled against the strict rules imposed by their parents, these same friends who now enthusiastically obeyed and worshipped the Nazi godhead.

The hours dragged on, the sky beyond the window black as her husband's uniform. She believed she heard an owl in the garden. She couldn't find a position which allowed sleep, but thought it just as well, for she feared missing the rendezvous with Ryan. Midnight was long past, the morning of their freedom still to come. The ornate clock on the opposite wall ticked incessantly, marking the hours and quarter hours with a soft thump. Leo so liked the reassuring cadence of his clock that the year before she had wrapped a small piece of felt around the hammer of the clockwork to soften the tolling. Now she waited anxiously for each muted strike of a new hour.

At four a.m. Erika left the boy's room. She moved quietly past the door to the study and stopped outside Horst's bedroom. Barely perceptible, his sonorous breathing was interrupted only occasionally by a muffled snort. From the study she phoned for a taxi and, keeping her voice as low as she dared, requested the cab wait outside the mansion's main gate at five a.m. She feared alerting Frieda or Oskar. She and Ryan had estimated less than half an hour for her and Leo to get to Lehrter station in the early morning traffic. She allowed some leeway. They couldn't afford to be late.

Getting a taxi dispatched at any hour to their upscale neighborhood never presented a problem. Most of the neighbors were also influential Nazis or barons of business and industry. The wealthy Jewish families had long since left the country, many leasing their splendid homes to powerful foreigners at ridiculously low rents. She had seen one neighbor standing before her residence surrounded by luggage and steamer trunks, awaiting transport to the station. Now she was one of those "running Jews" herself. For her it was to be only a small suitcase and a teddy bear for her son.

Back in Leo's room she reviewed the plan in her mind, looking for possible slip-ups that could put them all at risk. She felt much better knowing that Ryan would be there every step of the way, for saving her small family would be so much easier with his aid. It had been a relief to learn that he had a ready answer to that dilemma. *How stupid to have let him go and chosen Horst.*

At four-thirty Erika gently stroked the damp curls on his forehead until Leo awoke. He sat up and greeted her with a sleepy smile, and she switched on his bedside lamp. "Hurry up, little man, we're off on an adventure, and your grandparents are anxious to see you again."

"Is everything all right, *Mutti?* You look sad."

"Everything's just fine, Leo. We're just taking a little train trip, that's all."

Though still drowsy, he threw his arms around her neck and kissed her cheek. "Thank you, *Mutti,* let's go!"

Leo's sudden enthusiasm surprised her, following so closely on the heels of their recent Marburg visit. There, too, the boy had sensed her distraught mood. Quiet and reserved on the long train ride back to Berlin, Leo had repeatedly asked if she were all right. But now the boy couldn't stop talking about all the city lights they would see. It was very grownup to be up and out in the dark. She took him to the bathroom and dressed him for colder weather. Bending down to help Leo was painful, tearing at the aching muscles of her belly and the scabs already forming on her backside. She moved carefully. Out of her purse came a few squares of hazelnut chocolate, his favorite, to help with hunger until they reached the station. Erika didn't want to risk a visit to the kitchen pantry on their way out.

At a quarter to the hour she helped Leo with his overcoat, cap, and scarf. Erika stressed to him that they must be extraordinarily quiet and leave the lights off so as not to wake the household. *The others need their sleep, you know.* She pulled on her coat and scarf, adjusted her hat, and picked up the valise and handbag. His small hand in hers, they headed down the corridor and darkened staircase toward the front entrance.

"Fräulein Loos, are *you* coming with us?" Leo voiced disappointment at the prospect of adding another nighttime adventurer.

Erika was horrified to see the governess in the foyer, fully dressed and waiting for them. "What are you doing here?"

Frieda stood and pushed the button to illuminate the hall. "I always rise at five, Frau von Kredow, to look in on the boy," she said, her expression smug. "This morning I saw the light in his room and assumed you were planning to travel once again, so here I am to keep you company and look after the boy."

"That won't be necessary." Erika found it difficult to disguise both her nervousness and contempt. "I'm fully capable of taking my son on a little getaway."

"No doubt. But Herr von Kredow has made it very clear you're not to leave the house without me." Frieda gave a knowing smile. "Are you sure you're up for travel right now? You've already had such a strenuous day...and night."

*Malice in that smile.* The spying bitch must have witnessed her degradation and torture, and done nothing to intervene. Erika calmed her voice. "Very well, pack for a few days away."

"I can be ready very quickly, madam." She could not hide her surprise at Erika's ready surrender. "I'll just fetch my bag." She turned toward the staircase, switching on the hall lights as she went.

"Wait here, my darling," Erika whispered to Leo the moment the governess reached the upper landing. "And keep a close eye on our bag. I've forgotten one more thing to take care of."

"Is it Bruno?" he asked. Leo climbed onto the chair recently vacated by his governess.

"No, your bear's in the suitcase. You may take him out to play, just close it again when you're done. Back in a moment."

Erika moved swiftly up the stairs, avoiding the few carpeted treads which creaked. The door to Horst's bedroom was ajar, the ceiling light burning within. She approached with caution. Frieda was bent over the bed, attempting to shake Horst awake. He grunted and moaned in protest, but the drug and alcohol made his responses incoherent. The room reeked of vomit.

For the first time since the vicious assault, Erika felt empowered and she made her move. In four quick strides, her physical distress forgotten, she reached the fireplace hearth and pulled the coal rake from its stand. Distracted by futile attempts to rouse her master, Frieda never saw the iron rod which sent her sprawling across the bed. She lay unconscious next to Horst. Erika retrieved the stockings which had earlier held her captive and bound the feet and wrists of the nanny. She forced the same damp gag into the woman's mouth, tying it tightly around her head. A quick check found the ties secure. *This little whore isn't going anywhere now.*

Horst lay snoring once again. A small flow of blood crusted at the back of the nanny's head where the rod had done its work. If the morphine kit had not been downstairs in her handbag, Erika would have sedated his household spy, as well. *What a pretty picture,* her thoughts filled with venom. *I hope the two of you are very happy together.*

Erika hoisted the nanny under the arms. As she pulled the body off the bed she tensed at the pain. She dragged the unconscious woman down the hall and into the dressing room of her own chamber, shutting the door behind her. It would be some time before anyone searched for the missing woman, and the last place anyone would look would be Erika's closet. Horst always left in the morning without concern for wife and child, and Oskar didn't return from driving him until mid-morning at the earliest. By that time, if all went according to plan, Erika and Leo would be well on their way to freedom.

Downstairs, she hurriedly grabbed Leo by the hand and took the valise in her other, clumsily shutting the door behind them, not bothering to lock it. Leo hugged his bear to his chest with his free arm, smiling up at his mother over the excitement of the nighttime adventure. Their cab was waiting at the gate.

# CHAPTER NINE

In that unformed state between dream and awareness, Ryan already knew Berlin had changed. The usual din of the pre-dawn hours was familiar from his earlier years, when he had moved from the suburban tranquility of the von Haldheim mansion to a room in the heart of the city. He could expect to awaken to the clop of a brewery dray horse or the impatient honk of a passing delivery truck on the dark, cobbled street below. Cart vendors called out greetings to regular customers on their way to work, while shopkeepers exchanged pleasantries as they washed down the sidewalk in front of their stores. Heavy metal shutters clattered up to reveal shops ready for business. The familiar bell of the tram would clang on the thoroughfare beyond his narrow street.

But now a different clamor echoed in his mind, a harried rush of running feet, a racket of falling glass and splintering wood. And Ryan sensed a bite in the air, acrid smoke. Through the gloom he saw tendrils entering the casement window and sat up abruptly, only to hit the sloping ceiling just above the bed. He shook his head clear before stumbling to the window. In the still-dim street people moved through a yellowing haze of smoke, and his eyes quickly located the roiling clouds stabbed with flame which rose from a distant rooftop. Hints of a smaller fire danced in the storefront windows below on the street, and he saw frenetic movement in the crowd racing past the hotel.

Ryan recognized the source of the distant flames as the synagogue he had passed when looking for lodgings. The handsome temple had brought back memories of one near the university, of the resonant song of the cantor, and of the elderly street vendor, a worn strap holding his tray of matches, greeting him each evening with "all done for the day?" Ryan had brought the old man gloves to cover his red and chapped hands. Now a similar house of worship was burning, and he heard the sirens of the fire brigade.

He dressed hastily, grabbing his hat, woolen overcoat and valise. The tiny elevator failed to arrive, and he remembered why and took the stairs, two at a time. In the lobby he dropped the room key over the raised counter, now abandoned, only to find the clerk outside surveying the chaos in the street. "What's going on?" Ryan asked. Both stared at the wanton destruction before the hotel entrance.

"A party for all our Jewish friends." He turned away with a last weary glance. "Have a good trip."

The street lamps no longer burned and the overcast sky grew lighter. Dull amber tarnished the building fronts, and the harsh sound of shattering glass rang along the street. A gang of youths ran toward the synagogue fire, young men happily jostling each other as if on their way to a soccer match. Brownshirts marched past the hotel entry singing the Horst-Wessel-Song. Ryan stepped down onto a sidewalk covered with shards and made his way past overturned handcarts, scattered hardware and clothing, and broken display cases hauled into the street by the mob. Smoke bit at his throat and brought tears to his eyes. A smashed and forlorn cash register lay on the sidewalk, the surging crowd parting to either side as it raced to witness the major fire. A passer-by stooped to check the open cash drawer.

As Ryan entered the nearest cross street, three taxis pushed through with horns blaring. Rigid arms extended from the cab windows to meet upraised salutes and cries of *Heil Hitler* from the crowd. He ducked into the entryway of a camera shop and feigned interest in the photos mounted in the barred window, but two men spotted him and called out, and Ryan pivoted on his heels and raised his right arm.

Just then, Hitler Youth ran by, laughing and shouting racial slurs to no one in particular. Two boys pushed a handcart of paving cobbles and stopped before the street's Jewish bakery. A boisterous *eins, zwei, drei,* and palm-sized stones flew into the display windows. An older woman, likely the baker's wife, crouched behind the counter as panes shattered onto the sidewalk. Some boys picked up larger shards and hurled them back through the empty window frames. The baker and his apprentice, hands still white with flour, came running from the back room, only to retreat before the flying glass. Three youths entered the ruined storefront, re-emerging with baked goods in hand which they tossed to their comrades and by-standers. Now others entered to send loaves of bread sailing out into the street. Two of the vandals finally cornered the shop apprentice, dragging him out onto the sidewalk and beating him over the back with broomsticks. He shielded himself as best he could before escaping down the street, slipping and sliding on shattered glass.

The ordinances required all Jewish businesses to display signs warning Aryans away from the shops, and now those same signs beckoned the vengeful crowds. Ryan made his way cautiously toward the synagogue, recognizing that the crowd did not care whom it victimized. An eel writhed on the pavement, abandoned by a woman running from a storefront advertising "Live Fish & Poultry" in both German and Hebrew. The looter held a squawking chicken by the neck and carried a newspaper-wrapped bundle of fish under her arm.

A distillery store teemed with men and women, their arms filled with bottles and some lugging full crates, knocking aside other plunderers to get their prizes home intact. A Storm Trooper buttoned a slender schnapps bottle inside his uniform and took a swig from a second bottle before sending it shattering. He struck a match and set the spilled liquor afire, laughing at his own cleverness.

Ryan passed a furrier's demolished storefront, the mannequins in furs smeared with human excrement, the odor incredibly rank. An undernourished dog loped by with a string of sausages trailing from its mouth, taking advantage of the commotion to grab a needed meal. Two motorcycles, their sidecars filled with stones, cut a path through the shifting throng, the drivers sitting erect in civilian attire and making no attempt to hide the SS jackboots below their trouser cuffs.

An old man with a long gray beard and skullcap stumbled out of his dry goods shop, beseeching Yahweh for help and cursing the crowd in Yiddish. He appeared excessively frail in his nightshirt and robe as he struggled with a burden of stones which he dropped at the feet of the closest revelers. "Forgive me for asking, but I believe these are yours?"

Two louts grabbed him by the arms and dragged him into the street, his slippers scraping a path through the shards before breaking loose from his feet. The youths threw the man to the ground and repeatedly kicked him. Ryan pushed his way through the crowd with a shout of protest, but someone grabbed him from behind and forced him back from the fracas.

"Leave it! Not your battle!" a deep voice hissed in his ear, the man's breath sour. Ryan turned to face a neighborhood cop. "Let it be, my friend, just let it be." The officer now shouted over the jeering crowd, all the time drawing Ryan forcibly by the arm toward the opposite side of the narrow street. "It's for what they did to us in Paris, you know." Ryan seethed but said nothing, knowing this was a battle he couldn't win. Just meters away two other policemen stared at him and laughed at some shared joke, then turned to watch the beating of the old man but did nothing to intervene. "Just listen," the policeman yelled. "That's the *Volk* speaking, and God knows the filthy Jews deserve this...this, and plenty more." The cop's face showed true commitment and the certainty that all was right in his world.

Now one ruffian took the fractured leg of a chair and struck the elder across the back. The man cried out for help, curling up on the cobbles and shielding his head with arms and hands. As more blows rained down, his protest was lost in the jeering crowd. One attacker reached for the protruding, scraggly beard and yanked it skyward. "Shall we light a candle for Chanukah?" Ryan felt impotent, empty.

At that moment two Wehrmacht officers, hands propped on holstered side arms, forced their way forward and ordered the youths to desist. With hateful glares and protests the revelers backed off, and the remaining crowd seemed momentarily stunned by the intervention. Things fell eerily silent before most of the participants moved on to other sport. Almost immediately a young woman ran from the broken storefront to comfort the shopkeeper, still curled on the pavement with blood streaking his disheveled white hair. A yarmulke lay crushed beside him. She cradled the old man's head in her lap, her shoulders hunched as she rocked back and forth and sobbed.

Ryan pushed down the street toward the Ku-Damm. Firefighters directed water on the buildings to either side of the burning synagogue, but there was no attempt to extinguish the waning fire within the desecrated structure itself. The heat and smoke were palpable. Uniformed officers cautioned onlookers to stand well back from the fire crews and equipment. The stench of kerosene rose from overturned buckets and cans, and a hastily formed pyre of benches, tables, expensive cloths and Torah scrolls, all plundered from the now blackened shell of the synagogue, smoldered on the far side of the street. A few celebrants still hovered about the burning heap, a festival bonfire.

Two men held a rabbi fast while a third pulled off his hat, phylacteries and prayer shawl and added them to the now resurgent fire. Tears streaked the rabbi's soot-covered cheeks and ran into his beard, but he stood stoically without a struggle. A small gathering of sobbing Jewish women was forced to watch.

Out on the grand boulevard the early morning traffic of automobiles, horse-drawn wagons and streetcars gave some semblance of normalcy at first glance. But then a milling crowd gathered to chant "Out with the Jews" as soldiers forced a dozen men onto an open-bed truck. Trams and double-deckers rumbled past. From a distance Ryan watched a youth with a crudely-painted cardboard sign around his neck run a gauntlet of pummeling and cursing boys his own age. The legend on the sign was not legible.

Ryan pulled himself up onto the next passing streetcar. His progress on foot was too slow to reach the S-Bahn and connect to Lehrter Station on time. The tram windows, hazed from exhalations, blurred the phantom traffic outside. Occasionally the bright orange of a burning storefront tinted the misted glass. Raucous sirens, bells and blaring horns joined the metallic rumble of the tracks beneath his feet to form a discordant symphony. A mother held her hands over the ears of the frightened child who cowered against her.

Brakes squealed as the car came to rest at the next stop. Two young Brownshirts entered from the front and surveyed the crowded tram, their cheeks reddened from the cold morning and early exertion, their spirits obviously high. A young girl seated near Ryan clutched her schoolbooks tightly to her chest and lowered her eyes as she withdrew into the far corner of her seat. She pulled down the woolen topcoat to cover her knees and slowly lowered her hand to shield the Hebrew script on the spine of her books.

Ryan checked the watch at his wrist. He could do nothing here this morning, but later, once Erika's proof was in State Department hands, he would have done his part. And there was a train departing for Hamburg he couldn't miss.

The crowd surged fitfully through the vast hall of Lehrter Station. Steamer trunks and stacked suitcases, cardboard boxes hastily bound with cord, large wooden crates—all prevented easy transit across the concourse. Frustrated porters shouted warnings as they maneuvered overloaded handcarts and trolleys toward the waiting trains. In the morning hour no sunlight pierced the leaden sky outside to brighten the tall windows, and high in the barrel-vaulted ceiling a smoky haze enveloped the rafters. A single dove, lost in the stone and steel surroundings, rested on a flagpole. The white plumage contrasted sharply with a monotonous succession of crimson flags lining the walls.

Ryan threaded his way through the shifting throng, unusually aware of unwashed bodies and damp woolen topcoats. The overheated air felt thick. An occasional waft of coal smoke hinted at locomotives waiting on the tracks beyond the checkpoints. The hum of voices seemed unnaturally subdued, and anxiety showed on many faces, with departing parties in tears and children pressing to their parents' legs or sobbing at the uncertainty of the moment. Only the announced departures and arrivals and the distant whistles of trainmen pierced the colorless murmur. Ryan stepped atop a heavily-loaded luggage truck to search the sea of bobbing hats and caps, up-turned collars, and fur stoles.

Erika stood as agreed under the departure board. Nearby, long lines of travelers pushed forward to buy tickets. Her long gray coat reached to her ankles, and she wore a stylish hat with veil. Gripping her gloved hand, the little boy gazed earnestly up into the surge of tall strangers. Ryan approached indirectly, watching for anyone showing interest in the young mother and child. They shook hands, casual acquaintances meeting by chance at the railway station. Leo stood to attention and dutifully reached for Ryan's hand. The hint of a smile shone on the child's face.

"All went well?" Ryan, shaken by the tumult on the streets, feared her response.

Erika nodded. "Two tickets to Amsterdam, first class, and lightly packed, as agreed." The soft-sided cloth valise sat at her feet.

"The other matter we discussed?" Ryan fought an incessant urge to look around.

"In my handbag." Her voice was flat, toneless. "The camera, as well."

She began to remove the bag from her shoulder, but Ryan quickly shook his head. "Later, on the train."

"Then it begins."

It was a relief to finally reach this step. "Track two, central platform, the first carriage closest to the locomotive. We'll meet in the vestibule," he said. A shadow of uncertainty crossed her face. "Go on now, and no looking back. It'll work, the plan's solid."

Erika straightened her shoulders, gave her son a gentle smile and had him say "auf Wiedersehen" to her friend. The boy offered a parting handshake, then dutifully took his mother's hand and they made their way toward the departure gates. Ryan saw that she moved without her customary fluid grace, an unaccustomed stiffness to her walk. He watched the checker verify their tickets and wave them through before he followed. Agents in topcoats carefully ob-served every departing passenger who passed through the gates. Gestapo, clearly, with SA Brownshirts standing a few paces to the side, carbines at their shoulders.

Ryan joined the queue behind a family of nervous travelers—father, mother, two small girls—who caught the attention of the watchers. There was an angry bruise across the man's forehead. His long beard and the family's dress suggested Orthodox Jews, and the Gestapo immediately pulled them aside to review their papers. As Ryan waited his turn, he overheard one agent suggest loudly that Palestine would be the best destination for "this nauseating scum."

The wife and girls stared nervously at the tiled floor as their father handed over identification papers. The agent briefly reviewed the packet, removing an envelope which he slipped smoothly into his overcoat pocket. *Jewels or marks,* guessed Ryan. The agent sent the family out onto the platform with a dismissive wave. The policeman chuckled as Ryan handed over his documents. "Why we allow Yids to infect other Germanic countries is beyond me." He glanced at Ryan's American passport and waved him through with the comment, "Shame to have to deal with this scum, right?"

Ryan moved toward the massive steam locomotive fronting the six-carriage train, famed for record speed runs between Berlin and Hamburg. A swastika adorned the engine's snout, and streamlined coping gleamed in brilliant red livery with a *Reichsbahn* logo traced in gold. Heat from the huge boiler radiated out onto the cold platform. His watch showed only minutes to spare.

Erika and Leo stood as planned in the vestibule. Ryan mounted the step as a porter offered a friendly greeting and unneeded support to his elbow. A trainman's cry went out for all to board, and coach doors began to slam shut the length of the train. A piercing whistle signaled the imminent departure of FD24 for Hamburg, with connections via Amsterdam for Hoek of Holland and Paris, and a shrill response from down the platform acknowledged the signal. Ryan nodded encouragement to Erika as the trainman secured their door and left the vestibule.

She steadied the boy at her legs before the cars began to shift, and with a shriek from the locomotive, the coaches creaked into motion and the train crawled from the shed.

# CHAPTER TEN

Horst awoke disoriented, his head throbbing mercilessly. He was racked by chills, even though the radiator offered ample warmth. His lethargy suggested the mind-dulling effect of morphine, yet he had no memory of using his drug the night before. *Too damned much cognac,* he thought. He had also failed to set the alarm. It was close to seven, well past his usual time to rise.

With an expletive he dragged himself from the bed, avoiding the dried vomit, and moved unsteadily into the bathroom. The tiles were ice under bare feet, and the glaring fixture above the mirror made him wince. He rinsed his mouth and slung back three aspirin tablets, ignoring the deep black circles beneath his eyes. He gave little thought to his humiliation of Erika or to the identity of her lover. All that could wait. For now he needed to shower, shave, dress, and be in the office no later than eight-thirty. No time for breakfast. He had to get the report to the typing pool. This evening he would continue her interrogation. No worries, she would be in no condition to cheat on him today.

Oskar held the sedan door open as Horst left the covered portico. Despite the turmoil and excitement in the streets—the cause as yet unknown to him—they made decent time into the city, reaching headquarters by twenty after the hour. His driver dropped him off at the main entrance and left immediately to return home. Horst expected no further use for him during this busy day of in-office work. From the entry hall Horst ascended the broad staircase to the first floor offices. Salutes of *Heil Hitler* from the steel-helmeted SS guards seemed especially enthusiastic this morning, and all of headquarters was ramped up with activity. He couldn't recall ever seeing spirits at the *Gestapa* so high, with hearty congratulations coming from all sides. "What fun to see the people express their true feelings at last," he overheard an officer say.

At the top of the landing he headed directly for the stenographic pool. The clatter of typewriters jarred his edgy nerves. Despite nausea and a pulsing headache he was determined to make the morning's presentation a success. The SS non-com took the protocol in hand and ordered the work divided immediately over the entire available pool. "Ten copies for distribution within the hour, and anything less than perfection will disappoint the Reichsführer-SS." Horst left to prepare himself for meeting with Heydrich. His head throbbed despite the aspirin, and he noted he was sweating profusely. The personal aide waiting outside his office received an order of warm coffee and a roll, no jam or butter. Perhaps caffeine would help.

Klaus Pabst stood before the desk, a file tucked under his arm.

"Didn't I say we'd meet *after* my presentation?" Horst hung his coat and hat and remained standing, impatient with the interruption.

"Sorry, Horst, this can't wait any longer." He moved to shut the office door before placing a single sheet from the folder in front of his superior. Horst was ready to dismiss it out of hand. He recognized the standard form used to document Aryan purity for up to five levels of ancestry. As always, his eyes scanned first for the person whose lineage was in question.

He drew a quick breath at "Leonhardt von Kredow," his own son. Just above stood Horst's own name beside "Erika von Kredow, born Breitling." He ignored his family ancestry and moved up the right side past entries for Erika's parents, stopping at Johann Kessinger, her grandfather in East Prussia. Beside that name stood "Nadia Arens," boldly underlined in red ink. He stared at the further notation in the same pen: "Jewess/Lithuanian/Unmarried."

He eased down into the chair. Only the steady ticking of the wall clock marred the silence. Seconds passed. "A joke." Statement, not question.

"I wish it were, Horst."

The clock ticked on. Horst slowly reexamined each name on the family tree, piecing together the puzzle, considering the ramifications for him and for his career. *Blutschande.* Racial defilement. *Rassenverrat.* Betrayal of race. He sensed a trembling deep in his cheek and consciously steeled himself. *Mischling, 2. Grades.* Betrayed by a fucking Jewish whore. "Verified?" he asked at last.

"Beyond a doubt." Klaus withdrew a three-page document from the file and laid it before Horst. "The interrogation record of the grandfather, a pastor. It seems the holy man dipped his wick at least once in the Lithuanian Jewess."

Horst read through the record, line by line, comparing how he himself might have carried out the questioning. He reached the final notation: "Dispensation of detainee: succumbed to heart attack during interrogation." He looked up from the document. "Who else knows?"

"Our own man in Königsberg may have made the connection, and, of course, the family members in question."

"And you." Horst eyed Klaus carefully. The interrogation record was dated over a week prior. "How long have you known?"

"Some disturbing information came in nine days ago, an inquiry out of the civil records office over there in Königsberg. I hesitated bringing it to your attention, didn't want to distract you from your main project over some false report. Better to investigate first and quash the rumor, right?" Klaus straightened his shoulders. "Had the information proved bogus."

Horst raced through his options. Five years' work on the line—power, stature, career. He seethed. He felt contaminated. *Not even a German Scheissjude,* he thought, *but an Eastern degenerate.* He closed the file and slid it back across the desk, his path determined. His enemies would not hold power over him, and he would salvage the situation. "First, I must tend to Heydrich and the protocol. But I agree this couldn't wait a moment longer. Suppress the matter immediately."

"I'm on it."

"Isolate them both, woman and child, but not here. Get me a secure place outside the city for finishing this." He couldn't bring himself to use names, much less refer to them as wife and son.

"Marburg?"

"Take care of that immediately, as well." He looked at the clock, then stood and straightened his jacket. "I mustn't be late." The aide knocked at the door, breakfast tray in hand. "Later!" Horst barked, adjusting his tie. "And, Klaus?" He turned to regard his friend and subordinate. "Your discretion is appreciated, as always."

"It's what we Wachonians do."

Once Horst was gone Klaus ordered the aide to set the tray on the desk, then sent him off to fetch butter and jam. He sat behind his mentor's desk and poured coffee before lifting the receiver to connect with the switchboard operator.

Oskar received the radio call as he pulled into the drive of the von Kredow mansion. Within minutes he had searched the upper rooms. The pounding of feet on the dressing room wall drew him immediately to Frau von Kredow's bedchamber, where he found Frieda Loos gagged, bound and furious. Once able to speak, the governess told of being knocked unconscious, and revealed that wife and child had undoubtedly left before dawn. She insisted Oskar emphasize that she had made a vigorous attempt at intervention, which was duly noted on the record spread out before Klaus.

An aide's calls to the two taxi dispatch offices providing service to the wealthy neighborhoods near Wannsee confirmed that a woman and small boy had been dropped at Lehrter around five-forty-five that morning. The driver remembered the mother's rambling chatter about Holland, talk of windmills and wooden shoes. The woman appeared uncomfortable and nervous, and had kept the one small valise on the rear seat beside her rather than in its rightful place in the trunk.

A review of *Reichsbahn* departures for Amsterdam that morning focused quickly on the high-speed FD24 as the most likely candidate. Agents at Lehrter were ordered to give immediate attention to the matter. Within minutes Klaus knew that an attractive blonde with a small boy in tow had presented first-class tickets at the checkpoint and boarded the express, which departed Berlin on schedule at 6:55. Klaus relayed orders to Hamburg to have agents board the train upon arrival and take the pair into custody. *Highest priority with no interrogation of detainees; immediate and personal notification of arrest.* He checked the clock. The train was scheduled to arrive momentarily at the Hamburg *Hauptbahnhof.* Klaus leaned back. For years he had imagined proving to Horst that no other subordinate had his interests so fully at heart, that he was Horst's one true friend, the only man worthy of sharing his greatness. That opportunity had arrived at last.

Years before in Marburg, as initiates in the fellowship of the Wachonia fraternity, Klaus and Horst quickly found themselves drawn to the promise of the National Socialist cause. Both despised weakness, and yearned for a strong leader to cut through the selfish in-fighting and lead the country to rediscovered greatness. They shared contempt for the foreign powers that had brought their country down, and hatred of the Jews who controlled the world markets and corrupted the German race. With Horst paving the way, they assumed leadership within the student Nazi organization and began to weed out dissidents in the student body. If someone offended them, Klaus was only too ready to enforce Horst's will. And along the way Klaus found himself drawn under the spell of this remarkable leader of men. His admiration turned to adulation, his respect to devotion.

In 1932, a year before the Nazis gained power over the state, an outspoken member of the student council, an articulate young Jew known to attract Aryan girls, dared publicly ridicule Horst in his bid for the presidency of the council. Pabst saw an opportunity to win favored status in the eyes of von Kredow. He spent two weeks carefully observing the offending student, noting that early every Friday afternoon the Jew boarded a southbound train to Frankfurt, only to return late Sunday. In the third week Klaus made the trip, as well.

Klaus's inspiration came from a history class. Other more important teachings were long forgotten, but he remembered an insignificant aspect of Renaissance rivalries between opposing Italian clans: slender daggers crafted of fine Venetian glass used to assassinate enemies. The thin shard would slip easily in at the base of the neck, just above the collarbone, burying itself deep within the body before snapping off. Extraction was next to impossible without accelerating the already fatal damage. Klaus rummaged in the fraternity house cellar for a Christmas ornament, a glass icicle. He carefully chipped away the tip to create a sharp point, then wrapped the base in cloth to provide a protective handle. Its use proved far messier than anticipated, but the offending Jew caused no further problems for Horst. Or for anyone else.

Klaus became Horst's "dagger." When the leader entered the secret police, Klaus joined as a recruit, as well. When Horst moved to Berlin, Klaus joined him, always one step back, his advancement always a gift from his mentor. The third member of their team, Peter Brenner, was placed—again thanks to Horst—in the Kassel Gestapo office, for he had married a good local girl, a dedicated Nazi.

The behavior of Erika Breitling in Marburg had stunned Klaus. He could not imagine her debasing herself with an American when she had the epitome of German manhood in Horst. Klaus was equally shocked when his mentor married the bitch anyway, and resented that she had borne his child and continued her role in Horst's ascent within the SS hierarchy. She was a useless distraction and potential liability. Now was the moment to see the arrogant woman suffer for humiliating them both. He alone had unmasked her duplicity, and he alone would bask in Horst's gratitude for being the one true friend to save his career and free him of this whore.

Klaus placed calls to Königsberg and the small Gestapo office in Marburg. Satisfied for the moment, he ordered fresh coffee delivered to Horst's desk.

With an expressive venting of steam the locomotive came to rest on Track 3 of the Hamburg main station. The platform was eerily empty of passengers, given the time of morning and the number of travelers who would normally rush to board. Those planning to detrain in Hamburg faced a daunting rank of police and plain-clothes agents stretched along the length of the platform. Another impatient crowd stood behind armed guards blocking access to the tracks. The railroad employees watched from a distance. Their wait was not long.

Gestapo agents climbed swiftly aboard, entering from both the first-class coaches and the lesser carriages at the rear. Moving systematically down the aisles, they scanned each group of passengers. Every woman with a small child was questioned and her personal and travel documents reviewed. Upon seeing the new arrivals board the train the travelers had retaken their seats, hastily shoving luggage back into the racks or pulling it close to their feet. Most stared straight ahead, attempting to appear as innocuous and uninteresting as possible. No one wanted involvement in a police matter. One needed to have nothing to hide in order to fear interrogation and possible arrest.

Mid-train the teams met empty-handed. Notes were compared before the agent in charge placed a call to *Gestapa* Berlin. He reported two mothers traveling with sons at least eight years of age, one woman with a daughter still in diapers, and one governess taking a six-year-old boy to visit his grandparents. None traveled first class. No slender blonde woman with a three-year-old son.

# CHAPTER ELEVEN

The escape from the Amsterdam-bound express had gone as planned, just as the train pulled away from Lehrter platform. In one fluid motion, Ryan had released the latch and swung down onto the lower step of the rail carriage. Holding onto the railing, he dropped their luggage before hopping out. "Now quickly—the boy!" His shout faded beneath the metallic squeal of the turning wheels as the locomotive released another piercing whistle.

Erika held Leo in her arms at the open doorway, gave him a reassuring hug, then handed him into Ryan's waiting arms as he paced the rolling train. Her stomach muscles ached from the strain. With the train now creeping alongside the platform, she made the leap herself, landing with a stumble, her forearm braced tightly across her abdomen.

"You all right?" Ryan noted the grimace cross her face.

She gave him a quick look of reassurance. "Just need more practice at all this," she said.

Leo giggled, then laughed out loud, the first laugh Ryan had heard from the boy. "Let's do that again."

"Not now, my darling." She grabbed the child's hand. "Maybe later."

"Yes, please, every time!"

The hasty exit from the railcar left passers-by gaping in surprise. A trainman in blue uniform glared, offended by the violation of protocol. Erika's quick glance toward the gates reassured that the brown-shirted guards and Gestapo had taken no notice of their surprising action. As she and Ryan had hoped, the gatekeepers were too occupied with newly-arriving passengers to note activity on the platforms, and no alarm had been raised. An older gentleman in a bowler hat and bow tie had narrowly avoided the sudden emergence of luggage and then Ryan. He stopped to help with their two bags while his disgruntled wife huffed her displeasure. Erika offered a quick apology, "Sorry, wrong train."

"Glad to help," he said, tipping his hat to her.

The sullen matron lifted her nose at the impropriety and muttered to no one and everyone, "Unheard of, such behavior!" She led her husband by the arm down the platform, but not before he turned to wink at Erika, who returned his smile. Ryan picked up both boy and bags, and the three headed toward the subterranean passage leading to the S-Bahn interurban connection.

They hoped never to learn if Horst and his cronies had fallen for their ruse and pursued the train to Amsterdam. And should they be captured, nothing would save them anyway. But even a modest head start bought time for a crossing into Strasbourg as tourists, and should things get dicey, they would look to René to get them over the Rhine to France. Kehl may not have been the most direct route west across the border, but it offered the option of private river transport.

Erika told him that Horst knew of their meeting the previous day, but not Ryan's identity or the nature of their rendezvous. Her husband was sure she had taken a lover. Her hands trembled, and she shifted uncomfortably as she briefly described the departure from the house. Ryan realized the attentively-listening boy was preventing her telling the full story. That would have to come later.

With Horst now convinced of her two-timing him, he undoubtedly had agents tasked with her constant surveillance, so the Gestapo was certainly on their scent. Ryan knew from René that an unmatched network of internal spies, field agents and citizen informants made the secret police force nearly omnipresent. And the laws now made the Gestapo omnipotent, as well, free to arrest and condemn at will. The open question was how long it would take them to discover she had left Berlin. Erika suggested Horst might be fully occupied presenting his protocol, and the devastating trouble in the streets might also prove a distraction. And with the governess confined to the closet, it was even possible they might reach the border crossing before anyone raised an alarm. They agreed that was their best hope.

Ryan however was privately less confident that time was on their side. Horst was no fool, and he would know she would never leave her parents behind. The detour to Marburg could prove fatal, but he could not bring himself to object. They were after all her parents. Yet Ryan accepted his decision to risk all for Erika and Leo. He thought of his loss and regret after Isabel's disappearance, and he knew the brutality of the Reich. And now—more than ever—he was determined to send back to Washington proof of their diabolical plan.

They rode the elevated S-Bahn in silence, looking down upon the littered streets of the city. While the chaos of the early morning hours had abated, the destruction remained. Ryan caught himself glancing nervously around the interurban car. At the Friedrichstrasse Station they took a taxi to Potsdamer Bahnhof, the ride bringing them perilously close to Gestapo headquarters. Ryan bought first-class tickets to Frankfurt via Kassel, the group posing as a family. If the ruse at Lehrter Station had worked its magic, the Gestapo was on a wild goose chase toward Holland. However, if Horst was on to them, he might now assume his wife traveled with her "lover." He recalled the Nazi's unrelenting vengeance in Marburg. Were von Kredow to learn that his wife was with the same American he had tried to destroy years before, there would truly be hell to pay. And now a nation of thugs did his bidding.

Their compartment on the express out of Potsdamer Station was temporarily free of other travelers. Once the train reached the Berlin outskirts, Erika and Ryan moved to sit across from each other at the aisle door. From this vantage they could better spot the approach of any third party, whether passenger, train official, or police agent. Leo, fascinated by the heavy rail traffic, claimed the window seat vacated by his mother. Perched on the edge, he pressed his face to the glass to get the best view of the locomotives.

Ryan's concern for Erika's physical condition grew, but he held back his questions with Leo so near. Her movements lacked her customary grace, and occasionally she pressed a hand against her belly, her pain obvious. She had winced when changing seats, and now he noticed the ligature marks visible through her dark stockings. He repressed his anger, biding his time. "You doing okay?" he reached over the aisle to squeeze her hand.

She nodded, but her unease was apparent. He hoped Leo would sleep soon. Having risen early, he should tire before long.

"First, the camera," said Ryan, checking the corridor. Erika opened her handbag and handed him the Minox, masking it in the palm of her hand. Under the cover of his topcoat he rewound the film and removed the cartridge. Scarcely larger than a postage stamp, its value would be measured in countless innocent lives.

He spread out a newspaper picked up on the S-Bahn, *Der Stürmer*, a typical anti-Semitic caricature glaring from the front page. He unzipped his tobacco pouch and shook the contents out onto the newssheet. The previous afternoon he had purchased a similar pouch along with scissors and rubber cement. Now he slid the cartridge beneath the false bottom he had crafted, quickly refilled the pouch, and set the newspaper aside. He glanced over to see if Leo had noticed, but the child's eyes still followed the scenery racing past. Ryan hefted the small pouch and felt along its length and depth. Anyone looking at its contents would see only tobacco. Anyone grabbing the pouch by the mid-section would feel only tobacco. But anyone clever enough to squeeze along the bottom seam would undoubtedly question a solid object hidden there. It would have to do.

The next step was equally important. He nodded to Erika. Once again they checked the corridor. No one approached. She withdrew two small objects from her handbag which she handed over to him. The first was burnished silver in color: the oval Gestapo warrant badge assigned to Horst von Kredow.

To the German public, this badge, stamped with the Nazi eagle and swastika and bearing a distinctive identification number, represented unlimited power to arrest without provocation and convict without trial. According to Erika, Horst now found his badge unnecessary and rarely carried it. A man with his clout found no daily need for the identification disc, so his medallion rested routinely in the leather-covered case in his study. Until last evening. Ryan secured the gold chain to his waistcoat and tucked the ovoid disc into his vest pocket. He hoped he wouldn't have to use it, but Erika had told him during their planning session that he should carry it, "just in case."

"My father has one of those. Are you a policeman, too?" Leo watched Ryan with great curiosity.

Ryan glanced quickly at Erika, momentarily at a loss for words. "Can you keep a secret, Leo?" Ryan asked in a loud whisper, and Leo nodded. "Then sit here beside me, because we must be very careful who's listening." Ryan set the newspaper aside, patted the seat next to him, and lowered his voice conspiratorially. "I am indeed a secret policeman, and my job is to make sure you both have a safe trip. Will you help me with that?"

"I help *Mutti* all the time." Leo's eyes shone with excitement at sharing a secret. "So I can help you, too, because you're *Mutti's* friend." He smiled up at Ryan, all shyness gone.

"Well, here's how you help: not a word to anyone about our secret, and do exactly what your mother asks. You'll be my assistant policeman, all right?"

Leo nodded in agreement, obviously pleased with the prospect, before something more pressing came to mind. He turned to Erika. "I'm hungry." Erika realized they had not eaten anything since leaving the house that morning. With only a few squares of chocolate to satisfy his hunger, the boy had patiently passed several hours with no breakfast. She rummaged through the handbag in search of more chocolate.

Ryan smiled and took two wrapped sandwiches from his topcoat. "I hope you both like ham and cheese. I picked them up at Lehrter. Know what, Leo? I'm getting hungry, too." He handed one to the boy, the other to Erika, who smiled in gratitude for his thoughtfulness. "At Magdeburg we've a ten-minute stop. I'll jump off and get something more filling for everybody. Meanwhile, let me see if there's something to drink from the dining car."

Leo approved the idea with a nod, his mouth already filled with sandwich. He swung his feet against the bench as he chewed.

Ryan affixed the second object taken from Horst's study to his lapel. Its gold on burgundy lettering encircled a black swastika on white ground. Ryan was now a credible member of the Nazi Party, with an expensive pin to prove it. He opened the compartment door and disappeared up the corridor. As he crossed the vestibule he dropped a small package in a waste bin, the Minox camera, wrapped securely in the SS propaganda sheet.

Minna Breitling doubted Parisian breakfast rolls would ever be as appealing as the fresh poppy seed rolls she carried in a thin paper sack. Early each day but Sunday she left their home in the Barfüsserstrasse and walked four streets over to Lauschner's Bakery. The yeasty aroma of freshly-baked bread drew her from a block away, and Minna appreciated Frau Lauschner's friendly gift of two cinnamon buns, always added without charge to her standing order of *Brötchen*.

In the apartment, Joachim would already be taking the good china from the credenza and preparing their morning coffee. By now he would have set out butter and preserves, sugar and cream. For the last two weeks she had insisted they use the heirloom pieces every day, and this morning she directed him to also take out the fine silver cutlery for breakfast.

She had often said one never knew in life when things could change and finer things would have to be left behind. Now she knew. This day at noon, she and Joachim would join their daughter and grandson at the station and leave Germany. She could only assume forever. She fought back the tears, distracting herself by holding the bag of warm rolls to her nose, appreciating the aroma. She had asked Joachim to uncover the last of the marble cake, as well. It would be a hearty breakfast, befitting a long trip to who-knows-where and who-knows-what. But it was a journey fate had scheduled for them, and they would not miss their train.

The streets were littered with shattered glass. Crude graffiti marred the ancient stone walls and sidewalks. *Out with the Jews.* She wondered how many of her acquaintances actually believed that she and her physician husband—he who had unknowingly married a half-Jew—truly presented some threat to the Reich and their personal well-being. *The Jews are our misfortune.* It did not matter. Their being baptized Lutherans held no meaning, for this bigotry was all about perceived race, not religion. Their leaders had decreed it so, and the people were content to condemn the Jews and banish them from their midst, or allow others to do it for them.

Pallid smoke from Marburg's synagogue drifted through the narrow streets. The Krauthammers from 1A had stopped her on the landing to share the exciting news of the torching. "High time," they had said with great enthusiasm. Frau Krauthammer was their block warden and took her role very seriously, diligent in completing the monthly loyalty reports on each of the forty or so households in her domain. Minna had merely nodded politely in passing and hastened on her shopping errand.

As their apartment building came into view her heart missed a beat. A large black sedan rolled to a stop before her stoop and several armed men ran up to the entrance. Minna stood frozen on the pavement, her hand to her mouth, in full sight of the police. The bag of rolls lay on the cobbles. She knew there would be no final Marburg breakfast. She forced herself back into the side street and peered cautiously around the corner, her heart racing out of fear for her husband. The agents disappeared as someone buzzed them in.

She counted the familiar steps in her mind as she visualized their ascent to her apartment. She knew they would have no need to break down the door. She knew that dear Joachim would protest loudly, but not fight the inevitable. It seemed forever, but within minutes they emerged from the building, shoving her husband and forcing him into the back of the car. They had not even allowed him his hat. Frau Krauthammer followed on their heels, ever ready to help. Minna heard her shout while pointing up the street in her direction: "She's at Lauschner's, she should be right back." Two men stationed themselves just inside the entry as the car with her husband raced away.

Minna backed down the alley, her vision blurred by tears. She had left him this morning without a kiss. At the train station she took little notice of the milling crowds, the worried mood. She stood patiently in line and bought a ticket and immediately passed through the control gate onto the covered platform. There she sat hunched on a bench, watching and waiting, fearful of discovery.

# CHAPTER TWELVE

The insight struck Horst as he crossed the red carpet of Heydrich's office—*management of anger is no different than management of chronic pain.* Acknowledge that the anger must be dealt with over the long run. Focus instead on the challenges at hand to allow effective action. Make decisions to the steady drumbeat of the anger, but don't allow it to determine them. *A personal recipe for success.*

The presentation in Heydrich's ceremonial office went well. Heydrich, Müller, and Eichmann had kept Horst waiting briefly in the antechamber before an aide led him to the long conference table. There were a few other SS advisors present, and each attendee had before him a copy of the protocol. Horst laid out the basic concepts and reviewed the projections, and was well-prepared for their questions. The gravity of the moment overcame both his headache and pressing personal concerns. Heydrich appeared distracted, but pleased overall. Happily, the value of Horst's proposal was self-evident to all in attendance. Millions of Jews and agitators could not stand in the way of Germany's need for *Lebensraum,* material resources, and racial purity.

They congratulated him on a job well done, and at the close of the meeting the reason for Heydrich's somewhat somber mood became clear. Horst learned that *Gestapa Berlin* had been in the dark about the *Kristallnacht* project until around midnight. Since neither Himmler nor Heydrich were forewarned of Dr. Goebbels' vast propaganda undertaking, they resented the Führer's having by-passed them and their input. They had only become involved after the fact, and then only secondarily. Publically, Hitler was denying any support for this "spontaneous outburst" of anti-Jewish sentiment among the German people. They all knew better.

Only a few modest changes to detail, and Horst's plan would now move on to Himmler. Heydrich made clear that actual implementation appeared a long-term prospect, but they would be ready with training completed and contingencies removed, once Hitler gave his go-ahead to move east.

Now Horst sat once again in his own office and took more pressing matters in hand. Solving his personal Jewish problem was only a question of time. He controlled resources ready-made to apprehend anyone who thought to outwit or outrun the Secret State Police. His people could watch every airport, every rail station, every border crossing. Snitches and lackey block wardens were everywhere, anxious to please. He had authority to commandeer local police, SS, military, whatever necessary. But this action demanded greater discretion, minimal involvement, a subtler approach. And he would take advantage of the uproar across the Reich to cover his personal enterprise.

"Of course she'd try to save her parents. Don't be a fool; she'll head straight for Marburg." He looked up from the report and addressed Klaus. "Paris via Amsterdam? What idiocy to fall for that, and we certainly didn't require that show of force in Hamburg. The last thing I want right now is wide-spread attention. Discretion, Klaus, discretion!"

Pabst ignored the brusque tone. Horst's self-control was commendable—he had witnessed it many times before—but he could tell that his friend was deeply affected by the strange turn of events. "The Amsterdam lead simply couldn't be ignored, Horst. We now have agents checking all the other rail stations, as well."

"Tempelhof?"

"No one matching the description on any morning flights. I directed special attention to departures for Kassel or Frankfurt, but all passenger lists were reviewed. I'm thinking auto or rail."

"The roads are too slow except on the *Autobahn* stretches, but check the limousine services all the same. She's underway now for sure. I'd lay money on rail, so we'll take them at the Marburg end. What of the parents?"

"Father's detained, mother still unaccounted for. Out fetching baked goods when they nabbed the professor. But Marburg's small enough, she'll be picked up soon. We've put out a city-wide search, and our agents are waiting to welcome her at the station and then meet all southbound trains. A tight net—they won't get through."

"The orders still clear on no interrogation?"

"No interrogation, Horst. Detention without access until we arrive."

"Absolute discretion here."

"Understood."

"If someone does make the connection with my name, use the 'protective detention' cover. Say the damn Jews are trying to get at me. With all that's going on, anyone will buy that."

The only factor complicating quick containment was the ongoing action on the streets. Local and regional authorities had their hands full that morning. Reports verified a major round-up of Jews for the concentration camps, destruction of hundreds of synagogues and shops throughout the Reich, and an adequate number of fatalities to rattle all the Jewish cages. Fresh dispatches were brought in by an aide, and Klaus scanned the pages. He immediately glanced over to Horst but said nothing.

"Progress?"

"Report from a control at Potsdamer Station. Man, early thirties, American passport, accompanying a slender German woman, blonde, with small boy. They recall a 'von' in the woman's name."

"American?" His voice steady, neutral.

"American," Klaus nodded, "confirmed first-class tickets to Frankfurt via Kassel, departed at 7:53." A glance at the wall clock, then the train schedule. "Somewhere between Magdeburg and Göttingen by now."

Horst tapped a steady drumbeat on the desktop with his fountain pen. He reached up with the other hand and carefully drew his index finger down the length of his scar, fractionally above the raised surface. He almost smiled. *Ryan Lemmon.*

# CHAPTER THIRTEEN

D ieter Sprenger was on top of the world. It certainly wasn't the
weather that buoyed his spirits. Clouds hung low overhead, he
bent his head against a biting wind blowing in off the Baltic, and the
acrid smell of torched buildings still etched his sinuses. But Dieter
was pleased with his successful night. Informed of the national action against the Jews after midnight, he had taken it upon himself to
rally Brownshirts and Hitler youth to hit targets in the southern
district of the city. Now, as he strolled through the streets and took
in the devastation to shop fronts and plate glass, he congratulated
himself on his personal contribution to this spontaneous outpouring
of hatred on such short notice. He anticipated praise and perhaps
more when he arrived at Gestapo headquarters.

He had returned home to change clothes, the stench of smoke
deep in the fabric of his suit and topcoat. Strangely, he wasn't regretting a night of missed sleep. The adrenaline had not worn thin. His
dear Anneliese had prepared a hearty breakfast, supplementing the
usual fresh rolls and coffee with soft-boiled eggs, slices of Tilsiter
and Edamer cheese, and some fresh liverwurst from Heinlen's on the
corner.

Before he left home he peeked in on the children. Liesl had decided to keep them out of school today because of the destruction in
the streets. She didn't want to unduly upset them. They were both a
bit young to understand the real danger posed by the Jews, she felt.
And there was always the chance that they might encounter some
residual protests on the walk to school, or cut themselves on broken
glass. Both little Dieter and Leni still slept peacefully. Liesl had men-

tioned over breakfast that the loud cries and breaking glass during the night had disturbed their rest. Dieter kissed each on the head. Ah, the soft fragrance of well-scrubbed children. He then gave his wife a quick peck and a big hug before setting out into the cold.

Dieter Sprenger knew the day's work schedule would be full. Hundreds of Jewish agitators and political targets had been rounded up in the early morning hours. His role in operations would now give way to hours of interrogation in the basement cells, extracting confessions and finding links to other enemies of the Reich. It would be good, satisfying work. Liesl had once asked if it bothered him to use extreme measures on the detainees. He had laughed at the thought. He told her this *Dreck* would destroy her and the kids given half a chance. His work was for the cause of German purity and national pride, and she and the children should be proud of him in turn.

His spirits high, Dieter wrapped his woolen scarf a bit more tightly around his neck and pulled his hat down to keep the brim from catching in the wind. Only a few vehicles moved through the neighborhood, even though it was past mid-morning. He chose his usual shortcut along an industrial boulevard. The street, bordered by warehouse buildings, was nearly empty of life. He took little notice of the few vehicles parked along his customary route. The one most important in the life of Dieter Sprenger was a dark Horch sedan. It rolled quietly from the curb just after he passed. He barely noticed the movement, his thoughts on an anticipated promotion for the night's work. As the car gained momentum he heard the unexpected revving of the engine and turned his head in time to see the massive headlamps and grill just meters from the small of his back. His morning went dark.

Warmth flowed down his face and pooled around his head where it rested on the pavement. He smelled the ocean, the beach on a warm, sunny day. His eyeglasses were gone and his vision blurred, but he sensed a fire hydrant pressed against his body and considered the perverse notion that he was somehow embracing it. He heard gushing water, waves pounding on a distant shore. The Horch shifted gears and its right tire backed over his legs. The gears meshed once again and the sedan rolled up over his back as it sped away. He realized then that he had no feeling in his limbs. The day was far less glorious now. Dieter felt his mind graying, losing itself in the overcast. He thought of his wife, cleaning up the breakfast dishes. He thought of his children, still tucked in their warm beds. The taste of the fresh liverwurst lingered at the back of his mouth.

As he lay dying, there were no thoughts of the many detainees he had questioned so thoroughly in the basement rooms, and certainly no recollection of the old pastor whose wracked body had made such a mess of his table. He would never link that one interrogation to this unfortunate end.

The train slowed for the scheduled stop at Magdeburg. Ryan left his companions in the compartment for a quick dash to the station restaurant. No sooner had the carriage doors opened than he was on the platform heading for the canteen. Erika watched him carve a path through the throng of people, obviously offering apologies right and left as he pushed forward through the crowd.

The platform was awash in humanity. Many of the travelers appeared to be fleeing the turmoil in the city. She and Ryan had briefly spoken of the horrible Jew-baiting and destruction witnessed that morning, but they had hoped to keep Leo's attention elsewhere. It was an impossible task. Those hoping to board were harried by SA troops and plainclothes policemen, and many of the refugees were being turned back before reaching the trains. A woman collapsed at the gate in tears, her small children gathering about her trying to give comfort as two men brusquely grabbed her arms and forced her to rise.

Leo asked what those people had done wrong, and she was at a loss to explain. "Some people think they shouldn't be allowed to stay here, Leo, others think they shouldn't be allowed to leave." He looked at her quizzically. It all made no sense, and she knew it. So they just watched.

Her body ached from the brutality of the night before, but her focus was on saving her son and parents, so she forced herself to set aside her own physical suffering and concentrate on the moment at hand. She knew she would heal, assuming they got away.

The door to the compartment opened, and a middle-aged man asked if the empty seats were unoccupied. He carried an over-stuffed suitcase, its straps fighting the bulging contents and its colorful decals of tourist destinations helping hold it all together. His smile was warm and genuine.

"Of course," she said, seeing no option but to grant him one of the free seats.

"Then I'll join you," he said, hanging topcoat and hat on a hook and hefting the well-traveled bag into the overhead rack. "Quite the mess outside today, don't you think?" He gestured to the activity beyond the window.

"It's frightful," she replied. "One doesn't feel safe." Erika's words were ambivalent, the inevitable wariness with strangers. One never knew.

"I, for one, wish they'd ship the lot of them off to Palestine." The stranger smiled serenely. "And soon. I do hear they're doing a better job of it in the Ostmark already. Grab the bull by the horns, that's my motto." He took a seat next to the door. "But at least today's a good beginning." She remained silent. Leo looked at him with interest. She knew the boy appreciated the stranger's smile, a pleasant change from the downturned faces he was seeing that day.

Ryan suddenly stood at the door, his arms filled with sandwiches, salt-encrusted pretzels, bottles of beer and lemonade. Erika saw his fleeting surprise at finding a new passenger in their compartment. He greeted the stranger and took the window seat opposite Erika and the boy. The conductor called for final boarding, and the carriage doors slammed shut. Ryan distributed the food, offering one of the sandwiches to the man. He declined politely, patting his belly and protesting that he had just eaten. Leo chewed hungrily, while Erika nibbled distractedly at a pretzel, all the while trying to catch Ryan's eye and warn him of the danger.

"Are you enjoying a nice train trip with your mommy and daddy?" The man smiled at Leo.

"This is my *Mutti*," Leo corrected him politely, "but this isn't my father. This is a good friend of *Mutti*." There was an embarrassing silence, as Ryan and Erika exchanged quick glances. The stranger's face went blank.

"My father is a policeman," Leo continued undeterred. "But—and this is a secret, so don't tell anyone—Mommy's friend is also a *secret* policeman, too. They both have badges."

Erika held her breath.

The man smiled wanly and looked out toward the aisle. Silence ruled. Leo went back to chewing. Erika and Ryan stared at each other, polite smiles frozen on their faces. The man glanced nervously at his watch, as if remembering an important appointment elsewhere. Abruptly he rose from the bench. "You will excuse me, but..." The sentence remained unfinished. The stranger pulled down his bag, grabbed his coat and hat, and stepped out of the compartment. *"Auf Wiedersehen."* His voice was muffled by a swift retreat down the aisle.

"No one likes a secret policeman," Ryan said.

"I like secret policemen," Leo said through a mouthful of sandwich, not looking up. He took a sip of lemonade. Traveling with a three-year-old could spell trouble. Ryan and Erika shook their heads in relief.

Looking out at the passing countryside Erika picked out a plume of smoke rising from a town in the distance. On a railroad siding, armed Brownshirts shoved a small group of men up onto the bed of a canvas-covered truck. Their mouths moved soundlessly as the train sped past, a silent film with no musical accompaniment. But in their expressions and gestures she read rudeness, brutality.

Weary and desperate travelers thronged the station, their baggage heaped in piles left and right. If she waited too long, if too many trains arrived and departed, Minna Breitling feared drawing the attention of the police and Brownshirts milling about, hassling travelers who looked Jewish, or just distressed. The police dogs were especially disturbing. She loved animals, but these Alsatian wolf dogs, straining against their leashes, barking constantly and flinging saliva from their jowls, put her already tested nerves on edge. Smoke from the locomotives chuffing past caused her stomach to churn.

She thought of the missed breakfast with her husband. Now lunchtime had come and gone, but she had no appetite, no desire to enter the station and find something to eat. She wondered where he would be by now, what cruelties were already inflicted on the man she loved so much. Whether he would suffer long, or go quickly.

Huddled against the chill on a platform bench, she took a slip of paper from her handbag and began to write. Her hand unsteady, she held the paper firmly against the side of the bag to keep the note legible. Despite the cold she pulled off her gloves to better control the pen. Minna glanced once again at the arrivals board. In only a few minutes the express from Berlin would make its stop. She would see her daughter and grandson.

# DIE FALLE
## The Trap

10 November 1938

# CHAPTER ONE

Heavy-set and with tobacco-stained teeth, watery eyes and a nose distorted by multiple breaks, Josef "Sepp" Kreisler did not make a great first impression, and he knew it. Those who had a beer with him often regretted sticking around for a second or third, for he was a mean drunk. Only his partner Ewald Fischer found some pleasure in his company, for they shared similar tastes.

Sepp had been the grammar school bully, an unemployed thug when he dropped out. Finally apprenticed to a machinist, he lost his temper one day and took out his frustration on the journeyman teaching him use of the hydraulic press. He spent two years in prison for assault. The machinist would spend the rest of his days with only one hand. Once out of prison, he found his true fellowship in the budding Nazi party in Munich. What greater pleasure than the camaraderie found in drinking and picking on weaklings and traitors to the German cause? While the rousing speech-making of their leader Adolf Hitler went mostly over his head, he knew the long-winded harangues ultimately led to unrestrained head-bashing in beer halls and on the streets. Soon after the National Socialists took control of Germany, Sepp discovered his niche. Upon consolidation of the Reich police forces he was recruited to the Gestapo as a field agent in Kassel.

This past night Sepp had been in his element. A late call had summoned them both to the station house where he received a hastily-typed list of names and addresses. He and Ewald then spent long hours rousting Jews from their beds. Behind each new door on their list they hoped to find a young wife or attractive daughter still in her bedclothes. Twice they felt obliged to do "medical exams," as they called them, and while nothing incriminating was ever found hidden in those secret places, it was still far more entertaining than the mundane herding of protesting men to the curb.

By the first light of morning Kreisler and Fischer could not resist adding fuel to the fire at Kassel's main synagogue. A military motorcycle with sidecar had just delivered cans of kerosene to the site, and they bent their backs to help, dousing the wooden chairs and altar with fuel. A young rabbi tried to protect his precious scrolls from going up in smoke, and the strength of his resistance surprised the agents. Most Jews protested loudly but gave in to the inevitability of arrest when push came to shove. The two agents punished him all the more for not surrendering docilely to their blows.

Back at headquarters, Kreisler handed over his list to the duty sergeant with every name scratched out in pencil. Sepp and Ewald were ready for coffee and breakfast, and then some well-deserved sleep, but no sooner were coffee cups filled than Captain Brenner entered the break room, military posture perfect, as always.

"So you really are the only two in?" His expression soured.

"Just us. All taken care of, Captain, a good night's work," Ewald said.

"Well then, you two get the prize. You're headed out again, and take a car."

"But, sir—" Sepp was exhausted, ready to head home and hit the cot.

"Don't want to hear it, Kreisler." He looked around distractedly, making no effort to mask his disappointment at seeing his options devolve to these two agents standing at the hotplate. "Believe me, if I could pull in another team they'd already be on the way. This won't wait, so the two of you are it."

Sepp and Ewald saved their grumbling until the captain left the room. They were to proceed immediately to the main station and surveil all arriving southbound trains. Their target was a slender blonde woman in her twenties accompanied by a small boy, thought to be en route with an American in his thirties of above-average height and slim of build. The rules of engagement were simple: do not engage. Observe and follow, with regular updates to the captain for immediate relay to Berlin *Gestapa*. Should detention of the suspects become unavoidable, isolate mother and child from any male companion, then take no further action without specific instructions from Berlin. Under no circumstances interrogate. A reception team would be waiting in Frankfurt to make the arrest.

For the first time Sepp had an assignment of apparent top-level importance. If time off wasn't in the cards, at least he might finally be able to show he was more than just muscle, someone they'd have to reckon with.


The three engines of the Junkers-52 roared as the police Mercedes crossed the airfield and pulled up beneath one silver wing. Oskar stepped out to get von Kredow's door, but Horst was already bounding up the steps, signaling the pilot to get moving. Klaus barely had time to find a seat onboard before the plane was airborne from Tempelhof.

Horst admired his own self-control. Should word get out that his much-admired wife was a Jewess—worse yet, an *Ostjüdin*, her blood tainted with the racial characteristics of the degenerate Eastern European Jew—his rising star in the Nazi firmament would flame out. The ironic link between the morning's protocol presentation and his current dilemma didn't escape him. Some in the regime held less stringently to the Party's anti-Semitic laws and teachings, but Himmler certainly wasn't one to respect degrees of racial pollution, and neither was Horst.

The city below dissolved in cloud as the sky cleared to blue. The growl of the engines made conversation with Klaus impossible, but they had little to discuss for the moment anyway. Klaus had done well to uncover this treachery and bring it quietly to his attention. Anyone else in the Gestapa would have used it to manipulate him, to bring him down.

Erika's attempt to divert their attentions to the northern route through Hamburg had been simplistic, but would play into his hands, giving the fugitives a false sense of security. At Kassel his agents would board. At Marburg the Jew-bitch would find her parents missing, but have no option but continue on toward France, their obvious goal. In a couple of hours he would personally welcome the little group at the Frankfurt *Hauptbahnhof*.

His father-in-law, long held in contempt, was out of the picture. The professor had never favored the marriage, and made little attempt to disguise his dislike of Horst. Now he would pay for that impudence. The mother-in-law now in hiding would wait until the last moment before attempting a rendezvous with daughter and grandson. She would never reach the platform.

*Ryan Lemmon*, the name an obscenity on his tongue. How he had raged when the American made good his escape from Marburg, tail between his legs. And now the coward was screwing her again. Horst wondered how long she had been affronting him with impunity. Marrying the whore had seemed the best revenge for her first indiscretion. Then Horst had used her for his personal gain, and thereafter made her life miserable.

Obviously, that hadn't been enough, so this time he would crush her spirit before he eliminated her for good. Taking the parents and child would be the first step. The Führer liked a good family man, but Leo had proved a weak child of limited value to Horst's rise. A plausible cover story would be crafted—the accidental loss of wife and son—and the grieving father would be admired for seeing beyond his personal loss to carry on undeterred for the Reich.

So many tools and techniques to consider, many of Horst's own devising, others gleaned from medieval witch hunts and the Spanish Inquisition, efficient means to bring out exquisite agonies, wretched pleas, final cries for a compassionate end to the suffering. He had trained a lifetime for this moment. The parents, the lover, the child, finally Erika herself. It would be slow and exquisite pleasure for him.

Lost in these thoughts, he realized he had become aroused.

The station clock read 2:23 as the express from Berlin squealed to a stop on Track 2 at the Kassel station, precisely on schedule. Erika, facing forward as the train brakes shrieked, rose in surprise when she spotted Minna sitting on the platform bench. "Mother's here, not in Marburg!" Her whisper almost inaudible. "Ryan, watch Leo for me." She was out of the cabin before he could move to the window.

"Where's *Mutti* going?" Leo rubbed his sleep-filled eyes.

"She'll be right back."

He glanced at the timetable. Seven minutes in Kassel. While the child slept, Erika had finally described the torture and rape. He reached for his pipe, only to return it to his pocket. He leaned out for a better look. The air was chill, the skies overcast, a promise of rain not yet delivered. The crowd was not as frenzied as at previous stops, but numerous travelers and refugees were lining up to board. Erika dodged passengers and luggage handlers to fall into her mother's embrace. Minna's hair hung disheveled beneath her hat, and even from a distance she appeared distraught. Though he could not hear their words, they appeared to argue, repeatedly shaking heads and gesturing toward the train. Both dabbed at tears. Minna had no luggage and appeared to be alone. He scanned the length of the platform for the professor.

Leo stood on the seat, teaching his bear handstands on the luggage rack above his head. "Can you see *Mutti?*"

"Yes, she's with your grandmother. They'll join us soon."

"*Grossmutti's* here?" Leo bound past Ryan to the window. "*Omi!* Over here," he shouted, leaning halfway out the lowered window, "*Omi*, hurry up, the train's going to leave without you." Down the platform a large man in an overcoat turned toward the open carriage window and caught sight of the small boy. He followed the child's gaze toward the two women, and a smile creased his face. Turning to his companion, he pointed in their direction and mouthed something. His partner immediately cut a quick path to the public phone and grabbed the receiver. The warning came from the conductor to board.

Ryan pulled Leo from the exposed window into the shadows and held the boy firmly in his arms. Erika still tried to draw her mother toward the train, but the older woman refused, taking a stand. She gave her daughter some folded paper and prodded her to leave. Erika headed toward their carriage, then returned to Minna on the run and forced an object from her handbag into her mother's hand. Without looking back again Erika boarded the train as the doors slammed and the trainman's whistle pierced the cold air. Ryan watched the grandmother turn away before the train left the station behind. Standing well back in the compartment, the boy still in his arms, Ryan also observed the two men reunite and run to board the last car as the train slowly gained speed.

Minna had taken refuge behind a rusted iron column supporting the platform canopy. Through tears streaming down her face and a gap in the metal latticework she watched the train move out of sight. Her arrest was imminent. She could never return to Marburg and the apartment shared those many years with her beloved Joachim. There was no place to hide. Rumors of his arrest would have spread through the *Altstadt*, riding the morning gossip from the likes of the Krauthammers. Police would be watching for her everywhere. Hessen had been a hotbed of anti-Semitism well before last night's riots, and without Joachim, other options were not worth exploring.

Drying her eyes with a handkerchief, Minna sought out the women's room. She stood before the mirror and applied a little rouge to her cheeks, shaking her head in disgust at the swollen eyes and the deep worry lines of her brow. She fixed her hair in place beneath the hat. "Soon, my darling," she whispered to a memory.

She entered a cubicle and took from her pocket the small box Erika had forced into her hand. Thoughts of her days as a medical student flooded back. She imagined the hours spent in the clinic, falling in love with handsome Joachim as he made his rounds with her in tow. She removed the hypodermic and morphine, filled the syringe to capacity and eased the needle into a vein. Then, quickly, before she surrendered to the fear, she filled the syringe a second time and completed her task.

The paraphernalia fell to the tiled floor as she slowly sank to rest beside the toilet, drowsiness overtaking her quickly. *So much gentler than falling before a train,* she thought through the haze.

"Join me, my love," a murmur in the fading light.

# CHAPTER TWO

Erika slumped to the floor of the vestibule, sobbing. She unfolded the note and held it to the light, reading through her tears:

> *My dearest Erika,*
>
> *We know H. will never allow us to survive to speak of his "defilement." That he has had the privilege to be married to a brilliant, beautiful woman and to father an adorable son means nothing next to his bigotry and unbridled ambition.*
>
> *Your father's fate is sealed. He has helped men released from the camps, and knows of their mistreatment and degradation— of the deaths. He knows what awaits him, as do I.*
>
> *All that matters now is that you and Leo find refuge as this nightmare takes its chosen course. The outside world will not help us. Our own neighbors will disavow us to save themselves. This we understand. Fear rules our lives under these people.*
>
> *We have lived and loved as few others. We go together no matter what ensues. We are scientists, not believers. Yet I still sense I shall soon rejoin your father.*
>
> *This we have agreed, knowing that such a moment could come, and we will not slow you down in your flight. Be safe, knowing you are loved forever.*
>
> *Your adoring Mother and Father*

Erika was wracked by despair, her hope for her parents shattered, helpless in the face of such power and hatred.

Ryan found her slumped against the vestibule wall, face buried in her hands. He held Leo by one hand, the other grasping the valises. "What's the matter, Mutti, why are you so sad?" Leo put his fingers to her cheek and gently touched her tears.

She stood and picked him up, rocking him gently. "It's all right, everything's fine." Ryan handed her his handkerchief.

"We're out of time." Ryan's voice loud, the wheels rattling and squealing on the track below. "They're on to us."

"Who?"

"Two Gestapo, coming this way, now. Don't know if they saw me, but they spotted you and Leo. We have minutes at most."

"Where are *Omi* and *Grosspapa?*" Leo began to weep, wrapping his arms around her neck and tucking his head beneath her chin.

"What'll we do? We've nowhere to go on this damned train!" She shook her head in frustration and weakness.

"Go as far forward as possible with the bags. The agents boarded at the rear. They'll pass me before they reach you, and I'll stop them anyway I can. Whatever happens, the two of you get off at Marburg; it's the next stop."

"And do what? Where do we go from here?" Her voice now flat with resignation.

"Call René." Ryan jotted down the numbers. "Memorize this and destroy the paper. Now go."

"Ryan, I..." she bit her lower lip, "thanks."

"We're in this together. Now go!" He gave a smile he didn't feel and ushered them into the aisle. "We *will* make this work." Ryan watched them move up the corridor to the first forward compartment before he entered the rearmost cabin of the car, relieved to find it empty. He took the seat nearest the door. He would look the agents in the eye as they approached. Perhaps he would have a few moments to prepare.

The self-defense training in Virginia now seemed ludicrous. *An actual weapon would be nice.* He recalled a couple of schoolyard encounters with bullies, a black eye here and bruised knuckles there, a beer hall skirmish in Berlin. College boxing, welterweight, a lark, but these types were heavyweights, and no referee to call things off when things got rough. Track and field, that was his style: run like hell, vault over obstacles, go for the finish. Not pounding fists and broken limbs. *What the hell's keeping them?* Memories of Isabel flooded back: the fight in the warehouse, flailing bats and broken bottles, brass knuckles to the belly, Isabel's furious kicks, her love of danger. *Why had he let her go it alone?*

He had always been the diplomat rather than the soldier. Now he had volunteered to spy, and circumstances were forcing him to fight. At any moment licensed bullies would come to arrest Erika and the boy. Did they already know about him, as well? The Hamburg train ruse had bought them nothing. *What in God's name could be stalling them? They should've passed by now.* A small station clicked by, a blur of passengers waiting for local trains. He checked the pocket timetable. They had to come at any moment, the Marburg stop just minutes away. His heart raced. *What in the hell are they waiting for?* This time there would be no running.

Sepp Kreisler looked up in surprise at the sudden rush of sound as their compartment door opened. He bolted to attention, his partner following suit. "Heil Hitler!" His cigarette smoldered at his feet. The tall Gestapo officer wore authority on his lapel. The Party pin was richly tooled, jewelry rather than mere emblem. The suit of heavy wool appeared expensively cut. The man glanced around the compartment before stepping into the confined space. Sepp immediately spotted the finely-worked gold chain running from vest to the warrant badge in the man's hand. The officer rubbed the metal disc distractedly between thumb and forefinger.

"Identify yourselves, gentlemen." *A Prussian asshole, but one to be reckoned with.*

"Kreisler, sir, and my partner Fischer. Out of the Kassel office." He crushed the dropped cigarette with his heel. *These full-of-shit, educated SS types never dirty their hands with real street action.*

"As so often, what we have here is a duplication of effort. The woman and child are forward in first-class in my custody. Is headquarters up to speed?"

"Yes, sir, I personally phoned our captain." Ewald was looking to be named in the officer's after-action report. "He'll have let Berlin know by now, as directed. We're to observe only, at least till Frankfurt."

"And the older woman who made contact with the target on the Kassel platform?" He slipped the badge into his vest pocket. "Detained, I presume?"

"Our men will have her by now," Sepp said, knowing when to suck up. His partner would not get all the glory.

"Splendid, I'll take it from here."

"If I might ask, sir, what's the nature of the crime?" Ewald, trying once again for points.

"Only a domestic matter, but of interest to the Reich. It goes no further, understood?"

"Of course, sir. We're told there's an American, as well?" Sepp imagined some big shot's wife screwing a foreigner and now trying to avoid paying the piper. He gave a knowing smile.

"We snapped that one up in Göttingen."

"Anything further from us then, sir?" Ewald asked.

"My new orders are to remove the detainees at the next stop, rather than wait for Frankfurt. The two of you can help expedite things, then catch the next train back to Kassel."

"With pleasure, sir," Sepp said. "You caught our names, right?"

"Kreisler and Fischer." The officer gave a curt nod of recognition. "Well done, gentlemen. Your contributions will be noted, now let's get forward. Wait for me in the first compartment while I fetch the detainees, then I'll brief you further on my needs. Clear?"

The two agents nearly tripped over each other in haste to follow the SS officer down the corridor.

# CHAPTER THREE

The cafeteria in the Frankfurt *Hauptbahnhof* bustled with hungry travelers despite the mid-afternoon hour. A cold draft entered the buffet with every new client, and something warm for lunch suited Horst. He had waited until Pabst left to try the thick soup. Now Klaus was returning with a phone update from Berlin, so Horst pushed aside his meal, a frankfurter floating in lentils, a bread roll tucked beside the bowl: traditional fraternity house fare shared in honor of their Wachonian brotherhood.

"They arrive on the next express. We've two agents keeping an eye on them. The mother managed to get out of Marburg and meet up with them in Kassel, but she refused to board the train."

"Detained?"

"A tragedy—all very sad. Becker's surveillance team boarded to follow the targets, so another team came to pick her up. They found the body in the women's room, a suicide." He used the large spoon to cut off a chunk of sausage and placed it in his mouth. "Drug overdose. Her husband must have left her with a way out." He chewed.

"Such a pity. And speaking of Herr Professor Doktor Breitling, how's he doing?"

"En route to Dachau; said to be docile and uncommunicative."

"No surprise there. Must be a shock after a life of ease at the university."

"Well, now he's in with the vermin."

249

Horst glanced up at the canteen wall clock, its minute hand seemingly stalled in its track. "What about a *Bunker* where we can clean up this mess?"

"Locals have a safe house, secure, known only to the top brass here, and reserved for those special interrogation cases where discretion is the key," Klaus said.

"And certainly useful for illicit rendezvous."

Klaus laughed. "A warehouse office, just beyond the rail yard. Appears perfect for our needs."

"Anything else?"

"One more item...totally unrelated, of course." His eyes gleamed with self-satisfaction. "Sad story out of Königsberg: one of our own agents met with an unfortunate accident. Hit-and-run, fatal, no witnesses."

Horst pushed back his bowl and lit a cigarette. "So much tragedy these days, it's a wonder anything gets done." He checked his watch against the buffet clock. Once again.

Ryan left the Gestapo agents waiting in the rear compartment he had briefly occupied earlier and proceeded up the corridor. Few were traveling first-class on this day of upheaval, and Erika had found the cabin nearest the front vestibule free of other passengers. It was a relief to see the boy sleeping, his head in his mother's lap. Better he was well rested—no telling what was coming next.

Ryan kept his voice low. "Consider yourself now officially 'detained' by a powerful Gestapo officer, at your service." He tapped the Party pin, gave her a mock bow of introduction with a click of his heels and his most reassuring smile. The stage-fright was long gone, and he was alert and buoyed by his success. The role-playing had reminded him of the "passing for a German" game played with Isabel so many years back, and it occurred to him that—once again—it was life-threatening.

"The agents? You fooled the agents?" Astonishment and disbelief in her voice. Erika appeared wan, her eyes reddened, the tears now dry. He wanted to comfort her, but there was no time.

"Awaiting my orders, and so far, so good. Just pray that Leo doesn't start introducing his mother's 'good friend.'"

She smiled weakly and caressed the sleeping boy's brow, straightening a stray lock of hair.

"Here's the plan," he said, showing full confidence for her sake. "We'll get off now with the help of our cooperative Gestapo surveillance team. Leave the bags—only necessities in pockets or handbag. The rest we replace in France." He looked at Leo. "But bring the bear, he's good company." The train began its deceleration for Marburg. "Okay, wake him now, and hope he isn't in a talkative mood."

This time, the Kassel agents were watching for the SS officer and rose to attention as he approached the cabin. Both men looked haggard, their exhausting night finally taking its toll. Ryan's voice carried once again the commanding Prussian tone. "I need a vehicle as quickly as possible, my schedule's tight."

Sepp got the first word in. "Shall we ring the local office for a car?"

"Forget protocol. Just requisition whatever you can—a taxi will do—and make it fast. Also, clear out any agents at the station so we're not slowed down by explanations. If they have questions, you're both under my authority. I'll be on your heels with the detainees." He turned to leave. "So that's it, now get moving." As the train rolled to a halt, Ewald swung open the heavy door and the two agents shouldered their way through the platform crowd. Sepp immediately spotted a team from the local office and assured them all was under control: the older woman detained in Kassel, a high-ranking Gestapo officer now in charge of the operation. The locals headed to the canteen for a beer.

Luck was with the Kassel team. A black diesel idled in the front drop-off zone, behind the wheel a uniformed SS driver. His eyes were glued to a leggy brunette at the taxi stand who had just returned his smile. Sepp tapped on the glass and the young driver rolled down the window, put out over having his fantasy disrupted.

"What do you want?" The surly question barely out of his mouth, he wished it back. The Gestapo badge thrust in his face was hardly necessary. This wasn't one to mess with.

"This car, and it happens now!" Sepp already had the driver's door half open.

"Go see my lieutenant. He's inside for a coffee, and he won't like your taking his vehicle."

No one could miss the menace in Sepp's tone. "This is state business, and we're requisitioning whether you and your lieutenant like it or not." He pointed to the station entry. "Any moment you'll see a field-grade SS officer coming through those doors, and it won't be pretty. Do I make myself clear?"

The cowed driver nodded in acknowledgement, his fingers tensing on the wheel.

"Now get the hell out and go inform your asshole lieutenant," he yanked the door fully open, "and the key stays."

With a final glance toward the shapely brunette, the intimidated corporal disappeared into the crowd, passing Ryan without taking notice. Erika and Leo walked a pace behind the American, acting suitably subdued. Ryan spotted the agents beside the black Mercedes and pushed through to the curb. "Well done, Kreisler. I assume that was the driver?"

"He's letting his lieutenant know we're commandeering the vehicle. He's SS."

"Comrade-in-arms, so to speak, that should speed things up." Ryan reached for the rear door and told Erika to get in, his instructions polite but forceful. Leo looked up nervously before climbing beside his mother, unsettled by Herr Lemmon's stern looks and talk.

"Fischer, the lady left her valise on the train. Get back out there and see if it's still to be had. And you, Kreisler, go hurry up this lieutenant. Make clear I've a schedule to keep." The two made their way back through the throng.

The standard-issue Mercedes 260D was equipped with police radio, and the diesel was idling and ready to go. "How about a little trip?" asked Ryan, adjusting the rearview mirror and finally showing Leo his smile. The boy nodded in agreement, obviously relieved at his sudden change in demeanor.

Ryan swung the car out of the loading zone and headed first south, then turned west. He remembered these back roads well from his student days, when he had bicycled across this peaceful Hessian countryside from village to village, reveling in its beauty and gracious people.

# CHAPTER FOUR

Ewald Fischer exited the station without the valise. The express had long since departed for Frankfurt along with any misplaced suitcase. Sepp appeared with an irate SS lieutenant at his side, the young driver tagging meekly behind as he scanned the bus stop for the now missing brunette.

The Mercedes was gone, and the furious lieutenant turned his outrage on the agents. He and Sepp nearly came to blows, in each other's face with profanity and spittle flying, until Ewald managed to pull his partner back from the confrontation. The passing crowd and station vendors, realizing they had been gawking, turned attention back to business at hand. The crimson-faced lieutenant scowled at his driver and headed for the public phones.

"Forget that asshole, Sepp. Come on, we can do a number on his skull later. For now, let's give headquarters the word that the detainees are in good hands." They crossed the square to a café and ordered sandwiches and beer. The long night and trying day had put them on edge. Ewald volunteered to make the call while Sepp sought to unwind. He got Kassel headquarters on the line quickly and anticipated orders to return home for some rest. Instead he was told to wait for confirmation of new instructions from Berlin. Leaving the local number for a call-back, he joined Kreisler at a front table. It didn't take long, and the new orders were a disappointment: remain in place and wait for further direction. They grumbled as they scarfed down the last of the sandwiches, then ordered more beer and stared at each other in silence.

Sepp always saw a weasel in his partner—the pointed nose, shallow cheeks, and small, dark eyes. In the pale light from the café window Ewald's sharp features appeared especially feral. And that afternoon the stubble beneath those eyes was noticeably thicker than elsewhere. Sepp stared more closely and it dawned on him—his partner now relied on eyeglasses when shaving, and missed the spots hidden by the frames. Sepp rubbed his own tired face with his hands, and used a toothpick to scrape his coated teeth, then rose from the table.

"I'll be next door at the barbershop," he said, "I need a shave."

The locomotive stood at rest, panting after its long haul. Under the vast canopy of the Frankfurt station impatient passengers handed down luggage through the open windows as baggage handlers scrambled to clear the way for boarding travelers. Police and SA stood at control points, reviewing documents and eyeing those travelers they found suspicious. Some had hoped to pass through unnoticed and failed. A small, dejected group stood off to the side, isolated under Storm Trooper guard.

"They lost them," Klaus reported dutifully as he caught up with his mentor.

Horst stopped pacing alongside the sweating engine, suddenly aware of the gnawing at his gut and incipient twitch in his cheek. The train had pulled in with neither the fugitives nor the Kassel agents on board, and Klaus had just phoned Berlin. "Lost them?" Horst was incredulous.

"Your American presented himself as a Gestapo officer and took our agents for a ride. Those Kassel idiots even appropriated an SS car for his use, and nothing's been seen of the targets since."

"And how the hell did he pull that off?"

"Party pin and warrant disc—Frau von Kredow's contribution, perhaps?"

"The Jew-bitch thinks she's clever." Horst's mask remained rigid. "I'll show her clever once she's in my hands again." He ran his fingers through his hair and replaced his hat. "As for those Kassel incompetents, their heads are mine."

"Sounds like Brenner's on top of things: all-points bulletin, men at the main train terminals, telegrams to local and regional police stations and SS units. The civilian watch is alerted in the back road locales. Shouldn't be that difficult to spot them—SS staff cars are pretty rare in those rural areas, and the American's obviously not stupid, so he'll avoid main roads and the *Autobahn*." Klaus put away his notepad. "I'm told we also have people in direct pursuit by car, and military units are on watch.

"We can't have her mouthing off."

"All reports handled through Berlin, to be relayed directly to us, and still 'detain and isolate.' No interrogation absent your direct orders."

"The way these locals botch things, we'll probably hear Goebbels broadcast this fiasco as some spontaneous anti-Semitic action tonight."

"Nothing more to do for the moment," Klaus suggested.

"There's always more. They'll obviously head for Belgium or France, perhaps via Luxembourg. And east makes no sense at all. Switzerland's not out of the question, but those Kassel idiots probably told them we were waiting in Frankfurt, so I doubt they'll head south. Check the visa offices at the Berlin consulates, and put all border stations on watch. Now hand me your atlas."

Pabst drew a well-worn Baedeker from his briefcase, thumbed to the region west of Marburg, and gave Horst the map book. "Cover the stations at Siegen, Koblenz, Wiesbaden and Cologne." Horst's finger danced across the map. "Mannheim, too, in case they double back south. That *Scheisskopf* will quickly realize the car's a magnet and ditch it long before they make a border. Another train's definitely their best bet."

Horst surveyed the platform crowd as Klaus hurried away. *What a perfect day for all this—Jewish filth everywhere, all trying to get out. She blends right in.*

The roads through the Westerwald wound over hills covered in beech and down through well-groomed farmland. Rural villages spotted the landscape, their picturesque charm little changed through centuries of peace, famine, war and plague. Church steeples sprouted above the gray slate roofs, and courtyards steamed with man-high manure piles surrounded by pecking chickens. Farm wagons sat empty, their harvest loads already hoisted into the racks above the stables attached to the farmhouses, and smoke rose from countless chimneys.

Ryan knew they had a limited window to put kilometers behind them. The Mercedes would be the ideal escape vehicle were it not so recognizable on the road. The engine was reliable and the police radio a godsend. Erika monitored the frequencies from the front seat and tracked their pursuers' progress. Leo slept curled between them with his bear as a pillow.

The road atlas from the glove box proved invaluable once they moved beyond familiar biking distance from Marburg. They changed direction on the bumpy back roads with every new update squawking over the radio. Koblenz on the Rhine seemed their best bet to catch a new express south. At first opportunity he would call René to enlist his friend's help. With their description surely now widespread, crossing any border as tourists was no longer an option. All the fearsome reach and power of the Gestapo was on their tail.

The glove compartment hid an even better find, a Walther P38 automatic with full clip. "Show me how it works," Erika said, "if I have to face him again, it's on my terms." He acknowledged her determination with a grim smile. As he drove, Ryan walked her through its loading and use. She tried to stash the pistol in her handbag, but found no room among the toiletries, money, jewelry, and identification papers.

"Better in your coat pocket. Close at hand, and you might need to pass it to me in a pinch."

She handed Ryan a stack of the currency. "Just in case we're separated," she said.

"That's not going to happen, but it might come in handy for a bribe." As he slid the money into his jacket pocket he realized the strenuous day was taking a toll on his shirt, and wished for a freshly laundered one. Erika put the pistol away before once again seeking a more comfortable seating position. Ryan read the pain on her face. He was amazed by her ability to hold things together after a brutal assault and the separation from her parents. "You still doing okay?" he asked.

"Exhausted on every level, but okay." She forced her shoulders to relax. Another radio report crackled: a police unit in pursuit, heading for Limburg.

"I can't begin to imagine what you're going through." Ryan stared ahead at the winding road, watching for any slow-moving wagon or a road block. "You don't have to talk about it, but whatever you need, just let me know, and I'll find it for you."

She squeezed his arm. "Thank you, my dear American man. It's been worth it all to get away from him...with you."

Moments passed. When she spoke again, the words were barely audible: "They couldn't leave each other, you know. The Gestapo came for my father this morning. Horst won't let him live." Another long pause. "My mother knew she couldn't go on without him." She drew in a long breath. "It's what they wanted, it's for the best." Then her breathing came in soft, wet sobs that tore at his heart.

He forced his jaw to relax. This was the time for clear thinking, not rage. He felt for the tobacco pouch, reassured himself of the hidden film cartridge.

# CHAPTER FIVE

"We have trouble." Ryan spoke French to René, conscious of the observant innkeeper. The sour-faced woman idled at the counter within easy earshot of the telephone. He knew she was eavesdropping, indulging her curiosity.

His confidence had weakened with each new kilometer put behind them in the stolen sedan. The narrow roads and the unending zigzag across the countryside were taking a toll on their nerves. Every blind curve ahead, every tight path through a confining village seemed ideal for a dreaded road block. There would be no easy escape from armed men lying in wait. Weidenbach near Limburg was such a hamlet. Wisps of smoke rose from the chimneys, and light glowed from a few of the windows. A sign posted on a stone wall at the village limits reminded everyone passing through that Jews were unwelcome. Fewer than twenty structures huddled together, slowly surrendering to centuries of gravity and recent decades of poverty and neglect.

Ryan had driven down the narrow street slowly, noting a decrepit *Gasthaus*. Evening was fast approaching, and the warm light behind the curtains was inviting. The outside air had turned frigid, and he lowered his window to fight the drowsiness. They both needed a break, a moment to relax. Blurred silhouettes in the windows of the inn suggested few guests for the dinner hour. In front of the hostel sat a farm truck and against the wall near the entrance leaned a forlorn bicycle. There was no sign of police.

Ryan pulled off the road once they passed the last of the buildings and disabled the dome light. "You and Leo get in back, stay down low as possible and cover yourself with your coats. Anyone looks, they'll think I'm traveling alone." The rearview mirror reflected only deepening gloom behind them, nothing moving in the dark street.

Erika nodded her understanding. In the last half hour she had said very little. She slipped into the back seat and huddled down in the foot well, cradling Leo in her arms. "Not too long, Ryan. It's cramped and uncomfortable." He thought of her injuries, and of her strength. "And do bring some food if you can. Leo's surely hungry."

"Are we playing hide-and-seek?"

"Yes, Leo," Ryan said. "No one knows we're here, so you both stay down there out of sight for the moment." The boy snuggled up against his mother. Ryan pulled from the grassy shoulder and turned the car around, then parked a short distance up from the inn. "I'll hurry," he whispered to the backseat. The only response was Leo's muffled giggle from beneath the tent of her coat. Erika had tickled him.

The smell of onions frying in butter was inviting, but the human reception at the inn was far less engaging. Three men and two women seated at a round table glared at him as he entered. Ryan gave the obligatory Hitler greeting, and the stout, matronly type who stood beside their table appeared peeved by the interruption. She alone returned his salute. The others stared for a moment longer before one man muttered something unintelligible and they all returned to their meal. Ryan approached the bar, wondering if he should play his Gestapo card. He unbuttoned his overcoat to reveal the Party pin on his lapel. The innkeeper reluctantly took her customary spot behind a counter outfitted with cash drawer, beer tap, and a register for anyone unfortunate enough to overnight in this forlorn village. Three room keys hung on numbered hooks beneath a hand-lettered board advertising *Zimmer*. *No lodgers tonight,* he thought.

"Dinner and a room?" The woman's hair formed a tight bun, accenting severe features. Ryan could tell from her obvious once-over that she didn't care for his looks, either.

"Thank you, no, I'm in a bit of a rush." He remembered Erika's request. "But perhaps something to eat on the road?"

"Pork roast, potatoes, sauerkraut; take it or leave it—no big-city menu here."

"A couple of pork sandwiches and a bottle of cola, then." He sensed something more disturbing here than simple mistrust of strangers. Without responding she turned and entered the kitchen. Visible through a half-closed curtain, an apron-clad man labored over the stove, and Ryan watched her give instructions. The cook cleared his wire-rimmed lenses of condensation, returned them to the bridge of his nose, and glanced briefly in Ryan's direction. His face remained blank as he reached for a loaf of bread. Sour-face came back through the curtain.

"Something else?"

"Yes, if you don't mind, I'm running late and need to make a call. Is there a public phone?"

She pointed to a small alcove just beyond the bar. "It's the only one in town. Local call, I presume?"

"No, sorry, long distance, but in the *Altreich*."

"Reverse the charges," she directed.

"I'd rather not impose on friends, you understand." Ryan laid a ten-mark note on the worn countertop. "This will more than cover both phone toll and the food. The change is yours to keep." The woman glared for several seconds, as if memorizing his features, a school teacher with ruler in hand, plotting some fitting discipline for unruly behavior. She slipped the note into the cash drawer. Ryan turned toward the alcove.

"I'll expect to know those charges when you're finished," she said to his back.

He gave the operator René's business number at the docks, keeping his voice as low as possible. No answer. Ryan checked his watch, just past six. He had her try the home number. They needed a new plan, and now.

René answered on the fourth try.

Ilse Fleischer knew she was in the right place at the right time, once again. Block warden for Weidenbach and vicinity, her eyes and ears were always open. Barely an hour earlier a phone call had alerted her to a wanted fugitive in his thirties, driving an official vehicle and accompanied by a woman and a small child. Dressed for the city, his Prussian German abrasively crisp, this stranger was clearly up to no good. And he had ignored the space out front and parked well away from the inn. To top it off, he was now using French, obviously hiding something.

Fritz left the kitchen from the rear to verify the vehicle type and number, and he returned to report as empty car. *What's he done with the woman and child?* Ilse wondered. The flashy lapel pin did not impress her. Ilse knew poseurs on sight, late-comers who thought to ride the ascent of National Socialism only once victory was assured. She and Fritz had joined early, when others thought them brash fools. They had recruited among the disenchanted locals, organized meetings and events, sponsored speakers for the cause. When the government was theirs at last, no one dared question her power and authority, and she remained relentless in her vigilance. Now she could help bring this arrogant, educated type to justice, and further strengthen her own position. The stranger's French masked most of his conversation, but she recognized "Koblenz," and there was a name, "René." Little enough, but perhaps of value to the Gestapo, and she wasn't finished with her fact-finding.

The stranger's call was short. He told her the toll charges before leaving the inn with the sandwiches. The ten marks more than covered things, and the phone handset was still warm when she rang the operator. "Klara, here is Ilse Fleischer."

"Ilse, all goes well for you and Fritz?" Ilse knew that her grammar school classmate held no special love for her but respected the power she wielded.

"Indeed, everything's good, but now I need information. The call you just placed from my line, you have the number?"

"One moment, please." She relayed both numbers.

"Where do they connect?"

"Both to Baden." There was a momentary pause. "Kehl on the Rhine."

"Thank you, Klara. Now connect me to the constabulary, please. Oh, and one more thing, just how much was the toll on that call?"

Her duty done, Ilse stepped to the window and looked up the unlit street. The black sedan was long gone. Fritz came out of the kitchen to report it headed west.

Exhaustion finally overtook them now that dusk had faded to night. Ryan found his judgment affected on the dark and narrow roads. Several times he braked too quickly on a turn, or shook his head to clear his vision. Once he almost struck a deer. He longed for coffee. Erika remained in back with Leo as they finished off the sandwiches from the inn. Leo could drift asleep at a moment's notice, but now he was turning restless, and Erika suggested a break to stretch their legs. The police radio reported a sighting in Weidenbach, so they knew their pursuers were getting closer, but the car would have to serve a while longer.

Near the village of Montabaur they pulled onto an unmarked tractor path leading into a wood. Gloom enveloped them as Ryan switched off the headlamps. Once their eyes adjusted to the dark, he steered up the muddy path. A hundred meters from the road he stepped out into an eerie silence. He lifted his collar against the chill and trudged back down to the road to be certain lights from a passing vehicle wouldn't reveal their position. Once satisfied that their hideaway was secure, he made an emergency stop at a tree. Back at the car, he encouraged Erika and the boy to also take advantage of the dense growth. "You mean in the woods, like Bruno?" Leo had never used anything but a porcelain toilet. "That's funny."

"Yes, Leo, another secret of secret policemen, the woods work for people, too." Erika carried him into the brush, testing her way through the darkness. They hugged the path and returned almost immediately to the car.

Mother and son managed a half-hour's sleep. Ryan found only anxiety, frequently snapping alert and peering into the darkness. His breath condensed in the chill air of the car's cabin. Erika shifted fitfully in the back seat, huddled with the boy beneath her coat. Ryan turned on the engine and the heater sprang to life, but the two sleepers barely responded. Moments later he shut down the motor and the warmth faded away.

Surrendering at last to restlessness, he eased open the door and followed the rutted road to its crest. Beneath the hooded sky spread a woodland landscape, deep and brooding, reminiscent of a tale of the Brothers Grimm. Distant lights from a farmhouse on the edge of a field quivered through sparse foliage. A dog barked unhappiness at banishment from the family hearth.

Ryan felt very alone. He shivered, knowing the chill came from within and not his surroundings. In his hands lay the life of this woman and child. He lit his pipe and felt the smoke warm his face. He thought of the film in his tobacco pouch, a tiny cartridge that could affect the destiny of millions. His own life had been strewn with early and easy successes: academics, languages, sports, women. He'd earned a position on Wall Street, a European doctorate, a teaching appointment, all accepted as a matter of course.

And then along came this unforeseen opportunity to serve his country, an easy walk in a familiar park, or so he had thought. Perhaps it had always been too easy for him, never a challenge his natural talents could not overcome. But a new reality was settling in, and it frightened him to the core. He shuddered.

The dog in the distance fell silent.

# CHAPTER SIX

Sepp Kreisler was ready to pound heads. He had been duped by an American *Arschloch*, and would face ridicule and derision when they returned to the Kassel office. Ewald repeated the furious words of their chief, who had given them hell over the phone for allowing the fugitives to slip through their hands. Rather than immediately returning home in disgrace, they were to take a car from the Marburg pool and pursue—an unexpected and unearned opportunity to redeem their reputations. "Once we find them, he's all mine," Sepp said. They had reached Limburg. "I'll tear that son-of-a-bitch apart before the bigwigs get hold of this case."

"Did you get a good look at that blonde, those legs? How about a thorough 'medical exam' before we pass that one up the chain?"

For the moment they could do nothing but wait for a radio update, so they smoked and took turns dozing outside a storefront confiscated from some Jewish greengrocer, its old signage still visible despite hasty over-painting. Though exhausted, both were anxious to get on with the pursuit. Then toward evening the hoped-for sighting came in, and they were underway to Weidenbach.

The bitchy innkeeper there had not responded well to their interrogation. She gave as well as she took, and Sepp was tempted to knock her around, in no mood to waste time listening to her self-promotion. She had nothing new to add, other than the odd belief that the fugitive was now traveling alone. Within minutes they were out of that godforsaken hole, finally on a hot trail.

Koblenz was clearly the fugitives' destination. Sepp and Ewald made good time, expecting the target vehicle to appear beyond each new turn of the road. But disappointment crept in with every kilometer, and they reached the Koblenz main station with nothing accomplished. Sepp immediately notified the two teams on duty that the parties of interest were known to them by sight and that they had been authorized to take charge. A more specific briefing went to the team manning the control gate. The Kassel agents then split up, Sepp heading to the station canteen to down several shots of schnapps and dig into a hearty veal cutlet. With hunger and thirst satisfied, he relieved Ewald in the small police office and his partner went off to find his supper. The agents would need their strength for settling the score.

"That's perfect, absolutely perfect." Horst von Kredow offered only a thin grimace of satisfaction rather than an actual smile, but his pleasure was obvious all the same. "Now we get all three: the American, the Jewess, and that Frenchman, as well. Marburg once again, and this time we do it right."

Berlin had just relayed news. A backwater innkeeper had overheard the American place calls, and the phone numbers connected to *Gesslinger Rhein-Fracht* in Kehl on the Rhine. Memories of the duel gone awry came flooding back. Here at last would be the culmination of his revenge. He had thought the Frenchman destroyed, and had fumed when the American ran back home before he could take him down. And now the same merry little group thought to escape into France under the nose of his own secret police.

"How long ago?" Horst asked.

"They left some *Dorf* called Weidenbach barely an hour ago. She heard him mention Koblenz, but they could just as easily turn south toward Wiesbaden or Mainz."

"None of that matters. It's clear where they're headed." Horst slid the atlas across the canteen table and tapped his finger on the little town of Kehl. "Just make damned sure our agents hold back and surveil only. No slip-ups this time. The dockyards will be ideal to clean up this mess, and without distractions."

The large man with a boy engulfed in one arm approached the checkpoint leading to the platforms. He favored his right leg as he walked.

"Purpose of travel?" the official asked, regarding the man's papers which indicated ownership of a shipping concern on the Rhine.

"The boy's grandparents are ailing, so I thought the little guy here would cheer them up a bit." The child observed the agents sheepishly, a stuffed bear grasped to his chest. Then he looked back over the man's shoulder toward the crowd in the station, as if searching for someone or something.

The father shook his head with exasperation. "What a day for travel, with all that mess in the streets. You fellows sure had your hands full." He glared at a huddled family, sitting on their luggage as the other team of agents reviewed documents. The Gestapo agent grunted and handed back the burly man's identity documents, waving him through toward the southbound express just braking along the second platform.

"Very well done, young man," René whispered to Leo as they reached their carriage.

"Be sure to tell *Mutti* I did it right," Leo said to his new adult acquaintance, Herr Gesslinger.

It hadn't been easy convincing Leo to board the train with the intimidating stranger, despite the man's warm smile and easy manner. Ryan and Erika had watched through the glass doors from outside the station concourse as René purchased the tickets and made his way through the control, her son in his arms.

They had finally abandoned the police vehicle on a side street near the center of town. Ryan remembered to rip out pages from the road atlas covering the region they still had to navigate. After a brief walk they were able to flag a cab, and René waited for them as anticipated at the café facing the train station. Ryan was delighted to have his old friend's support, and Erika gave him a warm hug of welcome and word of thanks for his help. Leo had chosen to be his rare shy self, but Erika took him aside and assured him that this was all part of their "secret" plan. "Here's your chance to show what a grown-up boy you are, Leo."

The child nodded gravely, a look of uncertainty passing swiftly across his face.

"You must make Mommy and your grandparents—," her voice caught at the thought of her parents, "make us all proud by doing exactly what you're told." Leo glanced warily at the two men, busy discussing something. "Can you do that for me?" she asked.

"Yes, *Mutti.* Remember, I'm a secret policeman, too."

She explained that the friendly man would carry him to the train, while she and Herr Lemmon would follow a few moments later. "We'll be right behind you, and watching you all the time, all right?" Leo gave another uncertain nod. "But don't say a word to anyone except Herr Gesslinger."

Though the café was no longer serving, the owner agreed to make coffee and hot chocolate. The three fugitives took advantage of the facilities to clean up a bit from the rigors of their journey before rejoining René at the table. Ryan's friend unwrapped bread and cheese he had brought, as well as an apple and bar of chocolate for the boy. Leo hastily took both, his eyes lighting up, and put the chocolate in his coat pocket. He bit into the fruit immediately. "Thank you, Herr Gesslinger," he said, and his mother smiled in gratitude and praised his manners.

René and Ryan looked over a hand-sketched plan of Kehl showing the location and layout of the Gesslinger docks as they quietly discussed the difficulties facing them. Dividing up the group should throw off any watchers at the station expecting to see the family of three. It was agreed that, in case of trouble, they should act immediately and aggressively. "They'll expect us to be cowed, to surrender on the spot—intimidation and fear are their daily weapons— so we have to be ready to surprise them," René said. "I'll take the lead if things go sideways; I've dealt with them before. If we're separated, just make it to the docks."

He placed a finger on a small square drawn in pencil alongside the water's edge. "Here's an office shack with adjoining machine shop, midway along the dock. Hugo Gerson will wait there for us, all night if necessary. Once we arrive you go under canvas in one of my launches and we whisk you across to France. The water police might be out, but we know the river better than they do and we run without lights, so it shouldn't be a problem." He smiled at Erika in reassurance. "Unless one of you gets seasick, of course."

Erika gave the boy a final few words of reassurance before René hoisted him onto his arm and headed to buy their tickets. To her great relief, they easily passed the Gestapo gauntlet and disappeared out onto the platform. Ryan adjusted his overcoat to display the Party pin, placed his hand on her elbow and they moved forward. "You're sure no tickets are needed?"

"The Gestapo always travels gratis." Erika straightened her back and walked with an assurance she didn't feel. They stepped purposefully to the front of the short queue, jumping others before them.

"Gentlemen, my wife and I need to catch the Karlsruhe express," Ryan said, pulling the warrant badge from his vest pocket and pointing to the waiting train.

"Yes, sir." The agent gave Erika an appreciative once-over. "First platform to your right, sir, *Gleis 2*, and pleasant journey."

The express departed promptly at 9:27, following the scenic route along the Rhine toward destinations south. Kreisler and Fischer had watched with relief as the targets passed onto the platform, the gate control following their directions to the letter. Once the couple disappeared into their first-class carriage, the two Kassel agents boarded the last car and began to move forward. No watching and waiting this time. There was a score to settle, and now the fun could begin.

# CHAPTER SEVEN

The truck rolled beneath the archway and past the iron gates. Bellowing dogs strained at the leash, encouraged by the abusive shouting. Harsh overhead lights made day of night on the open field fronting the barracks as the guards dropped the truck's rear panel and ordered the prisoners out. The detainees squinted in the blinding glare after hours under the dark canvas canopy.

Two SS men climbed up into the truck bed and dragged and shoved those prisoners whose response proved too slow. Most tried to cooperate despite their exhaustion. Others—the sick, the frail or old—were dragged from the benches and thrown to the ground. The guards cursed and flogged them with metal switches, driving the prisoners toward a mustering point. One fallen detainee lay moaning after hitting the gravel. His leg or hip may have broken, for he was unable to rise to meet the baiting curses. A sergeant lashed him repeatedly over the head until he no longer responded. Two other prisoners were forced to drag the unconscious man toward the front of the assembly.

The men were filthy after the tedious journey. There had been no break to relieve their needs. Dark stains on crotches embarrassed those who had surrendered to the inevitable, and the stench of human excrement was pervasive. A few men wore rumpled suits of once obvious quality, others were dressed in working clothes, and still others had been dragged from their beds in pajamas. A few wore little more than underwear and shivered helplessly in the frigid air, no longer shielded by the covered truck and the body heat of fellow huddled prisoners.

The SS officer charged with overseeing the new arrivals watched as the men were forced into rank and file and ordered to remove hats and caps. He paced slowly up and down as the guards sought to bring some semblance of order, then stopped and flicked something from the sole of his jackboot with a riding crop. The injured man lay unmoving at the front of the assembly. "Is there a medical doctor in this impressive group?" The impeccably-uniformed officer appeared young in the garish light, certainly barely past twenty, and his voice was surprisingly juvenile.

An ashen-faced man in his sixties stepped forward. "I'm a physician," he said.

"Identify yourself."

"Doktor Joachim Breitling, Marburger Faculty of Medicine."

"I believe Jews no longer teach at our universities, Herr Professor, much less practice medicine."

"I'm not a Jew. However, I'll gladly treat anyone here who needs my services." He stood defiantly tall.

"Well, that's excellent, since I won't demean my camp doctor by asking him to touch that filthy scum at your feet." He strode over to the prostrate man and poked him with the crop. "So, be my guest, Herr Professor Doktor, show us what aid you can offer your first patient here in lovely Dachau."

Joachim crouched beside the bloodied man and placed his fingers to the base of the man's neck. The pulse was faint. Having been forced to leave without his eyeglasses, he squinted to see more clearly as he lifted the man's eyelid to check for pupillary response.

The crack of the pistol shot startled him, the immediate arc of blinding light as much as the sound. He did not feel the officer's bullet enter the back of his skull and end his life. The dogs bayed and lunged forward on their leashes as the other prisoners reeled at the unexpected brutality of the execution.

"Physician, heal thyself," the young officer said, amused by his own cleverness. He strode away, muttering to the enlisted aide who tagged along at his heels: "Tell Berlin it's done."

The tracks paralleled the Rhine on the rail line's southbound route, and the agents on board the express knew their prey were in the next car ahead. "No one gets past you, understood?" ordered Sepp. Ewald nodded but said nothing. "I'll signal when I've found them, so keep an eye out." Sepp left his partner standing guard in the rear vestibule.

Ewald never questioned that imperious tone. When Sepp was on a mission he could turn instantly, even on a comrade, and right now he was out for serious revenge. Sauer 38H in hand, he moved down the corridor, adjusting his pace to the cadence of the speeding train, steadying himself on the inner aisle wall as he cautiously peered into each compartment in turn. Once certain all was clear, he slipped forward to the next. Travelers aware of his progress fell silent and looked away at their own reflections in the dark windows. They knew better than to be too curious, especially after the violent day they had already witnessed. Meeting the conductor, Sepp brusquely ordered the man out of the way. The cowed trainman tripped over himself to reach the vestibule where Fischer watched and waited for the signal from Sepp.

The third-to-last compartment held their prize. Sepp could see the little brat near the door, the shoulder of the asshole American beside him, closer to the window. He signaled with his left hand. Ewald immediately moved up the corridor, stealth no longer needed and his own semi-automatic ready for action.

"No moves!" Sepp shouted as he burst in, locating each occupant with a quick glance.

The American rose in surprise, and the pistol followed a fast arc, cracking cartilage and spraying blood across the back of the bench. The boy burst into tears and cowered in the near corner as the injured man, stunned by the impact, dropped back on his seat, hands to his face. Across the narrow aisle, the larger man had also started to rise, but held back when he realized the pistol was now trained on his belly.

"I said no moves." Sepp grinned, pleased with the stream of blood pouring down the face of the SS poseur. All arrogance gone, head tilted back, the man applied pressure to his savaged nose. "Sorry, *Herr Kriminalrat,* it seems you ran into my barrel." Sepp tossed a filthy handkerchief in the American's bloody face. "Here, this should help."

Ewald Fischer now stood in the open doorway, his Sauer trained on the larger man. "The woman, where's the woman?" The American said nothing, using his own handkerchief to stanch the flow of blood. The eyes of the other man never left the two pistols, but he also remained mute.

The boy called out for his *Mutti*, his cry shrill. "Boy, where's your mother?" Sepp demanded. The child didn't respond, so he grabbed his collar and shook him violently. "Your mother?" The terrified boy trembled, and Sepp saw him glance repeatedly to the corridor outside. *The forward WC maybe?* He turned to his partner. "Keep them entertained here. I'm going for some fun." Ewald's expression was sour as he slipped into the cabin, keeping his pistol trained on the bigger man and ordering all three captives to the same side of the compartment.

Sepp moved up the corridor to intercept his prey. The next-to-last compartment held only a dozing man, chin sagging against chest. The final compartment stood empty, and Sepp positioned himself just inside to wait for the woman's return. He recalled those long legs and anticipated his coming pleasure.

Erika spent a few calm moments in the restroom, applying lipstick and rouge in the hope of feeling better about herself. *Twenty-four hours of horror.* She stared at her reflection, lost in thought, remembering how empowered she had once felt when her life was still hers to determine. She had become the tool of another, all for shallow desires.

Now she had suffered abuse and torture, her parents sacrificed on the altar of her choices, and her son at risk of an equally undeserved fate. Disgusted with her own weakness, she wiped away the tears. *It simply can't go on.* She steadied herself against the wall of the corridor, coat and handbag draped over one arm, and moved purposefully back toward their compartment, coordinating her steps with the motion of the rocking train. She would never be victimized again.

Sepp silenced her surprised cry with a rough hand over the mouth. Erika kicked back and struggled as he forcibly dragged her into the compartment and threw her into the far corner, her handbag and coat dropping to the floor. He slammed the door and trained his pistol on her. "Ah, and now we have my little slut," he looked her up and down, "such a pretty thing with such fine legs, shall we see how far up they go?" He slid the pistol into his pocket.

Erika trembled in shock. "Where's my son?"

"Oh, in good hands, safe hands, as you will be if you cooperate. You understand cooperation?"

"You've no idea whom you're dealing with," her voice low and menacing. "My husband is Heydrich's deputy, you fool." She tried to rise. "You'll pay for this!"

He backhanded her and she dropped to the seat. "Of course he is, and I'm married to Himmler's wife, you arrogant bitch." Kreisler towered over her. "No worry, that powerful husband of yours is back there with the brat and nursing a smashed nose, and he'll get a lot more of the same when you and I are done here."

His eyes strafed her body. "But for now, let's find out what you're hiding between those legs of yours." He unbuttoned his fly and thrust himself in her face, straddling Erika as his hand fumbled between her thighs. She drew back against the wall, beating at him in defiance, and he slapped her again. "The next one comes with the pistol attached, now get busy and make this worth my while."

She found focus in the thought of Leo's safety and forced herself to relax. "Perhaps we can work something out..." her voice now docile and yielding, "if you promise to leave my boy alone."

"No problem, I don't do boys, but it's been a while since I've had a woman with your class." He took his erection in hand and forced it toward her. "Come on, enough talk. Take it, now!"

She bit down viciously, ripping flesh. Blood sprayed, but she held on doggedly. Stunned by the attack, the agent jerked back off her lap, furthering the damage left by her teeth. He let out a furious howl and stared at the blood gushing from his groin, then clutched at his pulsing organ. Erika lunged for her fallen coat, for the pistol taken from the Mercedes. The attacker grabbed her hair and slammed her back against the wall. She was going nowhere.

"Before was just for fun," he said through gritted teeth. "Now you'll pay the price, cunt." Holding one hand against his bleeding crotch, he pulled the Sauer from his coat pocket and rammed the pistol between her legs, ripping her stockings and scoring her thighs.

Several compartments back, Ewald Fischer's world had also gone sideways. His delayed response to the sudden turn of events might have been excusable, exhausted as he was by a very long day and believing everything well in control. But he was pissed that his partner was now enjoying a pleasure he felt should be his, so his mind was elsewhere.

He had stood just inside the door of the compartment, his gun pointed at the larger man, the most obvious threat. The stranger stared back at him, pretending no involvement in the unfolding events, but Ewald wasn't fooled. He and Kreisler had seen this burly man carry the child through the control gate, so knew he was in just as deep as the other two. The child whimpered quietly now, his face sheltered against the injured American, clearly out of commission, his shattered nose buried in his hands. The man whose charade had made them a laughingstock now cowered behind a bloody rag, his arrogance long gone. In spite of explicit orders not to interrogate the fugitives, no one would protest their use of force in the face of resistance. Ewald and his partner would now make sure they all resisted.

Ewald took a step back through the door, keeping his gun trained into the compartment, and scanned up the corridor. He imagined his partner had the woman down by now, and Ewald resented being first to suggest a little sport with the blonde, yet his partner was now enjoying her. *The bastard always gets the best prizes.* Perhaps there was still time for him to get in on the fun.

That momentary lapse of concentration had a painful cost. The American suddenly slammed the door into his wrist, sending the Sauer flying. The larger man was out of his corner in a flash, dodging the rebounding door before ramming a fist into Ewald's belly, then grabbing him by the neck and slamming his head into the door frame. Stunned, he felt himself yanked back into the compartment as he saw the American reach for the lost weapon. Ewald's world went black.

"Take care of Leo," Ryan said. During the struggle the child had crept across the seats into the far corner and buried his head in his coat. "This job's mine."

"It's under control, go find her." René sat beside Leo and wrapped a reassuring arm around the terrified boy. With his other hand he massaged his right knee, his foot resting on the neck of the unconscious Gestapo agent.

Ryan raced along the corridor. His nose throbbed, but he had suffered worse on the sports field. At least the bleeding had slowed. He released the safety on the Sauer, but worried that using the pistol might put Erika at risk.

Distracted by his injury and fury, Sepp saw too late a man appear behind him in the cabin. He felt a blow to the base of his skull which left him dazed, and he swung around toward his attacker, knocking the pistol from the American's grip as he raised his own to fire. The woman lunged to the floor, grabbing his gun wrist with both her hands. Two shots reverberated in the narrow confines of the cabin, the bullets plowing through the seat cushions.

Now the American had one arm around his neck as he slugged him repeatedly in the kidney with the other. The woman worked to wrest the Sauer from him, but he fought on enraged, the pain in his groin forgotten but his sagging trousers hampering his movements. The bastard American now pulled his arm free of the bitch's grasp and wrenched it up behind his back, sending an agonizing jolt through his shoulder. He fired again, the bullet narrowly missing the son-of-a-bitch.

"The window!" he heard the American yell, "Open it now!"

Baffled by the barely-audible command, her hearing deadened by gunfire in the tight space, Erika scrambled loose from the tangle of limbs to release the catches and drop the window in its tracks. Frigid air burst into the compartment carrying a sooty cloud from the locomotive just ahead, the furious roar adding to the chaos.

"Out of my way," yelled Ryan, and she ducked aside as he wrestled the agent toward the open window. The weakened brute fought back with the strength of his legs, but Ryan deftly shifted to avoid the blows, all the while forcing up the gun arm to the point where he was sure bone would snap. With a brutal push and now aided by Erika, he forced the agent's head out into the whirl of sound and smoke. Bit by bit, shifting his weight with every shove to leverage the struggling agent, they worked him farther through the window.

They would throw him into the onrushing night.

There is good reason European railroads affix below the carriage windows a small metal plaque in several languages which warns passengers not to lean out. Such an action is always ill-advised.

Perhaps it was a semaphore column, signaling an "all clear" to the speeding express. Or possibly a catenary post, a tall pillar for the overhead lines which power electric locomotives. It certainly was a solid object positioned half a meter from the side of the passing train. And when that stationary post met an onrushing human head, the skull surrendered in a sticky spray.

The passenger in the second compartment had been jolted awake just moments before by bullets plowing through the cabin wall. Puffs of horsehair wadding shot forth as holes suddenly appeared in the upholstered seat to his right. Smoke rose from secondary entry holes in the facing seat. He had frozen in position, still drowsy and trying to make sense of the gunfire. He heard a fierce commotion from the next compartment, another shot, a pounding against the wall and voices rising to a fevered pitch. A woman's scream tore through to him, and then he saw a broad smear of fluid and tissue tracking across his window. It formed odd horizontal clumps and rivulets, driven at speed by the train's velocity.

Placing his head against the dark glass he blocked out his own reflection to take a closer look and came face to face with another's mortality. He reached up and yanked the emergency cord.

With a nauseating jolt, Ryan and Erika both felt the impact as the agent's head met the post. First the immediate wrenching of the body, slamming it toward the side of the window. Then, with all resistance gone, Ryan's unchecked shoving sent the body into the night. The legs and feet caught briefly at the edge of the opening before tumbling into the darkness. Erika let loose a piercing scream, a cry of victory despite her horror. Relief spread across their bloody faces as choking coal smoke swirled about the cabin.

Within moments a shudder passed through the train as the engineer applied the brakes, responding to the signal of the emergency cord. Ryan and Erika were thrown off-balance onto the forward seats as squealing metal on metal rapidly slowed the momentum of the train. Ryan trembled with coursing adrenaline; he was in a new element, had conquered his fear to protect what was dear to him. Perhaps he would question his response later, perhaps not.

"Leo!" her cry muffled by the ringing in his ears. "Where's Leo?"

"Safe with René," he said. "We'll get him now."

She grabbed her handbag and coat from the floor. The corridor was already filling with startled passengers, all talking at once, trying to make sense of the sudden deceleration of the train. A man in the next compartment stared vacantly at the smeared window surface. He then turned abruptly and forced his way past them without a word, heading toward the rear of the coach. His face was ashen, his expression unreadable.

René stepped from the cabin mid-carriage with Leo in his arms and limped his way forward, joining Erika and Ryan. No sooner had he reached them than a woman screamed. She had spotted the body lying prone on the compartment floor, then the bloodied faces of Ryan and Erika.

"Where's your guy?" René looked questioningly at Erika, seeing only a bruised cheek and smeared blood, but no other damage to her face.

"Got off unexpectedly," Ryan said, finally unclenching his fists.

Erika took the whimpering Leo in her arms. "My baby, it's all right..." the words of comfort as much for herself as for the child, "it's going to be fine, I've got you now." The child forced his head into the crook of his mother's neck, his arms wrapped tightly around her collar. She smiled at the two men and tears filled her eyes.

"Let's move," said René, "there's no time to waste, and this place will be swarming. Up front, quickly!" They could now hear the shrill whistles of trainmen outside, moving alongside the tracks and approaching their car. The conductor pushed his way past the fugitives without a glance, ordering them to make way on the vestibule platform. He opened the heavy door, barely touching the steps as he swung down to the graveled rail bed to join the others shining lanterns and flashlight up at the gore-smeared windows. The rhythmic throb of the resting locomotive reached them through the open doorway.

"One moment," Erika said, handing the quietly protesting Leo to Ryan. In the tiny restroom she rinsed her mouth, even though she knew the water wasn't potable. She drenched her handkerchief and took fierce swipes at her face. "Your turn," she said as she stepped back out and gently wiped at Ryan's battered nose before taking her son back in her arms.

"We have to separate," René said. "It's my weak leg, I wrenched it back there."

"We're stronger as a team, René, let's give it a try." Ryan protested.

"I know my own strength—I'll only slow you down. You've got the map and Hugo's waiting for you. Get to the dock and you'll be safe in France before you know it. I'll catch up when I can. Now go!"

"Then here, take this," Ryan unhooked the gold chain with the warrant badge and handed it to his friend. "They're on to me, but others won't know you yet."

René pocketed the disc. "Best hide the pin, though." He tapped Ryan's lapel. "You may need it later, but probably best not wear it for hitching a ride right now." Ryan grasped his friend's shoulders in a quick hug of thanks, then turned to the open door. "No, this side," René gestured to the opposite door. "Circle forward around the engine. You'll be hidden in the fog." He lifted the handle, and Ryan saw his friend wince as he put weight on his right leg.

Ryan took Leo from Erika and they climbed down to the road-bed. He turned to wave good-bye, but René was no longer in the vestibule. Through the windows he saw his friend limping back down the corridor at a rapid pace.

All the commotion was on the far side of the train. The locomotive headlamps cast parallel beams forward into the swirling mist, and the glow from the firebox warmed the ground outside the cab with a half-circle of light. The engineer and fireman were on the far side, watching the activity alongside the train. The fugitives stayed close to the wheels of the towering locomotive, feeling the heat from its boiler, and ducked around the front of the engine, keeping a low profile. Ryan noted Erika's difficulty negotiating the tracks in heeled shoes and he took her hand, and they moved tentatively down the incline and passed unseen into the blackness of a furrowed field.

Behind them the animated shouts of the train crew drifted through the fog. Ahead in the distance lay a roadway, its path marked by an occasional vehicle passing through the shroud coming off the Rhine. Ryan felt blood flow from his nose once again, and missing his handkerchief, he removed his necktie and wrapped it around his head, putting pressure over his nose to serve as a tourniquet.

The soil lay broken from a recent plowing and clung heavily to their shoes where rain had turned the dirt to mud. Several times they stumbled and nearly fell as he carried the boy in his arms. The fog occasionally revealed the road and just as quickly obscured it. He wished for a flashlight, but knew it would betray their escape. Reaching the roadway at last, he pulled his makeshift bandage down around his neck and suggested Erika take shelter with Leo in a small copse of trees just off the road.

It was nearing ten and vehicles were rare. Every so often headlamps pierced the dense fog and a vehicle passed, its driver ignoring the man waving both arms from the side of the road. At that point he remembered the bloody tie hanging like a noose above his collar and tossed it aside. *Better a bleeding fool and a ride than no ride at all.* There was little to be done about mud-caked shoes and trousers and the dried blood splattered across shirt collar and coat. The air was biting, and he wished for his hat, lost in the confrontation and quick escape.

For over an hour he stood by as an occasional automobile floated past in the drifting mist. No one braked for the lone figure caught in their headlamps. Erika and Leo shivered in the darkness, huddling beneath a tree.

# DIE ABRECHNUNG
The Reckoning

10-11 November 1938

# CHAPTER ONE

The truck announced its arrival long before its headlamps penetrated the fog. The lumbering Ford with canvas-covered bed had suffered questionable maintenance, one cylinder firing irregularly and the muffler overtaxed. Exhaust swirled acridly about Ryan's head as the driver downshifted, then braked to a screeching halt. The man at the wheel cranked down the window and Ryan moved around toward the driver's side. *"Guten Abend,"* he said, exhausted, forgetting his *Heil Hitler.*

"Move back into the headlamps to give me a better look at you," the driver's voice gruff, and Ryan obeyed, hoping charm and politeness would atone for his disreputable appearance. "Looks like you've had a bad day." He sounded middle-aged or older, his German thick with local dialect.

"You've got that right; a very rough day," said Ryan. "Our car ended up in a ditch. I was driving exhausted, and there was a deer. My wife and boy are with me, and we'd sure appreciate a lift."

"Anyone hurt?"

"Just bloodied and bruised, nothing serious."

"And that deer?" Ryan suspected the man was not buying his story.

"Never made contact, so I'd say it came out just fine."

A little warmth now tempered the voice. "Where you headed?"

"Mannheim or thereabouts, anywhere south. We can always catch a train from there."

"Why don't we pull that car of yours out of the ditch? It may not look that way, but this old truck of mine still has some strength in her, and I do carry a chain."

Ryan hesitated, pretending to consider the idea. "Thanks for the offer, but the car's pretty well banged up, so probably not worth the effort. The nearest train station would be a big help, though."

The driver got out and joined Ryan in the glare of the headlamps. He was in his sixties, his hair white, his face creased by life. Thick, wire-rimmed lenses made his eyes appear overly large. Ryan could see by the size of shoulders and arms that the man had done some heavy lifting. "Seriously, young man," he reached out to shake Ryan's extended hand, "as much as I'd like to believe your story—and it is a good one—I do believe there's something you're not telling me." He eyed the damaged nose and swollen cheek, already beginning to darken. Ryan started to protest. "No, no, it's not important. You'd be surprised at the 'accidents' I've seen today, and you're not the worst off by a long shot. So let's put this day behind us all." He smiled. "Go get your wife and child and find some room in the back. I'm going close to Karlsruhe; that's the best I can do with the load I've got to deliver."

"Thank you, sir, we'll gratefully take it." Ryan smiled in relief, flinching slightly from the pull on his swollen face. He waved toward the wood and Erika emerged into the headlamps with Leo and shook the older man's hand in gratitude. From force of habit she started to give her name, but quickly went still.

Noting her embarrassment, he chuckled. "No need for introductions on a night like this. Best we get moving." They headed to the back of the truck and the driver lifted the canvas at the tailgate and helped Erika climb into the bed. Ryan handed up Leo and pulled himself into the darkness. "I'll give a knock when we're close," the driver said. "Meanwhile, make yourself as comfortable as you can. I recommend up front behind the cab."

Ryan thanked the driver again as he secured the flap, then moved cautiously into the black interior. A flickering match revealed large wooden crates stacked to the ceiling, with barely space enough to stand between the cargo and the rear gate. A narrow passage ran alongside the load, just wide enough to slip through toward the front. He blew out the match as the flame reached his fingertips and lit another, just as the truck ground into gear and lurched forward. Erika grabbed for a crate with her free hand, and as they accelerated the canvas began a steady rumble.

"*Mutti?*" Leo wrapped both arms around his mother's neck.

"It's okay, love," she hugged him closer, "we're fine, no worries. The bad stuff's behind us now."

Ryan struck a third match. "I'll find us a spot forward." He squeezed down the narrow passageway, his back scraping against the wooden staves lining the bed. The truck smelled of old hay, motor oil, exhaust, sweat. They were not alone.

A family sat huddled against the front wall of the truck bed, all eyes watching him warily. One man lit a shielded kerosene lantern to help the new arrivals find a cramped spot, while the others obligingly moved closer together on the filthy floor. "Welcome to our little family," said the man with the lantern." No greetings, no introductions, just an unspoken understanding that they were all in the same boat.

Ryan recognized the same fear and disorientation that troubled Leo in the eyes of the Jewish children. They had all seen too much this day. Two mothers held the smallest children in their arms. A teenaged girl, her head covered with a scarf, stroked the dark hair of her smaller sister. The younger of the two men had an angry welt running from forehead to chin and crudely shorn hair extending beneath a rumpled hat. Once all were settled in, the man extinguished his lantern.

Erika leaned against Ryan with Leo on her lap. The old straw on the bed of the truck did little to cushion contact with the worn planks, and she tensed in response to the bumpy ride. The darkness was broken only by an occasional coursing band of light at the rim of the bed when they encountered another vehicle. The cold became increasingly bitter, and they huddled to share warmth. With every braking of the truck, with every town entered, the tension rose under the canvas shelter. Time passed to the steady rhythm of road noise, the creaking truck bed, the rumble of the engine, the thrumming of canvas in the wind.

A bottle of water and another of red wine moved from hand to hand. *"Mutti,"* Leo's voice a whisper, "I have chocolate." He tore open the bar and took a square for himself before passing the remainder on to the little girl beside him. It made the rounds.

The truck rattled across a long bridge to enter a larger town, and all the fugitives fell still. A group of drunken revelers left a noisy inn, a car horn gave a brief honk, then a distant siren, and the clip-clop of a horse-drawn vehicle, odd for the late hour. They passed a couple laughing, a rare sound of genuine happiness after that troubled day. The driver downshifted to a halt, and voices rose just outside, the driver answering stern questions, demands. His door creaked as he got down from the cab. There was muffled talk of papers and destination.

Ryan peered down through the narrow gap between canvas and truck and glimpsed jackboots moving toward the rear. Everyone tensed as someone stepped up onto the rear bumper and raised the tailgate flap. A beam of light crossed over the cargo to illuminate the roof above the huddled group. "All clear," came the shout. The man dropped the canvas and jumped down from the bumper. There was a collective release of breath, a momentary relief. The driver came back around to secure the flap before climbing up behind the wheel, gears grumbled in protest, and the truck lurched on its way.

An hour later they slowed for a series of tight turns, the roadbed now uneven and rocking the truck from side to side until they lumbered to a halt once again. A triple knock came on the window separating cab from the enclosed bed, and the rumble of the engine ceased. The children now all slept. The adults listened for sounds, voices, anything that would reveal what was happening outside. Only silence greeted them. Seconds passed, then minutes. Ryan watched the slow march of time on the radium dial at his wrist. Another quarter hour dragged by.

Somewhere an owl hooted and then let loose a screech. Moments later they heard the muted thump of wings as a large bird swooped over the truck canopy. The hair on his neck rose at the piercing squeal of the prey as talons sank home. Erika pressed herself to his chest. Ryan squinted through the tight opening in the canvas and surveyed the darkness, but saw nothing. The silence had returned.

Abruptly headlamps flashed on and off in a rapid three-beat staccato, silhouetting barren woods a short distance away. He tensed and waited, peering into the gloom. They flashed once again, and their driver responded in kind. The engine turned over and they rolled forward along the rutted track, every joint of the truck creaking with the shifting surface. The headlamps remained off. Meter by meter they worked their way in the direction of the signaling vehicle.

The stop came with a squeal of brakes, and almost immediately the rear gate of the truck dropped and the canvas was drawn back. "Hurry up, *schnell, schnell,*" a female voice called in over the cargo barrier. "We've little time! Quickly, now." She urged quiet and caution. The children, roused from their sleep, were guided forward by the adults. One by one they scooted alongside the wall of crates and were helped down by the two new-comers and the white-haired driver.

In the soft glow of his lantern the spokesman for the family reached out his free hand to Ryan and gave a nod of respect to Erika. Leo was in her arms, his legs wrapped around her waist. "*Shalom,*" he said.

"Is there anything we can do for you?" Ryan asked.

"No, thank you. What you see is what's left of our family, but we'll find a way out, thanks to these folks." He gestured to the couple and the driver guiding his group toward the other vehicle with the aid of a flashlight. "There are still many good people here—it's just getting harder to find them."

Erika shifted drowsy Leo to her right arm, pulled *Reichsmark* from her handbag, and pressed them into the man's hand. "Here, we have enough; this may help you on your way." The man protested briefly before accepting the gift. He blessed her for the godsend.

The driver rejoined them. The Jew handed him the lantern and made his way in the darkness toward the other vehicle. Across the clearing the dome light glowed briefly as nine people sought space in an old sedan meant for six. Erika offered the driver money, as well. "For your help and trouble," she said.

"Save it for those truly in need." He smiled. "My pay comes from sticking my thumb in the eye of those morons who run this country."

"We are eternally grateful." Ryan offered his hand.

"Happy to be in the right place at the right time, and sorry I can't take you the rest of the way, wherever that's taking you. As you see, we weren't prepared for so many passengers on such short notice. But for now I've just about reached the end of my route, so I'll have to say good-bye."

"Is there a train station close by we can walk to?"

"That load I'm carrying is for the SS garrison just up the road. Don't think you'll want to be hitching thereabouts. Let me show you on a map exactly where we are." He moved off toward the cab.

"No, wait," Ryan called him back and reached into his jacket, "I've what we need here." He spread out on the bumper the pages ripped from the road atlas and adjusted the lantern light. The driver pointed to the closest village with a local train connection, about a kilometer distant. Ryan was relieved to see they were now only about a hundred kilometers from Kehl, an hour or so by train.

"I head now directly to the caserne, as usual, or someone might get suspicious. Sorry, a detour to the train station is just too risky—people seem to remember my trusty Ford here." He patted the bumper.

"No, that's fine; you've done more than enough already," said Ryan.

"Tell you what—there's an inn just up the road, nothing fancy, but clean enough. Use your 'auto in the ditch' story. It's so good I almost fell for it. Get some rest and clean up a bit. It's getting late now, but I've seen an early morning bus out front of the place, heads right to the station.

# CHAPTER TWO

The dull-gray Zündapp KS600 with sidecar sat unattended before the village *Gasthaus*, the driver and his partner taking a break to wash down a beer or two before curfew. By all rights it was nothing extraordinary, a military vehicle seen almost daily in the Reich. For Ryan it was an open invitation. *After all*, he thought, *once you've stolen a police car, why not a Waffen-SS motorcycle?*

Through the curtained window he surveyed the pub and its last patrons before returning to propose his new plan to Erika. She waited with Leo in the deep shadows of an elm on the lower end of the graveled lot. "We're barely an hour from Kehl," Ryan said, "so there's little risk of Gestapo checkpoints—unlike the train stations— and the way those two are hoisting them in there, we'll be on the Rhine before they miss their machine."

"And roadblocks?"

"Who knows? But we're much farther south now, so less likely than before. And that motorbike can use open fields or forest paths if needed, plus the sidecar's made to order for the two of you."

"Okay, I'm game, let's do it." Nothing to be gained by indecision. "The sooner we get there, the better." She knelt down to speak with Leo. "Would you like to ride the motorcycle?"

"Yes, *Mutti*. May I drive?"

"Better Herr Lemmon does the driving, but I'll ride with you in the little sidecar, all right?"

Goggles and leather caps hung on the handlebars and the key was in the ignition—*after all, who steals a military motorcycle?* With a last glance to the door of the inn, he rolled the machine underneath the massive tree and unfolded a wool blanket to spread over the seat and onto the floor of the sidecar. Erika positioned herself with Leo sitting between her legs on the floor. She buttoned up her coat and put on goggles, wrapping the blanket over her head and around Leo. Ryan heard him giggle and marveled at the resiliency of the child. He donned the leather cap, turned up his collar and buttoned his over-coat to the neck, and positioned the goggles for minimal pressure on his damaged nose. Once his passengers were seated, he rolled the cycle down the slope of the parking area to gain distance from the inn. The engine rumbled to life on the first try and they left the lot.

Although the sidecar's added weight made it less agile than his Indian, the Zündapp was a pleasure to handle. He had scanned the map before leaving the truck and memorized the route to reach Kehl as quickly as possible. Much of the way took them through hilly, forested areas, then down across farmland. He was in his element at last, steering the solitary headlamp into the fog and darkness, sure of his destination, confident the worst was well behind them.

"My turn to wear the goggles, *Mutti*." Leo, barely heard from the belly of the sidecar.

Ryan lifted one hand from the handlebars and felt for the to-bacco pouch buried deep within his jacket pocket. Success would be theirs within the hour.

The landward approach to the Kehl boat basin led through dark woods, but dense fog obscured the forest stretches and Ryan was forced to concentrate on the road ahead. He stopped frequently to consult the map and René's drawings. Finally his navigating exper-tise and sheer luck brought them to the orange-black-white flags standing sentry at the high gates of Gesslinger Shipping. They were a welcoming sight in the shifting mists off the Rhine.

No one manned the guard shack at this dark hour. As arranged by René, the smaller gate off to the side was shut, but a bulky pad-lock hung open on the latch. They roused the sleepy Leo, lifted him from his nest in the sidecar, and he and Erika waited just inside the grounds while Ryan hid the road machine in the wood fronting the

access road. He came back carrying the teddy bear and handed it to
Leo. "Can't leave Mr. Bear behind, can we?"

"It's Bruno, Herr Lemmon."

Following René's sketch they headed left along the loading
docks, passing two barges and a company river boat rocking gently
at their moorings. The estuary formed a protected arm of water
reaching inland from the Rhine and lined by wharves. The fog carried the rank smell of backwater and diesel oil, and dock pilings
spread the heady odor of creosote. Massive coils of rope were spaced
evenly along the dock and metal cranes towered overhead. Industrial
fixtures alongside each of the warehouses cast diffused circles of light
onto the graveled surface below.

The machinist's shop and adjoining office shack were easy to
find on the water side of the railroad tracks. A solitary lamp burned
above the door, and a warm glow shone through the small mulli-
oned windows. The aged building was supported by pilings and surrounded by heavy wooden planking that creaked underfoot as they
climbed the entry ramp. A small motor launch bobbed gently alongside the wharf just south of the structure. Their transport would
seem even smaller once out on the dark river.

Ryan knocked tentatively on the door of the shack. Getting no
response, he eased it open and called out to Hugo Gerson in a quiet
voice. No reply. They exchanged a quick glance of concern before
letting themselves in. Happily, the interior of the office was invitingly warm. A coal stove in the corner worked overtime, its pot belly
glowing in the darkness. It had been recently stoked. Erika suggested
leaving the overhead bulb unlit, just in case someone—*a night guard
perhaps?*—got suspicious. Instead Ryan cracked the door to the stove,
sending a gentle flickering light into the room. They unbuttoned
their overcoats almost immediately, finally removing them altogether.

Two rolling office chairs stood to either side of a well-worn
table serving as a desk. Above it hung a wall rack with shipping invoices and river charts. A tray held soft cheese under a linen napkin,
a loaf of black bread with butter and a knife, and chilled bottles of
Gerolsteiner mineral water and local beer. A bottle opener and five
glasses sat nearby. Hugo had anticipated hungry and thirsty guests

upon arrival, a gracious nod to hospitality despite the hurried circumstances.

The sudden jangle of the phone on the desk startled them. Ryan suggested that perhaps they should answer—*Hugo, or even René?*—but Erika urged caution. *She's right,* he thought; *better not bring attention to ourselves.* The telephone rang itself to silence.

They used the sink in the small adjoining latrine to wash up, then ate open-faced sandwiches and quenched their thirst after so many hours on the run. Ryan placed chair cushions against the wall, creating a small, makeshift couch, and invited Leo and his bear to join them while they awaited the return of Hugo. Before long the exhausted boy was fast asleep again, head cradled in his mother's lap, his feet stretched over Ryan's legs. Ryan thought of the bench in the Tiergarten, the ducks, that moment when everything had changed for him less than two days before.

"He's been through so much," she said as she stroked Leo's forehead, damp with perspiration.

"You both have, but now it's almost done."

"He deserves none of this. I'm paying for my own bad decisions, but Leo only wants to please." Erika pushed his forelock to the side. "He's spent all his short life with adults, never had children his age to play with, so he's learned to keep still and do as told, especially around Horst. Such a good boy, who's now seen more than any grown person should." She sighed, her focus shifting to an uncertain future. "Oh, Ryan, what will we do with ourselves in France?"

No answer came to him. Europe stood on the brink of war. He carried proof that Hitler would never rest until Europe was under his thumb and the Jews annihilated. Refuge in France was an expedient first step, but no lasting solution. He only saw a future where barbarity lurked at every turn, biding its time until the next assault.

"Let's just take it as it comes, Erika, one step at a time, just as we managed to get through today." He was disappointed in his own banality, his lack of answers. She sighed once again but made no reply. He hoped René was safe in the aftermath of the violence on the train. How quickly the unforeseen laid waste to the best of plans. An unexpected wave of melancholy washed over him, a sense of foreboding, even now on the verge of their successful escape. "René was prepared with maps to get us this far without him..." Ryan hesitated, "I'm sure we'll be in France together by morning, but I need to know the two of you will be safe in Paris should we be separated along the way."

"But Ryan, we must get there together!" Leo shifted in his sleep.

"Of course we will, but 'just in case,' as you constantly say." Ryan smiled.

"I do?"

"Yes, you do."

"I say 'just in case?'"

"All the time."

"Then I'll stop using it immediately." She looked down at the sleeping boy. "Just in case you start to tire of me."

He laughed. "Okay, 'just in case,' remember the cabaret *La Chatte bottée* in the Montmartre and speak only to Marita Lesney. She's well connected to look after you and get you settled in."

"A 'special' friend?" Erika gave the hint of a grin.

"Just an old friend, but one who's prepared to help should the Nazis take France."

Erika's smile faded as quickly as it had appeared. "They will, won't they? Will any place in Europe be safe from them?"

"I suspect not. I'll do what I can to get you and Leo to America, or at least South America."

She reached over to take his hand. "I should never have let you go, you know, back then in Marburg. How different things might have been."

A question had tugged incessantly at his mind, but the words and right moment had not come in the last frantic hours. Ryan regarded the sleeping boy and decided it was time. "I must ask, Erika, was...*is* Leo mine?"

Her wry smile returned briefly in the warm glow of the stove. "I prefer to believe he's ours." She squeezed Ryan's hand and rested her head on his shoulder. "But we'll never know, really. Things were so different then. His nature, his inquisitiveness and warmth of feeling—those are yours, certainly not Horst's. And he does resemble you in the eyes, don't you think?"

Ryan examined the resting child's face—the high forehead, the long eyelashes, the rosy cheeks. He recalled his own childhood photographs, so carefully kept in a baby album by his mother in Lawrence. He slowly shook his head in bemusement. "Those Dreadnaughts we used, they were the new latex version, as I recall."

"Those things do fail sometimes, you know, and perhaps we simply weren't careful enough." For a moment she seemed lost in past memories. "But I wouldn't wish it any other way." She bent down and kissed the sleeping boy's forehead. "Was it his name that told you, or just his age?"

Ryan paused a second in consideration. *Leo's name?* "But of course—Ryan *Leonard* Lemmon. Leonhardt." He chuckled at the one clue of hers he had missed.

Erika smiled once again. "Horst never questioned my choice of names; it does mean 'strong as a lion,' after all." The smile faded. "But then, Horst thinks only of himself."

"Why didn't you tell me about Leo from the start? Didn't you think I would want to know, should know?"

"I didn't want to snare you with a sense of obligation. But in my heart I knew you would come, would help, because that's just who you are." She kissed him gently on the lips. "Thank you, my Ryan *Leonhardt* Lemmon." Ryan rested his head on hers. He chose to believe he had a son.

They ignored the ringing phone once again.

# CHAPTER THREE

It began with the low, steady thrum of an engine, a vessel approaching from the mouth of the estuary. The rumbling grew increasingly louder until it was unmistakable, and they heard the boat make a broad sweeping turn to dock just south of their shack.

"Hugo, at last," Ryan said. "Wake Leo and get him ready; it's best we leave right away. A shame René didn't make it in time to see us off."

"Ryan, the largest boat Leo and I have ever been on is a paddleboat on the Wannsee. Is this safe?" Erika helped the drowsy Leo into his overcoat and buttoned it up to his neck. "It's so foggy out, and there's bound to be river traffic."

"René said no worries; they do all the time." Ryan looked for his hat, only to remember abandoning it on the train. His suit was rumpled, his shirt held the rank odor of exertion, and he badly needed a shave. They would all put up in a nice hotel in Strasbourg, a room with private bath, ironed sheets, and no concern for bedbugs.

The wooden dock trembled as the arriving boat made mooring. Muffled voices confirmed lines tossed and vessel secured. Soon the decking creaked as footsteps approached the door, and there was a gentle knock. Ryan glanced at Erika in surprise, then stepped to the threshold and opened the door a hand's width.

The muzzle of a Walther P38 invited itself in.

"My, what a pleasant surprise." Horst's voice carried neither pleasure nor surprise, only menace. "Do step away from the door—no one is going anywhere...for the moment."

"Horst!" Erika aghast, bending down reflexively to pull Leo toward her.

The open door also revealed Klaus Pabst, flashing his pistol as he entered and expressing delight in the moment with a supercilious grin. Behind them two uniformed SS soldiers stood with machine pistols at the ready. Klaus flicked on the overhead bulb.

"Father," Leo called out in surprise, then quickly sensed the tension and pulled back to hide behind his mother's legs. "Are you here to take us home?" his nervous question muted by his mother's coat.

Horst ignored the boy, turning his pistol instead toward Lemmon's belly. "And here we have the Jew-loving wife-fucker from America. The years have treated you well, I presume?" Ryan said nothing. "Search him." Klaus patted down Ryan and secured the Sauer from his topcoat pocket. "No need to guess where you stumbled upon this, is there?"

Ryan saw no possibility of escape. "Horst von Kredow. You haven't changed a bit, I see," he managed to say. The pallid scar raking Horst's cheek seemed to hold all other features in place.

"Nor you, except perhaps for that ruined nose and those swollen cheeks. I remember your looking better in our university days. But enough pleasantries for now. We've been tracking your recent escapades, and you haven't changed in other regards, as well. You still lack respect for another man's property and you're still intent on saving the world's worthless Jews." He gestured with the pistol toward Erika, who had backed against the wall with the boy in her arms. "And you still stick your cock in this Jew-whore here."

"Be reasonable, Horst." Despite the strength in her voice, she trembled. "Let us go—we can't hurt you, and you don't need us."

"You dare talk about 'reasonable' actions, my treacherous little Jew-bitch?" Horst moved to the center of the room as Ryan joined Erika under the menace of the guns. Horst spoke nearly without emotion, and Ryan was struck by the unyielding mask of his face. "Was it 'reasonable' for you to hide your polluted bloodline from me, knowing I'm charged with purifying our race? Did you think I'd never find out? Was it 'reasonable' for you to use my seed to father that pathetic *Mischling* there?"

"Leo's no *Mischling*, he's your son!"

"You're mistaken, I have no son..." he shot a faint look of disgust at the cowering child, "...and no wife." He glanced around the room. "We anticipated another guest here this evening, but it appears your Frenchman ran into further delays. A shame, but don't give it a thought, we'll catch up with him. After all, we can't have foreigners—French or American, for that matter—disrupting train schedules and stealing vehicles with impunity, now can we? Who knows? My men at the front gate may be welcoming him as we speak."

Despite their dire circumstances Ryan was relieved to hear that René was not yet in their clutches.

"Horst, just let Ryan take the boy and leave," Erika pleaded, "I'll stay with you, and you can save your career. I'll do whatever you say."

"You think my career depends on your pitiful ass? No one will ever hear of this unpleasant episode, not a soul." He chuckled. "In fact, I will be offered the most heartfelt sympathies for the loss of my family in a tragic boating accident on the Rhine."

"Horst, no!" Erika looked to Ryan, who could only stare back in helpless fury.

"But we'll get to the two of you later, some fitting punishment before you suffer your unfortunate accident. In fact, I might have the boy witness his mother's penance. Obviously, you learned nothing from that little foretaste in Berlin." He turned to Klaus. "Have the bitch and her brat taken to the boat and kept comfortable. Tell the others to watch for the Frenchman. Meanwhile, we've work to do here. Let's see if our American truly appreciates what it means to be Gestapo."

Klaus opened the door and signaled to one of the soldiers. "Take these two and wait in the patrol boat." He pointed with his pistol to the woman and boy. "The guards remain at their stations." The youthful sergeant gestured to Erika with his machine pistol. She lifted Leo, his bear clutched to his chest, and gave Ryan a frantic look as she moved toward the door.

"Yes, do say good-bye to your lover; you may not recognize him later." Horst's lips tightened to a controlled sneer.

Erika looked back as she stepped onto the fog-bound deck, and Ryan could only respond with a desperate shake of his head. His mind raced for any solution and came up short. The soldier prodded her with the barrel of his gun, and Erika pulled Leo more tightly to her chest and looked away, tears streaming down her cheeks. Leo was sobbing, and then they were gone. Ryan scanned the room, searching for a potential weapon. No logic would persuade here, and no charade was possible this time around. The situation was truly hopeless.

"Make *Herr* Lemmon comfortable, won't you, Klaus? Oh, how could I have forgotten, it is *Herr Doktor* Lemmon now, isn't it?"

Klaus Pabst called in the sentry from outside and shut the door behind him. "Lose the clothing, *Herr Doktor* Lemmon." Klaus grinned at Ryan's surprise. "Lose it now, or we'll have to help you."

Ryan began to unbutton his topcoat. "That's a good American," Horst nodded, "Let's see what the Jewess found so attractive in you."

Ryan took off his topcoat and jacket and turned to place them on the table. "The floor will do nicely," suggested Klaus. Ryan removed his mud-encrusted shoes and socks and shoved them aside with his foot before dropping his pants to the floor.

"He's a bit less dashing in shirttails, don't you think?" Horst gazed around the room and gestured, as if addressing a party of on-lookers.

"Now the rest of it," ordered Klaus.

Ryan unbuttoned his vest, removed his stale shirt and under-shirt, and reluctantly dropped his shorts. He stood stock still and awaited the next command.

"Well, you certainly appear fit enough; except for that circum-cised cock, you'd make a decent SS recruit," Horst observed. "Do you suppose we have ourselves an American Jew here?" He turned for Klaus's reaction—a smug grin—and then returned his attention to Ryan. "But you really ought to do something about that face."

As if choreographed, Klaus grabbed Ryan's arms from behind and Horst swung his P38 in one fluid motion. Blood sprayed from the already-shattered nose, rivulets coursing down Ryan's face and across his shoulder. The assault was so fast, the pain so intense that

Ryan nearly collapsed. "There now," Horst said, "you'll look more symmetrical with both cheeks equally swollen."

Pabst released him and an unsteady Ryan put a hand to his damaged face and held back his head to try to stop the flow of blood.

"*Herr Doktor*, I believe you need to be seated; you're looking a bit pale." Horst gestured to one of the chairs. "Klaus, go fetch me some wire or rope from the machine shop. It's time we had a nice little chat with our guest, don't you think?"

Ryan slumped down heavily, lightheaded from loss of blood but still with enough presence of mind to swivel toward his adversary.

Klaus returned with a coil of rope and handed it to the soldier. "Tie each wrist to an armrest—palms up, it's more interesting that way—and each foot to the base. Nice and tight, now."

The sentry complied and Pabst tested the bonds. Ryan felt more than naked—with legs forced apart, he was totally exposed to his tormentor.

"Search his things," Horst ordered, as he picked up a cushion from the floor and placed it on the other desk chair. He rolled it around to face the American and sat with crossed legs, as if preparing for a casual conversation.

Klaus emptied all of Ryan's pockets, laying out the findings on the chart table. "Passport, wallet, Mont Blanc pen—very good taste, Herr Doktor—, a pipe and tobacco pouch, a comb, some maps, and a bundle of marks. And, of course, this attractive Party lapel pin." Klaus turned to the helpless American. "Hmm," he murmured, "I recall something we missed." He removed the heavy gold ring from Ryan's finger and set it next to the other belongings. "The collection is now complete."

"Almost, but not quite." Horst stared at Ryan. The swollen tissues and unstanched flow of blood were beginning to distort his features. "Now, *Herr Doktor*, judging by your recent actions, it seems your greatest wish is to join our secret state police. You certainly appear to have mastered use of the warrant badge, the one item not in our little inventory here." He gestured toward the tabletop, then rose from the chair. "Any idea where it might be? It was a personal gift, you know, so does have certain sentimental value."

Ryan said nothing, his head still tilted back to drain the blood into his sinuses.

Horst picked up the tobacco pouch and unzipped it, breathing in the aroma of the tobacco. "A strong blend. Nice choice." Ryan forced open his swollen eyes at the mention of the pouch, but remained silent. Horst zipped it shut and returned it to the table. "You're sure you don't recall where you left my badge?"

Ryan remained mute.

"Well, perhaps you'll remember shortly. Meanwhile, since you so want to be one of us, let me show you how to help detainees recall valuable information."

Horst bent down and pulled the fire poker from the scuttle beside the stove. He opened the iron door fully and stirred the coals to a frenzy of flame and spark, then left the pointed rod buried in the blazing embers. "Klaus, one more trip next door to the machine shop, if you please. Look for some implements that *Herr Doktor* Lemmon will find, shall we say, persuasive?"

In the cabin of the Water Protection Police gunboat, Erika did her best to soothe poor Leo as he whimpered softly into the folds of her coat, hugging his bear. "You're safe, darling, it'll be okay," she lied. She rocked him gently, hugging him with her free arm. "Be strong, my little man, I need you strong now."

They sat on a bench seat at the rear. The armed guard leaned against the boat wheel, eyeing her crossed legs. Her free hand in her topcoat pocket cradled the unfamiliar grip of the pistol. She was pleased it had not ended up in her handbag after all, which now hung uselessly on the wall of the shack. She had flicked off the safety as they crossed to the ramp of the police patrol boat. Horst's failure to have her searched had come as no surprise. He had always treated her as a harmless appendage to his male ego. Women did not act, they reacted. Women held no opinions; they mirrored the beliefs of their men.

Upon boarding the gunboat she had counted the armed men she had seen. Besides her SS escort she spotted two men on the forward deck, almost hidden in the swirling fog. Horst had mentioned men posted at the gates, and perhaps others were on board that she had missed. And, of course, her vile husband and the loathsome Pabst along with one additional soldier were still at the shack with poor Ryan.

But Erika was no longer a victim, and she fought the tears which threatened to weaken her. After the incident on the train she knew she was strong and could act in the face of adversity. She would not waste the certainty of the pistol. With luck there was still time to spare Ryan the pain coming his way. She imagined the horrors he would endure, for she now knew that Horst knew no compassion, respected no personal boundaries.

She would have to act soon or lose her advantage, but still she wavered. If she managed to shoot the guard—*it would be so simple to fire the pistol through the fabric, but how to aim it well?*—Leo would be endangered. She certainly could not return to the shack with Leo, and she could not leave her terrified son attended by a dead man while she went to rescue Ryan. Only one thing was certain. She would save a bullet for Horst. He would pay for this horror of a life.

First she had to handle the lecherous young SS trooper. She extended her legs a bit further, hiking her skirt to reinforce the distraction. Looking up to the guard, she smiled softly and he returned the attention with a grin.

Back in the shack, Klaus brought to the task an impressive assortment of tools in an oil-stained canvas tote. In his other fist he grasped the handle of a boat battery, and over his shoulder hung coiled jumper cables. He set the paraphernalia on the table, moving aside Ryan's possessions, and began to lay out the implements in neat order.

Horst appeared pleased with the selection, rising from the chair to run a finger over each tool in turn. "Let's see what we have here for your first lesson, *Herr Doktor.*" He picked up a set of heavy pliers with blunt ends. "First, you should know that compression and torque get good results. Sounds a bit like describing a motorcycle engine, doesn't it? Much like the *Waffen-SS* motorcycle you road-tested for us."

He set down the pliers and lifted a half-meter-long welding rod which he immediately slammed against the tabletop with a resounding thump. "Can you imagine, rods and whips do wondrous things to human flesh and can be very persuasive?"

He picked up a spoon gouge and tested its sharpness, his fingertip lightly following the u-shaped curve of the blade. "Then we have any tool that can take a fine edge. A well-honed blade tends to loosen tongues—no pun intended."

Horst turned to the battery. "And when all else fails, nothing compares to a satisfying jolt of electricity, especially on sensitive body parts." He attached the clamps and brought the cables together, releasing a cascade of sparks. "But enough introductory remarks, let's turn now to practical lessons."

He stepped over to the coal stove and withdrew the poker. "Here's my favorite of late, especially when it's so chilly outside." The tip of the poker glowed red hot. "We find it useful for delicate areas of discussion." Horst brought the radiant tip toward his fingertip, then drew it back the moment he sensed the fiery heat. Ryan gritted his teeth, determined to show no fear through sheer force of will. "Allow me to demonstrate," Horst said, "and, please, don't hesitate to speak up if this isn't warm enough for you."

Klaus approached from behind and held Ryan's chair stable, as Horst eased the smoking rod ever closer to Ryan's upper arm. His skin began to redden and singe. Abruptly, Horst forced the point into the bicep, searing the flesh as the pointed tip struck muscle. Ryan lurched back, but the chair hardly moved, and Horst withdrew the implement.

A sickening stench rose from the burned flesh. Ryan moaned and ground his teeth, but refused to cry out. The young soldier had turned aside at the first contact of the rod and now stared toward the far corner of the room, his face an ashen mask.

"Let's see if another spot is more sensitive." Horst lowered the tip of the rod to the crook of Ryan's elbow and branded him twice more in unhurried succession.

Ryan tensed each time in anticipation, then endured the flood of pain and involuntarily struggled against the bonds. He felt faint after each assault, nauseated, and tasted blood where he had bitten his tongue. He was drenched in his sweat. But he would not give them the satisfaction of hearing him scream or beg for mercy.

"Well now," said Horst, "perhaps I've misjudged you. I thought you'd be very talkative by now. Shall we see what courage you show when we bring your manhood to the party?" He returned to the stove and plunged the poker deep into the coals until the tip was once again glowing from within. "We don't want to do a half-assed job now, do we?"

Klaus showed his appreciation with a broad grin of approval and braced the chair once again while Horst approached with measured slowness. The glowing poker left a wispy trail as it neared Ryan's groin. He drew back convulsively to the limit of his bonds, every fiber of his body tensed in dread of the coming torment, and against his will his body began to twitch and tremble.

Erika first thought she heard backfire from an ill-tuned motorcycle, but then overlapping machine gun bursts answered in rapid succession. The guard recognized immediately the staccato of a fire fight and approached the door with caution, opening it a hand's breadth and peering out into the fog. A new exchange of fire drew his attention toward the entry gate of the compound.

The young SS man was obviously torn between obeying orders to babysit a harmless mother or find his first real action on the docks. Erika heard men race down the ramp in the direction of the fusillade. Now shots rang out from the bow of her launch and crossfire erupted from somewhere out on the water. Bullets struck outside the launch cabin and she dropped to the floor, pulling down Leo, abruptly wide awake, and covering his body with hers.

"*Mutti*, what's happening?"

"Hush, Leo. Just do as I say and we'll be fine."

The guard ignored his charges, his focus shifting to an attack coming from across the water. "Stay here," he ordered, and cocking his MP36 he slipped out of the cabin onto the gangway.

The cabin door remained ajar and Erika could see landside toward the warehouses and the main firefight. Gunfire rattled the length of the wharf. Several soldiers shouted to each other from the gravel below.

"Wait here and keep down," she whispered to Leo as she crawled on all fours toward the boat's wheel. She opened a tool box strapped to the wall and found a screw driver and a wrench. Pocketing the ignition key, she jammed the screw driver into the slot and pounded it with the makeshift hammer.

She motioned to Leo and he raced over with bear in hand and leapt into her arms at the open doorway. Heavy caliber bullets continued to ricochet from the portside cabin wall. She told Leo to hang on tightly, ducked down, and they slipped from the cabin. In her right hand she gripped the Sauer, its safety off.

The Gesslinger launch moored directly ahead suggested their best hope for refuge. To a cascade of gunfire from the direction of the gates, Erika ran down the ramp as fast as she could toward the smaller boat, clutching the boy to her chest.

The gun mounted atop the police vessel suddenly opened up, its heavy-caliber rounds splitting the air as the gunner found the range for a small motorboat closing at high speed from the boat basin and firing in their direction. A massive ball of flame churned high into the night sky, dispersing the fog in its brilliant aura as its concussive blast rattled along the row of warehouses. Erika saw two bodies flung high out over the water, silhouetted against the roiling blast as fire consumed the hull of the stricken vessel.

Reaching the launch, she stuck the pistol back in her pocket, tugged at the mooring rope to draw the boat closer to the dock, and then climbed gingerly aboard. Bending low, she pulled back the corner of the canvas deck cover and they both slipped under, now well hidden in the darkness. She dropped over the side the ignition key from her pocket and heard it splash.

"Stay here, my love, and don't move until I'm back," she whispered.

"But *Mutti*, don't leave, I'm scared."

"I'll be right back with Herr Lemmon and we'll get out of here, all right?"

Leo, obedient as ever, nodded before adding in a barely audible voice: "I'll be all right, Mommy. I have Bruno."

# CHAPTER FOUR

A secret police system immune to all laws and judicial review had one obvious downside— how to determine who was working on what, and on whose behalf. Denunciations were as prevalent among the relatively few police agents as among the great mass of informants who made the system function. The German people were as intimidated by the threat of "protective detention" as the police were of aggravating the wrong senior officer. René turned this confusion to his benefit in escaping the mayhem on the train.

Once his friends disappeared into the night, he had limped back to the compartment to confirm that the downed agent was still unconscious. And once certain no one was watching, he delivered an extra blow just to maintain that status quo. He then demanded to speak to the chief conductor, whom he found directing the search by lantern for further evidence of a body alongside the tracks.

Despite his limp and the uneven ground, René moved quickly to join the group gathered in their dark uniforms. Flashing the warrant badge and wielding the imperious tone of someone used to immediate obedience, he warned the train crew that any further delay risked charges of hampering official Gestapo business. He offered a simple explanation—a traitor to the Reich had attempted to exit the moving train via a window, and perished for his efforts. Case closed. Meanwhile his own partner lay unconscious on board, very likely suffering from a concussion, and any further delay put the survival of a Gestapo agent in jeopardy.

No one questioned the obvious authority of the man, nor dared risk detention for thwarting an official action of the Gestapo. The train official ordered crew and curious passengers back to the cars, the doors slammed shut, and a minute later the train was once again underway. Let the police sort out the mess later.

René called for a doctor or nurse, and a Wehrmacht medic traveling on family leave was assigned the oversight of Fischer. The soldier and a passenger recruited from the aisle moved the limp body from the floor to the bench seat, and the officious Gestapo officer with a pronounced limp left the medic behind in the compartment.

René exited the train at the next scheduled stop, and two hours passed before he could board the next express south with connection to Kehl. The Gestapo badge was his ticket.

At the Karlsruhe stop he phoned Hugo to warn of the fugitives' possible arrival ahead of him. He knew immediately something was wrong—the phone rang incessantly without response. René himself had arranged for the quick transfer of Ryan's party across the river, and the launch was already out of the boathouse and tied dockside before he left Kehl. Hugo was to have sprung into action the moment the "shipment" reached the docks. Hugo—always reliable, always on time. *Even to take a piss he'd use the latrine in the office shack,* René thought. *Answer, dammit!*

During the final nerve-wracking kilometers he considered his options, and at the Kehl rail station he phoned once more. No response at either the dockside shack or the main warehouse office. He placed two coded calls over the public phone to alert his network. His comrades were to meet him in forty-five minutes to review a plan of engagement, and they were to come fully armed.

René reached the wooded area above the estuary early. He moved with difficulty, his tweaked leg making the going painful, but the path was well-known since childhood. He quickly spotted two armed sentries just a dozen meters up from the gate. The soldiers apparently considered themselves well-hidden, but their cigarettes offered them up in the fog, and René was able to move close enough to recognize their Schmeissers. One laughed loudly at the obscene comment of the other. If all were as careless as these two, the assault would be over quickly. René returned to the rendezvous point.

His seven men gathered in silence. Each knew the dangers involved; each was committed to the cause despite not knowing the target of their rescue. It was enough to fight the tyranny of the system, enough that René had asked.

When the team was complete, René laid out his plan. Three would launch a frontal attack on the gate, firing from the woods and moving rapidly about to suggest a larger force. The goal was to draw out the SS so they could pick off the combatants one by one. If Ryan's group was already in Gestapo clutches, the firefight should lure out their guards and leave the fugitives open for rescue from dock- or waterside. Three other men would use a gate at the south end of the company grounds and work their way north behind the warehouses, then cross over toward the office shack and machine shop. René and his strongest fighter Uwe would sneak north to the boathouse beyond the storage yard, return by motorboat across the boat basin, and rescue the fugitives, then spirit them to safety in France.

The assault had begun as planned with a burst of gunfire from his men at the main gate and returning bursts from the Schmeissers. This signaled the teams situated to both south and north to move in. Then, from the vantage point of their boat as they crossed the basin at low throttle, all hell broke loose. An unexpected gunboat dockside suddenly towered out of the fog and fire coming from its prow caught René and Uwe off-guard.

The initial rounds glanced off the water and ricocheted into the darkness. Uwe raked the larger boat with quick bursts from his machine pistol, and they received stronger fire in return, their bow taking a few direct hits. His comrade let loose again with a staccato burst before René pivoted the motorboat to return to the cloak of dense fog. They cut quickly north and angled back in to attack from a different quadrant.

The unmistakable wail of incoming 57-mm Mauser rounds told René they were now outgunned by a boat-mounted MG34. He throttled up and spun the boat, but knew immediately that his response came too late.

The blinding flash and wall of searing flame tore apart his world as their boat's fuel tank exploded and the craft surrendered to a firestorm of burning wood and twisted metal.

# CHAPTER FIVE

Ryan held his breath at the approach of the glowing rod, his body tormented by an uncontrollable shaking. The searing wounds were forgotten in anticipation of what was yet to come. At the last second he tried to turn his head aside, but Klaus grabbed him by the hair, pulling back on his scalp, forcing him to watch. The mutilation would be burned into his visual memory as well as his groin. With his focus so intensely riveted, Ryan never heard the gunfire outside.

At the first burst of shots, Horst glanced toward the window. Only fog drifted across the dimly-lit rail tracks between shack and warehouse. "Ah, the final member of your criminal band arrives at last," he said to the trembling American. "Will he enjoy sharing your lessons, as well?"

Sporadic firing now echoed off the warehouses, but also to the south and from the water, and Horst realized his men had lost control. Such a simple assignment for the dozen SS soldiers and Water Protection Police recruited for the task: stay out of sight and take the Frenchman when he arrives. Either his men had all gone mad, or the new arrival had appeared at the gate with help. And the dockside action suggested that the police patrol boat was also under fire. Clearly not the simple arrest he had foreseen.

"It appears Herr Gesslinger has brought support of his own," Horst said, and buried the fire poker back in the belly of the stove, stirring the coals to flame.

Klaus and the soldier were peering into the night from the partially-opened door when a brilliant explosion out on the water to their backs rattled the shack, and the lagoon flared in orange light, casting a diffused glow across the warehouse walls beyond the cranes and tracks.

Ryan released his breath. His heart raced. He stared down at his blistered arm and heaving, bloodied chest, grateful for any interruption, fearing what would come next.

"I regret a brief interruption to go greet your clumsy French friend, but don't concern yourself." Horst strode to the door. "Do sit tight, and we'll be right back to pick up where we left off. Make yourself comfortable. You're my guest."

Horst drew his P38 and Klaus followed suit, taking off the safety. The three slipped out into the night, closing the door gently behind them. Ryan heard his tormentors move down the ramp in the direction of the main gate as the young soldier headed south toward the patrol boat.

Ryan struggled for composure, the trembling easing but his nerves torn raw. The bleeding from his nose had stilled, and he forced himself to ignore the agonizing pain along his arm. He knew he held in his bound hands one chance to rescue Erika and Leo and get them across the river.

Rocking against his rope ties, he scooted the chair within a hand's-breadth of the table. The tools remained invitingly close but just beyond reach. In a chair on rollers, he couldn't gain the traction needed to dislodge a sharp implement, and there was no guarantee anything useful would fall within reach anyway. He considered tipping his chair to topple the table, but realized the heavy load of tools spread across its surface made that impossible. The sharp blades taunted him. He was no closer to escape.

The obvious choice: the coal stove, glowing once again red at its belly. He scanned the room for other options, well aware that his tormentors could return at any moment. But he found no further choices open to him, and committed himself to the plan. Rocking himself in unsteady increments closer to the stove, he held his face back from the intense heat. For a brief moment he thought the handle of the poker extending from the firebox might be hot enough for his purpose, but regrettably it sat well below his grasp. Instead, he sidled back up to the belly of the stove and inched his left wrist closer.

His teeth clenched as the heat began to crisp the hair on his forearm. The stench of singeing flesh reached through the congealed blood in his nostrils. He worked his wrist closer to the stove, watching intently for the rope to catch fire, cramping his fist toward his body to spare it the worst damage. Sheer force of will suppressed the instinct to retreat.

His breath came in gasps as the skin of his wrist turned fiery red before beginning to buckle and char. But simultaneously the tight coil of rope burst into knots of flame, and Ryan jerked with all his might. An agonizing jolt ran through his arm, and the smoking strands finally gave way. The smoldering cord fell from his tortured wrist.

Ignoring the pain, he scooted the chair back to the table and found a sharp knife to cut the remaining bonds, then rose to his feet. Lightheadedness and nausea nearly felled him, forcing him to brace himself on the table. He afforded himself a moment to recover before dressing, stuffing his belongings and the tobacco pouch into his trouser pockets, abandoning jacket and topcoat as impractical for what he now faced.

Erratic gunfire and an occasional shout echoed along the wharf. Footsteps drummed on gravel to the front of the shack as he opened the window facing the water. The wounds on his arm and wrist fought for attention, but he focused on the job at hand, for any moment von Kredow would return to renew the torment.

He lowered himself feet first to hang three meters above the lagoon, anticipating a drop directly into the frigid water. About to release his grip, he found footing on a narrow ledge running the length of the pier and began to work his way toward the motor launch. His hands drew splinters each time he lost his hold on the weathered shiplap, but pilings every few meters jutted from the water, offering temporary relief to his cramping hands.

As he neared the Gesslinger boat the ghostly image of a much larger vessel loomed out of the fog just beyond. He remembered the heavy thrumming of the engines preceding Horst's arrival, and now knew where he would find Erika and Leo.

Angry shouts rose from within the shed. Horst had returned. Ryan quickly lowered himself down a piling to chest level in the icy water. He drew in a deep breath and then dropped beneath the oily surface and slipped under the dock.

The intense cold sent a shudder through his body. He lifted his head just above the lapping surface to draw air and tread water. The left arm ached and responded slowly to his mind's commands. The wash of creosote and fuel oil worked his tortured sinuses, straining his breathing. Once oriented to the murky world beneath the dock, he moved on with a clumsy breast stroke, his progress measured by pilings silhouetted against the fog-shrouded waters of the boat basin.

His advance was broken by a sodden mass which shifted in response to his forward momentum. His arm struck billowing fabric, and a lifeless hand rose up to graze his cheek. Ryan paddled aside abruptly in horror, and the kick of his leg sent the corpse floating outward toward the open water. The head bobbed just above the surface and the arms to either side formed wings of saturated wool rippling on the surface. Facing head down, the dead man appeared to search the floor of the lagoon. Pale, disrupted flesh encircled a dark hole in the back of Hugo Gerson's balding head.

Erika was worried. As she crawled from beneath the tarp where Leo hid, she spied Ryan emerging feet-first from the window of the shack. She observed his slow progress along the narrow ledge, followed by a rapid descent into the water as coarse shouts went up from within the shack. She then ducked quickly back beneath the tarp as armed men raced toward the gunboat to her rear. When she lifted the flap once again, Ryan was gone.

He had to be in the murky waters beneath the dock, working his way toward the police boat where they had been held. She knew Ryan would come for them. In the process he would pass right by her refuge, unaware that they were already free to escape this nightmare.

She looked for a way to signal Ryan when he swam by only meters away. A boat hook was attached to the wall of the launch, but she saw no way to extend it under the dock with any certainty that he would notice. She thought of tossing a lit flashlight into the water as a beacon, but found none. In desperation, and knowing that he must be very near, she slipped off her topcoat and shoes and prepared to enter the water.

"*Mutti?*" Leo whispered in amazement from the darkness. "You're going swimming?"

"Just for a moment, Leo, I need to find Herr Lemmon."

"Herr Lemmon's in the water?"

"Yes, darling," she said. "He's looking for us."

"Why's he looking in the water? We're not in the water."

"He doesn't want to be seen by the soldiers, or by your father."

"Wait here." Leo moved toward the opening in the tarp. "I'll just call Herr Lemmon over."

"No, Leo, hush! We mustn't let anyone else know we're in here, my love." She realized he had been through untold hours of inexplicable adult behavior.

"*Mutti?*"

"Yes, love."

"I don't want to be a secret policeman anymore. And neither does Bruno."

"Neither do I, darling, neither do I. Now sit tight here—no more questions—and I'll be right back with Herr Lemmon."

She eased herself into the icy water, shuddering briefly before taking the plunge. Her aching abdominal muscles rebelled and her teeth chattered, but her breast stroke brought her under the dock where she treaded water, hoping against hope that Ryan had not yet passed them by. With relief she heard the gentle wash of his approach and called out to him softly.

"Thank God, you're still here!"

He paddled over to her. "Where's Leo?"

"He's safe, just above us in the motorboat. I came for you."

The soldier responsible for binding the American and the guard who had left the Jewess unattended were already in custody and would suffer suitable punishment. That would come later. For the moment Horst focused on the damaged ignition switch of the patrol boat.

Only moments before, the small craft moored at their bow had sprung to life with a harsh roar. By the time he and Klaus arrived forward, the smaller boat was merely a blemish on the fog, carving a broad turn toward open water. Carbine shots fired by the men on deck had no apparent effect on the fugitive craft. "After them, now!" he had ordered the captain of the patrol boat. It was then they had discovered the sabotage.

"The ignition is *kaputt*, sir," reported the captain.

A livid Horst was in no mood for incompetence. "Then you damned well better fix it," he growled.

His uncompromising glare made clear no excuse would be tolerated. The captain grabbed tools and opened the console panel. The sounds of battle outside had diminished to a desultory exchange of fire. As long seconds ticked by, the nervous water police officer buried his head in the control panel, pliers and wire cutters in hand. Finally emerging with a look of satisfaction, he drew out the choke and brought together two extended wires in his hand. A spark preceded a deep, throaty rumble from the bowels of the vessel as the engines roared to life.

"Get us out of here, and now!" Horst commanded.

Two men freed the lines and the vessel swung out from the wharf into the fog-shrouded basin. The pilot gunned the throbbing engines and the patrol boat gathered speed in pursuit of the Gesslinger launch.

# CHAPTER SIX

Ryan shuddered, as much from the cold as from the pure terror of the moment. Soaked to the skin, his tortured arm and swollen face restricting movement, and exhausted by hours of struggle, he now knew with certainty that the larger boat would soon overtake them. His boating skills were no match for those of the professional seamen gaining on his launch with every second.

Near the mouth of the estuary they had decelerated in passing the overturned hull of a boat identical to their own, its shattered keel bobbing in the current. Erika told him of the destructive explosion and the bodies thrown free by the blast. An orange-black-white flag drifted on the surface near the charred wreckage, and he was forced to accept that Rene's best efforts at rescue had gone up in flames.

Reaching the lamps marking the confluence with the Rhine, they had been relieved that no lights were yet in pursuit, but they both knew Horst would never give up the chase. Their boat cut a channel through the shifting bank of fog as they entered the river. There was little traffic other than an occasional smear of light out on the water. But Ryan found it daunting to steer a course toward a goal he could not see, navigating solely by instinct. Hoping to lose his pursuers, he switched off their running lights, acknowledging increased vulnerability to any vessels that were challenging the fogbound shipping lanes.

Only the soft glow from the dash panel allowed him to see his companions on the seat beside him. Erika and Leo huddled from the frigid wind under the canvas tarp. Erika was as soaked as Ryan, but had donned her topcoat for additional warmth. She held Leo on her lap and rocked him in her arms as the launch pounded the choppy surface of the river. They heard nothing but the thrum of their engine and the thump of the hull.

Searchlights suddenly blinded them in a luminous wash. "Heave to," boomed a loudspeaker, and Ryan and Erika turned in despair. The fervent hope of the last twenty-four hours was dissolving in that all-encompassing glare. "Heave to," repeated the command, now clearly audible over the beat of their hull against the turbulent river.

The futility of further effort drained Ryan's will. Looking back at the hull now towering over his pitiful boat, he spotted the machine gun mounted atop the pursuing craft. At any moment Horst could order them blown from the water. He thought of the smoldering remains of the Gesslinger launch. Alive, they clung to a slim possibility of survival. Ryan eased back on the throttle and allowed the boat to drift in the forceful current. Despite several good battles he feared they had lost the war.

"No!" Erika's guttural cry of protest came from deep within, and Leo burst out in sobs at his mother's anguish.

"There's no choice, Erika," Ryan said. "We have to play this out."

Ryan let the engine idle and raised his hands in defeat. Under the wash of the spotlight he spotted Horst and his lieutenant up on deck. An SS man in green uniform stood to the aft with a line, and as the police vessel pulled alongside he tossed down the rope and ordered Ryan to secure their launch. The gun boat reversed engines to slow their movement in the heavy current.

"I'll find a way—" he said to Erika, "trust me, I'll find us a way out of this." He ached to believe his own words. "Believe me—I will save you."

The water policeman lowered a short rope ladder and joined the fugitives in the motorboat.

"Bring him up to me now!" Horst's voice was edged with fury. "We've unfinished business, *Herr Doktor* Lemmon and I."

At the prodding of the policeman's gun, Ryan climbed the rope ladder, his movements agonizingly clumsy as the two linked craft bobbed on the choppy waters and his damaged arm failed to respond. Topside someone grabbed him roughly by the collar and slammed him face down onto the deck, and Klaus forcefully pinned Ryan's neck with his foot. The policeman gestured to Erika to follow Ryan up the ladder, and reached down to take Leo.

"No!" Horst commanded. "Woman and child stay in the boat. You, sailor, get back up here, now!" The man appeared surprised by the order but complied, and skillfully ascended the ladder. Horst turned to shout to the men on deck. "Now cut them loose."

"Horst!" Erika's voice shrill in the damp air. "Horst, you don't want to do this!"

"Oh, but I do, I actually do." Horst turned to the crewman. "Cut them loose, tell your captain to back off, then send that Jewish scum to the bottom. Either ram the boat, or use the gun on top. Enough of this shit—I want them gone, and now."

"But, sir—" The man hesitated.

Erika fired twice in rapid succession, the first shot wide and striking the cabin. The second—by chance well aimed—entered just below Horst's chin, shattering both his jaw and teeth as it tunneled up to exit just above his pale scar of honor. His head thrown back by the impact, the long-damaged nerve reacted violently to the insult, sending him into a paroxysm of agony. Horst jerked to the left, and his mangled jaw hung loose as he crumpled to the deck. He twitched violently, hands at his shattered face.

The policeman dropped to the deck below Erika's sights. She crouched low, her left arm around Leo, her gun hand zeroing in on Klaus.

"You fucking Jew-bitch," he screamed, then drew his weapon and raced to the railing, extending his arm to fire on Erika and Leo.

The roll of the boat sent her next two shots wide.

Ryan sprang from a crouched position, putting full momentum into a body block to hit the Nazi before he could fire. Unprepared for the side attack, Klaus lost balance upon Ryan's impact and the two men tumbled overboard into the dark waters.

Erika screamed as the two men hit the water and slipped beyond the circle of the light. With Leo cowering at her feet, she turned, desperately seeking to sever the lines linking the two vessels. Instead she found the water policeman at her side again, wrenching the pistol from her grasp. Disarmed, she settled beside Leo on the deck of the launch and cradled him once again in her arms.

"I don't know your crime, madam, but you've just assaulted an SS officer in the performance of his duties," said the man, "and you are under arrest."

Erika remained mute. With her face held high, tears of fury and resignation streaming down her cheeks, she buried Leo's head at her breast.

"But you needn't worry, madam, your son will be well cared-for by the Reich."

# CHAPTER SEVEN

There comes a moment in drowning when survival loses its appeal. Muscles in thighs and calves cramp mercilessly, but pain becomes immaterial. The wrenching cold no longer sucks away the breath and the water no longer chokes, but rather soothes as it finds its way into tortured lungs. Mind and body yield to a calm acceptance that winning the battle is not worth further struggle, and the focus shifts from the life now receding to whatever comes next. Ryan was nearing that realization.

He had hit the water with Klaus Pabst flailing at his side and immediately fought the current which drew them relentlessly beyond the reach of the searchlight. He struggled back toward Erika and Leo, the halo surrounding the patrol boat a radiant target, but the powerful river and the sodden clothes hampered his best efforts, his damaged arm made him half the swimmer he once was, and he made no progress toward his goal.

An arm abruptly encircled his neck as the Gestapo agent sought to surface using Ryan as his buoy. The added weight forced him below the surface, and he fought panic as he worked to free himself. He sensed no aggression in his smothering burden, just terror at the immediacy of drowning and a single-minded intent to climb ever higher. Ryan repeatedly forced his own head above the surface to fight for air while trying to loosen the choking hold at his neck.

The target of light retreated into the dense fog, and gradually Ryan yielded to the inevitable. He kicked his cramping legs forcefully one last time to reach the surface, his movements directed now by

instinct rather than conscious thought. As he inhaled both air and
water, a new and expanding circle of light emerged from the darkness. It grew quickly to engulf him, and he realized that this was the
end of his life, a corridor of light to draw him in and spirit him away.

Aboard the Dutch river transport eight bells had already struck, and
Hindrik Kranz hoped the captain would take pity and send the mate
early to relieve him, but he knew it would never happen. His eyes
watered from the strain of staring into the deep fog. Other than occasional marker lights warning of bridge footings and hazards, all he
saw before him was the turbulent flow and the shifting banks of
mist. Most traffic had put in for the night, but Hindrik's captain,
running ballast back to Rotterdam, counted the lost income and was
determined to keep on schedule. Hindrik looked forward to the
Middle Rhine some hours ahead. Far less monotonous, and at least
by then it would be daylight and the fog partially lifted.

Hindrik had been nervous when they put in at Strasbourg just
past midnight. The talk among the river men was of synagogue
burnings and Jew-baiting in Germany, which had found an echo in
the streets of Strasbourg. Hindrik was himself a Jew. He chose not to
join the captain and the mate for a beer break on shore, begging a
cup of coffee instead from the captain's wife in the warmth of the
cabin.

But now the boatman's apprentice sat at the very prow of the
Rotterdam transport, his back to the railing, a coil of rope insulating
him from the cold decking. A bottle of *Grolsch* from the captain's
store now kept him company. The boat's engine rumbled faintly
from astern, turning at low speed to keep the craft under control in
the current, but allowing the flow of the Rhine to do the heavy
work.

The searchlight, normally devoted to nighttime transfer of cargo, was Hindrik's sole responsibility as the long vessel found its way
downstream. He swung its beam through the dense fog, picking out
a wallowing tree branch or a floating crate. Running lights from
other vessels passed from time to time as muted spots of brightness,
and another Rhine boat passed them heading south as they slipped
beneath the Kehl railroad bridge. Hindrik had already spent two

hours on watch by the time they left Strasbourg, and he faced another stint of equal length before he would be relieved by the mate. He yawned and forced his tired eyes to squint into the murkiness ahead.

At first he thought of some animal—*a stag, perhaps?*—struggling for the opposite bank. He directed the beam on the creature and blinked to clear his vision, but the animal was already gone from sight. Then the view cleared once more, and Hindrik saw in amazement a creature with two heads. At last—too late to react—he knew the boat was bearing down on two men, locked in a violent embrace in an effort to stay above the roiling waters. No time to signal the captain, no way to change course on such short notice. The struggling men were directly in the boat's path. Hindrik raced aft along the slippery deck.

As the radiant circle engulfed him, Ryan's dulled senses abruptly came alert. A river vessel approached relentlessly, its massive bulk now filling his horizon. He made a final futile effort to break the chokehold of the man on his back, for it was act now or never again. Drawing a great breath, and with what little strength remained, Ryan dove.

The churning waters tossed him from side to side and he tumbled, losing sense of direction in the turbulence. He felt a jolt at his neck and was finally free of the choking grasp. He kicked and kicked again, hoping he was moving down and away from the massive keel and pounding engine above him. The throb grew in intensity as the long vessel passed overhead, and he was briefly aware of striking something on the river bottom. But then—his lungs threatening to burst but his will to survive reawakened—he knew he had to surface.

There were no memories of those final moments in the water, only of the warm glow of the lantern, the rough wool blanket around his shoulders, and the acne-scarred young boatman—the one who had thrown him the life-saving ring—repeatedly asking in Dutch: "Are you sure you're all right?"

He was not. He had lost Erika and he had lost his son. And his promise to her had proved nothing but empty words.

# CHAPTER EIGHT

Intense depression plagued his waking hours, and nightmares woke him often through the long nights of recovery.

Once he dreamed of embracing Erika, the sleeping child between them, when something amorphous and terrifying tore them both from his reach. Another time he swam endlessly through a watery world of floating corpses, each lifeless body pushed aside to reveal the next. Again and again he struggled with an unseen man who forced Ryan's head from a train window to face a rapidly advancing column of steel.

He would awaken drenched in sweat and wracked with sorrow at his failure to save his friends. The physical and mental exhaustion slipped away, gradually and barely noticed, but the sorrow remained.

The Dutch boat captain had put in at the next port and seen him fed and lodged at a local inn. He had refused Ryan's offer of water-logged German currency and wished the American well. Ryan had insisted that some reward go to the boatman's apprentice, and the captain had resignedly accepted cash on the youth's behalf. A local doctor fussily dressed the brutalized nose, covered the burns with sulfa powder and gauze, and gave Ryan a sedative. The physician also refused compensation for his troubles. Ryan had then slipped into a deep and troubled sleep.

He never learned who had purchased a train ticket to Paris and placed it and five hundred francs in the pocket of his trousers, probably the same person who had dried and pressed them, laundered his shirt, and left a wool jacket hanging in his room at the inn. All of his other personal possessions were laid out on a dresser in his room.

When he awoke Ryan went first to the tobacco pouch. Its secret was safe.

His mind beset with grief, he remembered very little of the trip to the French capital. But by the afternoon of the first full day in Paris he was sufficiently recovered to see a physician, who repositioned the broken nose cartilage and applied ungainly bandages to both face and arm. He then made his way to the American embassy to meet with the cultural attaché designated his contact in the French capital. Once the story of his escape was told in detail, Ryan asked permission to reenter Germany to complete his mission. Several hours passed, cables exchanged with Washington, and he was informed that State had rejected his proposed return to the field. He was to be in D.C. at the first opportunity, once his health permitted.

The attaché reminded him that his cover was compromised by the attempt to bring out his friends, and State was concerned that a return would jeopardize the work he had done prior to the recent episode. After all, there was certainly a border watch at all German entry points for anyone matching Ryan's physical description and credentials, especially now with the obvious damage to his face.

He borrowed the use of a typewriter to write a brief explanation of the film's provenance, typing with one finger, his damaged left arm and wrist rebelling, then sealed letter and cartridge in a manila envelope addressed to his brother at the Department of State, highest priority. With great reluctance but recognizing the urgency, Ryan entrusted the envelope to the diplomatic pouch destined to leave that evening for the States.

The fate of Erika and Leo was never far from his mind and self-recrimination became his constant companion. Paris was gray and dismal to match his mood, and he holed up in his hotel room for most of the first week. He buried his beloved Berlin briar—now waterlogged and soured—beneath a tree in the Luxembourg gardens, as if burying his past. He drank Irish whiskey and smoked a new pipe. Occasionally he passed a restless hour in a café along St-Germain-des-Prés, combing the papers for any news from inside Germany. He visited Marita in the hope that her smile would cheer him up, but her valiant attempts at gaiety only depressed him further. He requested she write him immediately should she hear anything at all from his German friends, and she assured him she would.

Two weeks later he boarded the *SS Normandie*, departing Le Havre for New York. The embassy had made the booking and was sending him home first class to aid his recovery. All that meant nothing to him. He passed the stormy trans-Atlantic crossing alone in his cabin, or wrapped in a blanket on a deck chair, staring out to sea and speaking to no one.

# CHAPTER NINE

Washington reveled in holiday finery, and the wreaths on lampposts and garlands strung across the avenues helped spread the festive mood. Recent snow had turned to slush, but no one seemed to mind the inconvenience. Streets bustled with yellow cabs and busy shoppers, and come evening, well-dressed party-goers avoided puddles to race up the steps and join friends at elegant gatherings over punch bowls and champagne.

It was a world apart from the somber mood Ryan had left in Europe, where the specter of imminent war loomed in every headline and fervent radio broadcast. He felt uncomfortable amidst all the cheer. It was difficult to return smiles and Christmas greetings from well-meaning strangers as he and Edward made their way up the stone steps in the State Department building.

Ryan felt self-conscious with the small bandage across his nose. His face had swollen grossly in the first days in Paris, and as the swelling subsided he was left with a cast of deep purplish green. Now, several weeks later, his eyes still suggested a severe hang-over. Polite inquiries elicited a vague reference to surgical correction of a deviated septum. Scar tissue was rapidly replacing the scabs hidden beneath his jacket, and he exercised daily to keep the healing tissue from tethering and loosing elasticity.

Edward and Grace, their pregnancy now well advanced, had met the *Normandie* dockside in Manhattan and brought Ryan home to Falls Church for his first night. Edward hid his shock at seeing the unexpected changes in his brother. *Joie de vivre* had surrendered to a haunted look and cautious manner, and Ryan seemed uneasy in public, more nervously attentive to his surroundings and the actions of strangers than to his companions' words and questions. A melancholic bitterness crept into every response to inquiries about his travels, and he adamantly refused to speak in detail of the tragic events which had brought him home prematurely, always requesting more time to sort things out.

After dinner the brothers sat before the hearth in the sitting room of the townhome. Grace excused herself, mentioning the trials of pregnancy. Ryan took a dutiful sip of the warmed brandy before setting down the snifter to stare morosely into the flames. Edward had held his peace for as long as he could, and felt he deserved some answers. After all, it was his reputation in German Affairs that had suffered from Ryan's actions, and he had never been one to mince words.

"I have to ask, Ryan...so what in God's name were you thinking? Abandoning your assignment to meddle in the personal lives of a Nazi bigwig and his family? It appeared sheer lunacy from our end!"

"I had no choice; he would have had them killed. It was act and act immediately."

"One always has choices, Ryan. You were there to observe, record, report. Your assignment was clear: *covertly* establish a network." He lit a cigarette. "Instead, you risked an international incident."

"These were loving, beautiful people, not statistics. I can't expect you to understand, but they needed my help." He stared at the flames.

"There are groups putting their minds to solving this problem of the European Jews, and it goes beyond a few individuals, as you well know. The situation is too big and too troubling to be solved on a case-by-case basis. But your efforts put my work here at risk—I did vouch for you, Ryan—and your imprudent actions brought our assignment to an untimely close." He paused. "And in spite of all that, it all came to nothing."

Edward saw his brother cringe and wished he had not uttered that truth, but the words were out, and there was nothing more to be said. At least the work they had done before the unfortunate Berlin events had provided useful intelligence. His office was attempting to put the best face on this personal fiasco for The Group and ultimately for his father-in-law.

"And the photographic evidence, it's worth nothing at all? Have you yourself even looked at what we...at what I brought back?"

"The film went immediately to Kohl. Now it's up to the Secretary to decide how to best use it. He did express gratitude for that, and for the networks you managed to identify. In fact, few of the other operatives managed to do as well, but that's why your loss to the project hurt us all so much."

Edward then suggested they drop the whole matter until the detailed story could be properly recorded at State, so he spent a tense quarter hour making small talk about family and old friends.

Ryan appeared barely present, his unlit pipe in hand, the brandy long forgotten. When neither had more to say, Ryan rose from the wingback chair, excusing his exhaustion after the long days of travel, and retreated to his room. The next day Ed rescheduled the debriefing at State, giving his brother another week to recover.

Now that week had passed and Ryan sat in a closed conference room, his eyes often flitting to the wall clock as it trudged through the hours. One of his trainers from the farm camp was there, two newly-met functionaries from State, and Edward to help tie down loose ends in the rambling narrative. Large charts displayed linkages and contact data for the networks. If and when hostilities with Nazi Germany became a reality, and America or her allies needed the help, these would be resources to help wage a covert war. Edward referred to memos taken from Ryan's earlier dispatches and filled in the blanks whenever his brother's recollections became disjointed and his mood darkened.

Two secretaries took shorthand notes of Lemmon's rambling account of his months in France and Germany. His brother took silent note of Ryan's hazy mental focus. The sharp insight and dazzling memory which had been his trademarks had been sapped by recent events, and Edward hoped that time and distance would heal the wounds and restore his brother's strengths. He had the potential to be a valuable asset again someday if he just kept his wits about him and learned to follow directives rather than whims.

Ryan's depressed mood did not lift during the narrative and questioning, and soured noticeably late in the day when his account reached the now-compromised "Lone Ranger" network. It was difficult to know how much of the old friend's cadre was still untouched, ready to be activated when needed. Ryan was convinced that his failures had effectively destroyed that enterprise along with any surviving Gesslingers.

He knew in his heart the explosion witnessed by Erika had taken his friend. Letters had gone unanswered, one sent before boarding the Normandie and another upon arrival in New York. Both home and business numbers for René were now disconnected. The SS and Gestapo would not have ignored the Gesslinger role in Ryan's failed rescue attempt, and he was saddened to think that René's mother Jeanne had also paid for Ryan's personal shortcomings. And Erika and Leo's fate in Gestapo hands was already written large in the spilled blood of her parents.

Only the final hour of the debriefing focused on that frantic run from Berlin to Kehl. It was obvious to Ed—and quickly to the others present—that the emotional wounds were still too raw to allow a more detailed investigation into what had gone wrong. Ryan's normally resonant voice became brittle. His hands trembled. After an overview of the twenty-four hour odyssey and a few probing questions about security issues of possible value to future covert operations, Ed proposed calling it a day.

"What about the film, the proof of Hitler's plans for Eastern Europe? My friends died for that, and we're not even going to discuss it?" Ryan's knuckles turned white as he gripped the arms of his chair.

Ed looked up quickly from filing his notes into a portfolio. "Secretary Kohl wishes to personally express his thanks for all you've done." He consulted the wall clock. "I believe he can see you now."

Ed excused the others and they gathered up notepads and folders. Looking forward to the weekend, they hurried out with briefcases in hand, exchanging wishes for enjoyable holiday fun. The secretaries removed the charts from the walls and received instructions to get them to Edward in typed format first thing Monday morning.

After a brief call to Kohl's office, Edward assured Ryan that Deputy Assistant Secretary was waiting for him. He gave his brother an encouraging pat on the back before leaving for his own office. "Let's grab a drink afterwards before we catch the train."

Ryan found Kohl's receptionist behind a cleared desk and with time on her hands, obviously awaiting his arrival. She took his top-coat and hat and hung them on the rack before escorting him into the office. Nothing appeared changed since his last visit.

Kohl removed his reading glasses and rose from the chair to greet Ryan cordially, coming around to shake his hand, grasping it firmly in both of his. "Congratulations on a challenging job well done, Dr. Lemmon. You lived up to the promise we saw in you, and then some. Coffee?"

"Thank you, sir, but no coffee, I've had more than my share to-day." Ryan acknowledged the offer of a chair and sat down.

"No offense intended, but you're still looking a bit under the weather. Ed tells me things got a bit rough toward the end?"

"Things are rough for everyone over there."

"Yes, can't be helped, I'm afraid. Comes with the territory, so to speak."

"I hope today's debriefing will aid the Department's work."

"I'm sure it shall, Dr. Lemmon. I just hung up with your broth-er and he assures me that your groundwork will make our job easier in the coming months. Thank you for your fine service."

"Sir, the film I sent you? It's damning evidence, I know. Has the Secretary...has the President...put it to use, yet? Many lives are at stake, and it makes mincemeat of Hitler's claims to having no further territorial ambitions."

"Yes, we do thank you for your efforts there, as well." Kohl straightened the files lying before him on the desk, lining up the edges to perfection, then slid the pile aside and looked up. "But I'm afraid you overestimate the importance. Undoubtedly just another effort by a subordinate to impress Hitler with his zeal."

"Overestimate the importance?" Ryan was stunned. "How do you overestimate intent to conquer all Europe and annihilate millions of innocent people?"

"Now, Dr. Lemmon, please take it easy. We know you have a special concern—let's say 'affinity'—for these people."

"By 'these people,' you mean the Jews, correct?"

Kohl's look bordered on condescension. "Let's be honest here, Lemmon, shall we? If you hadn't put your personal inclination for a certain married woman ahead of your government's needs, you wouldn't be here now. And you wouldn't have risked an international incident contrary to your nation's best interests, now would you?" He left the question hanging and Ryan momentarily at a loss for words, his rage building. "Secretary Hull has bigger fish to fry than dealing with people the rest of the world has shown little use for. America, too, I might add."

"You must be kidding; millions of European Jews are small fish?" Eastern Europe doesn't matter?" Ryan felt the blood rush to his face, his bandaged nose throbbing.

"Let's set things straight, Lemmon. The Secretary and the President are well aware that Hitler is always less than candid when it comes to his intentions. But for now our interests—political and certainly financial—lie in Western Europe, and we still have to convince the American people that involvement over there will be necessary. Many prefer that Herr Hitler deal with the Bolsheviks and Eastern Europe first, rather than our having to deal with them later ourselves. These Jews are a secondary matter."

Ryan rose abruptly from his chair, steadying himself on the edge of the desk: "Did you even read that document? Those bastards are planning cold-blooded mass murder, town by town, village by village." His voice was a low hiss.

Kohl spoke as if comforting a child: "You must have missed hearing about July's international conference on Lake Geneva. The world's powers—including our own government and people—simply aren't willing to radically change immigration quotas just to take a bunch of immaterial Jews off the Germans' hands."

"You have no idea what those people are facing, do you?" Ryan felt his self-control going, his hands trembling. The image of Erika and Leo cowering in the searchlight haunted his mind.

"We'll all have to make sacrifices, and right now our concerns lie with what Europe faces as a whole." Kohl paused. "What the hell, just think about it, Lemmon, with that Jewish thorn in their side the Germans can't put all their energies into attacking their neighbors, right?"

Ryan slammed his fist down on the desk and Kohl jerked back in his chair.

"Dr. Lemmon, I must warn you—"

"You fucking asshole, you don't plan to use that evidence at all, do you?"

Kohl stood to put more distance between himself and Ryan. His hesitation was brief. "Well, come to think of it, I no longer recall what 'evidence' you refer to." He folded the glasses, put them in his breast pocket, and picked up the briefcase. "And now, if you'll excuse me, I must prepare for a holiday gathering. You may leave my office immediately."

Before his fury turned to a physical attack on the director, Ryan stormed from the office. The receptionist looked up in surprise as he grabbed his coat and hat and left the antechamber without a word.

He did not look back.

There was no drink in the bar before taking the train home for the weekend. He told Edward that he had no further interest in government work of any kind, and refused to discuss his meeting with Kohl. The following day he submitted his letter of resignation and made plans to return to the Midwest and teaching.

His career in espionage had reached a disillusioning end, and the memories of wasted lives and the prospect of millions of innocents yet to die tormented his soul.

# EPILOGUE

## Stockton, California
### 4 June 1941

The spring semester at the College of the Pacific was drawing to a close, the campus at its most beautiful and students' enthusiasm heightened by the end of exams and the imminent summer break. Ryan set the phone back in its cradle, pivoted away from his desk toward the sycamores which filled the tall windows of the Admin Building, and pondered what had brought Edward to California unannounced.

His brother's arrival awakened memories better left buried. It dredged up that burden of guilt which now only marred the predictable passage of the days when his mind was unfocused, or interrupted his sleep, leaving him struggling for air, drowning in the sweat-soaked sheets. Phone calls on special occasions such as birthdays had reconnected the brothers from time to time. Edward would speak of his sons' growth, and Ryan would think only of Leo. He had told no one of his connection to the boy, his shame and self-loathing too high a hurdle. Instead he would discuss the warm California climate and the fine city of San Francisco a short drive distant. Both brothers avoided mention of Washington and the war in Europe, and of Ryan's brief stint in espionage.

His nose had healed well, with only the slightest crook and occasional sinus problem to suggest what he had endured. The scars on his left arm and the larger pallid area on his wrist were explained away as souvenirs of a fraternity hazing initiation. He shared with no one the true story of that night with all its tragic detail, but it was never far from his mind.

He dated from time to time, but no woman he had met could compete with the memories of Isabel and Erika, the two he had lost. And he feared no woman could live with the depression he masked so expertly with a ready smile and confident demeanor in both classroom and faculty circle.

The staircase just outside his office creaked with a new arrival and the boards beyond his closed door groaned at the approach of a visitor. Ryan rose to welcome and embrace Edward. "What a pleasant surprise, brother."

"Baby brother, you look your old self once again, thank God. California's climate must be good for you." Edward looked fit in a stylish seersucker suit. He tossed his hat on the coatrack and took command of the chair in front of Ryan's desk. "No complaints about living so far afield from the East Coast and real life?"

"Not a one," said Ryan. "Long time no see, Ed. So what brings you out west of all places, and without your lovely wife and boys?" The warmth was projected, not truly felt.

"Business—" Edward's face darkened, "and the war in Europe. It's coming our way, as you well know, and very soon now." He leaned forward.

"Of course," Ryan's smile had also faded, "we've both known that for years. Bound to happen. Something new you can share?"

"Sadly, not right now, no. But—and hear me out on this, Ryan— I'm here to recruit you back east, back to Washington. And to Europe."

Ryan sat back involuntarily. "No chance. I came here to put as much distance as possible between me and that self-serving bunch in Washington."

"Look, Ryan, I understand your bitterness, but just listen to what I have to say and then consider any decision carefully. I do know how hard this is for you, whether you accept it or not. It's hard for me to even bring this up, but things have changed, and they're changing faster as we speak, so you at least owe me a listen."

"I'm listening," said Ryan, wishing for all his worth that he did not have to. He reached for his pipe, but set it back immediately on the ashtray.

"The Department needs men like you, now more than ever what with Belgium and France under Hitler's heel. We have some important people stuck in the Occupied Zone, a few in Vichy France, and we're desperate for trained people who can help them gather intelligence or even get them out...safely."

That final ill-chosen word weighed heavily, demanding acknowledgment. Ryan sensed that his brother regretted his phrasing, and he took a moment before he replied. "I'm not one of those you're seeking. I'm a German professor making ends meet at a small valley college, that's all. The school's admired, the students bright, the campus a rival to any out east, and I'm comfortable with this life." He swiveled in his chair and faced the trees beyond the window. "I was never cut out for espionage, and I'm certainly not now."

Edward sat back and lit a cigarette. "Look, I'm not here to make your life miserable, Ryan." He expelled a cloud of smoke from his nostrils. "But we need you back in Washington, and we need you even more in Europe. We'll be in this war for good within a year; all Washington knows it, despite protests from the 'keep us out' crowd and those who fool themselves into thinking we still have a choice. It's inevitable. Roosevelt now has a solid spy operation going, so The Group's out of business, and State's involvement in that area is far less direct. But we need knowledgeable operatives, trained assets who can repatriate both the people and the information we need. You're one of them, whether you recognize it yet or not."

Ryan turned back to his brother. "I'm sorry, Ed, but, as I said before, I'm simply not your man. I was an amateur who made major errors and it cost me more than you'll ever know. I live with it every day, and only fresh air and the absence of crowds keep me sane. Let's just drop this. We'll have dinner and wine tonight, you can visit San Francisco tomorrow, and then you can get back to saving the world without me."

"Listen, Ryan, I'll tell you what we're talking here and then you tell me to go to hell if you want, and I won't take offense, okay? We have our sights on important people who can help us win this coming war, but they're trapped in Nazi territory. And we have certain people here in the States and elsewhere they want their hands on. Right now we're still a neutral party, and we can make these trades happen with the right operatives who know their way around. We're setting up a program to deal with all this and it's tailor-made for you."

Ryan felt obliged to ask: "How's that?"

"We need diplomatic and language skills, plus geographical and cultural knowledge, as well. And above all else, State's looking for people who can think on their feet. You've demonstrated all those talents."

"Have you forgotten that I'm persona non grata in the Reich? The Gestapo and I didn't part on the best of terms."

Edward ignored the bitterness. "In the Reich perhaps, but Paris and the Nazi-occupied zone are still a different story, and Vichy France is quite independent in its dealings with us, even if the collaborationists are running the show. This time around you'll be on official State Department business, not undercover and off on your own. And you'll have specific assignments—closely monitored, of course."

"Ed, come on, I'm pretty much at peace with my life here now. And you know well enough I've never been one to be 'monitored.' You've been trying that without success since we were kids."

"Face it, Ryan, when this war comes, you'll be drafted along with all the able-bodied. It won't be just the young guys this time around. Sure, with your education and abilities you'll make junior officer, but would you rather slog it out with ground troops on the front, or use your wits behind the scenes? I don't say this lightly, but we both know it's only a matter of time."

Ryan stared out again through the canopy of trees. A magpie swooped down as two students abandoned a picnic site on the lawn below. He thought of his teaching. He thought of Erika and Leo, of René and Isabel, of the Old Major. As Ryan faced his own fears and regrets, Edward lit a new cigarette and said nothing.

At last Ryan turned back, his decision made. "Ed, I know you mean well...for me and for this country. But I had a good look behind the scenes. Your people trashed intelligence my friends died for, and I nearly died, as well. I swore I would never work for a bastard like Kohl again, and I meant it." He closed the test booklet he was grading when Edward called, effectively closing the discussion, as well.

Edward stubbed out his cigarette, and silence hung heavily in the still air of the office.

Finally Ryan spoke again: "You knew nothing would be done with the film I sent back, didn't you?"

"My duty was to pass along the cartridge. But Kohl did mention it, said it had no real value for our mission. It was up to him to send it up the ladder, and I was under orders not to speak of it further. Sorry, brother, my hands were tied—the job, you know."

"That didn't make it any easier. Or more wrong."

"In retrospect, I agree, but Kohl's gone now. Turns out your 'bastard' was a bit too close to the German-American Bund, and there's been quite a shake-up in our division. I hate to say it, but rumor has it he may have compromised contacts we served him up on a platter."

Ryan felt a trembling in his hands and slowly released his breath. "I should have thrown the son-of-a-bitch out one of those arched windows when I had the chance." He shook his head in revulsion and regret. "I nearly did."

"At any rate, as I said, he's gone now. A good man is in. You'd work in the new division that's just coming together, and we'd be a team again. Obviously on a tighter leash this time around, since the clock is ticking. We have to tread lightly, but we both would be doing what we must to fight this tyranny. Come on, Ryan, if we lose Europe, we've lost it all."

Ryan shut his eyes for a moment and shook his head. "I can't." His mouth felt dry. He forced back the vivid memories of the escape, the pain, the terror, the loss. "I simply can't."

Edward looked at him with a strange mixture of compassion and the smugness of a card player unlikely to be trumped. "I expected you to say that, so look here. I've something to show you." From his jacket pocket came a slender stack of envelopes bound with a rubber band. "These were found in Kohl's office when he was asked to leave last week. The new director passed them along to me, and I thought you should see them in person." He slid the thin packet across the desk.

Ryan hesitated, then slipped off the band and read the cover of the first flimsy. The postmark was Paris, 14 January 1939, the letter addressed to "Dr. Ryan Lemmon, Department of State, Washington, D.C., USA." The sender: "Gesslinger, *poste restante*, Lyon, France." It had been opened.

Ryan paused, the reality sinking in, then hastily shuffled through the remaining letters. The next two were now a year and a half old. It was the last cover that held his eye, not a flimsy but a small, travel-worn envelope. Postmarked in Gurs, France, stamped by the Vichy government, and dated 3 May 1941, just one month earlier, with no sender indicated.

"Gurs?" He held his breath, staring at the envelope, waiting for his brother's response.

"I needed an atlas. Basque region in the south of France, near Pau in the Pyrénées, close to the Spanish border."

The flap was loose. "You've already read it?"

"I had to know if it was worth the trip here to see you."

Ryan slid out a folded piece of cheap paper. The smudged French script was in pencil and appeared hastily written, a troubled hand at work:

*My very dear Ryan,*

*We have heard nothing from you in response to past letters. I can only hope you are well and this reaches you in a timely manner. Know that mother and boy are alive and in my care, but our time here appears short. Please do what you can.*

*With lasting affection, The Lone Ranger*

Emotion blurred his vision as he looked up to his brother. "Gurs—" he said, "Tell me everything you know."

"There's little to tell. A Vichy holding camp for foreign Jews and 'political undesirables.' Low-level security...pretty miserable place with lots of deaths due to living conditions, we hear." He stubbed out his cigarette. "We don't know how long detainees will be interned and where they'll go from there, but a concentration camp in the Reich is best guess."

Ryan sat stunned, silent in the face of a new reality. *Is Horst's protocol already in place, in practice?* He stared at the postmarks before unfolding each of the letters and reading them through in sequence, line by line. He ignored Edward, who smoked patiently as long minutes dragged by.

A quarter hour passed before Ryan finally spoke, his mind filled with his last promise to Erika, his decision carrying the burden of hope and the threat of nightmare:

"Get me in."

# AFTERWORD

In the fall of 1929 a young New York banker arrived in Germany to spend a year studying finance in Berlin. With the collapse of Wall Street and the onset of the Great Depression, he chose to remain in Europe and pursue academic goals. As the Weimar Republic buckled and Hitler and the National Socialists rose to power, the American became a favored guest of the old monarchist aristocracy, reported on Communist street fights and Nazi rallies, instigated a duel fought with sabers, earned a doctorate at a German university, and pursued the rescue of friends from under the eyes of the Gestapo. Later he performed wartime espionage on behalf of his government. And he kept a daily journal. That young man was the author's father, Leonard L. O'Bryon.

*Corridor of Darkness* is not his story, but it could have been. This is a work of fiction by a storyteller, not an historian. All names and characters are fictional, and any resemblance to real persons living or dead is purely coincidental. The words and actions of all the characters, including known historical personages, are the products of my imagination. But in writing this novel I have tried to present the reader with a realistic sense of life in those turbulent years, and I apologize in advance if an occasional inaccuracy has crept into the story.

Creative license was taken where the facts are still in dispute. For example, there appears to be no consensus on when and where a plan for genocide first arose amongst the Nazi hierarchy, so I have taken the liberty of ascribing this burgeoning horror to Heydrich and his team late in 1938. It most likely came into being piecemeal, and was not fully implemented until 1942. Similarly, some historians now believe that *Reichskristallnacht*, the "Night of Broken Glass" pogrom across the Reich, was instigated by Goebbels, undoubtedly with Hitler's approval, but came as an initial surprise to the Gestapo leadership.

Geographically, I have tried to stay true to reality. The tunnels beneath Marburg do exist, but I was never able to investigate what lay behind the wooden doors fronting the Lahn back in 1969 when I studied at the university. I did take liberties with the latch mechanism for the sake of the story. Wherever possible, I used contemporary train schedules to carry my characters across the Reich in an accurate manner. (As an aside, I once narrowly avoided losing my own head to a German catenary post while leaning out a train window to photograph a steam locomotive on a parallel track.) The hamlet of Weidenbach in the Westerwald is wholly imagined, and the Gesslinger Rhein-Fracht dockyard is, as the German would say, *frei erfunden,* a figment of my imagination.

With regard to Horst's damaged facial nerve, this trigeminal neuropathic pain is very real. I appreciate the specific anatomical information provided by dental surgeon Dr. John Orsi, who clarified how a misguided saber blade might lead to just such a medical affliction. Any factual errors regarding the affliction are attributable to me alone. And interestingly, it is surmised that Himmler himself may have been addicted to morphine. Nadia's fatal disease reflects an hereditary ailment afflicting some Lithuanian Jews.

Finally, academic dueling was indeed an established tradition in the thirties, and is still practiced today at some German universities. A computer search will show the interested reader exactly how a *Mensur* is fought. *Corps* Sachsen-Wachonia is wholly imaginary. My father did inadvertently insult a Nazified Marburg fraternity by failing to salute its flag, and a duel was fought and won on his behalf.

I thank my brother James E. O'Bryon for challenging me to quit talking about and finally start writing this story. I am very grateful to Roy Leighton Malone III, whose thoughtful suggestions regarding plotting and character development inspired a far richer story. My sincere thanks go also to Alexander Mackey and Olivia O'Bryon Mackey for their constructive and enthusiastic comments as readers, and to Gerda Tüchsen Brown, whose recollections of her childhood under Nazi rule added special insight to the portrayal of these troubled times.

I dedicate this book to my wife Dani, whose patience, loving encouragement and insightful critique have helped craft a far better story, and to my late father, who led such an adventurous life, and whose spirit hovers about me as I continue to record the saga he inspired.

Patrick W. O'Bryon
Cameron Park, CA

*If you enjoyed Corridor of Darkness, here is an advance look at the next thriller in the Ryan Lemmon Journals,*

# Beacon of Vengeance
## A Novel of Nazi Europe

*Future publication dates and historical materials relating to the novels may be found at the author's blog* ***www.corridorofdarkness.com.***

# PROLOGUE

## Kehl, Germany
## 11 November 1938
## 4:33 a.m.

The fury of the blast left René no time to react. As the incoming Mauser round pierced the fuel tank of their launch, his comrade took the brunt of the explosion. Uwe's body, lifted by the explosion, sent them both flying high into the air. René felt the searing heat and was momentarily blinded by a flash which shredded the fog, and then came impact with the water. By the time he regained the surface the shattered hull was in flames, burning fuel and oil slicked the surface, and Uwe's mutilated body bobbed face down in the choppy wash.

His fellow fighter had paid the price for shielding his friend and leader. A brief check confirmed what René knew instinctively— Uwe was a raw mass of blood and seared skin, and dead. One arm was gone. The signature thatch of coarse blond hair hung loosely from his head, and the curve of the flayed skull glowing dully in the flames from the wreckage. Large wooden splinters protruded from the flesh of neck and back, forcing René to think fleetingly of mariners' deaths in the days when cannon balls wreaked havoc on the tall sailing ships.

There was no sound. Or rather, only an incessant thrumming which filled his head, blocking all ambient noise. René could not tell if the firefight ashore was still ongoing. He treaded water and looked toward the docks, but the fog had gathered once again, leaving only diffuse pinpoints of light along the row of warehouses and a brighter glow from the police patrol boat which had been their undoing.

René was sapped of energy, resting on a floating hatch cover and cursing the death of his comrade as the current drew the mangled body away from his raft. He wondered if he had permanently lost his hearing, the constant buzz in his ears a distraction as he calculated his odds and those of his friends ashore. He wondered if he had been concussed again, if he would spend months recovering as he had after the brutal beating by von Kredow that had changed his life. His thoughts came so slowly. He was unaware of the cold.

Time passed, and René drifted aimlessly with his thoughts. Then he sensed a subtle variation, a rhythmic thrumming approaching across the water, and he abruptly remembered they might search the wreckage. He forced his dulled mind alert. The inverted hull, no longer aflame, bobbed several meters away as it drifted toward the Rhine. He left his hatch cover to breast-stroke over to the shattered wreck, where he dropped below the water to resurface under the capsized keel. A two-handed grip on the ragged framing above his head gave his weak right leg a rest, and there he waited. The backwash slapped against the hull as a passing craft slowed nearby, although the ringing in his ears and the dampening shield of the hull allowed little sound to penetrate. And then the vessel accelerated at open throttle, leaving his shelter bobbing violently in its wake.

He would swim to rejoin his comrades, with luck still rescue his friends. He thought of Erika and that little boy he had carried on his arm, and of Ryan. *If I still have any comrades to save,* he thought. He left the hull with a determined stroke toward the distant lights dimming and flaring in the shifting mist. His hearing had barely improved, but once again he sensed the throb of a vessel approaching and rapidly gaining speed. He knew it must be the Water Police gunboat, and in a big hurry. He submerged to let it pass.

She knew she had lost. Erika cradled Leo, his face buried at her chest, and fought against the numbness, both mental and physical. She imagined springing up from the bench, Leo still in her arms, and plunging overboard to join Ryan in death. She knew the future held no promise for her or her son. She would sink beneath the waters and not fight the pull of life, and this brutal ordeal would be over. But then she thought of Leo struggling to live, and she let the thought go. As long as she was still whole, still sound of mind and body, she *could* fight. As long as Leo was with her, she would not surrender, *would* fight. She hugged her three-year-old tighter and rocked him gently. *But we will both still die*, she thought.

The SS policemen out on the deck tended to the wreckage of Horst's face. It no longer mattered now what happened to him. She had seen his jaw shatter as the bullet struck home, the spray of blood and bone and flesh backlit in the glare of the searchlight. It had felt good. He had paid the price for destroying the future of the boy in her arms, for the death of her parents, for her torture and rape. Should he live, his face would be a horrific mask exposing him to the world, his mutilated features an indelible mirror of the monster within. Should he die, the world would be a better place.

Ryan had been so strong at the end, so certain of their success and escape to France. They had relaxed in the shack less than two hours before, sensing an end to the terrifying flight from Berlin, letting down their guard, and she had seen the pleasure in his eyes when she revealed that he was Leo's likely father. He had been a good man, a decent man, and she fought back tears, picturing his drop into the dark waters, the loathsome Pabst dragging them both beneath the roiling surface. *Ryan won't be back to save us this time, despite his promise.*

The tears finally broke loose, and she sobbed, pulling silent Leo ever closer to her breast. She wished she had the toy bear to offer her son as comfort, but Bruno lay abandoned on the deck of the motorboat which followed in their wake.

Horst now lay unmoving on the stretcher, his head a swath of bandages. His moaning had ceased, and the medic remarked on the inordinate amount of morphine it had taken to calm his agony. Little did he know that Horst routinely used the drug.

The young policeman stood over the captives, his machine pistol alert. He no longer tried to comfort her with assurances that the German state would look after her son once she paid the price for assaulting a high-ranking Gestapo official. She had read Horst's protocol, knew what that state planned for all Jews like her. If her husband did not manage their deaths beforehand for having "tricked" him into marrying a Jew, they would certainly still disappear into a concentration camp to ultimately perish there. But Erika would never go willingly without a fight.

René had found the Gesslinger docks in shambles as he climbed to the loading platform and limped ashore. Downed SS soldiers lay strewn across the gravel near the gate where his men had dragged the bodies. He dispatched the sole survivor—badly injured with a gut wound and unconscious—with a quick slip of his pocket knife.

The attack had almost gone as planned, but for the explosion and loss of Uwe, and the failure to achieve their principal goal. The police launch was away, and with it Ryan, Erika and the boy. His other fighters were unscathed, a miracle in itself. He found them consoling one another over his own presumed death.

The dockside shack had its own story to tell. The table displayed tools of torture. Ryan's overcoat and Erika's handbag still hung on the hooks. René noted the chair where his friend had suffered, the burned ropes and scorched wood of the arm, the cut ties which had bound Ryan's feet. Blood splatters streaked the floorboards, and the stench of burned flesh still permeated the shack. He doubted his friend could have withheld his secrets—few men could in the face of such cruelty—so the Lone Ranger network was likely exposed to the Gestapo. There was no sign of dear Hugo Gerson, but René easily guessed his fate, as well.

He sent his men home, warning that they were compromised and suggesting they escape to France, as well. His remaining boats were at their disposal, should they so choose. He burned with fury, but knew his job had just begun and fought the blinding rage which would render him ineffective.

René gave his mother no choice. Jeanne was in tears and resisted, but he helped her into her coat, reached her the handbag, and had his man escort her to the waiting Opel. She insisted on taking an album of photographs of her early married years. He quickly changed to dry clothing and gathered a few basics. Long ago he had stashed French francs at the Kehl home, for he had known this day would surely come. Within half an hour the family estate would sit abandoned, and he and his mother would be across the river before this new day fully dawned. They would head for the ancestral home south of Colmar in Alsace, take a few days to recover, then assess their situation and decide the future fight.

Erika expected that soon now some official would step in and seal their fate. Her mind raced as the gunboat headed upriver toward the police docks in Kehl. The long railroad bridge passed overhead in the fog, carrying others to the safety they had sought in France. The muted lights of the town beckoned as the launch made a sweeping curve toward shore.

The police station was understaffed—*Horst's welcoming party at Gesslinger Shipping had surely depleted their resources,* she thought with muted pleasure—so some confusion reigned. The ambulance awaiting their arrival quickly whisked Horst away, its siren pointless in that pre-dawn hour when no one dared the streets without official permission.

Her guard placed handcuffs on her wrists, the cold metal raw against the welts left from Horst's rape barely twenty-four hours before. It now seemed an age, an epic series of events which had taken all from her but her son clutching at her arm. Horst von Kredow, her sadist husband, the man she once believed she loved, the man who was destined to make her future in the new Germany.

They were placed in an interrogation room and told to expect the Gestapo shortly, and she knew she would soon be separated from Leo. He would go to an orphanage, at least until word got out of her Jewish heritage, or until Horst tracked them down again. She would face interrogation far more brutal than anything she had yet endured. *There is no future in this new Germany,* she thought.

The sleepy-eyed sergeant behind the desk—obviously resentful of the interruption in a swing shift watch normally devoted to dozing—insisted the woman give an official statement. He called for the key to her cuffs and placed it in his breast pocket. Despite her damp clothing, disheveled hair and makeup long missing, he still ran his eyes the length of her body and managed a lecherous smile, appreciating both her looks and her discomfort. Leo now clung to her bound hands.

"Well here's a nice piece of ass to grace our station," he said. "Don't worry—we'll get you out of that damp clothing as soon as possible, for your own health, understood? But first, I need a name."

Erika eyed the desk, the pen holder, the brass fire extinguisher affixed to the wall to her right, barely visible past the man's head. She quickly returned her gaze to the sergeant. His stubble and mustache carried remnants of something white and powdery and recently eaten—confectioner's sugar, perhaps. The fatigued eyes revealed nothing beyond the obvious leer, but his words made her decision easy. She remained silent.

"*Mutti, ich muss Pipi machen.*" Leo, pressing against her leg, looked up imploringly. He hadn't uttered a word since the shooting on the river, but now the immediacy of his need brought him back.

"A toilet for my boy," she said, a mother's demand, not a request.

"It can wait. He won't be coddled where you're both headed." The sergeant chuckled.

"*Mutti*, I need to go, I need to go now!"

"Remove these cuffs and I'll take him to a toilet, or you'll have a real mess to deal with. Your man there can stand guard."

"The cuffs go nowhere, and you'll remain right here even if you piss yourself, my dear. As for your brat—" he gestured to the guard, "Corporal Mannheimer, get this kid to the shitter and make sure he does his business."

The young policeman nodded and put a hand on Leo's shoulder. "Let's go, kid."

"*Mutti?*"

"It's fine, Leo, go with the man. I'll be here when you come back, don't worry." Leo read the truth in his mother's eyes, yet was hesitant to leave her, but nature called too strongly and he allowed himself to be shepherded into the hallway.

The sergeant returned to the typewriter. "Again, your name?" Erika remained mute, staring at the desk. "Listen closely, madam, we'll get it out of you eventually. Would you prefer the Gestapo way, or our way?" She said nothing. "Very well, we'll come back to that. You fired upon and grievously wounded a high-ranking SS officer before witnesses. The reason for your action?"

She finally spoke: "He deserved to die."

He looked at her with impatience and began to type, a finger of each hand tapping at the keys. He only got as far as the word "deserved."

The heavy bronze eagle in her bound hands met his skull, and Erika heard the crunch and felt the give and knew she had aimed true. The sergeant loosed a grunt and a fart and his head fell over the rank of type bars as blood poured from the head wound. She returned the eagle to its roost at the center of the desk, the bronze talons gripping the swastika now glistening red.

His two fountain pens lay scattered across the surface, the spilled ink forming sinuous patterns as it mingled with the blood from the sergeant's crushed temple. The scroll of paper in the typewriter was saturated, no name or mention of her relationship to Horst ever noted. The machine itself sat half-hidden by his drooping head, as if he searched within for his missing consciousness.

Erika withdrew the key from his pocket and freed herself of the manacles, then pulled the fire extinguisher from its wall bracket and positioned herself behind the hallway door to wait. She glanced over at the fallen sergeant and realized her error. Though the young policeman would not see her empty chair as he came through the door, he would immediately spot the slumped body of his sergeant. She quickly forced the unconscious man upright, positioning his elbows on the desk, his forearms over the machine. She wiped the blood from her hands on his uniform jacket. Two long paces and she once again stood concealed, the bulky brass canister at the ready.

She heard Leo's voice in the hall and then they were outside, just beyond the door. Leo entered first, the guard on his heels. "*Mutti*, I'm done. This man is nice."

One pace beyond the threshold and the young policeman would see her empty chair. She brought the extinguisher down on the back of his head and he slumped to the ground.

The boy turned in amazement: "But *Mutti*, I said this one was nice!"

The ringing of the phone startled René just as he closed the front door, perhaps more so because his hearing was now slowly returning despite the persistent drumming in his head. He knew the Gestapo would arrive unannounced and in force, so it had to be one of his crew. He stepped back into the foyer, picked up the receiver, and recognized the voice of Erika.

"We need your help, René," she said. "Please hurry!"

## ABOUT THE AUTHOR

Patrick W. O'Bryon has been a Fulbright Scholar
and Princeton Ph.D., a college professor, a command
military interpreter, a log cabin builder, a natural health
counselor, an investment property broker, an ad man,
and a rescuer of animals—both wild and domesticated.
It's obvious this writer has problems settling down.
For now, he brokers real estate and writes novels, travels
as frequently as possible to Europe, and shares life's
adventures with his wife Dani and their cats.